Alex Cohen Books 4-6

Leopold Borstinski

Published by Sobriety Press
Cover design and Illustrations by James, GoOnWrite.com
Edited by Melanie Underwood

##

ISBN 978 1 913313 42 5 ePub Edition
ISBN 978 1 913313 41 8 Kindle Edition
ISBN 978 1 913313 43 2 Paperback Edition

For more information please visit LeoB.ws

##

BOOK FOUR
CASINO CHISELER

November 1950

1

BLINK AND YOU missed it. Alex Cohen's life had flashed past him from the moment he took the bus to Rikers back in '36 and today. This would be his first time in front of the television cameras and an audience of millions.

He ate breakfast in his hotel restaurant—since coming out of jail, he had learned the value of a hearty start to the day because you never knew what your next meal would be. So a plate crammed with fruit, cheese blintzes, and a bagel, washed down with orange juice and coffee. Always with the black coffee. During the feast, Alex read the local paper—a habit he'd picked up from his teenage years in the old country. When he put the newspaper down, he smiled at his lawyer, Mendy Greenberg, who had been waiting all this time.

"Thanks for coming over and helping me with the hearing."

"My pleasure, Alex. It's been a while since I've seen you."

"My parole review. Before the war."

"A lifetime ago."

"Sure feels that way to me. Any last-minute advice?"

"The good news is that you are not on trial this time. But the same rules apply. Don't respond to anything anyone asks you without checking with me first. And do not rise to their bait. Kefauver's desperate to get a head on a spike."

"Just like old times. Different cops, but the same story."

"Remember that Kefauver is worse than a cop—word on the streets of Washington is that he'll stand for election soon."

Alex eyed Mendy, judging his words and considering his response, but before he could speak, he saw that his car had appeared and was ready out front.

As they headed over to the courthouse, he continued their breakfast conversation.

"One thing you never explained to me was why I only got five years."

"What do you mean?"

"You were expecting them to throw the book at me, but I was inside for three years, tops."

"Not everyone walked away from you back then. While nobody could be seen to support you, efforts were being made to ease your burden."

"Who?"

"Here we are. Don't speak a word to the press hounds. Do as I say and you will get through this just fine."

The car pulled over and Mendy leaped straight out, followed by Alex.

BULBS POPPED AND whizzed about his head as the crime reporters swarmed around him, hoping to catch the best photo of Alex for their front-page noon editions. Local cops lined his route from the curbside to the court entrance. Perhaps for the first time in his life, he was grateful to a bunch of flatfeet.

The crowd thickened at the bottom of the courthouse steps, forcing Mendy and Alex to pause their attempts to proceed.

"What you going to tell Kefauver?"

"Are you naming any names today?"

"How does it feel to be back in court?"

A thousand questions whirred around his ears as each reporter did their best to get a quote for their editor, but Alex followed Mendy's instructions and said nothing.

A handful of reporters stayed with them as they entered the hallowed portals of the courthouse building, and Mendy asked a nearby court official where they needed to go. The answer delivered them to a wide corridor packed with men and women standing around, looking like they had as much idea of what was going on as Alex did.

"Brace yourself, the world and his wife are watching us."

Into the courtroom and an usher showed them to the front right-hand benches. Alex surveyed the joint: an arc of seats, for the senators to question their witnesses, sat opposite with a bank of tables and chairs for them and their lawyers. Behind, the auditorium was packed with a mixture of concerned citizens, members of the press, and court ghouls who'd turn up to the opening of a paper bag if it took place in this building.

To the wings, either side of the tables in front of the politicians' pews, were enormous boxes on wheels—the television cameras. Alex swallowed hard. Mendy nudged him and leaned in.

"Don't worry about the TV crew. They are not your enemy—the senators are the ones who'll question you. Everything else is fluff. Stick to the script and if you think you will deviate from the plan, then stop and speak with me."

A HUSH FELL over the room and Alex twisted round to see what was happening. If he had remained facing forward, he would have seen a side door open and a stream of senators gush into the courtroom and take their seats in the arc in front of him. No sooner had they appeared than the lights on top of the television cameras glowed red, showing they were live on air across the country.

After an interminable wait for everyone to sit down, open their cases, shuffle their papers, and settle into their seats, the first witness was called. Alex strode over to the center of the tables with Mendy by his side.

A court official stepped forward and asked Alex to swear to tell the truth, the whole truth, and pretty much only the truth before his God. When this activity started, the TV cameras swung around and focused their rays on him. Despite being unsettled by this mechanical response, Alex sat down, leaning forward so that his elbows rested on the table and he interleaved the fingers of one hand in between those of the other. Then he exhaled and stared forward at the cockroach in front of him, Estes Kefauver.

"Let's keep this simple, shall we, gentlemen?"

Those beady eyes bore inside him and Alex swallowed hard again.

"Mr. Cohen, let me remind you that you are under oath. Are you, or have you ever been, an active participant in the organized crime syndicate known as the mafia?"

November 1941

2

ALEX'S PLAN FROM the moment he arrived in Sing Sing was to get out of there as quickly as possible. He listened to his lawyer's advice and they devised a two-prong strategy. Mendy appealed the sentence and Alex kept his nose clean and behaved like a model prisoner.

The first few months were the worst, in no small measure because he had hope to cling to—every time he saw him, Mendy talked about how he had found another line of argument, a different way to pursue Alex's freedom. By January, Alex realized this would not happen and instructed his lawyer to stop trying on his behalf—Alex was spending his hidden fixed income on legal fees with nothing to show for it.

Instead, he followed the guards' instructions to the letter. Never groused and always kept out of everybody else's business. In prison, that is not easy if you have a reputation like Alex's. Most of the cons believed he would sprinkle pixie dust over their circumstances, bribe a judge and get them out. As Alex explained repeatedly, if that was within his power then he would have done it for himself.

To pretend that he experienced ordinary prison time would be an exaggeration. Sure, he was locked in his cell and forced to do the bidding of the guards, but they also knew that he was connected to the most powerful criminals in the history of America and Alex let them hold that belief, even though those self-same syndicate members had left him beached, isolated, and with no support.

The other element that made his jail time more pleasant was his gelt. Alex had gifted two-thirds of his wealth to his ex-wife Sarah and their sons and had hidden his last million before he entered the portals of Sing Sing. That still left him with a small fortune to rely on in prison and grease any palms that needed it.

WHEN ALEX WALKED out of Sing Sing, nobody was waiting to meet him and he took a bus back to New York. This was a simple message from the syndicate that his time with them was over—his friends had turned their backs on him before his trial even began, and he'd expected no less upon his return to the outside world.

Still, there was a sinking feeling in the pit of his stomach as he realized he was on his own again. He considered looking up his old lieutenants, Ezra and Massimo, but thought better of it. Time had passed and they were best shot of him. Just like his family—Sarah hadn't visited him once, nor had he seen his boys since before the trial began. He was alone.

The smartest thing to do next was to leave town and head west, away from the sphere of influence of Charlie Luciano, Meyer Lansky, and Benny Siegel, as well as other members of the inner circle of organized crime like Albert Anastasia and Louis Buchalter.

While Chicago was an obvious destination, there were too many tentacles reaching out from the Eastern Seaboard into the Windy City so Alex chose Los Angeles as a fresh base from which to operate.

These thoughts permeated his mind as, years later, he sat on a train from LA to Detroit—he had a contract to fulfill in the city his old friend Abe Bernstein had called home. It was a lifetime since they'd spoken and, besides, the purpose of his visit had nothing to do with the leader of the Sugar Hill Gang and everything to do with a lowlife piece of trash known as Jem Cole.

WITH JUST AN address written on a piece of paper and the memory of the instructions issued to him by Jack Dragna back on the west coast, he found a fleapit hotel to rest overnight before doing the job the following day.

"The scumbag has shown me nothing but disrespect, Alex."

"I understand, Jack. Do you want him to suffer before he meets his end?"

"An apology would be nice, but don't sweat it. Just make sure he's deceased before you leave him."

From what Alex could figure, Jem Cole had taken a fancy to one of Jack's mistresses and had made the foolish mistake of being seen in a restaurant on Sunset Boulevard with her. Gili Earl was innocent in that she knew she shouldn't have agreed to the date, but she argued that it was only a bite to eat, whereas the kid had no such excuse. There was no way he only wanted to break bread with the long-legged brunette. So Gili's punishment was to no longer be Jack's skirt, and Alex was dispatched to Detroit in search of the guy.

He wasn't hard to find the following day because Jack had sent the boy on a fool's errand to isolate him from his crew—there was no need to put Alex in harm's way, and Jack reckoned Alex deserved a brief vacation, anyway.

The address Jack gave Alex was a residential building in the heart of the city and a quick check with the janitor confirmed the guy was in. At the top of the two flights of stairs, Alex pressed his ear to the apartment door to see if he could hear anyone inside. Nothing. So he rang the doorbell and waited.

After thirty long seconds, there was no response and Alex tried the bell again. Another wait and still nobody. He sighed—he surely didn't have the patience for this anymore and just wanted the job to be over with. Was he getting too old for bursting into people's apartments and shooting them in cold blood? Now was an opportunity to find out.

One swift kick and the door flew inward and landed on the hallway floor. Nobody stirred, and he considered the possibility that the concierge had got it wrong. He looked down at the number on the door and checked he had the right apartment.

Pulling out his revolver, Alex strode into the living room and found no one. Then he marched into what appeared to be a bedroom and discovered Jem, face down on the bed with several liquor bottles on the floor. The guy was out cold and Alex hoped it was only the booze and not that someone had got to the kid first. If somebody had made the hit before him, then he couldn't collect his fee in good conscience.

He bent down and smelled the whiskey on Jem's breath—just at the point when an enormous snore erupted out of his mouth, spewing a burst of air into Alex's face. He stood up straight and slapped the guy on the thigh with the side of his pistol.

A trip to the bathroom and Alex poured a glass of cold water on the fella's head and, amid much spluttering and swearing, Jem roused himself from his deep alcohol-fueled slumber.

"What the f—"

"Save it, Jem."

The barrel of Alex's gun was aimed right in the center of Jem's torso and the guy had sufficient presence of mind to remain still, and he eased back down on his bed, head resting on his pillow.

"Who are you?"

"It doesn't matter who I am. Instead, you should ask me why I am here."

Alex allowed Jem a few seconds to contemplate his suggestion, but as nothing was forthcoming, Alex continued the one-sided conversation.

"Last week you were seen out with Gili Earl. Do you remember that night?"

A nod confirmed Cole's memory.

"Did you have a great time?"

"Yeah…"

"Do you think Gili enjoyed herself?"

"Reckon so. There were no complaints."

"Was the food satisfactory?"

"Sure thing. I have never tasted such a great ribeye in my life."

"Wow. And how'd you fair later in the evening?"

"A fella don't like to brag."

"How very gallant. Did you get to first base?"

"Home run, my friend."

Cole winked at Alex as though they were compadres—for a moment, he forgot the situation he was in.

"Congratulations. Sounds as though you had a fabulous night all round—wonderful food, fantastic company, great lay. Things couldn't have worked out better, right?"

"I reckon."

"Wrong, Jem. Remember I asked you to think about why I'm here? Any ideas?"

Cole shook his head. This was all too confusing before his first smoke of the day. His eyes darted left and right until Alex offered him a cigarette, which he took, lighting it himself with a book of matches on his nightstand table.

"You made a mistake and I am here to correct that error."

"What was that? The skirt wasn't complaining when I left her, if you see what I mean?"

"Sure do, Jem, but that's not what I'm talking about. Did you know who Gili was before you took her for the meal?"

"One of the local girls. Why does it matter, and what are you doing hounding me in Detroit of all places?"

"She wasn't just any girl—she was Jack Dragna's skirt."

Alex allowed that idea to float in the air and mingle with the cigarette smoke being exhaled by Jem. The guy's expression shifted from youthful arrogance over his sexual conquest to wide-eyed fear at the implication that he'd messed around with a Dragna moll.

"I didn't know, mister. You gotta believe me."

"What I think about what you did is irrelevant—I'm just a hired hand. Are you sorry for what you have done?"

"Of course, Mac. If I had known, then I wouldn't have touched that ass with a six-foot pole."

"I guess that counts as an apology, doesn't it?"

"Certainly does, mister."

Alex inhaled, fired three shots into Jem's chest, and when the body stopped twitching half a minute later, he squeezed another shot into the guy's face at close range. Then he popped into the bathroom to make sure there were no blood spatters and left the apartment. He considered propping up the front door, still lying on the ground, but it wasn't worth the effort.

Down the two flights and out onto the street. Jem Cole wouldn't be ruining any more of Jack's women.

3

AS ALEX ARRIVED at the station, he looked up at the information board and spotted Hoboken as one of the many possible destinations from Detroit. The sound of his sons' laughter filled his head and he changed his plans—he'd visit them there instead of heading straight back to LA.

He dropped a dime to Jack to confirm that the contract had been carried out and then made a second call to Sarah to make sure he would be welcome when he showed up. The train was worth waiting two hours for if he had a chance of seeing his boys.

When he arrived in New Jersey, he hopped a cab and checked into a hotel near to Sarah's home, which he'd bought for her a decade before. Although she and her lawyer friend had moved in together before Alex did time, she had insisted Kameron Jacobs sold his place and she kept hold of her house.

He hung up his clothes in his room, dialed out, and, to his surprise, Sarah answered.

"Hi there. How are things?"

"All good. You?"

"Fine, thanks. I've just got in and have arrived at my hotel."

"Which one?"

"The Radcliffe, which isn't that far from your place."

"When were you wanting to come over?"

"I was hoping for tonight but I understand that's very short notice."

"And some. Why not pop round tomorrow at three?"

"Will Kameron be there?"

"No, Alex. He and I aren't together any more."

Alex was surprised—he'd figured they'd be an item for quite some time. The guy was a stand-up fella who brought in the money and made few demands on Sarah, from what little she had said on their rare phone calls.

"Since when?"

"A while. Let's sort out the details about tomorrow and you can cross-examine me when you come over."

◆ ◆ ◆

THE NEXT AFTERNOON, Alex arrived on time, sauntered up the path to the front door, and rang the bell. A young woman answered and let him in—he assumed she was the housekeeper, judging by how she behaved as he smiled on the porch.

He stood in the living room and edged toward the rear of the house where the sounds of youthful exuberance were bubbling away. Through the kitchen and out into the backyard until he bumped into the three youngest messing about with a football. Moishe and David, his eldest, were nowhere to be found.

"They'll be home later—they are at work."

Sarah's voice startled him for a second, but the calm tones set Alex at ease almost immediately.

"Living the other side of the country, it's hard to remember those two are old enough to earn gelt."

"Moishe insists on paying for his keep and won't take a single penny from me."

"We both know that's because he believes your money comes from a poisoned well."

"That has never been how I have described your generosity toward us, Alex."

"I understand that, but it is the way the boy thinks."

"The man is stubborn in his beliefs. Any idea where he might have got that trait?"

At that point, Arik spotted his papa and rushed over, forgetting himself for a minute. Then he checked himself the final fifteen feet and brought himself down to a slow saunter. His disappearance from the football field meant the game was over and the other two followed him in.

"Hey, Papa. What brings you to New Jersey?"

"To visit you fellas, of course."

"Yeah, right. I thought you were living in California."

"Don't ask your father about his business. Be glad he is here to see us. The man has traveled six thousand miles and you're giving him an inquisition."

"Aw, I was only pulling your leg, Papa."

Arik leaped forward and gave his father an enormous hug. As the youngest of the clan, the boy had yet to shed all his childish ways or be so concerned about how the others perceived him.

Asher and Elijah were a year or two older and were more cautious in their dealings with their father. Perhaps because their recollections were stronger of the shouting between their parents—or they had deeper memories of the night when their bedroom was strafed with bullets. Either way, they tolerated this man in their midst but didn't want to show much enthusiasm for Alex's existence. And even though it hurt him, he understood why.

They hung in the garden for the next three hours. The boys let Alex play in their ball games; other times he'd sit on the grass and take pleasure in watching them have fun near him. All the while, Sarah tried to remain indoors. True to her word when they got divorced, she always wanted to give Alex the best opportunities available to spend time with his sons.

SHE INVITED HIM to stay for dinner and he accepted—he enjoyed being surrounded by these people, his family. Holding guest status meant Sarah forced him to sit down in the living room while the boys laid the table and helped in the kitchen; their mama had them well trained.

She offered him a drink, but he declined and sat back, letting the domesticity engulf him. When was the last time he'd been in an ordinary house doing normal things? He had missed out on this by not being at home when he and Sarah were together and then being away after they split up.

David arrived back first and strode toward his father with arms outstretched.

"Good to see you, Pop."

"You're looking in excellent form, son."

"Can't complain, you know how it is."

Just before David embellished on his initial thoughts, Moishe's key jangled in the lock and David stood transfixed, aware of his elder brother's feelings about their father.

Moishe took one look at his old man and walked straight up the stairs, a blink of the eyes his only recognition that Alex was in the building. Alex sighed but had expected nothing less. David fake-punched him on the shoulder.

"Don't worry about him. He's just got some more growing up to do, Pop."

"He is living his life by his own set of rules. I can't fault him for that."

MOISHE WAS THE last to sit at the dinner table, but Sarah made everyone wait until he arrived before they started. She didn't admonish the man in front of the others, but she had followed him upstairs when he first got home. He was a man and needed to be treated accordingly.

"This is a fine meal, thank you, Sarah."

"You should have been here last week. The turkey was the size of a Buick."

Moishe shot daggers at Arik—the eldest son failed to understand why the youngest was prepared to even talk to their father. After all, Arik was the one who had been kidnapped at gunpoint—Moishe saw no reason to forgive the man for that traumatic afternoon in their lives.

"Last week?" What was so special about a meal several days before? Then Alex's eyes widened: Thanksgiving, a celebration he had never seen the point in. Takings were always down because every joe citizen stayed at home in the bosom of his family and, when he ran speakeasies and cathouses throughout Manhattan, Alex regretted that they didn't want to spend their free time in the bosoms of his *nafkas*. He smiled at his own joke.

"What's funny?" asked Elijah.

"Nothing much. Just happy to be here."

"Shame you didn't bother trying to be with us all the previous days of our lives."

"Moishe!"

"That's all right, Sarah. While his tone was disrespectful, Moishe is correct. I should have spent more time with you guys—especially when we were married."

"Cheap words, old man."

Alex's eldest son stood up and stormed out of the room.

"I am so sorry, Alex."

"Don't be, Sarah—you shouldn't apologize on his behalf. Moishe's a man nowadays and he must behave like one. And seek forgiveness like one when he needs to."

LATER ON, AFTER they tucked the kids up in bed, the adults remained and then David took his leave so that Alex and Sarah were alone.

"I find it hard to imagine he's working to be a lawyer some day."

"I know, Alex. It is hard to believe that any of them will do anything apart from play ball in the backyard."

"There is that. How's Moishe doing? Accountant, right?"

"Yes. It's taking him longer than David because he refuses to take a dime from me, like I was saying earlier."

"He's a fool to be so stubborn, but you have to hand it to him."

"I know. He can be annoyingly righteous."

Alex chuckled.

"The apple doesn't fall far from the tree, does it, Sarah?"

She grinned back and took a swig of her drink—a large Scotch on the rocks.

"How are you, Sarah? I'm sorry, but I had no idea that Kameron was out of the picture."

"Why would you? Since you moved to the west coast, we've hardly spoken."

"And before that, I was inside and my phone calls were limited… Who ended it, you or him?"

"Me. After a year, we had settled into a rut and I couldn't see we were going anywhere. He was a reasonable provider—not as good as you, naturally—but he was in the room yet not there for me. Kameron was the kind of guy who would always be more interested in listening to a match on the radio than talking to his wife. And now I'm alone."

"Has there been anybody since then?"

"No. I can't face putting myself through the dating scene and Hoboken isn't as metropolitan as Manhattan so people still stare at me, because they notice I have no man and look after all these kids. Some who don't know me very well assume I lost my husband in the war. Those who I have allowed into my life have some understanding of what it must be like for me to be your ex-wife."

"We could always get together again if you want," Alex chuckled, not knowing whether he was joking.

"I'll get back to you on that."

4

BACK AT HIS apartment in Boyle Heights in the heart of the most Jewish area of Los Angeles, Alex sat in an easy chair enjoying his newspaper after another heavy breakfast. He did the washing up and then sat back into the cushioning and flipped from page to page.

Just before he reached the sports section, there was a knock on his door. With nobody expected, Alex was cautious as he approached the entrance and squinted through the fish-eye before he relaxed.

"Come in. You were the last person I'd have thought would darken this cave."

Meyer Lansky walked in and took off his hat before carrying on into the living room, and settling into the couch. This middle-aged Jew was more than a guy from his past—he was the syndicate's financier and had been one of Alex's closest business partners before his incarceration, going all the way back to the start of Prohibition.

"Coffee?"

"Yes, please, and some cheesecake if you have it."

"You must be confused—this isn't Lindy's."

They both smiled and Alex popped into the kitchen to prepare their drinks. When he came back, Meyer had spread out on the couch and sat like he owned the place. Alex passed him his mug and returned to his easy chair.

"I almost drove past your block, Alex. I thought you'd have been in a different part of town."

"Richer, you mean."

"Well, I wouldn't have put it quite that way."

"I would. We used to say we live together, we love together but the minute Dewey came after me and threw me in jail, you all turned your backs on me. This isn't a complaint and I am thrilled to see you today, but there is a reason I'm no longer in clover."

Meyer sipped his coffee as he listened to his erstwhile friend.

"Remember, at that time, we were all nervous about how far the special prosecutor would go to nail all of us. People closed ranks, but it was always business and nothing personal."

"I understand. I'm hoping you can tell from my tone that while I was not happy about the situation, I do not bear any ill will—to you, Charlie, or Benny."

"We all did what we had to do—or could do."

Meyer's last statement made little sense, but Alex let it go. The truth was that he was horrified over the speed with which his friends had walked away from him when he needed help most.

"And I've been doing my best since I got out of jail too."

"How are things going for you?"

"I get by, Meyer. I've been careful to file my taxes each year and to make sure that Uncle Sam didn't shine a flashlight into my more private investments. So I don't flaunt my money, but I am doing all right."

"When I arrived at this building, I was concerned for you."

"This is a friendly neighborhood—there might be nothing as fine as Lindy's but I can buy bagels and cheesecake from the local stores."

"I'm glad you are making your way."

"I said I get by—and nothing more. You know that I work for Jack Dragna now."

"Why yes, he's mentioned it to me."

"Did he ask for a reference?"

Alex smiled and Meyer returned the favor.

"Let's just say he asked my opinion of you as a contract killer."

"Thank you for the kind word because he has kept me busy since I landed on this side of the country."

"*Gornisht*. It was the least I could do, and besides, you are a terrific marksman. Those years in France weren't wasted on you."

The weeks he'd spent cowering in fox holes in French and Belgian fields and the fact they had given him a Purple Heart for killing a kid in the middle of the war. Nothing made sense then, and not much more did now.

"And how is the old gang?"

"Charlie remains behind bars and Mendy has stopped trying to get him released. They gave him thirty years and it looks like he'll serve every one of them."

"Dutch Schultz was right—we should have killed Dewey while we had the chance."

"You reckon? Murdering the special prosecutor would not have stopped Charlie's trial. Now you are agreeing with Anastasia—he was hot for bumping off the cop back then, and I never thought I'd see the day when you two agreed on anything."

"Him and Buchalter. They still rule the roost in Brownsville?"

"Lepke went on the lam and then was arrested two years ago. You'll love this—they indicted him for the Joe Rosen murder and we hear the decision next week."

"I can't pretend to be sad that Lepke is in trouble. What about Anastasia?"

"He is still a syndicate member, although he has offered a six-figure reward to get rid of a little local difficulty he's facing."

"I wondered when you'd cut to the chase and tell me why you came all this way to make a house call."

"Alex, I have a proposition for you and it is worth one hundred thousand dollars."

"FOR THAT KIND of money, you have got my attention, Meyer."

"I thought I might. This is a hit like almost no other, which is why we wanted to go to someone we could count on to get it done, despite its challenges."

"You've stroked my ego, now tell me who are the people who trust me sufficiently to kill someone, but not enough to be invited back to the top table of the syndicate."

"Alex, I want you to listen to me and believe every word I say. The old guard know and respect you and almost all would like to see your return, but the newer members are nervous about accepting you into the fold since your time in jail. They hold a belief that your short prison sentence came at a price. Their words, not mine."

"I kept *schtum*. Dewey got nothing from me, other prisoners got nothing from me, and the governor of Sing Sing got nothing either."

"Don't shoot the messenger, Alex. You asked a question and I am giving you the answer you deserve."

"Yet they still want my help."

"The hit we have in mind is far from easy to achieve, and if it is timed well, it will be significant for the syndicate."

"Go on."

Alex wasn't so much sulking as deeply unhappy with the situation. For Meyer to assert the syndicate couldn't trust him was an insult. Under any other circumstance, or if he was any other person, the fella would be dead by now, but the two men had enough shared history—and personal respect—that Alex allowed the man the opportunity to pitch him a hit of a lifetime.

"An individual has named Louis and Albert as leaders of Murder Corporation and for being responsible for a string of murders. Their accuser is about to testify against them, and we wish this person to breathe no more."

"Let me get this straight, you want me to save Buchalter and Anastasia. The two guys who stole the heroin business from under me and Charlie?"

"Let's not rake over those coals again, Alex. If the hit happens before Louis' latest trial then he will be spared the chair. And Albert won't even get charged."

"This gets better by the minute. You want me to save the pair of them."

"Yes, Alex."

He was silent for a spell, mulling over the implications of Meyer's words. There had been a lot of time since he last saw his fellow directors of Murder Corporation, and the irony wasn't lost on him that he was being dragged back to New York to save their sorry asses. Given the number of killers in Brownsville, couldn't the syndicate have found somebody closer? The importance of the hit had driven Meyer to California and into Alex's home, but it didn't sit well with him.

"Who's the mark?"

"Abe Reles—he heard Louis issue the order for the contract on the trucker, Joe Rosen."

Alex was less than a week away from the start of his trial, and Rosen was the last contract he did for the Murder Corporation before being forced to step down by Anastasia and Buchalter. Funny how the syndicate's single biggest supplier of assassins for hire was the man to turn state's evidence. He'd always liked Reles—the guy had a simplicity to the way he behaved and no matter what the time of day or the distance that needed to be traveled, Abe could be relied on to know somebody who could down tools and perform a hit on the spin of a nickel.

"Where is the stool pigeon holed up?"

"He's in a hotel in New York. Before you agree to the job, you should understand that he is being guarded all day and night by cops. They will shoot you on sight to protect their star witness."

"Would a sniper rifle not be easier than walking into the place?"

"We've had a guy staring at the window through a scope for three days now, but Abe hasn't been seen at all. The police are smarter than they used to be, Alex, and this must appear to be an accident. There cannot be even a hint of foul play."

"If I do this, will I get back into the syndicate?"

"I can't promise that, Alex. It can only help your case but don't bank on it. The money is the payment and nothing more."

"Two hundred thousand, did you say?"

"No, I said half that."

"If you want me to save Anastasia's life, the cost goes up."

"But, Alex, if you hope to return to the syndicate then the price must remain the same. It is a generous amount by anybody's standards."

He stood up and walked over to Meyer to shake his hand and seal the deal. Lansky gave him the details of the hotel and an envelope with some spending money.

"After the job, you should visit Cuba—there are plenty of opportunities for a man like you and the lifestyle is so less squalid than the City of Angels. And if that's too big a trip for you, then swing by Benny Siegel. He's in Las Vegas nowadays and would be happy to work with a reliable fella like yourself from the good old days."

5

ALEX TOOK THE train to New York, his first time back since the day he got out of Sing Sing and passed through when he'd spent three hours in the station before heading west. He was too embarrassed to even try a visit to his boys in Hoboken.

With an overnight stopover in Chicago, the journey only took two days before he reached Penn and went about finding a bed for the night. The streets were all in the same place, but everything was different. Maybe it was the fact he was forced to stay off Times Square instead of a more upmarket location. Perhaps Alex was just completely alone—an experience he had not felt in Manhattan since the day his family arrived from the old country.

No expense was spared at the fleapit known as the Hotel Bristol on Thirty-Ninth and Sixth. In fact, no expense was spent either. The joint hadn't seen a lick of paint since the Great War, and the receptionist might have been witness to the birth of the nation.

Alex did his best to ignore the peeling wallpaper and acrid stench in the corridors. Instead, he threw his clothes in the wardrobe and hit the street to grab a bite to eat in a nearby diner before keeping his head down and taking every precaution not to be recognized—now or after the job.

The next day, he took a train and ferry out to Coney Island. As the vessel chugged its way along the Hudson, Alex's mind cast back to the time he and his teenage girlfriend, Rebecca, had made the same journey. He had won her a toy at the fair and they had got stuck at the top of a Ferris wheel. When the boat docked, the enormous ride still turned slowly and a bitter smile ripped across Alex's face. That afternoon had been one of the happiest of his life, but now this place meant nothing to him.

Two blocks away from the main thoroughfare was the Half Moon Hotel. The frontage comprised a brick wall and a crescent-shaped sign above the unassuming entranceway. There were four vehicles in the parking lot, all black saloons—reeking of cop.

Alex scouted around the perimeter of the Half Moon and found the hotel was split into two sections. The main building comprised ten stories and a second was attached to it, only four stories high. The rear hotel rooms overlooked the lower effort, but all he had was a room number and the sight of a plainclothes detective leaning against the back wall beside each of the two staff entrances.

Before he could hatch a plan, Alex needed to look inside, but achieving even that goal would not be simple. And he couldn't be sure having entered the joint that he could perform the same feat twice and not be spotted.

The only option was to wing it and wait for nightfall before taking the risk of breaking and entering. Also, he needed to go one block west to make sure the getaway vehicle was positioned where Meyer had promised it. Without that, he would have to stick around for the ferry to set sail and that was no way to leave the scene of a crime.

HAVING WALKED TO the car and chugged down a burger and fries along with a cup of coffee, Alex waited until darkness fell in a local bar. Old habits died hard because he spent the entire evening hugging a single beer at the back of the establishment, hiding in the shadows.

By eleven, he thought he had given more than enough time for Abe Reles to get to bed. Tomorrow was his day to shine in court, so the officers on his protection detail would have insisted he had an early night. Even if they hadn't, Alex's impatience got the better of him, so he threw two bucks down for a tip and headed out into the evening air.

A circuitous trip around Coney Island brought Alex back to the Half Moon. His natural professional caution prevented him from taking a direct route. Anyone seeing this gray figure in a fedora wouldn't think twice about him and would be hard-pushed to notice him heading toward his intended destination.

At the rear of the hotel, the two flatfeet remained glued to the walls, so that didn't look a promising start. Alex wandered round to the front and hung back at the far side of the parking lot, squatting between a low wall and a car that had arrived since his last sortie. A silence descended on the area, punctuated by the occasional distant whoop from the fair.

His patience paid dividends because fifteen long minutes later, a group of men and women appeared and made their way to the entrance. They were chatting to each other and, with so many people swirling around, nobody noticed Alex tag along at the back and join them as the party entered the hotel and lined up at the reception desk to get their keys.

Before they had a chance to disperse, he slipped to one side and made straight for the stairwell. Even though there was a cop sat in the lobby, there were too many moving bodies for the guy to see Alex peel off, let alone glimpse his face.

Up four flights of stairs and he hugged the wall next to the solid wooden doorway. He pressed his ear to the surface–nothing. First, he placed his hand on the handle, and then he turned it ever so slowly, waiting for the inevitable sight of another gumshoe on the other side.

With the door open ten inches, Alex popped his head into the residential space–two corridors met in an L-shape at the stairwell. Sensible location for a fire escape. Along the left were double doors fifty feet away and to the right was nothing but a long corridor filled with nothing but a pair of shoes at the far end, resting in the inky darkness.

Alex edged toward the double doors and monitored the room numbers—517, 519, 521… then the doors. One thing was sure: his quarry in 523 was on the other side and, therefore, there would be at least a patrolman from the protection detail five feet in front—unseen right now but present, nonetheless. He inhaled, felt for the piece in his pants, and pushed the door open.

A chair met him with no guard. Strange, but Alex was happy to take the good fortune. Keeping his hand on his revolver, he opened the door and, as casually as a hitman can, walked into Abe Reles' hotel room.

RELES WAS ASLEEP, sat up in his bed, clothed with a book on his lap. When Alex closed the door behind himself, Abe woke up with a start and his jaw dropped when he recognized his guest.

"What the…"

"Save it, Abe."

Alex pulled his gun and kept it aimed at Reles, while he circled around the room to make the guy's torso an easier target. Reles never took his eyes off him during this maneuver, even when he sidled over to the adjoining door and checked that the en suite was empty.

"Nice place you got here, Abe."

"They're looking after me just swell."

"The cops want something from you, that's why. It's not because of your charismatic charm."

"I know. You do what you gotta do."

"That may well be the difference between you and me, Abe. See, back in the day, I was up against that special prosecutor Dewey and he gave me the option to sing like a canary. I refused."

He shot daggers into Reles' eyes, a mix of deep disgust and sheer hatred.

"Look where it got you, though, Alex. The cops sent you up the river, and from what I heard, the syndicate turned their back on you. How long were you in jail?"

"Five-year sentence but out with good behavior."

Reles laughed—his book fell off his lap and landed with a thud on the floor.

"Good behavior? How much did you have to suck in to survive? And I'm not in your league—never have been."

"Abe, it is not a competition, but there are some things you just shouldn't do."

"In case you haven't noticed, we're not Sicilian. We are Jewish and the vow of omertà doesn't apply to us."

"It's the same code of silence, whoever you are. What the hell drove you to squeal, anyway?"

"Louis and Anastasia screwed me. Then they put a hit on me. I was trapped in a corner when the Feds offered me a way out. If I hadn't taken their deal, we wouldn't be talking right now."

His voice trailed off as he pondered what Alex was doing in his room—other than passing the time of day.

"I didn't trust Louis or Albert either—they stole from me too, but when I had the opportunity, there was no way I could squeal."

"You'd have done the same if you were in my shoes, Alex. It's easy to make pronouncements when there isn't a contract out on your head."

"That may be so, Abe, but I never squealed. Besides, what do you think will happen to you for the rest of your life? Are the Feds going to guard you day and night?"

"They've got plans to keep me safe—you don't have to worry about that... Hey, how did you get in here? Wasn't there a detective outside my door?"

Alex shook his head. Abe's question was a good one. The chances of the flatfoot taking a leak during his shift were close to zero. If Meyer could organize a getaway vehicle, then perhaps he could orchestrate other things too.

"No one was there to protect you, Abe. I walked straight in here. Nobody stopped or frisked me. Up the stairs and here I am."

Reles gulped and his fingers gripped the blankets at the implication of his guards' absence. Alex sighed and glanced out of the window. The room was at the rear of the hotel, on the side that overlooked the second, lower building.

"I need you to stand up, Abe."

"You don't have to do this, Alex."

"We both know that's not true. I might have been somebody in the syndicate when we last met, but now I'm just a hired gun. Get up."

The final two words were said with menace, and the icy glint in his eyes returned. Abe nodded and followed Alex's instruction.

"Open the window, Abe. It's too stuffy in this pit."

Reles walked over to the sash and heaved the pane of glass up. The drapes fluttered in the breeze and both men took a moment to enjoy the fresh air against their faces. In that instant, Abe bolted for the exit but Alex was too quick. Three paces and he reached Reles' hand on the handle and grabbed the guy's wrist, yanking it away from its grip.

Maintaining his hold on Reles, Alex punched the man in the jaw with his fist, which stopped Abe from struggling. Alex dragged him over to the sash and stuffed the gun into his pants pocket. With both hands free, he took Reles by the scruff of the neck.

"Perch on the windowsill, Abe."

A clear instruction issued with no hint of emotion, which Reles followed without hesitation, his legs dangling outside.

"Does it have to be like this, Alex? We both hate Buchalter and Anastasia."

Alex took half a pace back before pushing Reles with all his might, and the guy launched out into the blackness and landed with a crack on the flat roof of the lower building, some fifteen feet away from the side.

"Abe, when you sing like a canary, you must learn to fly like a bird."

6

AS ALEX STOOD in front of the information display at Penn, he was reminded of Meyer's parting words to him. While a plane ride to Cuba sounded exotic, Alex did not like the thought of flying, but a train journey to Vegas and the chance to catch up with an old friend would be a most welcome diversion before he returned to his hovel in LA.

"Meyer, it's me."

"Hello."

"That job has been taken care of."

"Good, and thank you. I will show my appreciation before the end of the day."

"Always glad to help… Before you hang up, could you put me in touch with Benny? I think I might pay him a visit on the way home."

"Sure thing. I'll place a call now and get him to pick you up when you arrive in town."

"You're a mensch."

"So they say."

WHEN ALEX STEPPED off the train in Vegas, there was no one on the platform. Maybe Meyer hadn't kept his word, or perhaps Benny wasn't as pleased to be associated with him as Meyer had implied. He sighed and wandered toward the exit and out into the arrivals area. The hustle and bustle of the transportation hub overwhelmed him as men and women jostled against him. It was worse than being at Penn.

He made his way to the grand entranceway enjoying the breeze on his face. Then out of the corner of his eye was a guy in a charcoal suit and black hat who was edging toward the door at about the same rate as him. Nothing unusual about that—apart from the fact that the fella had been waiting by the platform exit when he stepped off the train. His back stiffened as he poised himself, ready for action.

A fresh burst of travelers milled through the entranceway and he slipped inside the throng and doubled-back on himself, head down, trying to lower his height and become invisible. He had no idea who the guy was, but he wasn't the welcoming party Alex was expecting. Perhaps Meyer had dropped a dime on him and the syndicate was mopping up old vendettas.

Whatever the reason, Alex found a different way out of the joint. A quick look over his shoulder and the black hat wasn't around. The only trouble was that he was back in the ticketing area, about as close to the center of the building as possible. He ducked into the washrooms, walked into a stall, and shut the door to give himself time to think.

He lit a cigarette and inhaled to clear his mind and consider his options. The washroom entrance opened and closed—there had been two guys at the sinks, and at least one cubicle was locked, with a man standing at the urinal. Then a faucet was turned on and water gurgled. Nothing to worry about on that account.

Alex figured he should remain fifteen minutes and then head straight out. Black hat would have assumed he had lost him leaving the station and, in that case, there would be no point staying here to wait for a fella who had already departed.

A second cigarette consumed, he opened the cubicle to see a different mix of men by the sinks, so he headed out of the room to make a bid for freedom.

ALEX STEPPED INTO the main atrium and took two paces forward before a voice he recognized punctured the air.

"Got a smoke, Mac?"

He froze, and as he turned around, he placed his hand in his pants pocket to hold his pistol. By the time he faced back to the washroom, he saw the guy with the black hat and charcoal gray suit, head down, wearing a fedora. The only visible part of his face was the tip of his nose, and that gave Alex no clue who it was—but the voice.

He walked straight up to the fella and pulled out a packet of cigarettes from his jacket. Then he tapped the end of the pack to encourage a single smoke to rise out of the packet and offered it to the guy.

"Thanks, Alex. I don't suppose you've got a light as well?"

Alex smiled at his former lieutenant, Ezra Kohut, and fished out a book of matches with a picture of a half-moon on the front from another pocket.

"Keep 'em."

They shook hands and as they did, Alex placed a palm on Ezra's elbow to show the warmth of his feelings—he hadn't seen this fella since the judge pronounced his sentence.

"If you're here to whack me, better make it quick because I am damn hungry, Ezra."

"What're you talking about? Benny sent me to pick you up, but you've been running around the station ever since you got off the train. When you U-turned into the john I reckoned either you had an upset stomach or you thought you were being followed. So I waited—you had to leave the head at some point."

"Where are you taking me?"

"Benny's in a joint called the El Rancho."

"What kind of place is that?"

"You'll see, Alex. My car's parked outside."

ALEX HAD SEEN nothing like El Rancho before. His life on the east and west coasts—and occasional trips to Chicago and Detroit—meant the Tex-Mex experience had passed him by. The hotel oozed southern state charm, if you liked that kind of thing and cosmopolitan Alex was not such a person.

Ezra saw his expression as they drove into the parking lot and laughed. "This ain't no Richardson, that's for sure."

Mention of their old speakeasy sent an image flashing through Alex's head as he recalled his first date with his mistress, Ida, and the magic of that evening. Then a shudder down his spine as the memory of her limbs flailing as he suffocated her all those years later.

"Times change. People change."

As they approached the entrance on foot, the doorman nodded at Ezra and took him to one side for a quiet word before they reached the lobby. His former lieutenant must have some juice here.

Through the reception area, which could be mistaken for a cantina, crammed as it was with tables for the patrons and enough adobe pots to grow a cactus for every day of the year. Through a restaurant and out onto a patio laden with more adobe-based items and two grins at a table overlooking the pool.

"Good to see you, Alex."

"Likewise, Benny."

"Do you remember Massimo?"

"How will I ever forget my best Italian lieutenant from our New York escapades?"

Handshakes and hugs all round. Then they sat down and Benny Siegel ordered drinks as they jawed about East Coast times and the syndicate. Ezra and Massimo remained quiet during this because they were in the presence of two fellas who were or had been members of the nationwide board which ruled all major organized gangs in the country.

The glasses emptied and were filled again by the attentive waiters while the conversation turned toward the present day.

"How long have you been here, Benny?"

"I moved to LA two years after you journeyed upstate, but as you know I had visited many times before then. Hooked up with Jack Dragna and we did some work together. Last year I heard about what Vegas has to offer and thought I'd check it out for myself. Three weeks later, I relocated and have been here ever since."

"You're attracted to Tex-Mex fakery?"

"I know, but looks can be deceiving. If you strip away the pathetic attempt to mimic Texan casinos, what you have here is a goldmine waiting to be dug."

"Here we go again."

"Listen to me, Alex. All those years ago, did I not say we needed to find a new territory to plunder? Las Vegas is that place."

"And how far have you got following your dream?"

"I'm doing fine. This joint is just the start. I am learning the ropes and figuring out what'll work here for gambling."

"You told me you only needed a piece of green baize and a pack of cards and you'd set up a casino in a week."

"True, but I want more than a mere gaming house. I've got my eyes on a much bigger prize. Imagine a building where there are card tables, for sure, but also we provide a vast array of other entertainment opportunities—restaurants, bars, stage shows, and a room to lay your head so you can stay in the place for days at a time."

Alex recalled his own vision for his speakeasies when he combined drinking, whoring, and a cabaret show. He and Benny weren't far apart if he was honest with himself.

"I've been to Texas and seen how successful the ranch casinos have been and I want to do something similar here—but I realize I can do it better by making my venue more cosmopolitan. We both know that no New Yorker would come to a place that looks as though William Boyd is just around the corner."

"Do you own the El Rancho then?"

"No, not yet. Since coming here, I've spent my time taking control of some hotel services, like prostitution, skimming, and union extortion. Work was going so well that Meyer suggested Ezra and Massimo joined me, and as you were otherwise engaged, I invited them to stay in Vegas."

"Has he been looking after you?"

"Yes, Alex."

"A joke, Massimo. I'd expect no less of Benny, but I am glad matters have worked out for you guys—I never prepared you for my departure."

"Don't worry about it, Alex. Once you went upstate, Ezra and I carried on looking after our ventures under Meyer's watchful eye and protection."

Another round of drinks appeared on the table and Benny proposed a toast. "We live together, we love together…"

"…and we die alone," came the chorus from the others.

"Do you fancy joining the party, Alex? A man of your caliber will make his mark real easily, and there is a tremendous amount we can do in this town. There is no syndicate here—no other gangs jostling for territory. It's like the Bowery all over again. Work with me, Alex."

He weighed up his options in the time it took him to inhale.

"Come back after Hanukkah and we'll make big money together."

January 1942

7

BENNY HELPED ALEX find a place to stay after he arrived in Las Vegas with two suitcases and a pocket full of hope for the future. He had spent his time in LA treading water—not drowning, but not getting anywhere either. He considered that he had survived and that summed up his life from the moment he stepped on the bus that took him to Rikers back in '36.

Living in the City of Angels had been a monotonous experience. His apartment had been somewhere to sleep and eat. Without his ties to New York and the powerful friends he had counted on all his adult life, Alex felt adrift, and to make matters worse, the fire in his belly that drove him to succeed appeared to have been extinguished.

Meeting Benny and some of the old gang showed Alex the world continued to turn and that there was an opportunity out there for the taking. There were no sidewalks paved with gold on offer, but there never were. The only way to succeed is to seize the moment with both hands and not let go until you have squeezed the life out of it, just as he had done to his mistress. May Ida rest in peace.

The place Benny found for him was a block away from the corner of Las Vegas Boulevard and Sahara Avenue, the location of the El Rancho. Alex's third-floor apartment came with two bedrooms and a view of the desert—almost every joint in the city had a sandy vista because the town comprised only two streets and a handful of stores, along with a sprawled out residential area. And the funny thing was that Alex could walk to work because he was stationed at the El Rancho with an official job title of services manager, a phrase so meaningless not even Benny could remember why he chose it.

"You'll get a name badge and a regular paycheck, but you will earn through me too."

"Just make sure you provide me with enough documentation for my income statement to the IRS."

"And you used to accuse me of making jokes."

"Benny, I am dead serious. Every year since I left the joint, I have filed my taxes. There is no way they will drag me back to jail."

"Sure, Alex, but remember that if we are only half as successful as I predict, you will make much more than any hotel worker could generate."

"I'll figure something out when the time comes."

"You do that, Alex. Meantime, pop over to El Rancho's restaurant tomorrow afternoon. A friend of mine is coming into town I want you to meet."

"ALEX, THIS IS Mickey. You share two things so I know you'll get along. First, there's your name—you are both Cohens."

"And second, Benny?"

"You were both boxers. What are the odds, right?"

Alex shook hands with the stocky balding man a handful of years his junior and the three men sat down. He had a firm grip and a keen eye, but his abdomen had gone to seed since his glory days in the ring a decade before.

When Benny first headed west, he had worked alongside Dragna, eventually usurping his top-dog position. Then Benny brought in Mickey over Dragna's head, who remained unforgiving of the whole escapade–one reason Mickey was so eager to come to Vegas.

Alex didn't care about what had happened on the west coast—he knew Benny well enough from days gone by to understand how the fella operated. He blew hot and cold in the same breath. One minute the world was a joke, the next he'd hold a gun to a guy's head and shoot his brains clean out.

"The first thing we need to do is get this joint here sorted out. The name on the deed may not be mine, but I want to ensure that I dip my beak in every available trough."

"Benny, what do you want us to do?"

"Alex, you and Mickey should start with the hotel workers. Most of them are unionized—I do not judge—but we need to control this Hotel and Restaurant Employees Union. Nothing we do in El Rancho will succeed without the staff."

THE TWO MEN used the rest of the afternoon to sip coffees, get to know each other better, and form a plan of attack.

"I heard you worked with Capone back in the day."

"Yes, Alex. I spent a while in Chicago with Alfonse during the early years of Prohibition. Good guy. I got a lot of time for him and his brother."

"I never met a sibling."

"Mattie's a decent fella too. Quieter than Alfonse, but bright as a button."

"That makes both of them then. You heard anything about how Alfonse is doing?"

"Didn't you know? They put him into Alcatraz and then three years ago they paroled him. Word on the street is that he's a gibbering idiot—potatoes for brains. I met a guy who'd spoken to a fella who said Alfonse was retired in Florida waiting to die."

"He took a beating in Alcatraz?"

"Apparently not. Some medical condition or he just turned plain stupid. A couple of the old-timers think it's only an act to keep him out of jail, but I know for a fact that he went into hospital in Baltimore so I'm not so sure about that."

Alex mulled over what Mickey had said. If he ever got a chance, he'd head down to Florida and try to visit the guy. They weren't the closest of friends but jail, hospital, and a slow death weren't how Alfonse should meet his end. The man deserved a hail of bullets or a sudden heart attack on top of his wife or mistress. Not to lose his mind and fade into obscurity under the Miami-Dade sun.

ALEX, MICKEY, EZRA, and Massimo got to work the next day when they tracked down the local convener folding sheets in the laundry room. Hughie Mathews had constructed a fine pile of white cotton blankets before the four men surrounded him. He jumped as he looked up–their footsteps had been hidden under the clatter of the nearby machinery.

"Are you Hughie?"

The guy eyed Alex, unsure whether this was a shakedown, but certain he didn't recognize two of the group.

"Yes. Forgive me, I know Mr. Kohut and Mr. Sciarra, but we have not been introduced."

"I am Mr. Cohen, but call me Alex."

"And I am Mr. Cohen, which is why you should call me Mickey."

Mathews smiled at the lightness of touch and then his face soured as he reminded himself that Ezra and Massimo were in the group. Everybody knew they were with Benny Siegel, and that man was a gangster.

"How can I help you? I doubt if you've gained an interest in the cleaning services offered at the hotel."

"Hughie, you are right. We don't give a damn about the sheets, but we care about your members. When you get a chance, would you be so kind as to join us for a refreshment on the veranda?"

"Will there be liquor to drink?"

"If you want."

"Then I'll see you in an hour when I have my break."
"You can take it now if you'd prefer."
"Is that on the up and up, Mr. Kohut?"
"Sure, bud. Call me Ezra."

"THIS IS THE situation as I understand it, Hughie."

Alex had ordered everyone a beer, which Mathews consumed with relish. This was a working stiff who grabbed any opportunity that came his way.

"The El Rancho does its best to look after its staff, but it doesn't offer top-dollar wages and it could do better with sick pay. No disrespect to Ezra and Massimo who have been helping Mr. Siegel in the place for a while now, as I understand it."

"You new to town?"

"Came out this month and Mickey arrived yesterday, before you ask."

"Must be something big happening if such important men as you are crawling out of the woodwork."

Alex glanced at Mickey, who returned the gesture with a slight curling of his mouth. Mathews might be a small-time union sap, but he wasn't as stupid as he first appeared.

"We think the union can do better for itself and we would like to help. Would you be willing to accept two new members?"

"Always happy for people to pay their dues."

"We would expect to receive complimentary membership."

Mathews almost spat out a mouthful of beer.

"Now I think I've heard everything."

"Hear me out, Hughie. By having Mickey and me as representatives, you are very unlikely to find you have any problems with the hotel administration. In fact, I will provide my personal guarantee that is the case."

"We might only have been open for less than a year, but we have had no trouble yet with the management, so your offer doesn't mean very much."

"Hughie, my friend. You are looking at the past while Mickey and I are staring at the future coming down the tracks. James Cashman and Thomas Hull are fine men as management goes, but as time passes, you will find they'll need to cut corners to maximize their profit. And we all know that the first people to get it in the neck are the employees, right?"

"I guess… but why would Ezra and Massimo want to side with us workers when they've stood by Cashman and Hull since the place opened?"

"We represent outside interests, Hughie."

Ezra spoke softly, slowly, and his eyes were stone cold boring into Mathews' soul.

"I'm still not sure. You're selling tonic water to a healthy man."

"Hughie, let me make it easier for you. If you don't accept our invitation to help, then be certain of one thing: you will not be able to protect your members from the risks that prowl in every corner of a hotel. Who knows what accidents may befall an individual as they walk past this pool on the slippery surface of this patio…"

"Or what dangers lurk in the laundry machinery. Whoops, how did Hughie's hand get caught in the vicelike grip of that press?" Mickey offered this prediction while cracking his knuckles and that made Mathews swallow hard.

"Welcome to the union, gentlemen."

"Thank you. And one other thing—each Friday you will provide us with a small payment, let's say fifty dollars initially."

"What the hell for?"

"To protect you and your members from all these unforeseen circumstances we just mentioned."

"How am I going to afford that?"

"We are not asking you to put your hand into your pocket. That would be unjust. Raise your membership fees—that's what I would do if I were you."

8

ON FRIDAY, ALEX found Hughie in the laundry room, emptying large baskets of dirty clothing for sorting. Mathews caught sight of him early on this time, and Alex swore the man sighed from two hundred feet—shoulders raised and then slumped downward. He pretended not to notice Alex's impending arrival, but as soon as they were within shouting distance, Hughie nodded and stopped what he was doing.

"How's your week been?"

"Quiet, thanks, Alex."

"Just shows you what happens when Mickey and I get involved in the union."

"Yeah, right."

"Do you have the appreciation we asked for?"

Hughie nodded again and put his hand in a pocket to retrieve a bundle of notes. Alex counted the green and handed back a dollar.

"We are not thieves. I'm not going to stiff you, even over a single greenback."

"Mighty upright of you."

"Hughie, we are starting a long-term relationship and this journey best begins with each of us trusting the other. If we don't have that then we've got nothing."

"And I want you to understand that cash came from my pocket—I cannot ask my men to fund your theft."

"Harsh words, Hughie. Before you go slinging mud around, you better make sure you are on safe ground, my friend."

"Extracting money with menaces—that's extortion."

"I have not threatened you, Hughie, and I will not take kindly to anyone who spreads those kinds of rumors about me. Do you understand?"

Alex stepped one pace forward so that their noses were only inches apart–the fear in Mathews' eyes and the beads of sweat coagulating across his forehead.

"I told you before, if you prefer to have an easy time, raise membership fees. With the number of workers in this joint, adding a quarter on the current levy will get you my money and keep everyone nice and safe. There is no need for you to end up on poverty row for the sake of the staff here. You won't want it, the members wouldn't want that, and I have no use for you if you are destitute."

Alex leaned back to give Hughie some thinking space because the aim was to get the guy onside, not to intimidate him into making foolish decisions.

"I'm not sure they could all afford that."

"Then consider going on strike and demand more pay—nickel an hour would more than cover the extra and everyone would be happy—apart from Cashman and Hull. If they can manage to spend half a million to build this joint then the company should pay everybody a nickel more, right?"

"But nobody wants to lose a day's wage striking."

"It won't go that far. Remember, Mickey and I are on your side. A bit of chest-puffing negotiation and they will cave. You have my word on that."

Hughie smiled for the first time since he'd received a free beer. "Looks like we might get along just swell."

"For sure… and another thing before I forget, in the next week or two you'll have some more complimentary members. I'm increasing the number of working women in the resort and the union must get behind them from day one."

WHEN THE GIRLS arrived, Mathews needed no introductions–he spotted the nafkas a mile away.

"Hughie, if you want this hotel to thrive, we need to occupy our guests all the time. So we'll send families on a horse ride in the day and offer the men experiences of the flesh without their wives and kids."

"Alex, sometimes two blackjack tables, a roulette wheel, one craps table, and three rows of slot machines aren't enough."

"Playing cards is more fun when there's a woman on your arm and the promise of happiness at the end of your weary day."

Mickey understood that men liked to gamble and would do so on the spin of a coin. The local families who owned most of the real estate in the city took a piece of the action from each of the guys who ran a book in their bars and Mickey wanted to dip his beak in the same trough. So he went around the joints nearest to El Rancho to convince them to bend to his will.

The former boxer used a variety of means of persuasion, but by the time Alex's first call girls arrived in town, Mickey was getting ten percent from each venue. Then he turned his attention to El Rancho itself.

"You reckon the casino is as successful as it could be, Alex?"

"There's always room for improvement, but I think we need to watch the croupiers before we worry about anything else."

"Damn straight. I observed them all last night. Every single one is skimming from the take, and each croupier is palming cards and fixing winners."

"Let's both go tonight and find out if we can make everybody see reason."

ALEX AND MICKEY met up at ten to give the room a chance to get swinging. Massimo and Ezra were also there, but Alex had instructed them to keep their distance otherwise they'd be too easily spotted.

The advantage the two Cohens had was that they were both new in the hotel and not everyone had seen who they were. Alex's old lieutenants were all too well known. One Scotch later and Mickey nudged Alex and eyed a guy on a blackjack table. Alex nodded and they sauntered over to watch the game unfold.

Three men sat in front of the dealer, and to the casual observer, everything looked peachy. Nobody appeared to be winning more than the others, and the cards seemed to ebb and flow as a game of chance should.

To a more trained eye, each round involved at least one card being dealt from the bottom of the deck. Alex leaned in to speak into Mickey's ear in a hushed tone, "Middle player. Every time he exchanges money for chips, he gets more than he has paid for. They're working together."

"Yeah and he's winning way more hands than the other two. I'm surprised the other players haven't noticed."

"They're good. The dealer makes sure his accomplice loses enough small hands that it feels fair."

They stepped back and watched some more. Alex was impressed with Averill Cartwright's technique as he carried on dealing. A single finger raised in the air got Ezra to scoot around the edge of the room and pass by.

"When the middle client leaves, follow him out and don't let him leave the hotel. We need a conversation—bring your knuckleduster."

Ezra returned to his station near Massimo and shared the instruction before they split up to cover both exits—one to the lobby and the other to the guest rooms. There was nothing to do but watch and wait. An hour later and the other two card sharps gave up on the night and headed out. Within thirty seconds, the middle player cashed out and walked away without leaving a tip. Most unusual. Alex joined the guy and Mickey approached Averill.

The card sharp went up to the reception desk and asked for his key.

"There you go, Mr. Eady. Have a good night."

The beaming grin of the receptionist was met with a half-smile by Hollis Eady, who turned around to head to the stairs but faced Alex instead.

"I wonder if you'd mind spending two minutes helping us find out what our customers think of the hotel?"

"Not right now, Mac. I'm heading up to bed—it's been a long day."

"I understand, but I must insist you help El Rancho improve its customer experience."

Alex seized Eady's elbow with a vicelike grip and dragged the man across the lobby and through a side door then down the corridor of this staff-only area and into a room with a table and a few chairs and not much else—apart from Averill already sitting down along with Mickey, Ezra, and Massimo. Alex threw Hollis into a seat next to Averill, ensuring the force of the movement was too great, so he nearly toppled over as soon as he landed on the chair.

"You need to listen and you must listen good, the pair of you."

Alex pointed at both men while Ezra took out his knuckleduster and wrapped it around his fist. Hollis' and Averill's eyes followed Ezra's actions, but the way their eyeballs flitted toward him told Alex they were listening too.

"We will not tolerate people stealing from us at El Rancho—whether that is the staff or a patron."

"We done nothing…"

Averill didn't have time to finish his sentence because Ezra punched him in the jaw. Hollis' mouth gaped open and his breathing went into overdrive. A tooth landed on the table and splatters of Averill's blood reached Hollis' sleeve.

"This is not a discussion. This is a situation where you need to listen. Understand?"

Both men nodded and Alex continued.

"How much money you make tonight, Mr. Eady?"

"Dunno, mister. A couple of hundred."

"Empty your pockets and give me two C-notes."

Eady shoved his hands in his pants and jacket until he remembered where he kept his roll, and then he counted out the required amount. Mickey saw how much the guy had remaining in his hand and snatched the rest of Eady's bundle.

"And this is the money you owe me, you *gonif*."

"I've got nothing left."

Alex laughed and Mickey chuckled in reaction.

"We are leaving you with your life, little man… Massimo, please show this gentleman the way out. He's departing the hotel immediately so take him up to his room and help him pack. He needs to be gone in less than five minutes."

"Where will I go at this time of night?"

"Not my problem."

Massimo hustled Hollis out of the door as Averill sweated buckets.

"We watched you steal from us throughout the evening, Cartwright."

"It was Hollis' idea—I just needed the money. He told me that if we played fast and loose, then we could both make a little extra on the side."

"How many days you been playing this game?"

"It's the third night—and it was to be the last anyway, honest. You gotta believe me."

Mickey slugged him in the face and blood gushed out of his nose. Just before he delivered another punch to the dealer, Alex put a hand on his arm.

"Your punishment is that you will lose your job and I never want to see you again. Not in the hotel. If you notice me walking down Fremont then you turn and go the other way. Do you understand?"

"Yessir."

"Good. Ezra, please escort this thief from the premises and give him his severance pay."

His lieutenant looked confused for a minute until Alex explained. "Give him what we owe him." A raise of an eyebrow and Ezra got the picture—he buried Cartwright's body a mile out in the desert an hour after Averill's departure from the hotel.

Within a day, word had leaked out about the dealer's disappearance and the sudden exit of Hollis Eady from El Rancho. Mickey had no problems with skimming in the casino from that moment on.

February 1942

9

ONE INNOVATION EL Rancho brought to Las Vegas was what it called its Opera House. While Caruso had been dead twenty years, the venue was not aimed at his kind of performance. Instead, it offered a run-of-the-mill stage show, featuring a mix of singing, dancing, and joke telling—vaudeville in all but name.

The setup reminded Alex of what he had done at the Richardson blind pig when he needed to find a way of increasing early evening takings—during the time slot between the afternoon gamblers and nighttime whoremongers. A headline act would appear for a week and then drift away to an off-Broadway run in New York or back to Los Angeles and its theater district. In between was the Opera House and its audience of men seeking some respite from their losses at the casino.

Alex was no expert in the performing arts, but he knew what he liked, and time in the Opera House after work diverted his attention from his loneliness when he returned to his apartment to sleep. While the comedians' jokes didn't always hit their mark, they were more funny than not. The singers were passable and the hoofers moved well enough around the stage.

Thoughts of the performances in the Richardson took Alex's mind to Ida, his mistress, and then to her sorry demise. She had been the toast of Yiddish theater in her day, but that day was a long time ago in a city far away.

He liked to sit near the back of the auditorium so he could slink off whenever he wanted without getting in the way of any of the customers. He also believed it gave him the best view of the sweep of the stage on the rare occasion when the director did more than get the actors to stand in the center and bellow out their lines.

A comedian left—none too soon in Alex's opinion—and a lone woman skipped to the center and sang. The band joined in after the first phrase and then the Opera House filled up with a variety of dancers, all jiggling about in unison. Toes were tapping in the audience and Alex made a mental note they should hang onto the singer because the crowd liked her.

As the song drew to a climax, the chorus fluttered in front of the lead and returned to the wings to let the star shine in all her glory. That was the moment he almost dropped his Scotch. The fourth girl in the line looked familiar—her face, at any rate. He racked his brains to place where he had seen her before.

Perhaps he'd noticed her out of the corner of his eye, walking around the hotel or on the sidewalk—that was the most obvious answer. Maybe she'd been in Los Angeles and they'd bumped into each other there. While that was possible, it didn't chime with Alex. Then the answer slapped him in the kisser.

The last time he had seen the woman was in New York about twenty years ago when he was recuperating from the war and he and Sarah had gone out to a show. He'd seen her then for less than a second, but his heart had all but exploded out of his chest. And Alex was feeling the same response now. Singing and dancing at the back of the stage was his childhood sweetheart, Rebecca. He beckoned a waitress over.

"How long before the show's finished?"

"It's not that bad, is it?"

"No, I'd like to introduce myself to a member of the cast and don't want to be in the way until the performance has ended."

The waitress gave him a knowing smile and bent down so she could be heard over the music.

"The whole enchilada will be cooked in another ten minutes—fifteen at most. Would you like me to buy some flowers to offer her?"

"That'd be great. Could you?"

"I was joking, Mr. Cohen, but I'll see what I can do."

"Sorry, my mistake. Don't go to any bother on my account."

By the time the audience applauded all the performers as they took their final bows, Alex was standing too and clapping as loud as he was able, causing the occasional head to turn. He didn't care. He collected the bunch of red roses the waitress had acquired for him and headed for the stage door.

ALEX FOUGHT HIS way through all the acts as they tumbled into the narrow corridor which led backstage. First there was a closed door with a silver star on the front, and then there were a series of other changing rooms—some small, others large—and dozens of men and women casting off their costumes and make-up.

He checked out each room until he reached the far end of the corridor and the last door. Girls streamed in and out, which made him guess this was the location of the chorus line. He pushed open the door with his foot to preserve his roses and popped his head inside.

His eyes almost bulged out of his skull—Alex had never seen so much bare female flesh on display at once. And that included his time running Lower East Side prostitution for most of the twenties and half of the thirties.

"Hey, Mac, close your mouth and shut the door. If you want to stay here, we charge for a late show."

"Don't be like that. The john's got a bunch of flowers. He might be about to ask you for a date."

The two women cackled with laughter at Alex's expense, but he ignored them. Instead, he kept searching around the room for Rebecca. Three minutes later, he reckoned he had checked out every face in the place apart from one. It was hidden inside a dress that refused to go on over the owner's head; she had decided not to undo the neck before changing.

Alex stepped forward, at which point the unknown woman spun round with her elbows sticking out hoping a rotating motion would ease the transport of a skull through a hole which was too small. An elbow thumped into Alex, causing him to step to one side and to drop the roses on the ground. In response to bumping into an uncharted and unexpected body, the girl bounced in the opposite direction and landed on the floor, legs in the air with her panties visible to the world.

He bent down and took her by the arm while unzipping her dress by about five inches—more than enough to free her from her torment. "Thanks, Mac," she said without looking at who had given her liberty.

When she glanced at Alex, she stopped herself in her tracks and squinted at him. Then her cheeks went red and she sat up to regain her composure.

"Alex?"

He nodded and put out a hand to help Rebecca to her feet.

"What the fuck are you doing here?"

"I could ask the same of you, Rebecca."

"I work here. And you?"

"Me too. I pulled into town a few weeks ago and thought I'd catch a show before I went home."

"We arrived last night—and ship out tomorrow."

"In that case, let me buy you a drink—unless you have anyone waiting for you in the wings."

"I got nobody, Alex."

AT THEIR POOLSIDE table, he ordered another Scotch and Rebecca chose a Southside—gin and mint on the rocks in a tumbler. They chinked glasses and settled in for their conversation.

"You always yearned to become a dancer—all those hours practicing in your parents' apartment have come good."

"You're kind, Alex. Ever since I was a little girl, I wanted to dance and that's what I've been doing for the last twenty years—been stuck in the chorus line of second-rate shows across the country."

"I might not be an expert, but I recall you had genuine talent."

"In this business, it's not how well you can dance but who you'll sleep with that counts the most. And I won't put it about for just anyone."

Rebecca stared straight into Alex's eyes as she mouthed the last phrase. Was she implying that she maintained her high morals from their teenage years or was giving him a massive come-on? He only knew he had spent his life not understanding women at all well.

"You're doing something you enjoy, which is more than most of the saps round here can say. I mean, the customers here spend their lives earning money to gamble it away in a matter of hours and then return to their miserable jobs to repeat the process until the next year."

"That's entertainment."

She giggled at her own joke and looked round to find a waiter to refill her glass. Nobody appeared until Alex raised an eye and then a fresh Southside materialized pronto.

"Here's to you, Alex Cohen. I saw your name in the papers a while back and drank a beer to your memory. Since then, zip."

Alex swirled his drink in its glass, letting the ice whoosh round the sides, before answering.

"I've had my difficulties—like my trial five years ago. Uncle Sam wasn't happy about the amount of tax I'd paid."

"They threw you in jail, right?"

"Yeah, but that's behind me and I'm making a living in Vegas, working with some people I knew back in New York."

"I always told you I didn't want to mix with criminal types."

"You used to taunt me about my business." Rebecca laughed.

"Yes. Your cheeks turned a funny shade of crimson when I shamed you about your gangster friends. I couldn't help myself."

"I was on top of the world, Rebecca, before my trial."

"And here you are in Vegas, watching second-rate shows with third-rate actresses."

"Don't say that about yourself. Even if you haven't, I always believed in you."

"Always? During the two decades since we saw each other and I told you I wanted nothing to do with you while you were…"

"…sleeping with Sarah, who later became my wife."

"Wow. Forgive me—I never treated you fairly. I was too young to know what *momzers* were out there, to appreciate what I almost had."

"It is easy to be wise in hindsight."

"You have any children?"

"Five boys."

"Still married?"

"No, I divorced her before I went inside. She's in Hoboken along with the kids. They haven't flown far from the nest."

"Look, Alex, it's getting late and I've an early train to catch…"

"You don't have to explain. It was great talking to you, if only for a few minutes."

"You interrupted me. I was going to say that I have to run tomorrow and would like to invite you back to my place but I'm sharing a room with three other girls and that is not the after drinks party I had in mind. You got somewhere we could go?"

"My apartment's a five-minute walk away."

"Then what are we still doing here? We have a lot more… talking to do before the night is through."

"I know this is early in the conversation, but I'll put it out there. I have some juice with the management and can get you a full-time, hundred-dollar-a-week contract at the drop of a hat. Front of house, not in the chorus."

"First, let's go to your bed before we make any long-term plans."

"You've changed, Rebecca."

"Like you can't imagine."

She patted him on the arm and they strolled through the lobby and out onto the sidewalk.

May 1942

10

"I HAVE MY eye on a piece of land, Mickey."

"Alex, is that why we are standing in the parking lot of the 91 Club, in the middle of nowhere, a mile south of El Rancho?"

"Pretty much. There's talk that some Texan movie theater owner wants to build a casino here, and I want some of that action."

"What's stopping you?"

"A fella you might know from LA who's holding out on a price—Guy McAfee."

Mickey raised a smile and nodded.

"Guy and I go back a ways. He was captain of the vice squad and left town to run this joint when a new mayor arrived in the city. This looks a classic McAfee dive—unpleasant to the eye but serves a mean drink. Shall we find out?"

"I'm not in the mood for a beer, Mickey. There are a few matters I need to sort out, but if I can get things arranged right, would you like to share the investment with me?"

"Why not do this alone?"

"Because it pays to have friends and besides, you and I have worked well together this past year and I prefer to spread success. I wouldn't want you to think I tried to prevent you from making a pile of dough. Resentment does unpleasant things to a man's mind."

"Thank you, Alex. I appreciate your concern and generosity. Right now, I am cash poor and so I can't take up your offer. Unlike some, I didn't make millions out of Prohibition."

"Any fool can generate a million—keeping it is the hard part. Between my ex-wife and Sing Sing, you'd be surprised how little I have left."

"Especially as your new skirt has been hanging around for quite a while now. I doubt if her apartment was cheap."

"I've looked after Rebecca and don't you worry how much rent I pay each month."

ALEX'S PROBLEM WAS simple: like almost every business deal in Vegas, there was always a local family that had an interest and who needed to be accommodated before any handshake could occur. In the case of the real estate surrounding the 91 Club, there was the slight matter of the planning office. The leader of the committee, Jackson Garnett was also the brother of the county sheriff, Woodie—the soil was outside the city line so Benny had no influence over those local yokels.

For any transfer of ownership to run smoothly, Alex needed to grease the wheels of bureaucracy and he was happy to do that. If he was prepared to bribe Tammany Hall officials, sending a wad of notes to a pinhead in Nevada would not be a moral issue for him.

Yet this was Alex's problem. Jackson was a weak individual who'd spent his entire adult life refusing to think for himself. In any other managerial job, this would be a major hindrance, but the land office operated in a different way. Jackson did nothing without the approval of his older brother, and Woodie did nothing without a good reason.

"THANKS FOR SEEING me, Sheriff Garnett."

"Always pleased to meet concerned citizens, Mr. *Cohen*."

Had Garnett emphasized his name to remember it or because he wanted to stress the Jewishness of the word? Alex let it go for now and focused on the purpose of his visit to the policeman's office.

"I am hoping you can help me with a situation that has arisen."

"We like to serve the community, Mr. Cohen."

"Call me Alex. There's a tract of land I'm interested in purchasing, but I am concerned that the sale won't get through the onerous vetting process from the county office."

"Well, I don't see how I can help you with that, Alex. I'm here to uphold the law, not stamp pieces of paper."

He chuckled because he knew why Alex was here and what he wanted. For reasons best known to himself, he was making things difficult for this man stood in front of him, while he slouched in his chair with his feet resting on the desk.

"As you know how the wheels turn so well around these parts, I thought you would help me secure safe passage for my endeavor."

"They might let your kind buy land in Vegas, boy, but your sort are not welcome in my county."

Alex inhaled to stop himself from taking immediate action, tipped his hat, and left the police station.

MICKEY JOINED ALEX that night and sat in his automobile until Jackson locked up and plodded to his vehicle. With Alex behind the wheel, they tailed Garnett's car until it stopped in the parking lot of the 91 Club. The fat dude disgorged himself and propped up the bar for a beer or two.

"What do you want to do, Alex?"

"We wait. There's no conversation we can have with him in front of a bar full of witnesses. I am hoping to convince him to help us without grandstanding before a bunch of drunks."

Almost an hour after Mickey asked his question, Jackson staggered out of the bar and into his car. Then he lurched out of the lot and back onto the highway. Alex followed at a safe distance for two miles south of Vegas when the cop left the road and parked in front of the Nevada Ring motel and entered a room, which opened just as he arrived at the door.

"Our sheriff was expected."

"Could you tell if it was a woman, Mickey?"

"Not for certain, but do you think Garnett is meeting a man in the middle of the night at this rundown shack?"

"I was thinking it might be a poker game. Nothing more sordid than that."

They hopped out and scurried to the motel and followed the frontage over to Jackson's room. Alex bent by the draped window and tried to look through the sliver of a gap. Then he stood up and walked over to Mickey, flattened to the wall next to the jamb.

"He ain't going nowhere for a few minutes at least, Mickey."

They smoked a cigarette and then Alex knocked on the door. A few mumbled words came from inside, but nobody welcomed them in. Mickey shrugged and kicked the door in with one well-aimed heel to the lock.

The sheriff and a woman were naked on top of the bed and from what Alex saw, satisfaction had yet to be achieved for either party.

"What the…?"

"Sheriff Garnett, so good to see you again. And you must be Mrs. Garnett, I presume?"

The woman struggled to grab a corner of the blanket to hide her embarrassment, but the lump of a cop was more concerned with protecting his own dignity. She looked at Jackson and then switched her attention back to Alex.

"I'm not…"

"Of course you're not married to this, darling." Alex pointed a casual finger at Garnett. "Why would he waste his money on such a crummy motel if you were? I'd advise you to throw your clothes on and get the hell out of here. Pretend this never happened."

Mickey helped by chucking her undies at her while she was still in bed and within a minute Garnett's companion had left the building as the sheriff tried to find his shorts.

"Stay on the mattress, Mr. Garnett. We wouldn't want you to get lost in this sumptuous paradise you built for your queen."

"No need to be all sarcastic, Cohen."

"I told you to call me Alex and I would prefer it if you do. Understand?"

A nod of acquiescence.

"If you recall, earlier today we were discussing a trifling matter of some real estate and I asked for your help and you refused."

"It wasn't like that, Alex."

Mickey slapped the cop on the back. "Don't talk unless you're ordered to, boy."

"You told me you had no influence over your brother and that you didn't want Jews anywhere near your beloved county. Well, now you got two of them in the same room. Does that bother you, sheriff?"

Mickey slapped him on the back again. "Answer the question, boy."

"No, not at all. I was just horsing around with you before. I am sure we can come to an arrangement over that land matter."

Alex faced Mickey and laughed. "Now the *goy* wants to negotiate."

Meanwhile, Jackson tried to slither off the bed and put his shorts on. With one foot inside, Alex turned back to him and pulled out his revolver, aiming it at Garnett's head.

"Stop what you're doing, mister. I did not give you permission to do jack squat."

Mickey lunged over and punched him in the jaw, causing the overweight cop to topple over, with his feet caught up in his underwear. Alex took two paces forward, round the corner of the bed, and placed a hand on Mickey's forearm as he readied to land another punch.

"My friend here wishes you harm but I only seek resolution. Before he gets his way, put on your shorts because the sight of you on the floor with your balls in the air is not something I wish to experience for a second longer than I have to."

Alex waited for Garnett to right himself and sit back on the bed, doing his best to maintain what little dignity remained.

"Does your wife know?"

"About Phyllis? No. I mean, she might suspect something…"

"Let me give you a word of advice, Garnett. She knows. Mine did when I played around and yours will too. The way you walk back into the house after you've visited Phyllis in this motel or the smell of her perfume on your collar. She'll know for sure."

Mickey grinned as Jackson's cheeks reddened. Alex lit a cigarette and threw the match on the floor.

"You must convince your brother to let the sale of the 91 Club land go through without a hitch. If there are any problems or difficulties—if the paperwork gets lost or a signature is missing—then I shall find you and Mickey'll continue what he started tonight."

"And I will only stop when you are dead, you *fercockte dreck.*"

"You understand?"

"Yes, Alex."

"Now put your pants on and slink back to your wife. Buy her some flowers and do something nice for her. You don't deserve her, so show some gratitude once in a while."

"Yessir."

Alex and Mickey waited for Jackson to leave the motel and drive off before they left the room.

"Would you have killed him or were you just doing a scare act on him, Mickey?"

"He'd have been dead unless you wanted to save him. I didn't care. Either way, the brother would have seen the deeds through safely."

"Now all I got to do is convince the guys who actually want to buy the land that they need me as an investor and get Guy McAfee to decide he wants to sell."

"I can't help you with the buyers, but tell McAfee that Benny and I say hello. He'll do whatever you ask at that point."

"You got history, huh?"

"Guy ran gambling in LA for Benny, and I was the bagman. We have a shared past."

RICHARD E GRIFFITH was a smart businessman who recognized the opportunity in footfall that Vegas represented. He had selected a location outside the city line but on the way in from Los Angeles on Highway 91 before anybody reached El Rancho. The man had hired his architect nephew, Bill Moore, to draw up plans for the thirty-five-acre site. The only sticking point was that McAfee didn't want to sell for reasonable money. Alex paid Griffith a visit to see what could be arranged.

"Thank you for agreeing to receive me, Mr. Griffith. I appreciate that a man in your position has little time and many people seeking to squander it."

"You are very welcome, Alex, but I asked around and understand you have a certain status in the community, shall we say?"

"Very kind. Now that we have massaged each other's egos, may I be presumptuous and get down to business?"

"A man after my own heart. Do proceed."

"Word on the street is that you are seeking to acquire a piece of land south of Vegas and that McAfee is demanding silly money for the privilege of handing over his ramshackle fleapit of a bar."

"This is true. I want to make the purchase and the toad isn't playing ball."

"What if I told you I am able to not only get McAfee to accept a lowball price but I can guarantee that the county will smooth out any issues which may arise as the paperwork makes its way through the bureaucracy—locals prefer locals buying their real estate."

"Alex, that'd be mighty peachy, but I suppose you'll want something in exchange."

"Correct. I will pay for the land out of my own pocket—I don't foresee it costing more than a thousand anyway—and in return, I would like a thirty percent stake in the hotel complex you and your nephew intend to develop."

"That's a high price you want to charge me."

"The resort will cost money to build and you will fund that, so from the get-go, it'll make a loss. I'm asking for just under a third of an enterprise that'll be worth nothing. And I secure the deal in the first place."

"You are a smooth talker, Alex."

He finished his cigarette and allowed Griffith to mull over the proposition.

"Well?"

"I'd be more comfortable with twenty or even a ten percent stake for you. After all, I have to care for my nephew."

"Look after him as much as you want, but that always comes from your end of the deal. It is thirty percent or nothing. Take it or leave it."

"And if I leave it?"

Alex smiled and flicked a piece of fluff off his pants.

"Then you would lose a business partner and gain an enemy. All my partners have made money. You choose which path to follow, but I want to know before I leave this room today. My time is as precious as yours and I do not intend to wait around on your decision."

Griffith took a puff on his cigar, which had been burning steadily throughout their conversation, and balanced it on the rim of his ashtray. Then he spat in his palm and reached out to shake hands. Alex was about to own a chunk of the Last Frontier hotel and casino. Griffith cracked open a bottle of Scotch to celebrate and they shared a drink before Alex bade him good day and hustled over to McAfee to coerce him into selling for a paltry thousand bucks.

11

JAMES RAGEN HAD a singular vision—to provide the country's only racing wire. The Samaritan figured that if he controlled the only source of competition results to bookies from one coast to the other then he would dictate when anybody heard which horse had won and by how many lengths.

Why would this matter? Because there was money to be made from calculating the odds of an event when you already knew the winner. An unscrupulous bookie could alter the odds he was offering in between the race actually finishing and the result being announced in some hick town on the other side of the country.

Ragen invested in the phone cable and trained up staff to learn how to listen to a stream of racing results and updates while simultaneously writing it all down or dictating it for somebody else to scrawl onto paper. In racetracks where he didn't have the authorization, he'd rent a nearby room and station a guy with a pair of binoculars to read the odds off the tote board by the track. So long as Ragen obtained the information he needed, he did not care how he got it.

Benny Siegel understood the importance of the Nationwide News Service wire and wanted a piece of the action. He had run gambling in Los Angeles with Jack Dragna and Mickey, and he wanted to do the same in Vegas.

"Alex, I have a proposition for you."

"If there's money to be made, I'm all ears."

"Have you come across James Ragen in your travels?"

"Not yet, but I have a feeling that I will do soon."

"Funny, Alex. He owns and runs the Nationwide News Service and if we want to run gambling in this city then we must get our hands on the wire."

"Where does this Ragen live?"

"In Los Angeles last I heard."

"So what do we need him for? We have direct or indirect control of the only casinos in town and Mickey is working his way through all the bookies in the bars here too."

"Alex, sometimes you make me laugh. Running the buildings where gaming takes place is good because the house can charge for the privilege of owning a floor, walls, and a ceiling, but the real money is made by those who set the odds."

"The probabilities are all fixed in a casino, though."

"Unless our dealers are palming cards, yes. The chances of a queen of spades appearing in a pack are the same every time some poor sap plays, Alex."

"But with horses it is different."

"Exactly so. It is one reason many people prefer racing. The unknown is never far away."

"Great if you are a john but not if you're running the book."

"The calculation to price the odds so the house is guaranteed to come out in profit no matter who wins—is much easier if you take the risk out of the process. Knowing the winners minutes before the locals find out is the edge a bookie needs."

The jigsaw pieces fell into place in Alex's mind. They get access to the wire and feed their bookies the results so that the odds can be fixed before the races are over.

"Benny, back to the point then. Why do you want to know if I've met Ragen before?"

"Simple. We must convince him to sell his interest in the Nationwide News Service and between us, I reckon we can do it. To show my confidence in you, I'll offer you a fifty-fifty split of whatever stake we gouge out of him."

"You'd better finish your cocktail. We've got a train to Los Angeles to catch. I never thought I'd hear myself say this, but I can't wait until I get back to the City of Angels."

RAGEN'S OFFICE WAS in Burbank—a much more pleasant corner of town than Alex's old haunts, and the two men waited in the guy's anteroom. Benny had had the foresight to book an appointment because he figured a fella like Ragen would not want to be blindsided by two Vegas hoods.

"Very kind of you to see us, Mr. Ragen."

"Benny, no need to be all formal with me just because you've brought along a new friend."

He eyed Alex for an instant and ignored him in favor of his older acquaintance.

"What brings you to this fair city?"

"To grab some autographs and make an investment."

"I didn't have you pegged as a *Laurel and Hardy* fan."

"George Raft is more my kind of fella."

"I should have guessed."

"How's the wire business, James?"

"So-so. You know how it is. Everybody wants something for nothing and will pay you tomorrow for what you give them today."

"It's the same all around the country. I've set up a lovely situation in Vegas—casinos and other gambling operations in bars and diners."

"Congratulations. We missed you in Los Angeles."

"And this means we feed the bookies under our wing with sports results —I need not explain to you how that works."

"I wish you well. If you want to buy a wire, the Nationwide is second to none."

"Good advertising slogan, James, but as you've mentioned it, Alex and I would like to buy the wire."

"Benny, you didn't need to travel all this way to place an order. A phone call would have been more than sufficient. It's great to see you, but…"

"James, I think you misunderstood. Alex and I want to acquire the Nationwide News."

Benny stared at James Ragen until the man figured out the context of his remarks and then stopped in his tracks, unable to decide whether to take Benny seriously or if it was one of his many jokes of dubious taste and humor.

"Are you kidding with me?"

"No, James, we want to buy the Nationwide. I mean, a stake in it. We have no desire to lose you or your energy, but the growth of your business and our plans for gaming across the country have an alignment of interests. So we are asking for a piece of the action."

James lit a cigarette and puffed at half the stick before saying another word, all the while looking Siegel square in the eye and acting as though Alex wasn't in the room.

"Benny, we go way back, don't we?"

"Ten years or more. You were one of the first fellas I met when I headed out west when Prohibition was ending."

"That means I understand you are a serious man and you know the kind of guy I am. Have you ever known me to have a business partner?"

"Not so's I recall."

"Never, Benny. I create, I own, I manage, and I live off the fat of my land. No sharing with anyone, ever, for anything, and I do not intend to start now."

"I would make a generous offer based on future asset value, but you don't sound that interested in hearing my proposition."

"Damn straight."

"Mr. Ragen," Alex interjected, "Forgive me for saying, but I believe you and Benny have got off on the wrong foot here and I'd like to see if I can put you both right."

Ragen smoked some more and seethed.

"The Nationwide is a fabulous business that creates a more than healthy income for you and any family you may have."

"A wife and son, James Junior."

"That it generates for your wife and little James. We only wish to see it grow as an enterprise and to make sure that the venues under our control, now and in the future, are guaranteed to receive the benefit of the sporting information the Nationwide carries."

"And for this you want a stake?"

"How else can we be certain of always being a happy customer who pays the best rate?"

James smiled again.

"Alex, you have waited while Benny and I had our discussion and then you interceded on his behalf. Congratulations. You are a polite man who understands that there is a time to speak and a moment to be silent. You have wasted your breath because you did not seem to listen to what I said. I will have no business partners. Not with you, not with Benny—no one."

"Is that your last word on the subject, James?"

"You can bet your bottom dollar on it, Benny."

"In that case, we shall not waste any more of your time and will bid you a fond farewell. If at any point you change your mind, then my door is always open. Until we meet again, just one last thing…"

"What's that, Benny?"

"Got any good tips for the two thirty at Saratoga tomorrow?"

ON THE TRAIN back to Vegas the following day, Benny laid out his plan B.

"Without the Nationwide, we will need to establish our own wire service. There are several outfits around the country that would be happy to invest in a rival to Ragen, so we shall have the money to create an infrastructure of our own."

"Good to hear. Did you think Ragen would sell to you?"

"No, but it never hurts to ask. If you shove your hand up enough skirts, one woman'll eventually let you sleep with her."

"Well put, Benny. Always a gentleman. Is that why you're such a hit with the dames?"

"Leave my *shlang* out of it."

"I'm messing with you. Who have you got backing our venture?"

"Interests in Detroit, New York, and Boston—most of the syndicate. We'll build up our network of racetracks and sell into the legitimate bookies in Vegas to begin with."

"And then?"

"Mickey will unearth the less legitimate books and we can then roll out the model we create into other cities like LA or San Francisco."

"The places Ragen wants to maintain control over?"

"San Francisco is open territory right now and, yes, giving Ragen a bloody nose on his home turf would be fun—and good for business too."

12

BENNY HARDLY WAITED to step off the train before making arrangements in Los Angeles and New York for the Trans-American Publishing company to forge its way in the world.

"We will incorporate on the west coast because it'll deliver the message to Ragen that he has a fight on his hands, Alex."

"Should we be so open with him? Would it not be wiser to build the service and sneak up on him unannounced?"

"Are you feeling middle-aged because you're sounding like you are? When I attack a guy, I prefer to run straight at him, punch him in the face and kidneys until he is on his knees, and then kick him until he's unconscious on the mat."

"I'd rather poison the fella and not break into a sweat."

"Either way, that's what we will do and, don't worry, meanwhile we shall fund a bunch of guys to be our eyes and ears at the New York tracks. Then we'll move onto Boston and the other locations dotted around the country where they love to run horses ragged for the pleasure of man."

"You do not sound like you approve of the sport, Benny."

"I prefer games where it is you against the world. Clinging to the sides of a huge animal thundering along a narrow path doesn't appeal. The Big Bankroll loved it, but I'd rather play cards or dice. At least you're not bouncing up and down the entire time."

MEYER BREEZED INTO town seven days later. Benny was pleased to see him but seemed annoyed at him for not announcing the visit beforehand. Alex was just happy to see his friend again.

"Been a while, Meyer."

"But wonderful to hear you're enjoying life in Las Vegas."

"The place has been good for me—and Benny has looked after me too. Thank you for smoothing that over for me because I doubt I would have had the chutzpah to go to him myself."

"Don't worry about it. I told you then and I'll repeat it now: many in the syndicate want to see you succeed and I am one of them. What you and Benny have planned here will change the shape of gambling across this fine nation."

"He always said the future was in casinos."

"That he did, but he had a strange way of explaining himself."

"Still does, Meyer. He has a particular style of looking at the world. Spend enough time with him and you get used to it."

"Have you reached that point yet?"

"He still surprises me on occasion, but I understand him better nowadays. Perhaps he's just calmed down a little—he came across as jittery and impatient when he was a younger man. Nowadays, he understands about maintaining a watchful eye on the goal and not to deviate from it."

"Sounds as though he is as inflexible as ever."

"What I meant was that important matters hold his attention much more now. During those Prohibition years, one minute Benny would do a hit, the next he'd be chasing any old tail that passed before his eyes. He's more grounded."

"Is that because he has a steady?"

"There's his wife and kids, but nobody he's involved with at present."

"Nicely put, Alex."

"I have my moments. Do you have any plans for this evening or can I take you to dinner?"

"THIS MIGHT ONLY be Las Vegas, but this is a world-class restaurant, wouldn't you say, Meyer?"

"It is very good. There's no chicken soup on the menu, but this salmon is most pleasant."

"When we open the Last Frontier later this year, I will make certain we ship in some specialties from New York."

"Cheesecake from Lindy's?"

"Not my top priority, but yeah, if I can sort out the logistics…"

"I'm sure the man who brought hooch from Canada and heroin from Palermo ought to be able to get a takeout from a Midtown eatery in Manhattan."

"I'll do my best, Meyer."

"Only a fool would expect anything less from you."

"Too kind."

"And how is time with Benny working out for you?"

"Like I said earlier, all is good."

"Is he the right man to be running the Trans-American?"

"Why yes. What an unusual question."

"Not at all. Who do you think provided the investment capital?"

"I'm looking at him."

Meyer nodded in acknowledgment, admission that he was the prime financier for the syndicate—ever since the Big Bankroll met his untimely demise.

"So let me ask again, Alex. Is my money safe in Benny's hands?"

"Hand on heart, yes. He has a singular vision and an understanding of what we need to do to make it a reality. The *schnook* you remember has gone and a stand-up guy has replaced him."

"I believe you, Alex, but promise me something."

"Whatever you want."

"If at any point you believe this project is going south, tell me immediately. If the wire comes good then you would have an excellent reason to claim a seat at the syndicate top table. Who'd be able to argue against that?"

"Here's hoping."

"Bring in the big fish and you can worry about it then."

"Follow the money and doors will open."

"Right. Talking of cash, I've hired a new bookkeeper."

"And why should I care about an accounts clerk?"

"When it's Sarah, your ex-wife, I thought you might have an interest."

"Is she doing all right?"

"For sure. I figured if someone was to get visibility into my revenue then I should have somebody with an impeccable moral compass who I can trust implicitly."

"And then you chose Sarah."

"Nice joke, Alex. She left *you*, didn't she? So her judgment isn't that clouded."

"Girl done good, despite her time with me."

"You still see your boys?"

"When I get the chance, Meyer."

"Do you mind that Sarah works for me?"

"Not at all. I'm glad she's keeping herself busy now the lads are becoming men. Besides, there's a new woman in my life."

"Where d'you meet her?"

"In the apartment below my parents' when we first came over from the old country. Then we bumped into each other again in El Rancho. Rebecca is performing later at the Opera House next door if you want to hear her sing."

13

MICKEY HAD WORKED hard since he took over running the gaming in the city. Once El Rancho's staff came to their knees, he hit the road and approached the Vegas bars and identified all the guys who made a book behind a beer glass.

Many of the bookies rolled over with ease—the opportunity to receive protection from a friend of Benny Siegel's was an offer very few could refuse. Though, now and again, Mickey met a guy who was less enthusiastic about losing ten percent of his takings for the right to carry on plying the same trade he was doing before he waltzed in and declared the dive bar part of his territory.

Sometimes, Cohen responded with a slap around the chops and the fella figured the odds pretty quick. Other times, he'd find the need to get rough with the guy. On rarer occasions still, the cops would be called and Mickey would plead down the charges and pay a fine to stop the case getting too serious.

"What are you doing spending time in a jail, Mickey?"

"Who's been snitching to you about my affairs?"

"Relax, my friend. Nobody has been talking out of turn, but if you're going to beat on a guy so bad that he's hospitalized, then make sure there aren't as many witnesses."

Mickey smirked.

"As I was doing it, I told myself, I should drag his sorry ass out into the back alley."

"The least you could have done—placing a call with Ezra or Massimo to lay hands on the guy would have been a better option. That way, no one would see you doing anything and there'd be a separation between you and a bookie bleeding in the street."

"I disagree, Alex. There is nothing like a public kicking to send a simple message to all the scumbags out there who want to argue with me or not hand over their tithe."

Alex knew better than to create an argument with Mickey, but he also felt the fella was causing waves around Vegas, which he could do without lapping at his shore. Mickey might have only been held in a cell overnight, but word was out that he had beaten up a bookie and the guy's life was hanging in the balance at Clark County General. Two bruised ribs and a broken jaw were hardly a sign of imminent death, but that wasn't the point. People believe what they hear, and nobody needed the gaming community to be living in fear. That was bad for business.

"Will you do me a favor, Mickey?"

"What are you after?"

"Next time you pay a visit to a new recruit, do you mind if I tag along? It reminds me of my days in the Bowery."

"If you want to relive your past, be my guest—but don't get in my way."

CLAUD GARFIELD SEATED himself at the end of the bar and men would come up to him now and again for a conversation and a handshake. To the casual observer, Claud was a popular guy, but Mickey and Alex read the situation differently as they sat at a table on the other side of the drinking establishment.

Some of Claud's acquaintances walked straight into the Lucky Pepper, spoke, and left, so the beer was far from the main attraction. Others would mumble to the barkeep before making their way over to Claud. Mickey leaned into Alex for a private conversation.

"He's taking ten, maybe twenty, bets an hour and he isn't paying me a penny for the privilege of working in my town."

"Have you explained to him how the new world is operating?"

"I did as you suggested and let Massimo intercede on my behalf, but when he returned on Friday to collect Garfield's appreciation, he left with bupkis."

With that, Mickey got out of his chair and approached Claud. No rush—a quiet saunter over like he wanted to place a bet. Alex followed him over to the corner spot—Mickey's tone had an edge to it. Having caught up, Alex arrived in time to hear Mickey make his introduction.

"I'm Mickey Cohen—you might have heard of me."

"Your name is familiar, but we've not met."

"A colleague visited you to explain the new situation you find yourself in, but he received no appreciation from you at the end of the week."

"Listen, Mac. This is my patch and I don't pay no one to sit at this bar. Just because you walk in with your dago lackey and your Hebrew charm doesn't mean nothing. You outsiders are all the same to me."

Mickey stepped forward. "Listen to me and listen really carefully. What you do in the Lucky Pepper is your affair, but the minute you take a bet in

Vegas it makes it my business and you must compensate me for the right to run a book. I am not asking whether you agree to this—I am telling you how it is."

Claud dropped off his stool and towered over Mickey by a clear eight inches at least, but Alex was still taller.

"I will not pay you a penny. Not now, not ever."

Mickey did a quarter turn to face Alex, smiled, and spoke loudly enough so that most of the bar was in earshot. "Did you hear what Garfield just said to me?"

Claud's attention was focused on Alex who remained silent, looking at Mickey to see what would happen next. He rotated toward Garfield and raised a fist, using the momentum of his twisting to land a jab in the middle of Claud's face. A tooth flew out with the impact and the guy fell backward, caught off his guard, and landed on the floor. Mickey took another pace forward and kneeled down, landing a second punch into Garfield's nose.

The fella tried to shuffle away despite his pain and scurried on all fours toward the restroom twenty feet from the bar. Mickey laughed and remained still to allow his quarry an opportunity to escape—or believe he had a chance to flee. He'd catch up with Claud when the sap arrived at the head door.

Mickey picked him up by the scruff of the neck and threw him into the washrooms. Alex joined them in the tiny space because beating the guy into unconsciousness wouldn't get Mickey his money.

When Alex entered the washroom, Mickey had Claud's head in his hand and he was stuffing it into a toilet bowl, making him drink the water as he gasped for breath.

"That's enough, Mickey."

Alex spoke quietly though with firm conviction, but the hothead either didn't hear or did not want to.

"Stop it, Mickey. We need the guy to agree to make payments to us."

Still no reaction, so Alex placed a hand on Mickey's arm. He swung round with his fist clenched as though he was about to smack Alex in the mouth.

"Keep your nose out of this," he spat. Mickey would end up killing the guy for sure and there had been too many witnesses next door to smooth it over with a thousand-dollar fine and a misdemeanor.

Alex raised both hands, palms facing outward, showing he meant no harm while Mickey remained transfixed. He laid his palms over Mickey's fists until his business partner relaxed his grip. Garfield coughed water out of his lungs and tried to leave the area, but Alex had saved his life for a reason. He grabbed Claud by the collar and hauled him up until he stood on his feet.

"My friend has asked you politely to show him appreciation for allowing you to run a book in this dive. If you enjoy breathing, I advise that you pay ten percent every week whether or not you want to."

Alex eyed Mickey and stared back at Garfield. "Do you agree?" Garfield nodded consent.

"I need you to say it out loud."

"Yes, Mac."

Alex let go and Claud's knees buckled under him and he collapsed onto the floor. With a tap to Mickey's elbow, the two men walked away, leaving Claud to recover from the beating he had just received.

"You shouldn't have done that, Alex. I told you not to become involved."

"Your fists are lethal weapons, Mickey, and I couldn't risk such a valuable commodity as you ending up behind bars just for the sake of a shakedown. I'm not saying the guy didn't deserve to receive a bloody nose. I thought we should get the business transaction out of the way before he lost consciousness."

"Be careful what you do, Alex. I don't like fellas who make me appear foolish."

"I got you your money. Nobody made you look a fool."

Alex exited the bar, worried how Mickey was so quick to temper and the extent to which he seemed out of control as soon as he beat on Garfield.

August 1942

14

ALEX WAITED A while before making any plans because he wasn't sure he could trust Mickey not to blaze a trail through Las Vegas, beating up bookies like he was trying to fight his way to a championship boxing match. When he thought the former slugger had calmed down enough, he asked Rebecca to go on vacation with him.

"That'd be swell. Where to?"

"Somewhere to guarantee us some sun and the beach."

"Los Angeles?"

"I've spent too much of my life there, already—not that I stayed anywhere near Malibu."

"Cape Cod?"

"Maybe, but I had Florida in mind."

"The Keys. I've never been there."

"Me neither and Miami Beach is supposed to be a great place to stay. Do you fancy a few days alone with me?"

"Sure do. I'll just need to square it with Cashman."

"He won't object—if you remind him I'm the one who'll be whisking you away."

"This will require a whole new wardrobe. I haven't been on a vacation since I was a little girl."

"Here's some clothes money—buy yourself some pretty things and make sure you get a necklace. We can't have a beautiful woman walk around Miami without something sparkling around her neck."

"You're too kind, Alex Cohen."

"You ain't so bad yourself, Rebecca Grunberg."

THEY TOOK THE train to Miami and Alex rented a car under his own name at the station. This was a vacation, and he didn't need to hide his identity from anyone or set himself up with an alibi—an unusual experience for him. She sat in the automobile with a broad grin on her face as they drove over to their hotel on Collins Drive.

"I never thought this would be us in a thousand years."

"What do you mean, Rebecca?"

"When we were kids, did you imagine you'd be driving me around Miami, Florida with enough green in your pocket to never have to work again?"

"Hey, I've done well, but I'm not set to retire any time soon. You're confusing me with some other fella."

"You say that, but I bet you've put sufficient aside over the years to be comfortable for the rest of your life."

"Uncle Sam and my ex-wife took a massive bite into my savings. I gave gelt to Sarah—the Feds swallowed the money from my checking account."

"I didn't mean to open old wounds, Alex… This place is great. Look at the palm trees."

Rebecca pointed at a line of foliage by the roadside, and he glanced at the green fronds as he hit the gas to get them to their hotel before nightfall.

The Hopkins sported a white art deco frontage and a doorman wearing spats—old-fashioned in this day and age. The marble lobby boasted a sweeping staircase which led to a mezzanine floor with a breakfast restaurant, according to the bellboy who began his spiel almost before he'd picked up their bags to take them to their third-story suite overlooking the sea. A five-spot kept the guy smiling as he closed the door on the couple.

Rebecca ran around the suite, brushing her hands against the sumptuous furniture on show in the two bedrooms, living space, and dining room. She marveled at the oil paintings on the wall and the sheer size of the place.

"This must have cost more than a week's wages."

"Don't worry about the price of things. Just enjoy yourself while we're here."

She threw open the balcony doors and stepped outside, flinging herself at the balustrade and staring out at the ocean. "Amazing."

Alex unpacked while Rebecca soaked in the panorama, and then he joined her on the balcony, although he sat on one of the recliners.

"We have this place for the entire week, so the view will still be there after you've hung your things up and got ready for dinner."

"Where shall we go?"

"You tell me. Pick something and I'll get the concierge to organize a booking for us."

"Italian."

"We should be safe with that selection—we are in Miami, after all."

"Huh?"

"Let's just say that many people born close to Mulberry Street live in these parts."

"Is the place crawling with gangsters?"

"No need to be dramatic—but Miami-Dade has a high proportion of casinos and a ridiculously low crime rate."

Rebecca giggled and then froze for a second.

"We are here on vacation, right? You haven't dragged me here to be with your mobster friends?"

"I am here because I want to spend time with you away from Vegas. There is an old friend I would like to visit, but he has been retired for several years. Apart from that, every waking minute will be with you."

"And sleeping minutes too, I hope."

Rebecca's mouth broke into a leering smile and she padded over to sit on his lap. She draped her arms around his neck and they kissed.

TIME FELL AWAY from the couple over the next four nights. They devoted their days to enjoying the beach, the odd foray to stores to buy more trinkets for Rebecca, and hanging in the many coffee shops dotted around town. Every morning, they ate breakfast on the mezzanine or out on the front terrace to watch the world go by while he devoured cereal, scrambled eggs with lox, a bagel with cream cheese and she consumed juice and a slice of toast.

"What should we do today?"

"Hit the beach this morning and the concierge mentioned a place for lunch which could be interesting: Cuban—and I don't even know quite what kind of food that means."

"Sounds like fun. Thank you for all this."

"You can't imagine how much happiness you bring to my life. It is I who should thank you."

She squeezed his palm and he sipped his coffee from the cup in his other hand, emotion welling up inside him.

"Rebecca, this afternoon, why don't you go for a massage?"

"That's a new one. Would there be a female masseuse?"

"This hotel isn't a bordello."

"Will you have one at the same time?"

"No, I need to spend a couple of hours somewhere else."

"On business?"

"Not quite."

"Well? You're making it sound very suspicious—for a man who is meant to be on vacation, remember?"

"There's a fella I used to know who has moved here—I mentioned him when we arrived and I thought I'd swing by and see how he is. You do not have to come. You can but it won't be very interesting for you."

"Who's the guy?"

"Alfonse Capone. You might have heard of him."

REBECCA TOUCHED ALEX'S arm as they sat in their saloon outside a palatial mansion on Palm Island. She had remained by his side for the ten minutes since he'd parked and not left the vehicle.

"Are you all right?"

"Yeah. I was thinking about times gone by and got lost in my past life."

"What happened to Al?"

"Alfonse? He was on top of the world, and then Ness slammed him to the ground for tax evasion. Threw him in jail and left him to die."

"But he's out now."

"Because of ill health. I heard he was beaten up in prison and got his skull smashed—he hasn't been the same since."

They remained in silence as Rebecca mulled that thought over in her head and tried to imagine how bad the beating must have been. The fella was only a name in the headlines to her, but he meant much more to Alex.

"You don't have to come in with me if you'd rather not. I won't mind and he won't know."

"We've been together long enough for me to want to be with you all the time—not just for the shiny moments."

They stepped out of the car and walked up the front path. Almost as Alex rang the bell, the door opened and a guy inquired the purpose of their visit. A brief conversation and the man showed them to a sitting room where they waited only two or three minutes.

Alfonse and Mae Capone appeared and Mae welcomed them to their home and invited them to rest awhile in the shade on the patio by their pool. Alex had spent no time with Mae before—his trips to Chicago had always been on syndicate business and conversation was stilted at the beginning now, but Rebecca helped, drawing the woman into chatting about the weather and their son, Albert.

"He's doing well for himself, isn't he, Alfonse? We're hoping he will graduate and then the world is his oyster."

"Does he come to visit often?"

"When he can. You know how it is with children."

Rebecca looked askance at Mae, whose eyes darted to Alex and back.

"Mae, we don't have any… I mean, we've only been dating a few months."

"Sorry, Rebecca. I knew that Alex had a family and assumed…"

"My family is fine and they live in Hoboken. You weren't to know I got divorced in thirty-six. But you two are going great guns—I admire that longevity in a relationship."

"I supported him during his incarceration."

Without warning, Alfonse stood up from his abject silence and jumped into the pool with his clothes still on. Mae sighed and called for him to swim to the edge of the water. When he eventually followed her command, the butler cocooned him in towels and dried him off. An hour more and Alex thanked Mae for the hospitality and moved to shake Alfonse's hand goodbye, but the man refused, hiding his fingers in his pants pockets.

Alex drove to the Hopkins without uttering a single word, brushing an occasional tear from the corner of his eye. When they got back, he parked in the hotel lot and placed a hand on her leg before she left the car.

"I'm sorry to have put you through that, Rebecca."

"That's all right. He's not how I was expecting."

"Nor me. That was quite a pummeling he got in prison. He used to be so alive—all his faculties firing the entire time."

"Alex, I've seen people like that before and they weren't beaten up. It was the pox."

"Yeah, I figured."

"I understand if you want an early night tonight, Alex."

"No, we've only got three days left so we should squeeze every ounce of life out of our time here. I'll get the concierge to recommend a club—if you fancy trying your hand at dancing without a stage."

"Sounds like heaven."

15

THE SUCCESS OF Trans-American News was hardly remarkable given the amount of effort Alex put into the venture. He pounded the streets of Vegas mopping up every bookie he could find who took bets on any track race in the country. If Trans-American didn't have any eyes on the event when Alex walked in, then by his return a week later, he had the racecourse covered. There were no excuses to refuse his business proposition.

In a short time, Trans-American received payments of a hundred dollars a day from its bookie subscribers. As a director of the company, Alex had a legitimate reason to be rolling in cash. He imagined the advice he'd receive from an accountant like Meyer and stashed most of his extra income into deposit boxes and spent a little on himself and more on Rebecca.

Benny, Mickey and he perched at their usual poolside table at El Rancho and surveyed their world.

"Mickey, you've done well to tie in the bookmakers in Vegas—every single one pays protection to us. And Alex, you've convinced most to buy the wire from Trans-American."

All three smiled at the perfect business they'd built for themselves.

"It's a good start, Benny."

"You never were satisfied, were you, Alex?"

"So everyone else keeps telling me. I just don't want to leave money on the table."

"And what are we missing out on?"

"Vegas has been great for us. We've learned a lot—I know I have—but there are plenty of other cities in this fine country and we should sell Trans-American into those places too."

"Then we'd go head-to-head against James Ragen."

"Depends where we pick next, Mickey. But yes, if he's already got customers, then it's an opportunity for them to choose a different supplier."

"Where do you have in mind, Alex?"

"First, I'd like to go to Los Angeles, because we should hit him on his home turf. If he crumbles there, then other territories will fall in line much easier."

"And if we don't?"

"Then we'll know we've got a fight on our hands and can ramp up the aggravation, Mickey."

"You have all the angles covered, eh?"

"No, Benny. But I have an eye on a huge prize, and I mean to get it."

The three laughed because Alex meant every single one of his bold words and the other two knew it. Convincing illegal bookies to spend money on a wire service when they were already paying through the nose for Ragen's would not be a walk in the park, but nothing worth having ever is.

ALEX TOOK EZRA and Massimo over to LA with him because he needed fellas he could trust and who could handle themselves when trouble came knocking on the door. His lieutenants were all that and more.

A few hours on the train and the men arrived in the City of Angels and settled into a three-bedroom apartment Benny still owned from his days running gaming in the city. It was the perfect cover for a fella to travel round town extorting lowlife degenerate gamblers and their bookmakers.

They spent their first week creating a picture of the city and marked every illegal gambling joint that took bets on horse races. A cross represented a joint with no current wire and a circle was a venue where Ragen already had a client. Then they visited each place on the map they pinned to the living room wall to convert the shape into a square which meant the bookmaker was a confirmed Trans-American customer.

Two months and thirty-six gambling joints later, Alex stared at the picture and surveyed his victories. They started with the crosses because the ones who weren't with Ragen would be easier to turn and all bar two crosses were now a square, showing how successful the three fellas had been since their arrival. The next phase was to take aim at the circles and walk into Ragen territory. Alex looked at the map to decide where they should begin their assault.

ALEX, EZRA, AND Massimo walked into a bar in the heart of Chavez Ravine, the Mexican quarter in the middle of the city. They had to start somewhere and Alex had chosen this spot over all the others because it sounded a tough place to crack.

They ordered a beer each at the bar and hung a while to get the lay of the land. Near the rear of the venue was a guy seated at a table with a stream of short-lived visitors. Alex nudged Massimo and nodded in the general direction. Ezra scratched his neck to give himself an opportunity to view the situation. Having waited as long as his patience would allow, Alex stood up and ambled over to take his position in the informal line of men.

"I'd like to place a bet."

"It's a free country. What's stopping you?"

"No need for the attitude, Mac. Anyone with brains can tell you're the guy to see for these matters."

"Maybe I am, but I don't know you from shit on my shoe."

Alex stared at the bookie for two long seconds and then smiled.

"Forgive me. We haven't been introduced and I have forgotten my manners. My name is Alex Cohen and I would like to place a bet with you on the results of a horse race due to run tomorrow at Saratoga. Do you think you can help me with this request?"

"Señor Cohen, you are in luck because you are speaking to Rodrigo Sanchez and that is what I do for a living."

Both men grinned and the tension eased between them.

"What odds are you giving for fifty dollars on No Hoper at the four o'clock at Saratoga?"

Sanchez blinked and scrunched his face.

"There's no horse running of that name, mister. What do you want?"

"To see if you are as on the ball as I thought you were. Well done."

"What of it?"

"I wish to offer you an opportunity to get better quality track information."

"No deal, bud. I got myself a wire service and that's all I need."

"That is where you and I disagree at the moment, Rodrigo. The thing is I know you use the Nationwide, but that is in the past. From now on, the Trans-American will be your wire of choice."

"And why would I want to switch when I have no need?"

"You're wrong, Rodrigo. You have a pressing need to change because your health will be affected if you stay with the Nationwide."

"Listen, old man. Don't come into my joint and threaten me."

"Would you prefer if we go outside?"

Sanchez stood up and Alex followed him out the side door into an alley—Ezra and Massimo arrived ten seconds later.

The guy took a single glance at the three-against-one odds and cooled his tone before Alex spoke his next words.

"Understand, I don't care what news wire I get, so long as I got one and nobody gets hurt."

"Rodrigo, we want you as a client and not as a corpse—that is bad for business."

"Tell me about it. The thing is that I make my payments to Jack Dragna and he isn't the kind of fella to sit still while you walk around stealing his customers from under him. You speak with him. If he tells me it's okay to buy from you, then I will. If not then our conversation ends here."

Alex took two steps forward so he and Sanchez were only inches apart, pulled out a pistol, and thrust it into the guy's stomach.

"You are stuck in a difficult position, Rodrigo. I feel for you and I have a simple way out. You agree here and now to buy from Trans-American, and I will return my piece to my pocket. If you don't do that, then I shall put a slug in your belly and watch you bleed out before I leave this alley."

Sanchez didn't need more than three seconds to make the decision that saved his life. Even a stranger could tell that Alex meant what he said from the fire in his eyes and the tone of his voice. They settled on an introductory fee and Alex let him go back inside.

"Looks as though we need to pay a visit to Jack Dragna."

LIKE SO MANY bosses before him, Dragna lived in a penthouse suite in a swanky part of town. Alex reminded himself of the feel of marble underfoot as he entered the Brookfield hotel and went up to the reception desk to announce himself.

Up in a private elevator and a gorilla on the top floor frisked him before allowing him into the apartment. Jack Dragna sat at a long wooden table in a red leather chair and beckoned for Alex to sit near him.

"Thank you for taking the time to see me."

"Happy to meet a friend of Benny's."

"Likewise, Jack."

Dragna offered Alex a coffee, which he accepted, but he declined the opportunity to chew on a Danish pastry, although the cinnamon swirl caught his eye more than once during their dialog.

"The primary reason I agreed to this conversation, Alex, was that my men tell me you have been selling your wares in LA and we both know you have omitted to offer me any appreciation for operating in my territory."

"Benny sends his regards and wishes you well. He told me to inform you of his intention to compete with the Nationwide News wire, and Benny understands how you have a lucrative financial arrangement with Ragen to prop him up in Los Angeles."

Dragna stared at Alex and sipped a coffee, occasionally nibbling at a sugary delight on his plate.

"Benny and I have no interest in interrupting your cash flow. All we request is that you support us as we compete with Ragen on our own terms. What does that mean we are asking you to do? Nothing. We are happy to show you our appreciation, and in return, we do not expect you will interfere with our endeavors."

"Alex, let me be clear to you. If you weren't a friend of Benny's, you and your colleagues would be dead by now. In fact, you'd have been killed within days of arriving in my town, but I allowed you to live because of my excellent relationship with Benny Siegel. If you make restitution for not coming to me sooner then we can negotiate in good faith on the matter of the racing wire."

"Let me know what sum you think is appropriate and I will organize the amount to be in your possession before the end of the week, Jack."

Alex didn't begrudge paying a syndicate member a small fraction of his income in LA to keep the business line secure, but why had it taken Jack so long to react to their arrival in town?

April 1943

16

WITH THE LAST Frontier opening in October, Alex offered Rebecca the chance to move to his new hotel and continue her singing career closer to his home, but she refused. While the idea was tempting, as a performer she was happy where she was and he was still welcome to come to any of her shows.

He took that opportunity at least two or three times a week because he loved to watch her perform—just like when they were kids—and that was magnified by the warm glow he felt when the audience applauded at the end of one of her numbers.

Even before the place opened to the public, Alex moved into a cottage in the grounds. It had been designed as a manager's dwelling so had been built to a very high spec.

"If you won't sing on my stage, would you live with me in the Last Frontier?"

He and Rebecca were lying in bed one Saturday morning.

"I'd like to, but I'm not sure. I need my own space. My time with you is great, but there is something healthy about being apart and meeting up again, don't you think?"

"We wouldn't be handcuffed together—you would continue to be the performer you are and I'll carry on with my business interests. The only difference is that we'd share the same living space. I mean, you spend most nights over here, anyway…"

"Let me think about it, Alex. Your suggestion is wonderful and the fact you are prepared to spend so much of your life with me is fabulous. Only…"

"Only you are afraid that this is a slippery slope. One minute you are in my bed, next you're in my house and then you think we'll get hitched and you will be tied to me forever."

Rebecca was silent in response.

"You have nothing to fear on that score—at least not from me. I've been down that road before and I am happy to remain single. I'd be even happier if we were to move in together, but I won't be proposing to you unless you want us to get married, in which case I'll think about it but make no promises."

"Could I have my own room too in the resort? Somewhere I would call my own. I wouldn't spend much time in it, but it'd be there if I needed it."

"Like a security blanket."

"Exactly."

"Sure, why not? The place will not be full to the brim for the first while, anyway."

Alex shrugged in agreement and that settled the matter.

THE FOLLOWING WEEKEND, Alex finished transporting his belongings to the Last Frontier cottage. It was situated five hundred feet away from the main building, surrounded by a small wood and a dozen other cottages, designed as exclusive dwellings for the high rollers at the casino or other elite guests. The manager's residence was the smallest, a mere four bedrooms, with living and dining rooms, as well as a kitchenette, and boasting a veranda that overlooked nothing but a beautiful woodland scene.

Rebecca arrived with her two bags and a painting the next day and put her things in the second bedroom.

"I could use this as a dressing chamber and if we keep the bed here and bring in a table from somewhere, then we wouldn't need to reserve me a room in the hotel. This works great as a private space just for me."

"Are you sure? I've already issued instructions for the front desk to expect you to check in later today."

"It's fine, Alex, but thanks for your understanding."

"You don't want to be cooped up here, trapped with nowhere to go. I think that was Sarah before she walked out on me, and I do not want you to experience the same crap I put her through."

"You're a better man than that, Alex."

"Don't be so certain. I've had several life-changing moments and not one of them has been pleasant—apart from the births of my sons."

"Not for Sarah, I bet." He grimaced and nodded—childbirth was no laugh.

The couple found a new balance with Alex popping over to El Rancho to watch Rebecca sing and dance, his mind almost always harking back to those halcyon days when the most he hoped for was the sight of an ankle beneath a swirling skirt. In the intervening years, the woman had altered her attitude to revealing more than just a thigh.

THREE SATURDAYS ON and Alex went straight to the cottage after catching Rebecca's first show of the night. He didn't have the energy for the midnight performance—it had been a long week and he needed some rest. At two in the morning, the front door burst open and Rebecca stood there, clinging to the jamb, sobbing.

Alex woke in an instant and ran to her, but she wouldn't let him touch her. Instead, she staggered and collapsed onto a couch, still crying her lungs out.

"What's happened?"

The tears only lasted for five minutes, by which time Rebecca had calmed down enough to utter a handful of words.

"He put his hand up my dress."

"Who?"

"I pushed him away, but he wouldn't stop."

"Which guy? Where?"

"He dragged me to his room."

"One of the guests?"

"Tore my robe."

"Which guest?"

"Huh?"

"How did you get away?"

More sobs, and then they abated.

"He had me sit on the bed. When he stood up to take his pants down, I punched him in the balls and ran out the room."

Rebecca loosened her folded arms for the first time since her arrival in the cottage. The front of her blue satin dress was torn from top to toe and was only held by a thread at the bottom hem.

"I want to be sure you are okay. Did he… do anything else?"

"No. If I'd stayed there for more than a few seconds, then he'd have done far worse than a hand on my leg."

"Tell me who did this, Rebecca."

"I can't."

"If you didn't catch his name, we will figure out which room he took you in."

"Can I have a shot of vodka?"

Alex strode into the kitchen, found a bottle, and poured two glasses. She gulped hers down in a single swallow.

"I know which room and I know who did this, but I cannot tell you the name."

"Why?"

Rebecca stood up and walked into their bedroom to return a moment later in a housecoat. The trail of her blue dress lay on the floor.

"If I give up the name, then you'll do something about it—I cannot allow you to do that on my behalf. You will be sweet and protective of me to want to take action, but it is not your fight. It is mine."

"Why would you not want me to act?"

"Have a think for a minute, Alex, and answer the question for yourself."

Alex pondered for a short while, and then he understood.

"It was Benny."

Rebecca looked down and nodded, a shudder rippling through her body. Alex's hand formed a fist and he bit into the knuckle. Siegel was a renowned womanizer despite having brought his wife and kids out to Los Angeles, and then Vegas, with him. The stories of his conquests were varied and many—entertaining anecdotes when the men were sharing a drink. Until now.

"He is my boss, your business partner and ally. What happened to me shouldn't change your relationship with him. It'd cost you too much."

"That's not what's important, Rebecca."

"I'll deal with Siegel in my way. I don't need you to fight my battles."

"When a friend behaves badly, his friends should call him on it. Do you think I can ignore what he has done to you?"

"You must."

"Right now, I want to go to his room and shoot him in the…"

"And that is why you can't take any action. If you work with Benny, then you'll return to the syndicate. Whacking him is not the way to win friends back home."

"So, Rebecca, you want me to sit on my hands?"

"Don't make this about you, Alex. Benny assaulted me and I am the one who will deal with the *verstinkener momzer* in my way and in my own sweet time."

17

ALMOST EVERY SMALL-time bookmaker in Las Vegas paid for the opportunity to get the Trans-American wire and avoid being on the receiving end of an arson attack. But there was one lone voice of dissent and it came from a large establishment, which meant Alex needed to take them under his wing as soon as possible. The longer they didn't pay their dues, the greater the chance that the other bookies might dispense with his services.

Gavin Wolff operated out of the back of a bar on Fremont called The Red Pheasant. As a drinking venue, it was pleasant but nothing fancy. People popped in for a beer, but they stayed for the betting. Alex brought his lieutenants to check out the joint.

There were four cashiers in a row receiving the wagers, and behind them was a huge blackboard stretching the entire wall. Scurrying along with stepladders on wheels were three guys writing and rewriting the odds on every race taking place across America that afternoon.

"This is quite an operation they've got here."

"And some, Ezra. Either of you two spotted Wolff?"

His men shook their heads and the three continued to watch the room. While his lieutenants concentrated on the people, Alex's eyes were drawn to the cables attached to the wall and skirting.

At the far end of the cashiers was a fifth man, whose ear was glued to a telephone receiver while he scribbled onto a notepad. Each time he finished another scrap of paper, he threw it behind him and a boy picked it up and distributed it to the three guys on ladders.

The cable coming out of the phone stretched to the wall ran on top of the blackboard and out into the back. The power in this room lay in the racing wire, and that was why Wolff couldn't be seen. This guy wasn't taking bets, he was running the joint from behind closed doors.

Alex nudged Ezra and the two lieutenants joined him as he walked over to the door which was shut and had a gorilla with no neck to prevent unwanted guests being foolish enough to wander in without permission.

"You got two options right now. Let Wolff know he has visitors or don't. Either way, we are going in and *you* are not stopping us."

Alex stressed his point by digging what felt like the barrel of a gun into the fella's belly and he went inside to announce their arrival. The three pushed past the gorilla and stood in Wolff's office while the man himself sat at a large oak desk, in front of which were a handful of chairs—a long couch, armchair, and coffee table were ten feet away but nobody looked as though they would get comfortable and chat.

"Freddie tells me you do not have an appointment and that you were insistent that you should see me anyway. For what do I earn this approbation?"

"I want to offer you a business proposition and I believe you will find it so compelling we shall sign a contract before my associates and I leave this room."

Wolff put his feet up on his desk, leaned back in his chair, and chuckled.

"You have this place confused with somewhere else. This isn't backstage at some theater show, even though you are acting like some comedian. Get out of here before Freddie causes you some discomfort."

Alex nodded at Massimo, who grabbed the hapless Freddie by the throat and pinned him to the wall, raising his arm slightly so that Freddie's feet barely touched the ground. Within seconds, choking noises emanated from his larynx. Alex turned to face Wolff.

"Now that we have got the pleasantries out of the way, why don't we introduce ourselves. I am Alex Cohen and you are Gavin Wolff."

The guy let both feet drop off the desk to the ground and he let out a whistle, pushing his Stetson to the back of his head.

"I did not realize who you were."

"No matter. If Massimo releases his stranglehold on Freddie, can we assume that the chump will leave us in peace?"

"His only job is to prevent riffraff from entering my inner sanctum."

Alex issued another nod and Freddie scurried out of the room to let the adults talk. After the door was shut, Alex perched on the couch, forcing Wolff to walk out from behind his desk and sit on the easy chair nearby. Massimo maintained his position near the exit and Ezra sat next to his boss.

"You are a busy man and I do not wish to waste your time. The business proposition is simple and I hope you find it amenable. I want you to cease your contract with the Nationwide and subscribe to the Trans-American wire instead."

"The Nationwide covers more tracks and their service has worked fine for me from the start. My margins are at least ten to twenty percent fatter thanks to James Ragen. I do not need to leave him."

"Gavin, we are both men of the world and understand how business is conducted. Sometimes it is not the quality of the service that dictates who beats the competition, but the overall package on offer. You are correct that the Nationwide has marginally greater coverage, although we will narrow that gap within the next six months."

"You see—"

Alex raised a finger to halt Wolff.

"And it is the package on offer that you should focus on and not the details of which tracks we can offer a results facility today."

"What package? You're selling a news wire."

"Ragen sells a racetrack news service. I sell racing news and insurance cover."

"Why put those together?"

"Gavin, they are inseparable. How can you be certain you are calculating the best odds if a corner of your mind is worrying whether your place of business is mysteriously going to be subjected to an arson attack?"

"Mr. Cohen, I have no such concerns. My competition is small fry and won't assault my premises. They are more likely to do something dumb like undercut my odds until they can't make any money."

"Gavin, you are wrong. In fact, word on the street is that this bar will go up in flames tonight."

Alex sniffed the air for smoke so much that Wolff looked around and inhaled himself. Then he stopped himself—much to Ezra's amusement.

"If you buy from the Trans-American, then your subscription includes an insurance against such events occurring. More than that, you receive my personal guarantee that your business will be trouble free from this moment on."

Alex waved a hand in the air and Ezra revealed a bunch of papers he had stuffed inside his jacket pocket.

"The contract is here and all you need to do is put a signature on it."

"Mr. Cohen—Alex—forgive me, but I cannot sign paperwork unseen and unchecked by my lawyer, even if the terms are first class."

Another wave and Ezra procured a pen and placed it on top of the papers on the table next to Wolff. Alex stared at the man, waiting.

"I want you to understand something, Gavin. Unless I have your signature on that contract before I leave this room, then you had better pray the fire service can get over here in good time before you lose your livelihood."

"You're threatening me."

"I am advising you of the consequences of your actions. Nothing more. I hope to help you reach a sensible commercial decision. Your bookmaking operation might be expendable, but my reputation is not, Mr. Wolff. I mean what I say and have given you fair warning—choose between this contract or a pile of ashes. I would prefer us to become business partners, but if that is not possible then you will have no business. Those are your options, and you must make a choice now."

"This is daylight robbery."

"I am not stealing from you—we are exchanging money for a service. Please do not utter libelous statements about me. I do not appreciate those who tarnish my reputation. Will you sign?"

Alex pushed the contract three inches nearer to Wolff, who looked at the front page and licked his lips. Five, ten, fifteen seconds and he picked up the pen, opened the document, and signed in all the right places.

"An excellent decision, Gavin. Thank you for being our latest customer. You won't regret this. My people will be around tomorrow to help you move over to Trans-American News."

Wolff stood up and shook Alex's hand—still on autopilot—he couldn't believe he'd been forced to buy a wire service without even finding out how much it would cost. As Alex and his associates walked out of the room, Wolff reminded himself that he still had his health and the place would not burn down any time soon.

18

BENNY WASN'T THE only fella who had difficulties keeping it in his pants. Alex hadn't spoken with Mickey in almost a week which was unusual. He enjoyed talking about the old days and reminiscing about times in Chicago and New York—places and people they both shared from their past. Alex didn't mind chatting over times gone by, but having seen Alfonse only recently, memories of the Windy City held less of a luster for him nowadays.

"You know where Mickey is holed up?"

"No, boss. Haven't seen him for ages."

"Massimo, tell me if you hear anything from him."

A day traveling from one bookmaker to the next delivered more sightings than Alex and his men could possibly track down, as so many of them had him in two places at once. That evening the three sat in the Last Frontier bar to figure out a plan.

"Are there any bookies or bars we haven't visited?"

"Not that I know of, Ezra—but the fella can't have vanished. And if he has to be somewhere, then it is our job to find him."

"There is always the possibility that he's buried out in the desert."

"Massimo, you're right and although Mickey has a brusque manner, I am unaware of anyone who would bump him off—assuming we ignore any disgruntled bookie who thought the subscription rates to Trans-American were too high."

"When we looked into the whites of their eyes this week, we'd have noticed if someone wasn't kosher."

"I agree, which means we have been looking in the wrong places. If Mickey's not in a bar or a bookmaker's, where would he be?"

"Brothel."

Massimo and Ezra gave the answer at the same time and smiled at each other in acknowledgment. Alex nodded.

"Looks like we'll have to wear out more shoe leather on the fella. At least, let's think smart. Use your crews to search all the nafkas we run in Vegas and we'll see if we can get a lead before we are forced to go into every bedroom and check under the mattress."

JUST BEFORE ALEX settled down for lunch the following day, he received a message from the desk clerk at the Frontier. Ezra had found Mickey, who had been resting in the same boudoir from the moment he first disappeared. Alex figured the chances were that he would remain in the same location for another hour while he went to the restaurant to grab his food before meeting Ezra in the lobby and heading out.

They drove past El Rancho and continued north for half a mile until they reached a building on the edge of town. As with many of the most vibrant places in the city, it didn't look like much from the outside. Although this bordello was owned by Alex, he hadn't imagined this was where Mickey might have gone. Lois greeted the men and started her spiel but halted in her tracks when she recognized Alex and Ezra.

"You here on business or pleasure, gentlemen?"

"Work, Lois. Ezra's heard there's a john in one of your rooms who has been here for best part of a week. That true?"

Lois sighed because her gravy train was about to go off the rails.

"Yeah. He's on the second floor—at the far end."

"You know who he is?"

"If I didn't when he walked in, he sure made certain we all learned within a minute of his arrival."

"But no call to inform either of us that our mutual friend had his pants around his ankles as a room guest?"

"I'm not being funny, Alex, but I didn't think you'd want me to bother you every time one of your fellas turned up to have a private party."

"Good point, Lois–although you might consider it was worth dropping a dime after the second entire day, though?"

"Uh-huh. To be honest, we've earned more from him than from the rest of the rooms put together this week, and we were hoping the party would last forever."

"They never do, Lois. You should know that."

She nodded and shrugged because Alex was right—a phone call was the least Lois owed him.

"Anybody with him now, or is he resting?"

"He's paid us for a full day's company in advance and he handed over more dough just before lunch. So if he is awake or asleep, then there's a girl in the room with him—it's what he's paying for."

"Will you take me to him now, please, Lois?"

SHE OPENED THE door and Alex stepped in. Ezra made to follow him, but Alex asked him to remain outside.

"If you hear any ruckus, then come in, but let's try to leave Mickey as much of his dignity as remains."

Ezra dragged a chair from further down the corridor and settled in and waited–this was a job that would not be hurried.

The interior wallpaper comprised red stripes, and the swirls in the carpeting hid a multitude of stains. Alex surveyed the scene of Mickey flat on his back on the bed with the nafka sat at her dressing table sneaking glances at a book on her lap. She turned her head as Alex entered the room but registered nothing more of his presence. He walked over and took her novel, flipped a look at the front cover, and returned it.

Alex placed a single finger over his lips to show the girl should remain silent and when she acknowledged that instruction, he pointed at the corridor and indicated she should walk over there and vamoose. As she closed the door behind her, Mickey snored so loudly Alex believed he saw the walls shaking. The noise was disturbing enough to wake Mickey from his slumber, and he blinked twice until he found his bearings. Then he sat up and searched the bedside table for a smoke.

"Where's Bernice?"

"Went out for a breather. She couldn't keep up with you."

"Figures. None of them broads got the stamina to spend much time with Mickey Cohen."

"That so?" Alex looked around and threw Mickey's shorts on his lap. "You must be the only john in the world who's paid for the day and not the hour. I admire your prowess—if that's the right word."

"Sounds mighty fine to me."

Alex popped his head out the door and asked Ezra to hustle up a pot of coffee. Five minutes of listening to Mickey's boasting and Bernice came in with a tray containing the drink and a pile of sandwiches. Alex gave her a hefty tip.

He poured two mugs and offered one to Mickey, who seemed more interested in locating some vodka he'd mislaid from earlier. Alex picked up an empty liquor bottle peeking out from under the bed.

"This what you're looking for?"

"Yep. Anything left inside her?"

"Only your own spit, Mickey. Have a coffee instead."

"Don't want to. Wanna bottle of hooch and Bernice sat on top of me."

"Mickey, you've had enough fun to last most men a lifetime. I need you to sober up, take a shower, and come back to work. Why d'you go on this bender, anyway?"

Mickey eyed him cautiously, the way only a drunk can—his head swaying because his balance was shot to hell. Mickey's eyes weren't working well enough to let him focus on Alex, as his neck refused to stay still.

"None of your goddamn business, Alex. Bring Bernice to me, and perhaps I'll tell you all about it."

"No dice. Coffee and a shower—that's what you're getting. You won't be seeing Bernice for a while. There's a gaming operation you are supposed to be running."

"Leave me alone, Alex. You're not my boss. You seem to forget that you used to be somebody, but nowadays you are nothing—just one of Benny's crew. And that means you can't go ordering me about. I do what I want and it is none of your business."

Alex remained seated and had no desire to argue with a drunk Mickey. He smelled the guy's verstinkener breath from the other side of the room.

"I've been very patient with you, Mickey, but that is wearing thin now. You have been out of action for an entire week and it would appear that all you have achieved is to empty the bar downstairs and give Bernice a chance to finish *War and Peace*."

"Huh?"

"Never mind. Take a shower and get to work. I will be on the first floor finishing my coffee. If you are not down in thirty minutes, I'll hop over to El Rancho and inform Benny that his right-hand man is banging his girls."

Mickey rolled off the bed and staggered over. He drew back a fist. "Don't you tell me what to do. You are no better than me. If you give me one more order, so help me I'll punch your lights out."

Alex stood up and headed for the door. Just before he closed it behind himself, he turned and said, "Thirty minutes, Mickey."

19

BENNY SIEGEL CONTINUED to maintain a hand in some gaming operations in Los Angeles. Without Guy McAfee to look after business there, he was drawn to take matters into his own hands now and again.

Most of the time this was just the way of the world, but occasional difficulties would ensue and the cops would arrest him on a variety of charges. Then he would appear in court, express his sincerest apologies for his misdeeds and, with the help of a generous donation to the judge's benevolent fund, would pay a fine and move on in his life.

For Benny, it was the price of doing business, but he did not appreciate the attention he received from the newspapermen and the nickname they gave him. He did his best to leave it alone and Alex advised him not to respond in public, even though Mickey told Benny to smack any guy in the kisser who called him Bugsy.

"Alex, they made up the phrase because in the last court case, a bookie said I had acted all crazy—bugged out—but I'm never too sure they're not talking about my eyes."

He looked at Benny and didn't quite get what he meant, and then he stared again by squinting at him and understood why he was so sensitive. In the half-light, his eyeballs appeared to push out from his face, but in all the years Alex had known Benny, he had noticed nothing about them before. Alex could write a long litany of the problems he had with Siegel, but the fella's eyes were not on the list.

ONE EVENING ALEX and Benny met up after dinner. Rebecca was performing in the late show at the Last Frontier, having left El Rancho several months before, so Alex planned on catching up with Benny and then hoofing it back to the Frontier to catch Rebecca's act around midnight.

At the El Rancho bar, Benny had hit the sauce early, judging by the extent to which he was slurring his words when Alex arrived at nine. The chances of business getting discussed reduced to zero by the time he heard him speak.

"Did you see the sheets today? My name is all over the papers—in LA and here too. It's like the press wants to hound me to death."

"The one thing I've learned about them newspaper boys is that it is never personal and always about what sells their stories. My picture was on the front page of every New York news rag for weeks—or at least that's how it felt to me. Truth was that I had three days of notoriety and a month of people squinting at me as they tried to figure out where they'd seen my face before. It all passes over."

"Might be true for you, but not for me, Alex. The trial they've dredged up again took place last year, and still they're going on about it."

"Is there an election soon? Candidates like to sound strong on law and order—you and I are the people they'll name because johns have a perception of what we do and how we behave."

"Just businessmen, right?"

As Benny finished speaking, he raised a solitary finger and the waiter appeared—he ordered a vodka martini, straight up with a slice, and Alex asked for a Scotch on the rocks. While this was happening, Alex picked up Benny's newspaper and read above the fold.

The article was a rehash of Benny's trial with the added twist that a cop was on the take and had been in the same bar as Benny at some point in the past when Siegel lived in LA. The whole piece was tenuous and just a feeble excuse to slap Benny's photo on the front page to make a few more sales. The johns liked to read about their hotel owners and the families who owned most of the land in Vegas, and gained pleasure in hearing about the downfalls of the recent arrivals in the neighborhood, especially if they were Jewish.

Benny forgot about sipping martinis and emptied his glass before Alex tasted his liquor. The waiter delivered another cocktail in short order.

On the other side of the pool, a group of four nudged elbows and pointing in their vicinity. Were he and Benny making a scene or had the foursome recognized the syndicate members?

The two couples meandered toward the men, and Alex monitored their journey while he listened to Benny complain about the state of the nation's press.

"Hey, we think you're famous. Are you, bud?"

They aimed the question at Benny, but the way the guy swaggered, Alex could have been forgiven for thinking the inquiry was aimed at him. Benny ignored the kid, as he was so wrapped up in his own misery.

"Mac, I'm talking t' ya. You famous or something?"

Benny raised his head and glanced at the guy.

"What's your name, son?"

"Hal Bishop."

"Listen to me, Hal. I am not famous, but you might have seen me around. Now go back to your table with your friends and leave me the hell alone."

Hal's smile dropped from his face and he scowled as he took in the instruction. Then his eyes widened when he saw the newspaper next to Alex.

"You're Bugsy Siegel."

Benny leaped out of his chair and pounced on Hal. Before the guy knew what was happening, Siegel pushed him to the ground and kicked him in the kidneys. Alex attempted to pull his friend off the tourist, but Benny was in no mood to be dragged anywhere. The two women in the group screamed and a huddle of waiters surrounded the melee. Meanwhile, the steel toe of Benny's shoe made contact with Hal's stomach and head three times.

Alex got a better purchase on Benny's arms and hauled him five feet away —far enough for his legs to no longer be able to kick his hapless opponent.

"Everyone, calm down. You too, Benny."

Alex shot a glance at the nearest waiter. "Give everybody here a drink on the house as we have disrupted their evening."

Then he continued to hold onto Benny, who he felt was trying to slip from his clutches to begin the second round. Hal remained on the floor and his woman cradled his bleeding head. The other two stood there like chopped liver.

"Why don't we move this disagreement outside?"

"You need to call the cops. That guy can't go around beating on people." Hal's girlfriend had a point, but now was not the time for an argument.

"Tell you what. Let's all go out to the lobby and take things from there. Are you able to stand, Hal?"

Bishop nodded and fumbled his way to his feet, assisted by his friends. The six exited the restaurant and meandered over to reception—all the while, Alex kept pace with Benny, who was still seething and was in no mood to discuss anything.

Near the entrance, the waiters had called ahead and the concierge, along with two security guards, were waiting for the group. Alex indicated for them to hang back because his plan was to diffuse the scene as much as possible as tempers were running high and more hotel staff would only inflame the situation.

"I understand this has put a crimp in your day, but I also hope you appreciate that Mr. Siegel has a right to privacy."

"Look what he did to Hal." The girlfriend sobbed and the other couple shuffled nervously. They had gone out for an evening's fun and the night had turned sour. As they had read the papers, they knew that Benny was a gangster and that made them very nervous.

"We should go, if that's all right with you, Hal?"

Bishop nodded and spat more blood onto the floor. Alex couldn't tell if the guy was aiming for their shoes or just trying to clear the gunk from his mouth.

"Benny, if you don't mind, I think we should offer Mr. Bishop some form of compensation for the evening's misadventure. Would you be willing to discuss the size of this consideration, Mr. Bishop?"

"You mean money?"

"Why yes? You have been inconvenienced and should receive something to acknowledge it. In return, we would like this matter to stay among ourselves. There would be no need to involve the local police."

Alex's eyes bored into Hal's, gauging how likely he was to take a few shekels for his silence. Benny understood what Alex was doing and stopped seething for a short while.

Hal wrestled his elbow from his friend's grip and found he could stand by himself, despite the blood and bruises to his torso.

"I would be happy to come to an arrangement. How much are we talking?"

"Hal, why don't we hop into Mr. Siegel's office to iron out the details? We'll all be more comfortable there."

Hal's girlfriend interjected. "I think I'll go home now, dear. This whole situation has left me feeling queer. Will you be all right without me?"

"Sure, but this'll only take a minute. You could rest here while we men talk business."

"Could you call me a taxi instead? This has all been too much."

Even if Hal couldn't figure out what was happening, Alex sure did. The girl had no appetite to spend time with Hal any more this evening because he looked wretched and bloody—and would just need tending to.

She wasn't married to him and felt no desire to act like his mother. She was with Hal to have fun and nothing more. Meanwhile, Hal had dollar signs coming out of his eyes and had forgotten he had taken this woman out for an evening to show her a good time. Alex nodded at the concierge, who organized a cab within a minute. The girl pecked her boyfriend on the cheek and was gone. Alex, Hal, and Benny walked into his office and they all sat down.

"How about five hundred dollars and we call it quits?"

"The trouble is, Mr. Siegel, that you hurt me and I might need medical attention. I don't know if that will be enough to cover my expenses."

"Then a thousand should provide for a hospital bill and still leave you plenty to buy a fabulous meal for you and your girl."

Hal thought for a second and held out his hand to shake on the agreement. Benny sealed the deal and got Hal to sign a sheet of paper that said this was full and final settlement of the matter. Alex and Benny knew it wouldn't stand up in court, but Hal was happy enough—especially when Benny produced the gelt out of a petty cash box.

"Let me walk you to your car to show there's no hard feelings."

Alex went with them as far as the lobby and watched the two men leave the hotel. When they were three hundred feet ahead, he wandered outside until he caught up with them, as they stopped at a vehicle that Hal unlocked. A brief flash erupted from nowhere in the dark and a split second later, a bang of the revolver. Hal had learned the hard way that nobody ever used the name Bugsy around Benny and lived to tell the tale.

December 1943

20

"I THINK YOU'LL want to come over and pay me a visit."

Alex listened on the line and tried to decide whether Jackson Garnett was on the level. It was the first night of Hanukkah, the Jewish festival and while he was disinterested in such things, Rebecca still enjoyed the traditions of her childhood and wanted him home in time to light some candles, say a prayer and exchange a small gift.

"For real?"

"I wouldn't bother you if this didn't matter—you'll understand when you get here."

He warned Ezra and Massimo to stick near a phone in case he needed the cavalry and headed out to Garnett's office a few miles down the road, south of the Last Frontier. When he walked in, Jackson was nowhere to be seen and the desk sergeant acted like it was his life's goal to be the biggest pain in the ass in the world.

"What business do you have with Sheriff Garnett?"

"He knows why I am here."

"That may be so, but until you tell me, I can't allow you to pass to the other side of that gate."

The cop indicated a small wooden swing door which separated the desks from the waiting area.

"In that case, I'll wait for Jackson to show. If he's in the joint, let him know that Alex is here."

Fifteen long minutes later and Garnett appeared from a doorway that led to the cells. He smiled when he saw Alex and walked over—his weekly extra paycheck might prove a useful investment this early evening.

"Thanks for popping over. You should have told Bill to get me instead of hanging around here and waiting."

"Sergeant Bill thought he wanted to know my business and even though I explained to him to keep his nose out of my affairs, he insisted on doing nothing without everything typed in triplicate."

Jackson glared at Bill who was oblivious to the offense he had caused, but Alex knew that hick cops didn't understand city ways and ignored the flatfoot.

"Let's forget about old Bill and deal with the matter at hand. Will you come into my office?"

Jackson led Alex through the little gate, past the desks and their typewriters, and into his room with a frosted glass door. He invited Alex to sit down and offered him a coffee.

"Tell me what was so damn important that I had to get into my car and drive over here?"

"Before we start, I want you to know that I had no part in this happening."

"What has happened that's nothing to do with you?"

"We've got a fella in the cells downstairs."

Alex blinked twice, but Jackson seemed to think he'd given enough of an explanation.

"Who is this mystery felon?"

Jackson looked quizzically back.

"I thought you knew—we arrested Mickey Cohen two hours ago."

"WHAT THE HELL happened, Mickey?"

Alex had demanded to see Mickey immediately, and Jackson hustled him down the stairs. When they reached the cells, Alex soon spotted Mickey because the others were just kids caught making mischief.

"I got pulled over by some greenhorn who didn't recognize who I was and the next thing I knew, he had me eating the paint of my car hood and had slipped cuffs on me."

Alex let Mickey continue his tirade of complaints for a while until he couldn't take it any more.

"Why did the cop stop you in the first place?"

"He reckoned I was weaving over the road."

"Did he have just cause?"

"I don't know, Alex. I can't remember, but the gumshoe had no reason to use handcuffs."

"Did you threaten him or act in any way that he might construe you intended him any harm?"

"You joking with me? When he asked to see my license, I passed him my wallet and left an appreciation for him. That's when he hauled me out of my vehicle and ran me in."

"You know what the charges are?"

"They haven't told me zip since I got here. The cop processed me, Garnett showed up, and the guy threw me into this cell and I've heard bupkis after that."

Alex surveyed the scene as the three young men in the adjoining cell craned to hear Mickey's whispering. He might have been angry, but he was no fool.

"Let me talk to Jackson and figure out how we can straighten this out. I'll get you a coffee or something."

"I don't need a coffee—I need to be free."

"One step at a time, Mickey. And no disrespect, but you stink of booze and need a hot drink."

BACK IN GARNETT'S office, Alex sat down opposite his host and sighed.

"Mickey said your flatfoot processed him. What happened?"

"Denzel Waterman followed Mickey for over a mile as he was swerving all over the place. When the officer stopped him, Mickey was verbally abusive and tried to bribe him. At that point, Waterman asked him to leave his vehicle and Mickey refused. Then he cuffed him and brought him in."

"How long has Waterman been in the squad?"

"It's his first week—his first collar, actually."

"Where were you when Waterman arrived here with Mickey?"

"Out dealing with a domestic dispute. By the time I returned, Waterman had fingerprinted Mickey and was typing up the paperwork to book him. That's when I figured the best thing to do was get Mickey in a cell and to call you before this got more out of hand."

"You said it. What made Waterman feel the need to create a file before interviewing Mickey?"

"Your friend was so far gone that Denzel thought it was an open and shut case."

"Have you had a word with the greenhorn and explained who Mickey is?"

"I didn't have to. Even old Bill knew Mickey as soon as he walked in and tried to convince Waterman to play it quietly, but Denzel was psyched up with his first ticket and refused to listen to reason."

"Where is the boy now?"

"At his desk. I told him to check everything he'd typed up and suggested first drafts of forms can find themselves in the trash sometimes."

"And do you have a good answer why that wizened old crow of a sergeant didn't intervene and stop Waterman in his tracks? I mean, they fingerprinted Mickey. Where's that record sheet?"

Jackson waved a piece of yellow paper from his desk and Alex beckoned for it to be handed over. Garnett followed the instruction and Alex tore the card into fingernail-sized pieces, emptied the trash on the floor, threw the bits into the receptacle, and tossed in a lit match. Then he took a second one to light his cigarette.

"What do you want me to do now, Alex?"

"Bring in Waterman."

"Would it better if I deal with him so he doesn't see… our relationship?"

Alex pondered for a moment and agreed.

"Make sure Waterman understands this is his only mistake with me. The next time he arrests one of mine, he must explain his actions to me directly."

"I understand and I appreciate how you're handling this. It's mighty big of you."

"And have a word with Bill—he might have known Mickey, but he did not show me any respect when I walked in today and that has incurred my displeasure."

"I'll see to it, Alex. Nobody intended any disrespect."

Alex raised an eyebrow but let the comment go. Bill knew better than to poke his nose where it didn't belong, even if the rookie had blundered into a dangerous situation of his own making.

IN THE CAR, Mickey and Alex sat having a smoke before they headed back to where Mickey had been forced to abandon his vehicle.

"I will pay a visit to Officer Waterman's home when he goes off his shift."

"And, Mickey, what will you do then?"

"Put a bullet through his brains and bury him in the desert with all the other scum."

"Let's not get ahead of ourselves. The guy made an honest mistake in refusing to take your money, but he doesn't deserve to meet his maker for being too upright a citizen."

"Alex, that's where you are wrong, but then you weren't the one handcuffed in the back of a traffic car."

"Mickey, you were driving under the influence. This never would have happened if they'd had the good sense to keep the Volstead Act."

Mickey's expression showed he thought Alex's whimsy was misplaced.

"Alex, don't get high and mighty with me. The kid disrespected me and he needs to be taught a lesson."

"That may be so, but death is not what you should be teaching. I've had a word with Garnett and Waterman will soon see the error of his ways."

"Eye for an eye, Alex."

"If that is true then as you are not dead, there is no need for him to be whacked. You have been waylaid for two hours and he will spend at least a month stuck in the station house doing filing for the squad. You'll get your retribution."

"I still think he deserves a shallow grave."

"Let's return you to your car and we can decide then. Just remember that we do not need any heat from a cop-killing haunting us right now. Bill saw you in his cells and if Waterman is hit, even an old-timer desk sergeant will want to know whether you had an alibi."

"I guess—but I don't like it."

"Who does, Mickey?"

February 1944

21

VALENTINE'S DAY HAD a special place in Alex's heart ever since he traveled to Chicago and assassinated seven members of the North Side Gang in a botched attempt at killing Alfonse's enemy, George Moran. That was 1929, and this was now—Rebecca had a different relationship to February 14.

Having spent so many years on the road and alone, she got a real buzz out of the day. She left a brief note in Alex's pants pocket and gave him a card almost as soon as he woke up.

"You must wait until later for your present."

"Rebecca, there is no need to buy me something. Being with you gives me all the pleasure a man could want."

"Does that mean you haven't bothered getting me anything?"

She scrunched up her nose and put her hands on her hips, as though admonishing him. But they both knew better than that. Besides, whenever Alex noticed any pretty trinket, he'd buy it just because it was there. Rebecca was not lacking in gifts from her man.

When he got home that night to get ready for their evening together, she had sprinkled rose petals in a path from the hallway of the cottage. A muffled voice asked, "Is that you?" and Alex answered in the affirmative. "Wait a second and come on through."

He counted ten elephants and sauntered along the steady stream of petals, through the living room and into their bedroom. And there she was—the most beautiful woman in the world, kneeling on the bed, wearing only a giant red ribbon across her chest tied in an enormous bow and not a scrap of clothing more.

"Don't you want to open your present now, Alex?"

HE HAD FOUND a chi-chi restaurant at the edge of town—a family-run place with an Italian menu and a solid reputation for its desserts. Although he had only phoned the joint a week before, they could, of course, accommodate his booking on this special day—which was his way of life in Vegas nowadays.

He drove them over and from the moment they stepped across the threshold, they were treated like Hollywood royalty. The attention to detail was second to none—from the place settings through to the specially printed Valentine menus.

Rebecca ordered a grilled sole with all the trimmings and Alex took the veal. Before they had settled in and sipped their first cocktail, a violinist had serenaded her with what he assumed was an Italian folk tune. You knew this was a classy joint because the guy didn't ask for any money.

"We've been good together, haven't we?"

"Sure have, Rebecca. It's almost two years since we met."

"Again. Our boat ride to Coney Island when we were kids still leaves me with a smile when I think back to those times."

"I'm glad because for me that day was the beginning of the end, Rebecca —until you cruised into town on an overnight trip to stardom."

"Let me apologize for the way I treated you all those years ago, Alex. I did not understand about the world back then."

"None of us did—and no need to say you're sorry. I threatened your boyfriend to keep him away from you."

"My fiancé, you mean."

"Yeah. That wasn't right of me either."

"I always knew it was you, but nobody had any proof. I resented you for a long time after that."

"Rebecca, who wouldn't? That's water under the bridge. The amazing thing is that we are with each other now."

He gazed into her eyes–a warm glow in his belly from being in the same room as her. Then he pondered the impossible question of whether he felt more deeply for Rebecca or Sarah—and shook himself out of his reverie. He was divorced from Sarah, and Rebecca was his present for the evening. She had literally given herself to him earlier.

"We are fools under the stars and they watch us and laugh."

"Who said that?"

"It's from a show I was in when the Yiddish theater was still a thing on Broadway."

"Did you play a duchess or a princess?"

"Neither; second maid, but they were beautiful lines even though I didn't speak them."

Alex smiled and they held hands while the waiter cleared their plates and offered them cheesecake on the house. When that course was polished off, the couple continued to talk and stare out of the window. Despite Alex's late booking, they had the best table in the place.

"It's quiet around here. There's hardly been a car go by."

"Almost as though we weren't in a city like Vegas, Rebecca."

She sneaked a glance at him and carried on staring outside into the night.

"There are still too many lights to see the stars properly."

"We could nip out to the desert if you like. Five minutes further north and we'll be in the middle of nowhere."

"Would you mind, Alex?"

"Who's complaining? A guy with his girl, alone in the dark. Sounds good to me."

ALEX GRABBED A blanket from the trunk and covered Rebecca's shoulders as they stepped away from his car and stood in awe of the pitch black which engulfed them. With an arm over her shoulder, he stared upward and within a few seconds, small pinpricks of light emerged from the night's sky and they played a game of spotting different shapes in the twinkling stars.

"Rebecca, I don't believe they are laughing at us. Not tonight. Maybe they are smirking at the johns in Vegas, but they are grinning at you and me."

"Do you think so?"

"I am looking at them right now, aren't I? I've seen enough of this world to know how it feels to be laughed at—and I'm not feeling that. Are you?"

"I suppose not, Alex."

Their conversation trailed off as the two stared at the patterns up above. Every so often, Rebecca would point at a string of lights and explain to him the name of the constellation they were from and give him the ancient Greek story that went along with it. He'd had no idea she was filled with such knowledge.

"How long have you been fascinated by astrology?"

"By astronomy—since I was a little girl. When we were on the boat coming over to America, there was one night when I got to look out of the window in the middle of the Atlantic Ocean. And in the midst of the horror of that crossing was a single moment of light—when I saw the stars and imagined being a million miles away from that ship and the verstinkener families crammed into that tiny space."

He kissed her on the forehead and they embraced for a short while before Rebecca's gaze headed upward again. Another fifteen minutes and they both felt the cold of the night seep into the bodies and Alex suggested they return to the city. With chattering teeth, she agreed, and by the time they drove back to the parking lot at the Frontier, feeling had returned to all their fingers.

"Do you fancy a nightcap in the bar or shall we go straight back to the cottage, Rebecca?"

"A cocktail to warm our souls might be lovely."

He drove into his named space twenty feet from the hotel entrance and leaned over to kiss Rebecca as a car backfired in the distance. Alex tensed for a second, instincts on overdrive, and then relaxed. They sauntered over to the entrance with its revolving doors and two uniformed doormen, eager to help and ready to receive a gratuity for their services.

Arm draped on her shoulder, Alex looked up at the sky once more and Rebecca stopped to do the same.

"You still sure the stars aren't laughing, Alex?"

The headlights of a parked car switched to full beam and white light engulfed the couple. An engine sparked to life and the vehicle lurched forward, turning sharply to avoid Alex and Rebecca.

Then brakes screeched the saloon to a halt next to them. Alex twisted round to find out what was going on as the passenger window wound down and a black metal barrel emerged. He hit the dirt because his life depended on it, and as the first shot rang out, Alex used the momentum of his descent to drag Rebecca along with him.

As soon as he landed, he seized his pistol from his jacket and squeezed out a slug at the passenger who retaliated with second and third bullets. Then the car squealed off, out of the parking lot and into the night.

Alex stood up, holding his piece in both hands, firing slugs at the all-too-distant vehicle. When the gun was spent, Alex turned round to find both doormen kneeling next to Rebecca. He blinked, shut his eyes and stared out again. Red seeped onto the concrete forming a pool around Rebecca's limp body. Alex closed his ears to the screaming around him and zeroed in on his love's death throes. He pushed the doormen aside and held her still-warm body. Blood gushed from Rebecca's head and pulsed out of her chest. A well of emptiness engulfed the pit of his stomach as the gnawing understanding flowed through his head. Alex had lost the woman he loved more than life itself.

22

ALEX BURIED REBECCA in the Woodlawn Cemetery on Las Vegas Boulevard two days later. Although it tore his insides apart, he was forced to wait more than twenty-four hours for the initial police findings before he got the paperwork together and the ceremony organized. Garnett tried to intercede on his behalf, but the sheriff held little sway with the city force—and they saw no reason to speed up their process for a gangster Jew.

On Wednesday she was laid to rest, and that afternoon Alex received telegrams of condolence from Meyer and Charlie Lucky, who was still stuck in Sing Sing with no hope of parole. By Thursday, Alex was in a blue funk which stayed with him for the remainder of the week and only lifted when he thought about the shootist. He called Ezra and Massimo to his cottage—he hadn't left his home since he returned from the burial. Benny and Mickey had attended, along with Massimo and Ezra.

A handful of the hoofers had also turned up at the funeral out of respect for Rebecca and in acknowledgment of Alex's importance in the casino community. He had paid for a rabbi to come over from Los Angeles to officiate the ceremony, and Benny had ensured ten Jewish men were present to make the shiva—the evening prayers—kosher. That night, Alex cried his eyes out like a little boy and only spoke with the reception desk to order room service over the next two days.

"What have you found out for me?"

"The saloon had out-of-town plates. One of Garnett's men pulled a similar vehicle over about twenty minutes after the hit for speeding and let them go on their way. Nothing wrong there because the medical examiner hadn't even pronounced her dead at that point."

Ezra glanced at Massimo and wondered if he'd overstepped the mark at all, but his friend nodded and Ezra continued.

"There were two men and Waterman gave me good descriptions of both of them."

"Denzel Waterman?"

"You know him?"

"Our paths have crossed, but no mind. Anyone recognize them?"

"I called back east and Meyer is checking whether there is a Brownsville connection."

Alex nodded at the implication that this might have been a hit with instructions issued out of the Bronx—his old home from home.

"Is there much of Murder Corporation left?"

"Not like it was when you were in charge, Alex. But there is still a need to settle disputes between syndicate members, and there's a pool of fellas willing to pull a trigger for a price."

"I assume the hit was aimed at me. Rebecca never mentioned anybody who might do her harm."

"Correct, Alex. You were the target and for reasons we can't explain, the guy missed you and caught her instead."

"Twice. One in the chest, another in the head."

"In which direction was the car heading when Waterman let it go?"

"Los Angeles, but we all know that doesn't guarantee it was their destination. They could have turned around and hightailed it through town ten minutes later. No one was on the lookout for a black saloon with unknown assailants then—apart from you and the doormen."

Alex swirled his Scotch in its glass and knocked back the remains of the contents.

"As soon as you find the location of either of the two men, you tell me. Day or night—I don't care. You hear me?"

"Loud and clear, boss."

THE SCENE PLAYING out before Alex was the same as so many situations where he, Ezra, and Massimo had discussed matters with an assailant in an empty warehouse in the middle of the Lower East Side. The only difference was that the location was in the heart of the desert, where nobody passed by to hear the screams of any prisoner. And that was how Alex wanted it.

Trussed on the floor was a guy in a black suit and white shirt, his mouth stuffed with Massimo's handkerchief bound with twine. The sound of the man's nostrils inhaling and exhaling filled the open space—a single-story shack reached via a solitary track running from the highway.

Alex had got a call from Ezra to tell him that one of his fellas in Los Angeles had dropped a dime and suggested they pay a visit to Rico Piovene, who had come into money and boasted of its origins. Ezra and Massimo had driven to the City of Angels, grabbed the guy, thrown him into their trunk, and brought him to his current location.

"Sit him upright so we can converse like men."

Alex dragged a wooden chair next to Piovene's body and let his lieutenants haul the man up and dump him on the seat—making sure his wrists remained tied behind his back. While they sorted out the wheezing captive, Alex found more furniture so everybody could be seated if they wanted, although the other two remained standing to tower over Piovene.

"Do you know who I am?"

A shake of the head.

"Do you know where you are?"

A second no.

"Any idea why you are here?"

Naught for three.

"For a guy who's opened his mouth in a Los Angeles bar telling the world about your business, you don't know much, do you?"

Alex stared into Rico's eyes, spearing into his soul—not letting his gaze break, even for a second.

"My friend tells me you came into some gelt. Did good fortune smile on you?" Alex indicated to Massimo that Piovene needed to speak and to remove his handkerchief. "I asked you a question and unless you want a beating, you'd better give me an answer."

Rico looked at the two lieutenants and returned to staring at Alex.

"Yeah, I got some money. What business is it of yours?"

"We will get to that in a minute."

"I didn't catch your name, Mac."

Before Alex responded, Ezra stepped toward him. "That's Alex Cohen, you schnook." And he landed a punch in the stomach before Rico could digest the information.

They waited for Piovene to recover from the blow for a minute.

"Now you know who I am, you should be aware of what forces I can unleash against you. So let us try again. Why do you think you are here?"

"I must have displeased you."

"Interesting understatement. Any idea what that might have been?"

Piovene shrugged and stared into the middle distance, just above Alex's shoulder.

"I ain't done nothing."

"If that is so, why were you telling anybody in earshot that you'd earned money from a Vegas hit a few days ago?"

"I say things, but it don't have to be true."

"So you weren't involved in a hit?"

"Not me. You got me confused with some other fella."

"Rico, I want you to understand something, so listen carefully. Everyone in this room knows what you have done. That is not the issue. What I have to decide is what'll happen to you because of your involvement in the hit. And that depends on what you say and what you do during this conversation."

"I have already said it was not me."

"Let's pretend for a minute you are telling me the truth. We know you're not, but work with me here. If it wasn't from the hit, where did your extra gelt come from?"

"I won it on the horses."

"Gambling? And yet you told the bar you'd been to Vegas on a hit, like you were a big shot."

"I ran my mouth off and I'd been drinking. The story sounded better than I picked a horse and it came in first."

"Did you pull the trigger or was it the other guy?"

"It wasn't me. I placed a bet and it came good."

"If you were the driver, then I will let you live. If you continue to lie to me, then I cannot guarantee the state of your health."

Alex remained silent for a minute to give Piovene a chance to think through his situation and to make the right decision.

"Well? I have given you an opportunity to reconsider your ridiculous story. Were you the trigger man?"

"The driver."

"That's better. There's nothing worse than having your intelligence insulted. Who carried out the hit?"

"Art Nicchi."

Alex turned to Massimo. "You heard of this guy?"

"No, but it won't be hard to find him."

"Well done, Rico. Now here is one more question and then you can go."

A smile flitted across Piovene's face.

"Who hired you?"

"Art asked me to help him with some out-of-town business. He didn't say who was paying the bill and I didn't ask. You know how it is."

"That I do, Rico. Are you sure this Nicchi didn't mention a name at all?"

"If I could tell you, I would, because I want to get out of this place alive."

"You're a stand-up man, Rico, and I believe you. Art was the brains of the outfit and couldn't trust you with the name of the person who hired you."

"Am I free to go then?"

Alex smiled and stood up.

"There's just one more thing, Rico."

He walked over and bent over the man as if to have a private word, whispering to him so that neither Ezra nor Massimo heard.

"For you, this was business and if Art'd only clipped me, then that would be the end of the matter. But you guys made the mistake of killing my childhood sweetheart."

Alex straightened up, pulled his piece from its resting place in his jacket, jammed the barrel in Rico Piovene's mouth, and shot him in the head. Blood splattered out the rear of his skull and the body lurched backward, falling on the floor.

"Bring me Art Nicchi and make sure no harm befalls the momzer before I speak with him."

23

THREE DAYS LATER and Piovene's body was no longer lying in a bloody mess on the floor. Most of him was in a shallow grave a mile away from the shack. Now in Rico's seat was Art Nicchi—a man sufficiently smart not to inform Rico who was paying the bills but not clever enough to leave the country and never return.

"Art, you know why you are here so let's get to it. Who hired you to kill me?"

"Cohen, you should understand I can't tell you."

"There is a world of difference between not being able to do something and refusing to do it. You assassinated someone very dear to me, and there are consequences."

"The skirt?"

"My girlfriend. My childhood sweetheart. Yes."

Ezra glanced at Massimo—they hadn't known Alex and Rebecca's lives stretched back to their days in the Bowery.

"And, Art. I need to understand why she died. Rico told me you were the hired hand and he was the driver. Is that correct?"

"I pulled the trigger, but I can't say who paid me."

"I suppose they never gave you a name. Just a middleman acting on behalf of a silent partner."

"Lying to you won't do me any good. I owed a Shylock some money—way more than chump change—and they passed my betting slip up the chain until it landed on a certain someone's desk. He told me I could wipe the slate clean if I did one job for him."

"How d'you obtain the gelt to pay Rico?"

"What I was being asked was priced higher than my sizeable debt so there was spare on the top. I gave most of that to Rico because I figured he'd helped me get out of a big hole."

"And now he's dropped you into an even bigger one."

"Sure looks like it."

"You walk out of here by giving me a name. Anything less and we get to work on you. Understand?"

"Listen, Mac. If I give up my boss today, you will find me in a ditch next week."

Alex smiled. "And if I don't hear the name this afternoon, you'll be buried in the desert by nightfall. Your options are limited and unpleasant—unless you spill who needed me dead."

Nicchi stared out and kept his lips shut. Alex could tell he wished to say, but old allegiances die hard and the guy hadn't dealt with the fact that Alex needed more than the organ grinder—he wanted revenge on this monkey too.

"Art, I'm giving you one last chance to offer me the name before I insist on you saying. Who put out the hit and was it authorized by the syndicate?"

"Oh no. This was a local matter from what I understand, but I won't give up who."

Alex believed Nicchi and knew that within the next sixty minutes, the guy would sell the souls of his grandchildren as yet unborn to stop the pain Alex was about to inflict. He stood up and walked over to two bags lying on the floor twenty feet away. One was a sack and the other a tool bag. He yanked Piovene's head from the sack, dumping it on Nicchi's lap, causing the man to scream with fear. Then Alex removed a hammer from the tool kit and slammed it into Nicchi's right knee.

AN HOUR LATER and Art Nicchi fell back into unconsciousness and Alex had what he was looking for; Jack Dragna had called for the hit. The guy who owned Los Angeles wanted him dead even though they'd met only once, and then Benny had done almost all the talking. It made little sense.

"Throw some water on him," Alex instructed and Nicchi was dowsed with a bucket and came round. Alex grabbed him by the hair as he sat, strapped to the chair, fingers and toes broken, torso slashed several times, and cigarette burns on his hands and feet.

"I woke you up to let you know that you will die."

Alex executed Art Nicchi with a single shot to the head and then he stepped back three paces. Ezra and Massimo moved in, cut off the straps that bound the man to his seated position and the corpse fell to the floor and splashed into the bloody pool which had formed over the intervening hours since his arrival.

"Is it too much to send their heads to Dragna?"

"Yes, Alex. Please don't let your anger overcome you."

"I know. It's more important to get to the bottom of why the hit was called than have revenge for Rebecca."

"The body count is rising, Alex. I doubt if she'd want you to kill more people in her name. You've buried her, and Massimo and I will make this carcass vanish for you. Go home and let us do our jobs."

Ezra was right. Rebecca was dead and nothing he did would bring her back to life and he must deal with Dragna. Alex needed to figure out how he had offended the boss of LA.

"BENNY, WHY WOULD Jack Dragna want me dead?"

Siegel sipped his coffee and settled back in the seat positioned behind his desk in his office. Alex sat opposite, barely able to concentrate on the matter at hand, his loss sitting in the pit of his stomach like a bowl of lokshen.

"Alex, it isn't anything personal—he hardly knows you. So it must be business."

He thought for a minute and tried to list their interests in common. His mind was blank on the matter as snippets of conversation with Rebecca wafted into his head instead.

"There's prostitution, the hotel, a casino, and the racing wire. Anything else you run, Alex?"

"That's about all." His voice trailed off, dulled by sadness. "But it's only the news wire that goes beyond the city boundary. The rest is local."

"Let me have a talk with him and see what's going on. If it is the wire, then I wonder why he didn't attack me too."

"Benny, you are a member of the syndicate and I am not. I was a much easier mark."

"And you won't be able to get your revenge either for the same reason, Alex."

"I am painfully aware of that, but we buried the trigger man and the driver in the desert."

"May Rebecca rest in peace."

Alex drilled a hole in Benny's head with his eyes—did Siegel mean what he had said? He had been the one to try it on with her, and Alex had never called him on that. He had respected Rebecca's wishes to not pursue the matter, but it had not sat right with him. And here was another occasion involving her when he wouldn't be able to act the way he wanted.

March 1944

24

"WE'RE FIGHTING THE Japs and Nazis now. Sometimes I wonder if I should have enlisted again and returned to France."

Alex and Benny sat by the pool in El Rancho as the late afternoon sun headed toward the horizon.

"I thought you had enough of the army life in the Great War. You told me that experience broke you."

"True, but I went over there hoping to save Jewish lives. I might have been wrong last time, but Hitler means our people only harm. We need to stand up to him."

Benny sipped at his cocktail and considered Alex's suggestion, then shook his head.

"War is a young man's game. I met Goebbels before the war started, when I was involved in a spot of gun-running—total prick for sure. But the reports you hear are that the Nazis have internment camps for the Jews. You fighting on a beach ain't going to save anyone from those workhouses."

"Don't you want to do something though?"

"You earned yourself a Purple Heart last time. Leave it for some other upstart to take the glory."

"There are people closer to home who are dying too."

Benny eyed Alex, checked his watch, and intoned, "Louis must be dead by now."

Alex raised his glass to make a simple toast. "To Louis Buchalter, syndicate member, Murder Corporation director, and friend to Benny Siegel. Rest in peace."

"Please God, may we be in Israel next year."

Even though Alex had thrown Abe Reles out of the Half Moon window, there was other testimony and other murders that had brought Louis to his knees. Now he would be remembered as the first gangster to fry in the mercy seat.

"Do you feel responsible, Alex?"

"What do you mean?"

"The Rosen hit—that's what Reles testified about and that was one of yours, I thought."

"Yes and no. I carried out the contract, but Louis issued the instructions to me in front of Reles. I barely remember, but the fella walked in and out of our meetings in Brownsville. Stupid thing is that if Anastasia hadn't been so keen to choose the venue, we'd have been in Lindy's and Reles would have heard jack."

"I know you were inside, but Louis gave himself up to the Feds in thirty-nine. He'd been on the lam for a year or two."

"Then he was a fool. If I'd been him, I would have left the country—or the state at the very least. Sometimes a field in Wisconsin can be appealing."

Benny smiled because Alex was right, even though he was talking ill of a guy he'd known since he was a kid.

"The afternoon edition said that they flipped the switch on Alfonse's brother after they did for Louis."

"Well, Alex, at least Alfonse won't bear the pain of hearing about the death."

"Brains like mush."

The men soaked in the decaying rays of the setting sun as they considered the deaths surrounding the people in their lives. After several minutes, Alex broke the silence.

"Did you get anywhere with Jack Dragna?"

"You've met him…"

"Briefly…"

"And you must pick your moments with him. He is liable to fly off and act crazy."

"We are talking about the man who organized a hit on me and ended up killing my girlfriend."

"I know, but as soon as the time is appropriate, I'll speak with him. From what you found out, this was business and that makes it to do with the wire service. For Jack to strike out like that means we are doing something right and he feels threatened."

"Lashing out at me was not the way to go, Benny."

"No, of course not—but we have to carry on, even if we apply a level of caution. His actions might have set us back a small amount, but there is an enormous amount of money to make from Trans-American."

Alex had expected more from Benny than a half-promise to speak to Dragna at some point. This was a syndicate matter as the guy was attacking one of Meyer's key investments. There must be some reason he didn't want to push things harder, and Alex doubted it was because Siegel was worried whether his erstwhile underling would get his nose put out of joint.

That night, Alex lit a remembrance candle for Alfonse's brother but refused to do anything to commemorate Buchalter's demise. Just because the fella was dead didn't mean how he'd behaved when he was alive was any different.

June 1945

25

ALEX STAYED AWAY from the war in the Pacific and the one raging against the Jews in Europe. For reasons best known to himself, Benny stayed away from Jack Dragna and Rebecca's death faded from everyone's minds apart from Alex's.

Six weeks after peace was declared across Europe, Moe Sedway and Gus Greenbaum arrived in Vegas to manage Benny's latest acquisition: the El Cortez resort on East Fremont. This venue had all you'd expect from a Siegel establishment—casino, hotel rooms, and prostitutes, restaurants, a stage with dancing girls, and a lot more besides.

"I will turn this joint around and make it as successful as the dumps I've seen in Texas."

"What's the difference between this place and El Rancho?"

Alex admired Benny's reach but was concerned that the fella's attention should be focused on the racing wire, which had languished over the past year, rather than expanding his entertainment interests. That said, Benny had wanted to create a gaming empire here twenty years ago, so Alex shouldn't have been surprised by the way Siegel's head was turning.

"I'll refurbish the interior so there's a lot less Mexican ranch to the place. We want to appeal to the johns who live on the coasts of this great nation, not just those who have a land border in the south."

"Benny, you sure are living the dream."

"It's the American way, right? I'm making a million a year out of El Rancho and Trans-American. By next year I want to double that—and again, every year until nobody can touch me."

ALEX DIDN'T QUESTION where Benny got the money to make the purchase–he received a cool half a million from the news wire annually—

and as an equal partner, Benny was getting the same. The rest of Benny's income was a mystery, not that it was any of Alex's business what Benny earned.

Gus and Moe came across as upright fellas when Alex met them a few days later. They had a classic New York Jewish mobster feel to them—gray flannel suits and fedora hats. Their eyes burned with suspicion but, to hear them talk, you'd think they were ordinary businessmen with a hawklike eye on profit margins. For those who cared to look, the bulges in their jacket pockets showed they packed heat.

"Benny wants to run an elite joint for the high spenders in the country. But Moe and I think we can all make more money by opening the place up to anybody with some greenbacks. He's the boss, so we'll do whatever he says."

Moe nodded in agreement and Alex smiled. The three were having a coffee in El Rancho, comped by Benny as always.

"Benny has a nose for gaming, that's for sure. When I first met him in New York, he talked about building a casino out west with a deck of cards and a piece of green baize."

"Alex, that's funny because he carried that story around with him wherever he went. I must admit I thought the idea was goofy, but what did I know?"

"Moe, the fellas back east never took Benny seriously and now look at us all."

"MEYER. HOW'S THE hustle and bustle of New York?"

"All is good here, Alex."

"Pleased to hear it. And how is your accounts clerk doing?"

"Sarah is well—I've promoted her to my executive secretary. I shall let her know you inquired after her health."

"No need to bother her, Meyer. Was this a social call or have we something to discuss?"

"How is business, Alex?"

"Are you on your own or have you put me on a squawk box?"

"Both. I wanted to drink my coffee and speak at the same time."

"Meyer, the Last Frontier is doing well—and Trans-American is catching up. As you know, it has taken much longer than anyone thought to make it work outside of Vegas, but we are getting there. I'm going on a sales trip soon to break open San Francisco—there has been interference from Jack Dragna which has slowed us down, but Benny must have kept you apprised of all that."

"I'm sure he has. Can you be more precise for me? I want figures, Alex."

"You know my numbers because I always show my appreciation, right? There's half a million from Trans-American and the Frontier generates about the same for me, including my interests in prostitution."

"How about El Rancho?"

"I can't be certain but I would expect El Rancho to clear more than the Last Frontier—it's bigger and better established."

"That's what I thought—very helpful. And as far as you are aware, El Rancho is profitable?"

"Yes. Is there something I should know, Meyer?"

"How are Moe and Gus? Have they settled in yet?"

"We've helped them secure places to stay and they seem fine—but they've only been here a handful of days, so it's too early to say."

"They'll find their feet soon enough. Good guys."

Alex put the phone down. Meyer knew all the numbers at every second of the day or night—he had no need to hear it from Alex. Instead, he wanted to listen to him speak the sums out loud. And the way he changed the topic when Alex asked if anything was up showed him that there was something going on—only Meyer didn't want to talk about it.

ALEX CALCULATED BENNY'S income and the difference between what he'd told Alex a few days before and the implications from Meyer that El Rancho wasn't wiping its own ass. If Alex was right, Benny was underplaying how much he was making to the syndicate, because Meyer implied there was little money coming out of the resort.

These thoughts lingered in his mind the next time he hooked up with Mickey. Almost like the rear booth at Lindy's, Alex took his seat at a table by the El Rancho pool, only there was no need to have any of their lieutenants sit by the entrance because the local cops were in their pocket and there were no rival gangs in town.

"How's tricks, Mickey?"

"All going fine, Alex."

"My prostitution numbers have flatlined these past two months. Has the casino income suffered the same way?"

"Nah. Since the start of the year, things have picked up. We might be in the middle of a war, but the high rollers are still piling into town and gambling like there's no tomorrow."

"Is that only in the hotel or are takings up with the other bookies?"

"Across the board. Why d'you ask?"

"No reason. I was just wondering where we should expand our efforts with Trans-American. We can gouge more in Vegas or hop on a train someplace else."

"Buy your ticket today. This town is full—I'd be surprised if there is a single track bookmaker in the city limits who isn't paying us through the nose. Where are you thinking of going?"

"The two hottest options are San Francisco or Los Angeles."

"You and Dragna have unfinished business, right?"

"That's one way of putting it, Mickey. Could I count on your support if I were to go after Dragna?"

"I beat him to the punch when I came over here to work with Benny, but Jack and I go back years and as much as I disagree with what he did to you and your skirt…"

"Rebecca."

"Whatever… that still doesn't mean I want to raise a gun to the fella's face."

"And what about Benny?"

Mickey laughed. "Well, I ain't going to be firing no shot at him either."

"No, I meant, how would you feel if you'd heard that Benny was making a little on the side from your hard work?"

"I wouldn't be happy—who would? But is that what you are saying is happening because whoever's pouring out those kinds of rumors needs seeing to. Does Benny know these lies are flying about town?"

"One barfly spouting his mouth off is not worth lifting a finger over, Mickey. I was just thinking out loud and nothing more."

"Well, do it in your head and don't let your lips move so much."

Alex marveled at Mickey's loyalty to Benny—and how poor he was at counting. The amount of money Benny said he was making far exceeded anything that Mickey was seeing, but it did not rankle with him. Perhaps he didn't care what his boss did, provided he himself was in gravy, but Alex minded and Meyer had chosen him as the person to talk to on the matter.

26

EZRA, MASSIMO, AND Alex took a train to San Francisco and grabbed a hire car at the other end—there's nothing like local plates to stop heads from turning when you drive down the street. They spent the first week creating a map of the bookies—just as they had when they tried to open up Los Angeles. In stark contrast to the earlier attempt to break new ground, Alex also chose to piece together who ran the different parts of the city before making a move.

Anthony Lima had been running the town for about ten years, although he had focused his attention on extortion and prostitution. Alex arranged an appointment with Lima and brought with him a bottle of imported Italian wine.

"Thank you for taking the time to see me, Mr. Lima."

"I am happy to be with a friend of Benny's and, please, call me Anthony."

"Your time is precious and I do not wish to waste a drop of it. There is a business proposition I'd like to offer you."

"Let's crack open your vino and I will hear what you have to say."

"The syndicate is making a significant investment in the Trans-American racing wire and we want to introduce it in San Francisco. My understanding is that you do not have long tentacles in gaming, otherwise I would not be so presumptuous as to come here at all."

"Alex, what little betting takes place in my city isn't worth my while. If one day it becomes significant, I shall dip my beak in that trough."

"Anthony, I have mapped out where all the track bookies do business in town and I want to make them Trans-American customers. This will benefit me, naturally, but also the syndicate, and I would like to ensure our interests are aligned by sharing revenues with you personally."

Anthony smiled because he'd heard what happened when Alex tried to muscle into Jack Dragna's territory with the racing wire—it took him years to recover from that slapping.

"You have considered this well and I am always interested in making money, so what would be my end?"

"Like everyone else, I give my tithe to the syndicate to show appreciation. I am offering you ten percent of my gross share and I am asking you to do nothing in return—apart from allow me free passage around town as I generate gelt for the pair of us."

"You are a thoughtful and caring man—I wish there were more like you in this world, but a tithe is not much to offer. I understand it is proposed with respect, but I have lived without gambling revenues fine so far. Twenty percent would elicit a different response from me."

Alex smiled because Anthony was negotiating over price and that meant he was hooked.

"Fifteen percent is my highest offer—no matter what amount we agree, I still have fixed expenses that must be met. A racing wire is an expensive operation and there are other cities I could go to."

Anthony raised a hand to signal he had heard enough of Alex's spiel.

"I can live with that. You are offering me free money, after all."

"You better believe it."

WITH LIMA ON his side, Alex had received the green light to exploit gambling in San Francisco as much as he was able, but he knew two things—his priority was Trans-American and as soon as any other gaming revenues became significant then Anthony would step in and take it for his own.

The map of bookies in his hand, Alex instructed his lieutenants to hover around and see which were taking any serious racetrack bets. The other aspect for consideration was how susceptible the guys would be to buying from Trans-American. A second week and the three men assembled in Alex's hotel room—they'd had the good sense to bring in coffees and cake for the afternoon's meet.

"The important thing is to close the deal with every bookmaker in the city—I don't care who does it or how it is done. The contract is what we require."

"So we can use as much encouragement as we need?"

"No corpses, Massimo—and they must pay each week without us having to chase them for the gelt. It's the same as any other racket we've ever been in. We need them to bend to our will and not break."

All three men knew what was expected and how far to press a man before he'd reach for a gun or throw a punch. With Lima's backing, Alex hoped they'd meet less resistance than in LA.

"YOU THINK A bunch of Jews from Vegas will scare me more than a bunch of Italians from Chicago? Get outta here."

Alex, Ezra, and Massimo stood in front of their last catch of the morning, a guy who ran a book at the back of a bar overlooking the bay. Tourists and locals alike popped in and placed a wager with Luke, who didn't bat an eyelid when the three men approached him with their proposition.

"We are offering you the chance to get in on the ground up with a new wire service."

"I got one already and I make a pretty penny out of it. I don't need two."

"We aren't suggesting you use both—you should replace your current provider with Trans-American."

Alex had seen this conversation play out three times before on the same day and could sense how it would end up.

"I'll buy from you if you are much cheaper and the Chicago outfit tells me they are happy for me to do so—otherwise you're putting me in an impossible situation."

"We are backed by Anthony Lima and he would like you to go with Trans-American."

"I'm sure he would, but he doesn't have to deal with no Chicago mobsters, does he?"

Alex sighed—it had been the same all day. The most lucrative bookies were signed up to Ragen's Nationwide wire and coercing them to join Trans-American wouldn't mean they'd stay for very long. In fact, the only way would be to install a team of heavies in San Francisco to shake down each payment out of every bookmaker in town. This was not a viable business proposition from Alex's perspective.

They left Luke to give him time to reconsider his position and with a veiled threat they'd burn his home down and attack his family, but from what he'd said the Chicago outfit had made similar claims and not acted on them either.

"We might as well split up—three of us standing in front of one gonif just wastes time."

ALEX'S NEXT PORT of call was Frederico, who perched in the back of a bar near the Golden Gate Bridge, not that this meant he was any more amenable to the Trans-American service.

"Don't get me wrong, mister. If you were the only game in town, I'd buy from you—but the Nationwide got to me first. I've seen what they are capable of and have no interest in encouraging them to come to visit me."

"And a beating from them at some point is worse than a definite bashing from me later on today?"

"No disrespect, but I'd suggest not—just because the Nationwide fellas won't stop demanding money from me, no matter what I say."

"Frederico, how about this? Let me install our service for free. You use it without charge for three months, and then we can talk about our fees again."

"Put it in but I won't switch it on. The Nationwide will crack my skull open and I'll be lucky to wake up in a hospital."

That evening, the Vegas men shared war stories over a bite to eat.

"The Chicago mob has tied up this city tight—no wonder Lima was so susceptible to you coming into town, boss."

"Ezra, Anthony sure was happy for us to do the donkey work—now it makes sense. He'd already ceded gambling over to Chicago before we arrived."

"What are we going to do, Alex?"

"Let's stick to our original plan and keep hustling for a week and then we can take stock. If we've made little headway, then a fresh approach will be needed. The syndicate appears to be split into two factions with competing interests around the two wire services and we sure don't want to get caught in the middle of that shitstorm."

27

WHEN ALEX CAME back to Vegas, Benny was in no mood to hear about the inability of Trans-American to take hold in San Francisco. Instead, his head was filled with desire for a new woman in his life—Virginia Hill. Benny had brought his family over from New York when he first relocated, but like many powerful men, this never stopped him from playing around. He kept a mistress even though she was based in Beverly Hills and Mrs. Siegel was ensconced in Arcadia out in the San Gabriel Valley, Los Angeles.

Alex had a vague memory of seeing Virginia tending to some men when he visited Alfonse, and she had a history with the Chicago outfit before she ran prostitution in Mexico for some other of the syndicate's interests. But Alex did not judge her on how she earned a living—he didn't operate at that level, especially as his ex-wife was a former nafka, his mistress back then was an opium fiend, and his most recent girlfriend had been in the chorus line. None of these jobs could be mistaken for anything respectable. Yet at some point, to a greater or lesser extent, he had loved them all—although not at the same point.

They met over a cocktail, much as Alex might have predicted, by the pool in El Rancho. Benny was beaming and besotted—Alex couldn't remember seeing the man so happy.

"So how did you guys meet?"

"Charlie introduced us in New York years before."

"And then we bumped into each other again at a Hollywood party two weeks ago."

Benny looked at Hill as she added the detail to provide the information Alex wanted to know—how long had they been dating and why had she flashed onto the scene in Las Vegas. Alex nodded approval and Benny ordered another round of drinks.

"Do you act, Virginia?"

"I got myself an agent, but I'm between roles right now."

"And who held the party where you met again?"

Benny and Virginia looked at each other, neither wanting to go first. In the end, Siegel relented. "George Raft threw one of his blowout affairs and we got together that evening, but we've known each other off and on for years."

Alex was teasing Benny because the couple had been seeing each other ever since Hill was sent by Charlie Lucky from Chicago to New York to keep tabs on syndicate member Joe Adonis back in 1937. Their relationship had been a closely guarded secret, although Charlie informed Alex and Meyer after Hill arrived in town so they'd know not to stoke any unnecessary fires with Benny.

"For a woman who wants to smash into the movies, you got a low profile in Hollywood, Virginia."

"I should change my agent."

"You just haven't had your big break yet, Virginia."

"Kind of you to say so, Benny, but I've been to enough auditions to know these producers are interested in me, but not for a part in their movie, if you get my drift."

Benny ground his molars at the thought of another man laying a hand on his skirt and Alex marveled at the double standard—given how Benny had behaved toward Rebecca—when he had his wife at home and Virginia in an LA apartment somewhere.

"I am sure your talent will reveal itself soon." Was Alex's acid remark aimed at Virginia, who slept with anybody the syndicate instructed her to or with Benny and the old scars still unhealed?

"Shall we go for a bite to eat? There's a new Mexican opened up nearby, which is meant to be awesome."

"Sure, Benny, but if you two want to be alone together, I'll understand."

"Of course you're welcome, Alex. Isn't he, babe?"

"Yep."

Virginia stared at Alex when she spoke, her eyes beaming into the back of his skull, almost like she was trying to convey some other meaning than what she said. Alex took her at face value, at least for now.

THE RESTAURANT WAS fine but nothing special despite the hype. By the time dessert was served, in a perfunctory manner given the importance of the men sat at the table, several bottles of wine had been consumed and neither Benny nor Alex took offense. Virginia's indignation made up for both of them.

"You're not going to pay the gratuity, are you? I thought we'd need a catcher's mitt for our entrees."

"It's not the waiter's fault."

"Benny, who do you think is responsible for the delivery of the food from the kitchen to our table?"

Alex remained silent during this lovers' spat. Virginia made a good point, and she knew Benny well enough to understand that was not how she would get him to change his mind—almost as if she was saying it to her audience rather than to Benny.

"I know how restaurants work, babe—I own two. If you want to decide on the tip, then pay for the meal, otherwise, it doesn't concern you."

Virginia opened up her purse and rifled through to see how much money she had on her. When her shoulders slumped to signify how little gelt there was, her indignation got the better of her and she lashed out.

"I don't know what you are staring at, Alex. If you were a gentleman, you'd have said something by now and told Benny how foolish he is being."

"Virginia, I make it a rule not to express an opinion in differences between two people as close as you and Benny. Second, Benny is my business partner and I have known him for twenty years. You and I met today, so I will show him more loyalty than you."

"You are useless, aren't you?"

She spat each word out with genuine venom and eyeballed Alex for five, ten seconds. He ignored the outburst, took a sip from his drink, and lit a cigarette, careful not to blow smoke in her face, despite his childish desire to do so.

Until this point, Virginia had appeared all right to hang out with, but now she had revealed a darker side to her. The stories Alex had heard of how she manipulated the rich and powerful men in her sway made more sense. There were tales of the Chicago outfit sending her off to sleep with bosses from other cities to find out their plans and to shift their opinions. She had been so good at that, they sent her to Mexico to run some narcotics angles down there.

The time she met Benny in New York was around when she was sleeping with Adonis—under instruction from Chicago. A high-class nafka with business talent, and now she had her clutches into Siegel.

Benny pulled out a roll of notes and put some down by his plate. Then he counted out a smaller amount and, while staring straight at Virginia, threw the second bunch on top of the first pile of greenbacks. His point made, Virginia tutted, grabbed her coat, and stormed out.

"I'd better go after her."

"If you say so, Benny."

He ran out of the restaurant and Alex smiled as he witnessed the couple through the glass frontage having a stand-up row in front of a room full of diners. Neither Sarah nor Rebecca had behaved like that. Then he waited until the fight was over before walking out the joint and taking a stroll back to the Frontier.

October 1945

28

LAS VEGAS ATTRACTED many kinds to its city borders. The more astute money men recognized what Benny had known since the twenties—a resort where you could gamble, enjoy a decent meal, and sleep on the premises is a potential goldmine. Billy Wilkerson had a vision of a new hotel, focused on gambling with lodging rooms, a stage, and a restaurant.

He had only one issue—gelt. He calculated that the cost of the land combined with the build meant he was short by some way and the banks were not prepared to take on the risk—gaming was still a no-no for most of the country. Meyer Lansky came to town and met with Wilkerson, Benny, and Alex.

"So, Billy, on the phone you said you had funding issues that you wanted us to talk about."

Wilkerson looked around the table and shivered as he saw he was surrounded by these gang bosses. It is one thing to ask a known crime financier for money—it is quite another to be sitting face-to-face with the Jewish mob in your own hometown.

"This is the deal, Meyer. I own a thirty-three-acre plot south of the city line where I can develop my entertainment vision how I see fit without the Vegas elders sticking their noses in my affairs. The cost of materials has skyrocketed because of the war, and to achieve any return on my investment, I need to get the complex built and open."

"What makes you think your place will be successful so far away from the action?"

"No offense to El Rancho, El Cortez, or the Last Frontier but these are aimed at a different customer to mine. I want to reach the rich and the famous—develop a casino and hotel venue where you can smell the money dripping down the walls."

"Billy, I invested in El Cortez with the same aim as you, only I inherited the Tex-Mex facade. Our ideas are aligned and I would be happy to work with you on this new venture."

"Thanks, Benny. I have the advantage that I am starting with fields of dirt and nothing more."

"How much gelt are you seeking for the investment?"

"Meyer, to get the buildings up and ready for customers, hire staff, and open the doors? Six hundred thousand."

Billy eyed the three men and settled his gaze on Meyer. Nobody was showing any outward signs—these were not fellas to play poker with if you wanted to keep your shirt.

"You know what'll happen if you can't meet your financial obligations?"

Wilkerson gulped, imagined the worst, and nodded.

"Yes, that is clear to me."

"Punitive interest charged per day. When I invest, I want everybody to walk in with their eyes wide open."

"Sure, Meyer. I wouldn't come to you and ask for your help if I wasn't aware of the consequences of doing so."

"And what would be the size of my stake?"

"I thought you were offering me a loan?"

"Billy, you said you wanted an investment and I told you that was acceptable. If you prefer me as a creditor then we can reach an arrangement along those lines but I'll need collateral and the only thing worth my time and energy would be the thirty-three-acre site and I wouldn't release that until every dime was paid back. Plus my interest rate is not what a bank'd charge you—I have my costs to underwrite. So an investment is cheaper and safer for you. Once the place is up-and-running, you'll need everything to be plain sailing with unions and suppliers. And the last thing you want is for the place to burn down. My investment secures insurance against all these potential difficulties."

Meyer smiled at Billy, whose furtive glances at Benny and Alex showed he hadn't engaged with what it meant to do business with a syndicate member.

"Yes, an investment sounds the best option."

Benny cleared his throat. "Meyer, if you don't mind, I would like to put some money in myself."

"Fine by me, but only once Billy here tells us how big the stake will be."

"Fifty percent?"

"Without our capital, you have a gigantic pile of earth, some blueprints, and nothing much else, right?"

Wilkerson nodded agreement.

"In that case, our gelt is worth more than half of nothing. Let's pretend we asked for the whole thing, you refused and we end up with two-thirds. Would that save us wasting our time haggling?"

Another hard swallow from Billy and he consented.

"In the hope we'd come to an arrangement, I got Mendy Greenberg to draw up the paperwork for us. All we have to do is fill in the blanks for the cash sum and stake. You can have the money before you go to sleep tonight."

They shook hands on the deal and signed the contracts which Meyer whipped out of his briefcase.

"Benny and Alex will work with you to ensure everything runs like clockwork from now on—any problems then see them. They will be my eyes and ears on the ground."

Once Billy had thanked Meyer profusely, he walked off to leave the three men alone by the El Rancho pool. Meyer was the first to speak.

"Congratulations, Benny, we each own a third of the new hotel. What shall we call it?"

"That's easy, the Flamingo. It'll remind me of Virginia's lovely long legs every day I go to work."

Alex smiled because that was Hill's nickname, but most people called her that because her cheeks went flamingo pink when she hit the booze too hard.

"Works for me, Benny. The next item on the agenda is that you must buy out Wilkerson's remaining stake. We don't need this schnook to build and run a gambling joint. Reach an agreement with him by the end of the week or a terrible accident will befall him."

AFTER BENNY WENT back to his office to sort out some problem with a hotel guest, Alex asked Meyer if he could dip his beak in the Flamingo trough, but he would hear none of it.

"As much as I respect your desire to make money out of this matter, I must decline your request, Alex. The syndicate needs no other business partners."

"Is that what it comes down to, Meyer? I'm still not a member of the syndicate so you will shut me out of the juiciest deals."

"Be patient. There are reasons why you can be no part of this and they will become clear later, but until then you must bide your time and trust me, I have your best interests at heart."

"You don't make it easy for me."

"Alex, nobody told us life was a walk in the park."

MOE AND GUS were brought in so Benny could delegate the day-to-day activities and focus his attention on all the hotels under his ownership. Alex was asked to keep an eye on what the two men were doing, but they followed Benny's orders and Benny made all the decisions.

One of the first things he did was to stop buying from out of state. The architect's drawings were explicit and called for the finest of all materials, but Benny changed suppliers at almost every turn.

"Are you trying to make the investment capital stretch further, Benny?"

"What are you talking about, Alex?"

"The specification was for imported marble in the lobby, but it's only traveling from California. So I figure you're being careful with the syndicate's gelt."

"And what business is it of yours?"

"No disrespect—I was just asking."

"All you need to do is make sure Moe and Gus get on with their jobs—and nothing more."

"I haven't seen Virginia for a few days. Is everything all right between you two?"

"Alex, you're in a curious frame of mind tonight. She's off on some business for me in Paris if that's acceptable to you."

Alex gave up talking to Benny at that point. The next day he popped over to the airport and made a few inquiries. Virginia had flown out by private jet two days before, although the destination on the manifest was Geneva.

29

HILL'S RETURN TO Vegas was called through to Alex, who had asked a contact at the airport to keep a lookout for Benny's friend. When she arrived at El Rancho, Alex was already in the lobby and feigned surprise at bumping into her.

"How are you, Virginia?"

"Fine, thanks. What are you doing here, Alex?"

"Passing through. You know what it's like—there's always something to do for Benny."

"He likes to keep everybody busy, that's for sure."

"You've been out of town—I haven't seen you here for a while."

"Yeah…"

Her voice trailed off in abject disinterest.

"Do you have time for a quick drink, Virginia?"

"Well, I don't know…"

He smiled and looked in the general direction of the pool and the position of his usual table. Virginia hesitated and then shrugged in acceptance. Alex led her to the poolside and she slipped her sunglasses on. As they sat down, she ordered a cosmo and he asked for a coffee.

"Did you pop back to LA for a few days?"

"No, Alex. I was out of the country."

"Anywhere exotic?"

"I wouldn't say so—it depends if you are used to international travel."

"I've seen more than my fair share of France and Belgium."

"Really? I had you down as someone without a passport."

"Well, I don't have one of those."

"So how come?"

"I was stationed there during the war."

"No offense, but you were too old, weren't you? Besides, I'd have heard if you'd only recently got back from Europe."

It was Alex's turn to be confused until he realized Virginia's mistake.

"I was talking about the First World War, not the one just passed."

"That must have been quite something."

"Haunts me even now. They gave me a medal, but that is no substitute for returning home with all your friends in one piece."

"Did you leave many behind?"

"Far too many. Have you been to France?"

"Several times—I'd love to make Paris my second home."

"Yeah? Is that where you went on this trip?"

"No, I was elsewhere. Alex, why are you so interested in my travels?"

"To be honest, I am trying to look after Benny's interests and I don't want you to take this the wrong way, but I know that when you came back from wherever you went, your baggage was several pounds lighter. And that got me to thinking that perhaps you had left something behind."

"Did it? You're sounding like you are a cigarette paper away from accusing me."

"Not at all, Virginia—just commenting. If Benny is getting you to carry out errands, that is none of my business and I am not prying into his or your affairs."

"Funny, because that is what it sounds like you are doing."

"Nope—you must be mixing me up with some other fella. I'm only happy when Benny is happy and if you are facing any difficulties with these trips of yours, then all you need to do is ask and I'll be there for you."

She looked at him, trying to decide whether to believe him. Alex smiled back and sipped his coffee, which was cooling down.

"There is nothing to worry about, Alex. A few years ago I worked down south with some friends from Chicago and they have some interests in Switzerland, so I fly out to help them because, like you, they don't have a passport."

"Do they speak French over there?"

"Yes, they do, Alex."

He reckoned that meant she would be in Geneva rather than Zurich, where they spoke German. Alex's tour in Europe wasn't entirely spent in the trenches, despite the worst of his memories. And Geneva was renowned for its discreet private banks. Either Virginia was squirreling cash away for the Chicago outfit or the source of the gelt was closer to home. Besides, Alex would have known if there were regular Italian Illinois visitors in town.

ALEX LAY IN bed that night–not everything Virginia had told him added up. The Chicago outfit supported James Ragen's news wire, and Benny was in direct competition with those fellas. Would his girlfriend work with them and look after their overseas interests?

Although Alex preferred not to deal with the possibility, Benny had been playing fast and loose with the truth about the amount of money generated by his ventures compared to the gelt he was sending back east.

If there was a hidden surplus, then Benny may well wish it removed from Vegas so nobody else could get their dirty mitts on it. Geneva would be as good a place as any—these were six and seven-figure sums—as Swiss private bankers asked no impertinent questions like from whom did you steal this money?

But all Alex had at the moment was his belief that something was up—there was no evidence to show Meyer or anyone else from the syndicate. The other issue was whether he wanted to be the fella to rat out Benny. He was one of Meyer's and Charlie's oldest friends—should he really be seen to throw the man to the wolves? Alex met up with Virginia the next day on the pretext of some security matters.

"I'm hoping you'll let me know when you are heading over to Europe again, Virginia."

"This actually isn't any of your business, Alex."

"I agree that what you do is your own affair, but I am responsible for what goes on in Vegas and we believe there are thieves at the airport targeting lone women. We both know you can handle yourself with no help from me, but I would rather be safe than sorry."

"Yesterday you accused me and today you want to be my bodyguard. Why the turnaround?"

"Virginia, let me apologize for the manner I spoke to you then. Part of what I do is to look out for behavior I don't understand or think is unusual. I didn't explain myself to you well enough and came across badly. All I care about is that you and Benny are happy—and you both remain safe."

She looked at him for a while—he was so hard to gauge.

"You were only doing your job, I guess."

"Exactly right. And the best means for me to know you are out of harm's way is if you'll be kind enough to inform me the next occasion you hit the airport. You don't have to say where you are going or why you are heading there, but the date and time of your departure means I can help you between here and the flight."

"Benny is lucky to have a friend like you, Alex."

"You reckon?"

"Too many of the fellas only look after number one. So few understand the bigger picture."

"We live together, we love together, but we die alone."

"That kind of thing, yeah. You guys have a proper sense of camaraderie—I haven't seen that for some time."

"I found that out during the war—those of us who survived did so because we looked out for each other and were damn lucky."

"Benny told me you got a Purple Heart."

"But I did not deserve it. I killed a kid to save a friend, only he was already dead before my shot rang out—big deal."

"I doubt if that's quite what happened. They don't give those things out like candy."

"So you'll let me know your flight plans?"

"Sure, Alex. You've got my back—I understand."

June 1946

30

DESPERATE TIMES CALL for decisive action and Benny had reached the end of his patience with Trans-American.

"We've been scratching away for years, Alex, and I'm sick of fighting with the Nationwide News wire. It's time we dealt with our competition once and for all."

"What are you planning, Benny?"

"James Ragen is on a business trip to the Windy City and we need to ensure he doesn't make it home in one piece."

"He's supported by the Chicago outfit, right?"

"I have syndicate approval for the hit—a majority of the fellas fund us and they want to see an increase in revenue too."

"Have you issued the contract?"

"Not yet, Alex. That's why I wanted to speak with you."

"I don't know anyone who we could call on—my time running Murder Corporation was years ago. My little black book is light of paid killers."

"I wasn't asking you for a recommendation. Instead, you pack a bag and head off to the Windy City this afternoon, Alex."

"Are you sure, Benny?"

"Is there anyone better for the job than you? Get outta here."

ALEX INVITED MASSIMO to join him on the trip and they arrived in Chicago in time for the sun to set over the skyline. They holed up in a cheap hotel—if Alex's life was anything to go by, places like the Hotel Muldrove were only kept solvent through the one-night stays of contract killers. In every city in the land, there were fleapits located close to the station, which were surrounded by low-rent nafkas and guys hooked on brown powder. The Muldrove proved the stereotype.

"Our friend is expected tomorrow morning at an appointment on State Street, so that will be our best opportunity."

The two men made their plans over a simple meal on the edge of the South Side—Alfonse Capone's old stomping ground.

"Tonight we'll boost a car on the north of town and then we can fly by and get the guy, Massimo."

"Works for me. Am I driving or squeezing the trigger?"

"You go behind the wheel—Benny was clear he expected me to do the deed."

Massimo didn't mind either way, he only wanted to know there was a plan to stick to—he was not one to make things up on the spur of the moment. So they waited in a stolen car on East Pershing Road until Alex spotted Ragen's vehicle, just as Benny had described.

Massimo tucked in behind Ragen's black saloon and they carried on south a block until he came to a halt and parked on the right-hand side of the street.

"Steady," warned Alex as he raised the barrel of his rifle to peek out from his window, which he'd wound all the way down. Massimo timed matters perfectly as he pulled up to stop beside Ragen just as the guy hopped out of his car into the road.

Alex fired off three slugs before the racing wire tycoon hit the ground. People screamed and every passerby looked around to figure out where the shots came from and who had been the target for the assault.

Massimo slammed on the gas and they tore away, waiting four blocks before heading back north to the city center and the railway station. Before they got on the train, Alex had the presence of mind to check the late edition and found that Ragen was down but not out. Somehow the weasel had survived being shot at point-blank range and was being treated for leg and arm wounds at Mercy Hospital.

"Let's get some poison and put this scum out of his misery."

"Alex, you want to take him out from his hospital bed?"

"The longer he's alive, the greater the chance he'll remember details about the car that pulled up alongside him and the faces of the fellas inside the vehicle. We need to get this done tonight."

THREE HOURS LATER and the two men entered Mercy clutching a bunch of flowers each, fedoras clamped as far down at the front of their heads as they could. They both knew the score and Alex kicked off the plan by sauntering up to the reception desk to speak with a nurse behind the counter.

"Sorry to bother you, but I'm looking for a friend of mine. They brought him in earlier today, but I don't know where to find him."

"What's his name?"

"James Ragen."

"He's on the third floor—just ask someone when you get there, but I doubt if they'll let you see him. He is under police guard because of his circumstances."

"Oh no. The least I can do is give him these flowers from me and the fellas. That way, he'll have something to remind him he's not alone."

The nurse feigned interest in Alex's sob story, but she stopped listening almost at the same time as Alex ceased caring about the details of his lie. Up to the third floor and Alex separated from Massimo, who had his own task to complete.

Meanwhile, Alex headed to the desk in the male surgery ward hoping to get close to Ragen. There were cops at the counter and a quick glance showed two officers standing outside a room, which must contain Ragen otherwise what were Chicago's finest doing in the Mercy?

Alex's shoelace mysteriously came loose and he put the flowers down to sort out his shoes. Almost to the second, a loud bang ripped out from the far corridor and the cops in the waiting area raced over to investigate the commotion. Then the two guards ran past and followed their colleagues toward the noise of the blast. Massimo had done well to create such a controlled explosion in the stairwell in such a short amount of time.

In Ragen's room, Alex closed the drapes to hide his activities from any prying eyes. He only had a minute before the cops realized they were chasing a flash in a pan and returned.

The fella was sleeping, so Alex fumbled in his pockets for the syringe and the silvery-white liquid he'd purchased earlier. He didn't need to be that adept with a needle as he poked through Ragen's skin in his upper left arm. Then he plunged the syringe deep inside and squeezed the mercury into the guy's body.

As soon as the spike pierced Ragen's flesh, he woke bolt upright, but Alex placed one palm over the guy's mouth to prevent any sound reaching unsuspecting ears and held him in place while he writhed in agony as the toxic metal took hold. Thirty seconds and he was dead—Alex checked his pulse twice and listened to his heart too.

Five minutes after James Ragen breathed his last, Alex and Massimo met up around the corner and headed to the station.

"You hear about Charlie Lucky, Massimo?"

"What?"

"Dewey commuted his sentence and set him free—only Charlie has had to go home to Palermo."

"Why did that scumbag relent?"

"Charlie helped him during the war on the New York waterfront."

"Stand up fella. Has he had to give up on the syndicate?"

"Not at all, Massimo. He will run things from Sicily."

WITH THE RACING wire king in the ground, Benny and Alex visited the widow within a week of the funeral.

"Mrs. Ragen, we are sorry for your loss and appreciate this is a tough time for you."

Benny was focusing hard on behaving as well as he could, and Alex echoed his manner.

"There is nothing to do to erase the terrible way in which James met his demise, but there is something we can do to ease your anguish over the coming months and years as you learn to live again."

"He was gunned down in the street and then someone walked into the hospital and murdered him in his sleep. What can you offer me to make that pain go away?"

"A million dollars so you will never have to worry about money ever again. It can't bring James back, but it should take the sting out of the day."

The woman eyed Benny suspiciously, but she let him continue—her grief was balanced by the prospect of a sizeable amount of gelt.

"Talk to me about the sting."

"My partner and I would look after the running of the Nationwide News wire that James worked to build up from nothing. That way, you wouldn't have to worry about organizing all those men and the technical equipment, and can find some solace knowing that you will benefit from all of James' hard work. I'm sure that's what he would have wanted."

"Don't be so certain, mister. If you knew my husband as I did, you wouldn't go shooting your mouth off singing his praises. He was a mean, cold-hearted bastard who was only interested in himself and his wealth. He ignored me and the kids from the moment he created that news wire of his. If you're not jerking me around with talk of a million, I'll sign the paperwork right now."

BACK AT EL Rancho, the two men enjoyed a celebratory cocktail.

"Alex, I have a side proposition for you. How hungry are you for the wire?"

"We've spent years trying to build Trans-American up to something and have always been beaten back by those with allegiance to the Nationwide—Jack Dragna and the Chicago outfit. Now we control the only two racing wires in the country, coast to coast."

"Would you like to have it all?"

"What do you mean, Benny?"

"This is the situation. I need to make some payments for the Flamingo and I'm short on gelt, now that Ragen's wife is swimming in small bills. So I'll sell you my fifty percent stake for cash, but I must have the money this week. This is no gentle buyout. You get to dip your beak in every racing bet in America and I have my dream hotel complex."

"How much are we talking?"

"Two million."

Alex whistled through his front teeth.

"I thought Meyer had invested sufficient capital to get the place up-and-running?"

"Don't go concerning yourself about Meyer Lansky and his money. Let's just say we hit some unexpected snags and needed to buy our way out of certain situations. Are you in or not?"

"Mickey and I will own gambling in Nevada and California, and I'll get a percentage of every track bet going. What's not to like?"

"When can I have the gelt?"

"Tomorrow, Benny?"

"Tonight would be better."

Alex shrugged and agreed. He just needed to make a few stops around the outskirts of Vegas to collect his investment capital. He'd been out of the Bowery for longer than he could remember, but he still kept his money in a bunch of holes in crumbling walls.

December 1946

31

A BROWN ENVELOPE arrived at Alex's door, shipped special delivery by an unknown courier. Five minutes later, he received a phone call and recognized the voice as soon as the first syllable landed in his ear.

"I sent you a gift. Have you opened it?"

"Yes, I've never had one of those before. How did you know I wanted one?"

"Because you're taking a trip overseas tomorrow and I remember you telling me you didn't need a passport when last you traveled abroad."

"No passports necessary in the American Army."

"A car will pick you up at nine. Be packed and ready to go."

Meyer hung up and Alex was left listening to the buzz at the end of the phone line. He found a case, threw in some clothes, and folded a spare suit on top. Then he had a light supper, watched a show at the Last Frontier, and went to bed early.

His limousine arrived on time the next morning and took him to the airport and within minutes, Alex was walking up the steps into a private plane. Meyer was already sitting inside, reading a newspaper.

"Good to see you. Where are we going?"

Meyer smiled. "To visit Charlie."

"We're off to Sicily?"

"Don't be ridiculous. In this twin prop? He moved to Cuba in October, and he's called a meeting of the syndicate. I think we need you there to hear what you know."

MEYER AND ALEX hotfooted over to the Hotel Nacional de Cuba when they landed in Havana, where Charlie Lucky met them. He gave Alex a massive hug—Alex didn't realize how much he had missed his friend until they were reunited. The three friends headed out to Charlie's residence in Miramar, an area of the city filled with foreign embassies and uptown money.

"So how did Mendy spring you, Charlie? I thought Dewey meant for you to die in prison."

"The special prosecutor wanted my final breath to be the stinking air inside Sing Sing, but he forgot I had connections on the waterfront. During the war, the navy needed eyes and ears focused on any suspicious activities near New York's ports, and I helped."

"In return for an early release?"

"That's right, Alex. Mendy cut me a great deal and then Dewey welched at the last minute and deported me as soon as I stepped outside the prison walls."

"Did any of us ever like that guy? You could never trust him."

"Alex, that man clipped both our wings."

"He still walks free—and they talk as though there's justice in America."

"Listen to the pair of you—calm down and be thankful you both have your health and your wealth."

"Right, Meyer. We live together, we love together…"

"…and we die alone."

The three men nodded and fell to silence. Meyer was right—any fool can complain about his lot. It's what you do with the hand you're dealt that makes the difference between the winners and losers in this world.

"Are you staying a while in Cuba, Charlie?"

"As long as I am able. I like the place—it reminds me of Florida, only in Spanish. Also, I am a handful of miles from America and I can manage the organization easier from here."

"Meyer said there was a meeting planned."

Charlie smiled at how much Alex wanted to be back inside the syndicate.

"That's right. We're inviting you as an advisor which means you will attend and observe all that happens—and make any comments you want, but you have no voting rights."

Alex was close to returning to the inside track, but no cigar.

"And, Charlie, why call the meeting in the first place?"

"I couldn't think of a better excuse to come to Havana and see Frank Sinatra—he's in town this week. Besides, we can hold our discussions without worrying about the cops and the Feds."

THE AGENDA FOR the Havana conference was straightforward—there were only three matters to discuss: heroin trafficking, gambling in Cuba, and the Flamingo. One syndicate member was notable by his absence—Benny

Siegel, but apart from that, there were the usual suspects at the Hotel Nacional de Cuba.

Along with Meyer and Charlie were Jack Dragna representing the west coast and a host of fresh faces that Alex didn't recognise. These were the fellas Meyer said were unfamiliar with him and hence reluctant to let him back at the top table, although he was close today. He sat behind Meyer, near enough to lean in and offer private advice where necessary.

"Thank you all for coming to visit me here in my home from home. It ain't Little Italy, but it'll do. While I may have stepped down from running the syndicate when I was in prison, there is still an alignment of interests sitting in this room."

Charlie eyed the attendees one by one—Joe Adonis, Albert Anastasia, and Vito Genovese, along with at least half a dozen others from New York, Anthony Accardo from Chicago, and gang bosses from New Orleans, Buffalo, New Jersey, and Cleveland. Alex looked out at the sea of strangers and returned his gaze to one man: Anastasia, who didn't even offer him a flicker of recognition. This was the fella who had stolen Alex's drug operation from under him before he visited Sing Sing. All water under the bridge, apparently.

"I have set up supply lines from Africa and South America to guarantee a free flow of heroin into the US."

The men spent the rest of the day hammering out who would get what percentage from the narcotics supplies until everybody was content with their cut. That night the entire group had front row seats at a Sinatra show which took place in the hotel. Meyer explained how he had asked the singer over as a special favor and they all agreed the guy had a voice on him.

THE NEXT DAY, Meyer whizzed through a discussion on some investment plans he'd unearthed in Cuba.

"I am an indirect joint owner of this hotel with President Batista—he's a man who cares for his people but is more interested in the dark art of making money and I hope to work with him as we open up gambling opportunities in this country."

"We all know Meyer has a sharp eye for a deal and the joint we're sitting in is ripe for growth, which is why I invested a hundred and fifty yesterday in the place."

"Thank you for your vote of confidence, Charlie. Just as we have reached into Nevada and California, thanks to Jack and Benny, Batista wants to attract tourists to this island and sees casinos as a way of achieving this goal. He runs his country with an iron fist so the good news is that whatever he wants, he gets."

"And how long do you think he'll maintain his interest in gaming?"

"Albert, I have spent the last two years working with this man and I can guarantee one thing—while the money flows, he will remain interested because he ensures he lines his pockets as well as the vaults of his treasury."

While all these matters had been of mild interest to Alex, there was no need for him to be in the room. Meyer had been kind to invite him, and the fact the others allowed him in showed his star was rising. The next day, he discovered the real reason he was sitting in this room in a luxury hotel in the middle of Havana.

EVERYBODY SAT DOWN with their coffees and Charlie opened the third day of discussions.

"The last item for the meeting is Las Vegas. Talk us through the situation, Meyer."

"Thanks, Charlie. We have four million invested in the Flamingo being built by Benny Siegel. The hotel-casino will open later this week and several of you have expressed concerns about the size of the investment and when we are likely to receive a return."

Every man nodded and a general murmur spread around the room. Alex had no idea that Vegas was the object of such scrutiny from so important a group of people—he operated as though his little empire in Nevada was of no significance to these fellas, but he was wrong.

"The Flamingo was only meant to cost six hundred thousand—that's what Siegel told us he'd need when we first bought in."

"Albert, when I lent Benny the gelt initially, that is what I believed was happening. When more requests for cash came through, I thought we should all have an opportunity to invest."

Meyer was shrewd enough not to take on all the risk himself, even though he and Benny had been childhood friends.

"Now there are other considerations beyond the money for us to discuss, but first I'd like to ask Alex Cohen's opinion on the situation. He is based in Nevada, running the Trans-American racing wire—and he owns two hotels, so he understands the business thoroughly. What do you think of Benny's handling of the Flamingo?"

Alex grabbed a sip of coffee and lit a cigarette—his moment had arrived.

"I've worked with Benny for years and he has supported me with Trans-American very well and his vision for gambling in Vegas is second to none."

"Alex, we all know how Benny was the first to spot the opportunity for building casinos out west, years before the rest of us. He claimed all he needed was a pack of cards and some green baize. What we need to hear from you is whether Benny is playing with a straight deck. Be honest here—you are among friends."

Alex looked at Albert—was Meyer right? It had been so long since he trusted Anastasia, he thought he might have forgotten how to do it, the *farbissener* momzer.

"He has chosen his suppliers, sometimes using locals instead of our out-of-town friends. Also, I am unaware of the extent his attention has been taken away from the Flamingo by his girlfriend, Virginia Hill."

"Many of us know Virginia—you need not explain any further in that regard." Meyer glanced at Joe Adonis and then at the Chicago representatives. She had either been in their beds or on their payroll.

"Would you say Benny has invested our money wisely?"

"Meyer, I haven't seen the accounts and I know little about putting up a building."

"Has it ever crossed your mind that there might be a discrepancy between what is spent and what Benny has received?"

Meyer had lifted his own ideas out of his head and dropped them into this meeting.

"The costs Benny mentioned to me do not tally with the expenditure. And if I must talk about another fella's finances behind his back, I am not sure his earnings from his casino investments have been accurately reported to the syndicate. Again, I don't know for certain, but it has crossed my mind."

Silence. Alex's heart raced inside his chest. As the words came tumbling out of his mouth, the men in the room lapped up his every syllable. Once he'd stopped, he felt enormous relief—like he'd needed to share his concerns but had no one near enough to listen until now.

"Thanks, Alex. Does Virginia make any trips out of town?"

"About once a month, maybe. She goes to Europe and comes back lighter than when she flew out."

"Alex, how do you know? That's a very specific claim you're making."

"Charlie, when Virginia first came to town, we didn't hit it off, so I kept a watching eye on her in case I needed to protect Benny's interests. I used plane manifests and confronted her, but she said she was looking after the business of our Chicago friends, so I let it go."

Accardo's eyebrows raised to the roof and Alex saw that she had lied to him. Meyer turned his head to face the syndicate.

"As we discussed earlier, there is some evidence that Benny has been skimming a proportion of our investment into private bank accounts in Geneva. I think he has also been omitting some of his income from the casinos and other operations and has been transporting it to Geneva too, with a little help from Hill."

"You think she knows what he's up to?"

"Joe, she's flying to a bank in a foreign country in a private plane. She knows what she is doing, but we don't know if she is in on the scam or just doing what Benny has asked of her."

"She maintains her own apartment in Los Angeles even though she spends almost all of her time in Vegas," Alex added. "I'm not sure she is as committed to Benny as he'd like her to be."

"Let's take a break and when we come back, we need to decide what we will do about Benjamin Siegel."

Charlie stood up and walked out of the room, followed by Meyer. As Alex had no desire to jaw-jaw with the fellas left, he sauntered out and hoped to catch up with his old friends.

HE REACHED THEM before they left the floor to walk around the block.

"Meyer, I felt as though you knew the answers to the questions aimed at me before I opened my mouth."

"We've had our suspicions for a while, Alex, and I needed you to confirm them in front of the others—or show why we were wrong."

"You could have warned me before we walked into the room."

"Alex, what I wanted was for you to give us an honest account of what you saw and what you believe. The syndicate members were clear they didn't want me to coach you. Benny and I go back a long way."

"What now?"

"That's for the syndicate to decide, Alex."

Back upstairs, there were no speeches before the vote and a unanimous decision in favor of whacking Benny for non-payment of monies.

"Charlie, may I make a simple request?"

"What is it, Meyer?"

"Please let us wait until the Flamingo opens before we carry out the contract. If the hotel is successful, then we could recoup the gelt that has been stolen from us and maybe come to some arrangement with Benny over the whole affair."

"As that is only a matter of days, I can accept the wait."

Albert spoke for all of them. As much as Benny needed punishing, everyone knew the last time the syndicate agreed a hit on one of its own was with Dutch Schultz. Charlie broke the silence.

"Let's see if Benny can turn the Flamingo around. If he does, then we will sit down with him and talk. If not then, Meyer, you'll need to organize the contract—that way we'll know the hit has been carried out without malice. This is just business."

With those words, Charlie glanced at Albert Anastasia, who had always had difficulties with Jewish members of the syndicate; a Sicilian, whose prejudices were shaped in the old country and not in modern America.

That night, they broke bread with Sinatra in a private dining room in the hotel and the following day, Alex returned to the Last Frontier.

32

"ALEX, HOW IS my six million investment doing?"

"Meyer, we're getting there. Everything is complete apart from the hotel rooms, and Benny plans to open after Christmas."

"There should be gold leaf on the walls, the amount this thing has cost us."

"Benny wants it all to be perfect."

"Perfect is good, profitable is better."

When the lobby doors were finally opened at the Flamingo, the casino was ready as was the restaurant, but there were none of the promised hundred and five hotel rooms—the second floor was not safe for customers yet and the third comprised a series of floorboard supports and not much else.

"Why didn't you wait until everything was completed, Benny?"

"Because I need to generate some revenue to keep the syndicate off my back, Alex, and we both know you can run a roulette wheel without offering the johns a bed to sleep in afterward."

"Put like that…"

"It cost me four million to get this joint looking as it does on the first floor." That was another number that Alex couldn't make add up—a two million or more gap between what Benny had spent and what he owed Meyer.

Despite Alex's best efforts to round up some johns, Benny refused to give him any gelt for advertising—not one red cent to send a few girls out onto the street with even a flyer and a willing smile.

So Alex was hardly surprised when nobody appeared in the first hour and only two families rolled in to eat at seven. Benny and his Hollywood friend, George Raft, showed up too. The guy seemed down to earth, unlike many of Benny's showbiz connections, but then Raft had started life in a New York gang.

As soon as he saw the chance, Alex slipped away from Benny, Raft, and Mickey who looked set to drink into the night while the Flamingo staff tried to keep the joint running. The chef couldn't handle the three table orders which had rushed at him all at the same time. Alex attempted to offer some direction and a sense of calm to the paying customers and the waiters alike.

At one point, he leaned against a restaurant wall to find the plasterwork crumbling beneath his shoulder. For a man who had taken so much money, Benny didn't look as though he'd spent it on the Flamingo.

"WE ARE GOING to have to shut the place down, aren't we?"

Benny sat nursing a hangover by the El Rancho pool on the following afternoon. Raft and his entourage had shipped back to Los Angeles, and all was quiet in the hotel complex. Alex sipped a coffee and thought about the Flamingo.

"It's not yet fit for purpose, is it, Benny?"

Alex was right and, although it hurt Benny's ego to close the doors so soon after opening night, it was that or watch the place hemorrhage gelt—Benny needed the builders back in to finish the hotel rooms. Only then would families be able to stay over while the husband played cards and the wife watched a show.

"Is there money in the pot to complete the work?"

"Yes, Alex—we only ran out of time. And I must admit I'm my worst enemy, what with me always demanding excellence and not letting second-best be good enough."

"Perfection is a tough beast to ride." Alex wasn't too sure whether he was being sarcastic because of the crumbling plasterwork the night before, but Benny seemed to be sincere in what he said. Perhaps the fella was throwing him a curveball to take his eye off the financing.

ALEX HAD A quiet word with Gus and Moe. Benny had brought them over to Vegas because they knew how to run a gambling joint and keep the other lines of business running alongside the ordinary johns—their expertise covered prostitution, money laundering, and extortion. The list went on, but he didn't want to blow smoke up their asses too much.

"What do you say, fellas?"

"Alex, you know we are always happy to help, but the Flamingo is Benny's show, not ours. I can't speak for Gus, but I wouldn't feel comfortable stomping all over Benny's shoes without his permission."

"I understand, but I'm not asking you to walk in there and run the joint—just keep an eye on it and offer some friendly advice now and again. I've done my best but I have my hands full running the racing wire. What do you think, Gus?"

"Same as Moe. I won't set foot across the threshold without Benny tipping me the nod—unless it's having a drink at the relaunch party."

"You're a funny guy, you know that?"

"I have my moments."

Alex pondered the situation. These two men were the best hope they had of helping Benny land back on his feet. Although Benny hadn't spoken to Meyer since Charlie sailed to Palermo, the fella was under tremendous scrutiny by the syndicate—given the enormous amount of gelt they'd poured into his dream. The place might have been named after the color of Virginia's cheeks, but Benny would be the one blushing if this venture didn't come good. And soon.

"What would it take for you to visit the building four times a month and help keep Benny on track?"

"A small consideration only."

"Five thousand a week until the place reopens and a bonus of fifty if that happens before Pesach in April."

"Each?"

Alex snorted. "If that'll make the difference, then yes."

March 1947

33

"WE GOT THERE, Alex."

"Well done, Benny. You've made it."

They clinked their champagne glasses as they stood in the Flamingo lobby. A parade of famous, renowned, and rich faces flowed past—Benny had invited some of his Hollywood pals, various syndicate members, and other gang bosses, as well as the well-heeled and well-funded citizens of Nevada and beyond.

Alex nudged Benny as Clark Gable wandered by and nodded in their general direction. "I thought you only knew George Raft."

"That once was true, but I've spent enough time in Los Angeles supplying the film studios with cocaine and skirts to know a few other A-listers."

To reinforce the point, Lana Turner broke away from the group and pecked Benny on the cheek, blew a kiss to Alex, and returned to her conversation with Cesar Romero. In the background, the orchestra played on stage—the auditorium had been converted into a dance floor just for the launch night, and couples were already taking advantage of the Cuban band.

Alex's eyes maintained surveillance around the room, noticing when johns walked up the stairs to where the nafkas were stationed, ready to offer a special experience to select guests later in the night. Mickey Cohen's men provided security, so there would be no disturbance from the ordinary citizens and this was a syndicate-funded party so any fella who wanted to cause trouble would make enemies of the most senior criminals in the country.

"How much did it all cost in the end?"

"Six million."

"And boy does it look as though you spent every single cent?"

"Ever since I was a kid, I dreamed of opening a joint like this, where high rollers can lose their dough at poker while their wives watch a show and have a meal."

"You deserve everything that you get, Benny."

"Thanks, Alex."

WITH THE STARS from the silver screen sipping cocktails, Benny moved further inside—he wasn't expecting any other important guests and had timed matters so that the Hollywood names walked into a buzzing, lively venue. He threw a few words out to the press hounds and then Mickey's guys ushered them off the premises so that everyone could enjoy themselves away from the watchful eyes of the news reporters.

Alex stayed in the lobby a while—he was in no mood for the biggest party of the year and, given the discussions in Havana, he couldn't face spending the night listening to Benny brag his way through into the early hours. Instead, Alex took a walk in the grounds to draw some fresh air into his lungs, hoping to clear his head.

Once you left the frontage and followed the path around the side of the hotel toward an entrance to the pool area, the glitz fell away mighty quickly. The walls were painted, but the concrete of the passage was already beginning to crumble—poor quality materials or roughshod work. Neither was a sign of six million dollars spent on the building, despite Benny's claim.

Alex arrived at a patio area near the pool and a waiter swooped up on him and offered some champagne. Armed with the Californian sparkling wine, he wandered past the guests in search of he didn't know what. He sat down on a diving board because he'd had enough of overhearing snippets of other people's conversations.

On the other side of the pool, he spotted Meyer, who was in deep conversation with Moe and Gus. Each time he spoke, he leaned in, preferring to speak into their ears than announce his thoughts to the world at large. Leaving his glass behind, Alex zigzagged in between the party guests until he arrived at his old friend and the other two.

As he walked up, the three fell into silence for a second and Gus glanced at him, before finishing his sentence in Meyer's ear. Alex couldn't hear a word that was said because of the noise of the band.

"I wasn't too sure if you'd show tonight, Meyer."

"You know me, Alex—I love a good party and we are here to celebrate such success."

"That's you all over, Meyer." Alex's deadpan response made Meyer smile, but soon the accountant in him took over again.

"If you'll excuse me, gentlemen, there's someone here I'd like to introduce to Alex."

Gus and Moe nodded acceptance if not consent, and Meyer led Alex over to the other side of the patio, near the entrance to the dance floor.

"Is Sarah still with you, Meyer?"

"Of course. She is well and wishes you kind thoughts—she assumed we'd meet this evening."

A man in a white tux stood holding hands with a woman in a black cocktail dress. The sparkle in the jewelry around her neck and wrists showed these guys were loaded. Although there was a fixed grin on the woman's part, the man's countenance improved as Meyer walked toward him.

"Senator, let me introduce you to a wonderful friend of mine, Alex Cohen."

They shook hands.

"Alex, this is Senator Merrick Townsend. He represents the good people of Massachusetts."

"Do you come from that state, Merrick?"

"Born and bred. If you ever get the chance to visit, let me know and I will show you the sights. Boston is beautiful in the fall."

"Very kind, Merrick. I shall bear that in mind. Although I've been to the city a few times over the years, no one has been gracious enough to treat me as a tourist."

"I am always happy to help a friend of Meyer's."

"And do you find yourself out in Nevada often?"

"First occasion for my wife, Sylvia, but I have been here twice—for business."

"You should sit at one of our poker tables before you leave. Legal gambling is not something you have back home."

"My constituents would not appreciate my spending time occupied in such habits." Alex didn't like being admonished by this bureaucrat, but he kept his peace, knowing Meyer would only have put them together for a good reason. Townsend touched his elbow and hovered his lips near Alex's head. "Once I've ditched the old girl, I'll join you for a few hands if you can organize a private room."

"No problem. If you don't mind, I might invite some of Meyer's friends to come too—only trusted individuals, you understand?"

"That'd be most enjoyable."

AFTER MIDNIGHT, THE crowds remained, although Alex was still far from being in the humor for the festivities surrounding him. As soon as he was able, he hightailed it over to the second floor ostensibly to check that everything was running smoothly with the nafkas.

He walked down the main corridor and all the doors he passed were shut, which meant they were occupied. Any hotel guests had been placed on the fourth floor, so this showed the girls were being kept busy, earning an excellent hourly rate for Alex, who ran all prostitution in town.

At the far end was a room with its door wide open and Alex stepped inside. He had given strict instructions that this was his space for the night so he would have somewhere to hide from the johns. He sat on the bed and nursed his Scotch.

The sounds of the band and the guests mingling around the hotel permeated through the walls and got inside Alex's head. The jollity of the noise contrasted with the stone-cold fact that Alex missed Rebecca. This life had killed her and had driven Sarah away from him. What did he have to show for it? Piles of cash hidden in the Vegas and LA area, and not much else. His real friends in America were extradited or dead—apart from one: Meyer remained.

While he'd trusted Benny with his life when he first came to town, now things weren't so simple with the syndicate waiting to decide whether to execute the man for wholesale stealing and the way the fella had behaved toward Rebecca. Alex finished his drink just as a knock resounded from the door.

He checked through the peephole and let the girl in–she was one of the women he'd brought in for the night but he didn't know much about her apart from that.

"The girls said you were on your own and, no disrespect, but I thought I'd check on you to see if you wanted a good time."

He cast a glance up and down her body but absorbed nothing of what he'd seen.

"Sure, come on in."

As he closed the door, she removed what few clothes she was wearing and slipped under the crisp white sheets.

"What's your name?"

"You can call me anything you want in the whole wide world."

"Rebecca, then."

He could afford to spend a few minutes more in this room before he'd have to go downstairs and let Townsend win at cards.

34

THE ADVANTAGE OF running the Trans-American news wire was that nobody batted an eyelid if Alex left town for a day or two for some far-flung corner of the country. The Saratoga racetrack was hardly obscure and was a natural place for Alex to want to visit. Its proximity to Manhattan gave him ample cover to hide the fact his real purpose was to meet up with Meyer Lansky.

Having conquered his fear of flying with his Havana jaunt, Alex took advantage of this newly found transportation option and hopped on a plane to New York so that the trip didn't take forever. Meyer had hired a private room, and Alex only entered when he could be sure all the waiters had left.

"Good to see you, Meyer."

"Likewise, Alex. I'm glad you could pop over at such short notice."

"For you, anything."

Both guys smiled and Alex sipped the Scotch Meyer had ensured was waiting for him on his arrival. There were plates of sandwiches and chips too, in case either of the men became hungry during their conversation. Two pots of coffee were sitting at the ready as well.

"How's life in the syndicate?"

Before Meyer parted his lips, the crowd roared as the next race started and a bunch of thoroughbreds shot along the track with the sole aim of getting past the post before any of the others.

"Same old. You know what it's like. How is Vegas?"

"Quiet. We've soaked up all the racing wire business there is to get in town and Ezra and Massimo spend most of their time on the road, either encouraging new customers to join or collecting subscriptions. Mickey keeps the gambling ticking over and Benny looks like he's turned the corner with the Flamingo."

"Really?"

"He said it had made a quarter of a million, which at its first launch, I never dreamed was possible. The fella appears to have got it together."

"That's good. I'm glad Benny's dream hasn't been for nothing."

"But I doubt if you asked me to fly halfway across the country just to hear what you already know about our activities in Las Vegas."

"You are right, Alex. There is a specific item I need us to discuss."

Another roar as the race reached its conclusion and a rank outsider won, much to most people's annoyance. Alex sat up in his seat, not because of the excitement of what was happening on the track but because of Meyer's words and the serious expression on his face.

"What is it, Meyer?"

"At the end of last year, you watched as the syndicate agreed to hold back on taking action against Benny. I did my best to protect him, but the others have lost patience."

Alex inhaled because he thought he knew what was coming next, but he didn't want to say it out loud in case he was wrong.

"I appreciate the Flamingo has turned a profit, but it is nothing compared to the amount Benny owes us. At this rate, it will be at least two years before we get our money back and, even then, there is the matter of Benny's robbery from his friends."

Alex swallowed, feeling Meyer's pain as he spoke. A sip of coffee eased the dryness in his throat.

"And what have they instructed, Meyer?"

"Charlie has made it clear that the group will proceed with the contract and it's my job to make sure it gets done."

"By your hand?"

Meyer looked out at the race as the horses thundered past, almost as if he couldn't bring himself to answer Alex's question.

"That would be ideal, but I don't think I can do it. He's saved my life too many times over the decades."

"Is that why I'm here?"

"I'd like you to take on the contract, yes."

"You want me to kill Benny Siegel?"

"That's what I'm asking. Will you?"

He nodded his consent—he had been the one to hit Dutch Schultz all those years ago, but that didn't make it any easier. His relationship with Benny was different—they had spent so much time together, working closely in Vegas and New York before.

June 1947

35

"HOW HAVE YOU been, Virginia?"

Alex and Hill had spent little time in each other's company and hadn't been in the same room together since the opening night of the Flamingo. He had eased off his dislike of her when he realized she was only doing Benny's bidding—knowingly or otherwise. Once that idea had permeated his mind, Virginia diminished in Alex's esteem but he was more sympathetic to her situation.

"Not so bad, Alex. Life keeping you busy?"

"As ever. There's always someone to see—the race wire business doesn't run itself."

"I suppose not." She looked around the Flamingo bar area, in search of Benny, but he wasn't there.

"Drink?"

"A cosmo would be most pleasant."

They passed the time of day amicably enough for a few minutes and then lapsed into silence. The only thing they had in common was Benny, and that didn't stretch conversation beyond an initial hello. They sipped their cocktails and Alex inquired about LA.

"Do you still keep that apartment in Malibu?"

"Beverly Hills," she corrected him. "Yes."

"I'd like to entertain a guest somewhere discreet but homely. Are you planning one of your trips soon?"

Virginia eyed him suspiciously.

"That's not an issue—you want my place for how long?"

"Only a night. Maybe two."

"You often meet business acquaintances of an evening in an apartment? Alex, I thought you men used bars and backroom gambling dens to talk over work."

"Who said anything about business?"

Virginia smiled and touched his arm briefly before taking another sip of her cosmo.

"You can't fool me, Alex. If there was a woman involved, then you wouldn't want me to know about it and you'd hire some suite—with a better view of the beach."

"The reason isn't that important—I just would prefer to go somewhere discreet and not one of our usual haunts. The guy is from out of town and I'd like to set him at his ease. He thinks it is dangerous to hang out with men like me."

"You expect me to believe that?"

"It's the best answer on offer."

She looked at him again and decided.

"I hope she's worth it. Yes, you can have my apartment."

"Will you be out of town in a week or so, do you expect?"

"While you won't admit to having a girlfriend, I'll tell you I'm planning a trip to France. I might not have told you before, but I am seeing a guy there."

"Hence all your flights to Europe?"

"Pretty much."

"What does Benny think of the situation?"

"He has his wife, I have my man in Paris. And because he's in another country, there will never be a time when he and Benny cross paths."

"You've got it all worked out."

Her story didn't chime with what Meyer said was going on, but at least she would be out of the way.

"I will let the super know to expect you once we've confirmed the dates and I'll leave a key for you with him."

"Perfect. When did you say you were off?"

"I didn't, Alex—Guillaume is waiting for me to arrive so I can leave whenever suits."

"How about Monday?"

"That'll give me the weekend to get ready."

"Just make sure you're flying on Monday."

Perhaps Virginia noticed the change in Alex's tone, or maybe she caught a hint that he wanted her out of the country. Either way, that Monday Virginia Hill stepped onto Benny's private plane and flew to Paris. If Guillaume was a fictitious character, it didn't matter to Alex. The guy was as real as Virginia needed him to be and the LA apartment was secured.

36

MONDAY LUNCHTIME, ALEX arrived at the outskirts of the City of Angels and entered a diner for a bite to eat. His rental car contained an overnight bag with three changes of clothing, a case containing a pool cue, and a pack of playing cards.

He spent the next two nights in a motel near Long Beach, only stepping outside to grab some food, never going to the same place twice. Alex read the LA newspaper, made some calls to Ezra and Massimo to ensure that business was running smoothly, and played numerous games of solitaire.

On Wednesday, Alex swapped his rental for a local automobile and drove over to Beverly Hills, where he settled in an apartment with a clear line of sight onto Virginia's home. He unpacked his clothes, hung them in a wardrobe, and placed his playing cards on a coffee table in the living room. Then he went back to the car and drove to Fairfax, where he met Jimmy the Hawk in a pool hall.

Jimmy was one of those characters you saw on the other side of a joint and knew to avoid. It wasn't his appalling body odor, although he suffered from that affliction no matter how many times he showered. And it wasn't his gruff manner which annoyed people almost before they began speaking with him.

Jimmy's nickname was a clue—due to an accident while street fighting as a kid, his right eye was not pointing in the usual direction, the eyeball having been twisted out of its normal countenance. So his face was distorted in a way that made women avert their gaze and men wonder whether or not they were being stared at. Alex knew him as one of the most reliable fellas for firearms, and that was the purpose of his visit.

He spotted Jimmy sat at the bar near the entrance and stood by until the one good eye noticed him. They walked to the rear and found a table away from any other customer. Alex ordered a coffee and Jimmy got another beer.

"Thanks for meeting me, Jimmy."

"Always glad to help a friend, but are you certain you want anything from me at all? You look like you're only here for a game."

Alex looked down at his cue case and smiled.

"This is for you or one of your guys to play with until the end of the week. Make certain it gets used as it's brand new so any marks they produce will stand out well."

"Understood. I'll give it to the worst player I know."

"Fine but it needs to be returned and still be usable. If anyone were ever to ask, this is evidence to corroborate my alibi."

"I get it. And I assume you are seeking something in exchange?"

"That was what we agreed. Have there been any issues with my requirements?"

"No, Alex. I would have preferred more time to acquire the principal item, but we both know that I factored difficulty into the price."

"It is what it is. Before you hand the cue over to your lunk, check the lining of the case and the gelt will be there as requested."

"Too kind, Alex."

"Where are the goods?"

"In the trunk of my car, which is parked in the lot."

"Finish your beer and then we can close out our arrangement."

They spent the next five minutes in small talk as Alex watched the contents of Jimmy's glass drain away. Once the last vestige of amber liquid journeyed down the guy's throat, Alex took a swig to finish his coffee and the two left the building.

Alex drove up to Jimmy's vehicle and in a twinkle of an eye, a bag was removed from one car and deposited in the other's trunk. They shook hands and Alex sped away with the promise of dropping Jimmy a dime when he wanted his cue back, probably Friday but by Saturday at the latest.

HIS BEVERLY HILLS pad was better appointed than the first fleapit he'd landed in. There were two bedrooms and the living area had more space. There was a coffee pot in the kitchen and that was all Alex wanted for cooking. Best of all was the view.

The living quarters possessed a glass wall that led onto the balcony, and even if you didn't step outside, you could still see forever. Or rather, with a scope sight clamped to your eye, Alex had a direct line into Virginia's apartment.

He set up the tripod supplied by Jimmy right by the balcony entrance so if he opened the double doors, the barrel of his semi-automatic wouldn't need to stick out of the building in view of prying neighbors, but Alex could still get a clean shot. Until it was needed, he kept the firearm in its case, only taking it out to check the mechanism.

Today was only Wednesday, and Meyer would place the call to Benny tomorrow and arrange to meet him on Friday. Alex had plenty of time to kill. He whipped out his playing cards, put on a pot of coffee, and settled in for a long wait.

ALEX WOKE UP on Thursday to discover himself still lying on the couch, but he shook himself together and took a shower to wash the cobwebs away. He popped down to a diner five blocks from the apartment for breakfast and visited a general store on the way to grab some snacks and buy more coffee.

Back in his lair, he hunkered down, played cards, and stared out of the window. His life in Vegas had been mixed. While he had made more money than he had ever known in New York, he had found and then lost Rebecca. In between, Benny had gotten fresh with her and Alex'd done nothing in retaliation. Although he hadn't told himself this, Alex had never forgiven himself for that lack of action—it was so unlike him. Sometimes he wondered who he was. Some jumped-up *lobus*—all words and no deeds?

He stood on the balcony and stared out at the anonymous panorama in front of him. Los Angeles was a sprawling mass of humanity, but with no heart. Every other place he had been in, Alex knew where the city center was, but not here. It was just a set of jigsaw pieces with no picture. That night he made sure he slept in a bed so he'd be able to come out all guns blazing the following day.

AFTER BREAKFAST IN a different diner in the other direction from the apartment, he went to a pay phone and called New York.

"It's me." Alex relied on Meyer recognizing his voice.

"Hi. All good?"

"At my end, yes. Did you make the arrangements?"

"I did."

"When?"

"Today. At the time we discussed."

"Good. I'll speak later when everything has happened."

"Thank you."

Alex checked his watch in reflex–he had hours before his quarry would be in Virginia's place, so he went home and waited some more.

THAT EVENING, HE removed the M1 carbine from its case and propped it up on the tripod. With the drapes drawn, nobody casting an eye toward his balcony would see anything to make them concerned. Alex had instructed Jimmy to modify the rifle so that a scope was mounted on the top. This had cost a considerable penny, but Alex wasn't a kid any more and being a sniper was a young man's game. Anything to give him an edge was most welcome.

As the light faded, Alex used his scope to check on Benny's arrival. Meyer had called him and asked for a private meeting in Los Angeles. Knowing Virginia was out of town, Benny suggested her place as a safe, discreet location—as predicted. They had agreed that Meyer would show at ten and that he'd explain everything when they were in the same room, but it was a tremendous business opportunity.

What Alex did not expect was for Benny to appear with another man. He didn't recognize the fella, but judging by their body language, they knew each other well. Maybe Benny wanted to hook this guy up with Meyer as an extra investor. Whatever the reason for bringing a stranger to a private meeting, this would add complications to what he needed to do.

Virginia's living room comprised a long three-seater couch with two armchairs opposite, separated by a low coffee table. On the sideboard on the left was a radio set next to a cocktail cabinet. Judging by Benny's frequent trips, it was well stocked.

At the allotted hour, Benny sat at one end of the couch which faced the window, and the other man perched in the direct line of fire between the muzzle of the rifle and Benny. Why was the guy even in the room? There was no time for Alex to consider this question because the minutes were ticking away and Benny would only stay for a while before he got impatient with Meyer's no-show and stormed off.

Alex stood with the butt of the rifle wedged into his shoulder. As he put his finger on the trigger, readying himself for action, Alex felt the rifle shaking in his hands. Was he going to be able to kill his friend? All his other hits had been strangers, more or less. Then a memory of Rebecca's torn blue dress lying on the cottage floor flitted through his mind and Alex exhaled and gripped the rifle once more.

Fat Max refused to do anything but sit in his chair and stare at Benny, who would pop up out of his seat to grab another drink and scurry back. Alex needed more time for a clean shot. He took three deep breaths to calm himself down and stared back into Virginia's apartment. Fat Max was sitting down and passing a newspaper over to Benny. Damn—a golden opportunity missed.

Max tapped at a particular story he wanted Benny to read, and as he leaned forward in his chair, Benny's entire body became visible. Alex put his finger on the trigger and squeezed off a shot that passed through Benny's right cheek and out of the left-hand side of his neck.

Blood poured out and Max spun round, having whipped out a pistol. Then Alex released a second slug that caught Benny in between his nose and right eye. His body remained pinned to the couch as more red pulsed out of the fella's head. All this time, Max stood and swiveled around hoping to find the assailant.

To ensure he didn't have another James Ragen on his hands, Alex fired off several more bullets into Benny's body—one way or another that man would not survive this assassination. Then he aimed the rifle at Max who continued to face the window and, for a moment, it felt to Alex like the guy saw straight into his balcony. He considered dispatching Fat Max but decided against it—he was a witness who had seen nothing and wasn't worth killing.

Alex closed the drapes, packed the rifle away, sat back on the couch, and lit a cigarette. Before he inhaled his second puff, Alex sobbed and then he cried, muffling his mouth with both his hands.

He had murdered his friend and was no better than any of the street scum he had spent his life trying to rise above. What's more, the syndicate viewed him as only a gun for hire and he would never return to the top table.

And then there was Rebecca. She was gone for good and it was only now that Alex allowed the empty gnawing in the pit of his belly to ooze out of his eyeballs in salty tears. His thoughts raced on and arrived at Sarah. Why had he been so stupid for so many years when he had the chance for happiness? Alex was alone in the world with only one friend whom he'd seen a mere handful of times in the past decade.

He pulled himself together, emptied the apartment of any personal items, and headed to his car. Although he had told Jimmy he would return the rifle, Alex knew this would never happen, which was why he had agreed to Jimmy the Hawk's ridiculously high price.

He drove around the city, stopping to throw pieces of the now-destroyed firearm into various dumpsters across town. Then he dropped a dime.

"There's been a change of plan, Jimmy. You can keep the cue as I can't trade your item back."

"I thought you might say that. Did everything work out for you?"

"Peachy."

At a different phone booth, Alex called Meyer to utter one sentence.

"It's done."

"Thank you."

Then he settled into his rental and drove all the way home, stopping only once to freshen up and grab a coffee and a piece of cheesecake.

37

ALEX FLOPPED INTO his bed at the Last Frontier and grabbed three hours sleep before he had to wake up and face the dawn. He found he was still wearing the clothes he'd had on when he murdered Benny Siegel, so he hopped into the shower and threw his sweat-encrusted shirt into the trash. Then he called down to housekeeping for them to get his suit cleaned and pressed and settled into his day.

Under these circumstances, routine is everything and although he wanted to eat in his room, Alex forced himself to go to the hotel restaurant as he did every other morning he was in town.

The newshounds had been busy while he was driving back from LA because the lead headline declared Benny was dead, killed by an unknown assassin. The second paragraph claimed he'd been shot in the eye, but that wasn't true—you can't believe everything you read.

Some people took a different approach to their newsgathering and accepted every word as solid. Mickey Cohen stormed into the restaurant clutching a copy of the paper and threw it down on Alex's table, only just missing his coffee and juice.

"Have you seen this?"

He stabbed a finger at the headline, which was identical to the one in Alex's hand; he placed the newspaper on top of Mickey's to emphasize the point. Before Alex answered, Mickey replied for him.

"Someone's done for Benny."

"You know who?"

"What're you trying to say? Of course, I don't know the trigger man. How about you?"

"No clue, Mickey."

"I thought you were tight with all your syndicate pals."

"Mickey. From the moment I went inside, I've been waiting to get back to the top table, but they don't want me. So, no, I have no idea who whacked

Benny and if it was a Murder Corporation hit, then they didn't bother to ask my permission first, despite what you may think."

"I'll put a contract out on whichever scumbag did this."

"Even if it was sanctioned by the syndicate?"

Mickey thought for a minute because Alex had asked a good question. The fella might have red mist in front of his eyes—the ex-boxer in him meant he was a fighter and a survivor—but he didn't intend to get on the wrong side of the men who ran America's organized gangs.

"I will kill the *pishers* who did for Benny but then I'll leave it there. I've no beef with the fellas in charge."

A waiter hustled toward Mickey and asked if he was available to take a phone call.

"Who is it?"

"The gentleman preferred not to give his name, but he insisted I find you and that you'd be interested in the information he has to offer."

Mickey tutted and followed the guy out, returning two minutes later.

"A connection says the momzers are hiding in the Hotel Roosevelt."

"They capped Benny and had time to get over here?"

"If they drove all night, they could have."

"I guess..."

"I'm going over to make some inquiries."

"Mind if I tag along? We might not always see eye-to-eye, Mickey, but Benny was my friend too."

A nod from the squat man seething before him and Alex swigged back his coffee and followed Mickey out and over to the Roosevelt.

BY THE TIME Alex arrived at the hotel, Mickey's sedan had halted at an angle in front of the main reception entrance and the driver's door was wide open. He ran inside before Mickey did anything stupid. Alex knew for sure that whoever Mickey was gunning for was as innocent as the day they were born—and might not deserve to be killed by him based on the testimony of some guy's phone call.

As Alex stood in the lobby looking around, Mickey pulled out two handguns and fired several times into the ceiling. "The guys who whacked Benny Siegel have ten minutes to come outside to account to me for their actions." Then he stormed out and paced up and down by his car.

Alex glanced at his watch and leaned against Mickey's sedan while the two men waited for the non-existent gucsts to leave their rooms and volunteer to be shot down by Mickey Cohen. This was not a brilliant plan by anybody's standards.

Fifteen minutes later and even Mickey was sensing that it wasn't working, especially when they heard police sirens in the distance.

"We need to get out of here, Mickey. The last thing either of us needs is to have to explain to the cops why you were shooting indiscriminately in the hotel lobby, shouting about Benny Siegel."

Mickey glanced at the road and then fixed his gaze on Alex.

"Yeah, let's get outta here."

AS THEY DROVE out of the parking lot, Mickey turned left and zoomed down the highway. In contrast, Alex went right and paid a visit to the Flamingo as Meyer's investment was leaderless.

When he arrived, Alex found Ted Bean, the manager.

"Judging by the downbeat mood, you've all heard about Benny?"

"Yes, it is so shocking."

"It sure is. The trick is to keep going. Take every day as it comes, but the Flamingo was Benny's dream and there is no way he would want the place to go to hell just because he wasn't around to look after it."

"I told the staff the same thing, Alex. And at some point, once all the furor dies down, we will find out who our new owners are. Someone is bound to buy up his stake, right?"

"You can be sure of that, Ted."

A call came through from reception that two men were asking for Bean. Alex accompanied him back to the lobby and found Moe and Gus waiting.

"Good to see you. You heard the news, right?"

"Yes, Alex, that's why we're here."

"Oh?"

"We're looking after the place now."

Meyer hadn't wasted a minute before installing his new management. Ted Bean might have the job title, but the decisions would be made by Meyer's men.

"Congratulations. Couldn't have happened to a nicer pair of fellas."

Benny was dead, the Flamingo was in safe hands and the syndicate would control its most expensive asset until it had rung the place dry of gelt. Alex was left back where he had been—running prostitution in Vegas and the racing wire across the country for Meyer and the boys out east.

38

"THERE IS A tough choice to be made, Alex, and that is why I dragged you down from Vegas."

Meyer and Alex sat in a pair of casual dining chairs on a patio area overlooking South Beach in Miami. Meyer had explained during their brief phone call that he was spending much of his time at present in Cuba and that Miami would be a convenient location for them to meet up.

Alex didn't mind too much where they held their discussion. While Moe and Gus were running the Flamingo—and doing well by all accounts—there was the bigger picture to focus on.

"We need someone to oversee Las Vegas for us, Alex, and there are three names we are looking at. Jack Dragna, Mickey Cohen, and you."

Meyer sipped his coffee and stirred in a small amount of sugar.

"Dragna has wanted a piece of Vegas ever since Benny first headed west in search of his gambling fortune."

"The guy is hungry for it and competent."

"Would you say the same of Mickey?"

Meyer smiled. "What do you think of the fella? You've seen him operate the last few years."

"To be honest, there's too much of the boxer still in him. He is quick to temper and acts before he thinks through the consequences."

"So your money would be on Dragna?"

"If it were a two-horse race, yes. But that says less about Jack and more about Mickey's shortcomings as a leader."

"The tension in your voice implies there is some bad blood between you."

"Meyer, we had a few run-ins, mainly over Trans-American."

"That must be all in the past though, right?"

"If you are asking me whether I could work with him then, yes, I would suck in my animosity toward him for the greater good."

"Did things get that bad?"

"We had our moments, but that is all water under the bridge."

"Alex, whoever gets the job will need to be trusted—after Benny's thieving hands, the syndicate is concerned that all and any tribute winds up in their pockets."

"You know what happened to Virginia Hill? I haven't seen her in town since Benny's demise."

"She won't be coming round Vegas soon."

"Was there a contract?"

"Oh no, nothing of the sort. I just meant that without her sugar daddy, she will seek some other fella to nest near. She's a nafka in all but name."

"Harsh. She only ever had one john in play at a time."

"Says who?"

Meyer's question stunned Alex—he had always assumed that the woman was soaking Benny for all he was worth, and that was all. He had never considered that she might have several men in tow around the country—or that her story about a French lover was anything but a tissue of lies.

"Meyer, did anyone pay to clean her apartment?"

THE CONVERSATION CARRIED on over dinner. His friend found the perfect venue—a restaurant that served Italian-Yiddish cuisine, just like being back in Midtown during Prohibition. By the time they'd consumed the last cannoli, Alex wasn't sure he had any space for the cheesecake, which Meyer assured him was to die for.

As they savored their coffees, Meyer returned to the earlier topic.

"As I was saying, we are down to three candidates for the Vegas job."

"Am I still in the running?"

"What makes you think you've dropped off the list since this morning?"

Alex considered a minute–if they were going to hand Vegas over to Jack Dragna, then Meyer wouldn't have made a special trip over to Florida or got him to fly down from Nevada.

"We spent all the time talking about Jack and Mickey, I assumed I was out."

"There is a world of difference between discussing your competition and losing the race, Alex."

"To be honest, if you give the place over to the ex-boxer then I will leave town and never come back. I don't mean to be dramatic, but the guy is a flake."

"He was always Benny's man, not mine."

"If I wanted somebody to organize security or run a team of killers, then Mickey would be the fella I'd call."

"For sure. So that leaves you and Dragna."

Alex frowned at the same time as Meyer smiled.

"I've been messing with you, Alex. There's wonderful news and some not so good news—which would you like first?"

"Always the bad news, Meyer. What gives?"

"You are not yet a member of the syndicate. There remains a whiff of concern about trust from some newer members. I know and you know that it is nonsense—they believe the rumors about you from before you did your time. Whatever the basis, that is the decision."

"Well, that's a punch in the belly. What's the good news?"

"We want you to run Las Vegas for us. You report to me. Congratulations."

NOVEMBER 1950

39

MENDY GREENBERG HIT town two days before Alex was to appear in front of the Kefauver committee hearings in Las Vegas. He had been Alex's lawyer when Dewey took him down and had been Charlie Lucky's advocate too.

"I haven't seen you for a lifetime—you're clearly keeping out of trouble."

"Mendy, I have spent my career trying to keep my nose clean—and once you have been in prison, you know how important it is to never go back."

"It must have been hard, but you've done well since you got out, so Meyer's told me."

"We had some tough rides, but now that Trans-American is ticking over, I can keep an eye on my other interests."

"No need to be coy with me, Alex. We have client-attorney privilege to protect us."

"Mendy, forgive me but I'd rather not talk as though I dip my beak into every piece of action in the city, but there isn't a nafka on her back or a bet being placed that I don't receive some appreciation for. If a union official sneezes out of turn, I get paid."

"How's the hotel business?"

"You ask even though you know already. Benny was right—the Flamingo's been a superb model and the syndicate has made several investments in the casinos here. It is a license to print gelt and also, with so much cash floating around, money laundering becomes a cinch for our other operations."

THE TELEVISION CAMERAS turned to face Alex in the committee room as he returned to his chair after taking his oath to tell the truth, the whole truth, and not to deviate from that plan of action at any point in the proceedings.

Estes Kefauver was enjoying all the new media attention because smugness oozed out of every pore–each time the cameras trained their lenses on him, he sat up ever so slightly straighter.

"Let's keep this simple, shall we, gentlemen?"

Alex stared at this man from Tennessee with his track record of cleaning up malpractice and wrongdoing wherever he went. This was no Thomas Dewey hoping to make a career—this guy already had juice.

"Mr. Cohen, let me remind you, you are under oath. Are you, or have you ever been, an active participant in the organized crime syndicate known as the mafia?"

"No, I have never been a member of the mafia."

Mendy leaned over to Alex and covered the mike with his hand. Ten seconds whispering in his ear and Alex continued.

"While the senator might wish to rush through proceedings, besmirching people's good names as he goes, I would like to remind this committee I am a hard-working immigrant, who owns a service used by millions of law-abiding citizens every day. I appear before you of my own volition."

"Thank you for the edited highlights of your life, Mr. Cohen, but you have omitted to mention that you served jail time for federal tax evasion."

"Everybody makes bad choices at some point—mine was not to keep good paperwork. I haven't made that mistake again. Have you performed any errors of judgment over the years, Senator Kefauver?"

"You are here to answer my questions and not the other way around, Mr. Cohen."

"Then ask your questions—I will help as best I am able."

"Did you know Arnold Rothstein?"

"Yes, I met a fella of that name, but he died over twenty years ago."

"Do you, or did you, know a man named Charles Luciano?"

"Again, there was a guy who left the country a decade ago with that name with whom I was acquainted."

"And how about Bugsy Siegel?"

"I knew a Benjamin Siegel, but not this bug you talk about, although call an exterminator as there are cockroaches all over this room."

The onlookers behind Alex laughed, but he didn't turn around and kept his gaze on the man in front of him. Mendy leaned in again.

"Don't get too fresh with this guy. He tears men limb from limb if he chooses."

"The committee appreciates your concern for its health and the environment in which it operates. Cockroaches are attracted to utter filth and we are in Las Vegas."

Alex smiled and kept schtum, following Mendy's advice.

"Mr. Cohen, Benjamin Siegel is dead, is he not?"

"This is true."

"Your colleagues are dead or deported. You admit you consort with criminals?"

"All I told you was that I knew people of the same name as the individuals you mentioned. That does not mean I was friends with any of them, Senator."

"But the man sat next to you was Luciano's counsel until the felon was sent back to Sicily. Are you telling this committee that you only knew a man of the same name as Charles Luciano?"

Alex inhaled as he prepared to answer the direct question, but he was interrupted by Merrick Townsend, sat to Kefauver's right.

"Senator, forgive me, but I must leave shortly on some Massachusetts business. Before I go, I wanted to put on the record that I have known Alex Cohen for several years personally and have found him to be nothing other than polite, charming, friendly, and the epitome of the American way. This is a man who came to this country with only the clothes on his back and is now responsible for Trans-American, a nationwide news service, used by many God-fearing and taxpaying citizens every day of their lives."

Kefauver stared at Townsend as he stood up and walked out of the room. Alex made a mental note to comp the senator an extra nafka when he came to town next. Then Kefauver continued as though the interruption had not happened.

"As I was saying, Mr. Cohen, do you not know Lucky Luciano?"

"Senator, my belief was that you were interested in rooting out the contagion of crime that has blighted this land ever since the Pilgrim Fathers stole turkeys the first winter after they arrived. From what I have read in the papers, Mr. Luciano is no longer living here and therefore can have nothing to do with any criminal activities which may or may not take place here."

"Answer my question."

"I will respond to any accusations you wish to make about crimes that have occurred but I do not see any value in confirming whether I know some men who are dead or gone from this country. The viewing public expects more from their elected officials, I would imagine."

Kefauver looked at the cameras then flitted his attention to Alex. Then back to the cameras with their red lights shining out, and on to Alex again.

"Mr. Cohen, if you don't change your attitude, I will hold you in contempt."

Mendy took this opportunity to speak.

"May I remind this committee that my client has come here of his own free will and has said he is prepared to subject himself to your questioning. There is no contempt here—only a genuine interest in furthering the aims of this board as it investigates crime."

"Then get him to answer my query."

"Senator, tell me what the question was and I will gladly respond."

"Do you know Charles Luciano?"

"As I have already told you, I used to know him before he left for Sicily. Your question is designed so I cannot give you a straight answer. It is almost as if you want to make me appear evasive in front of this committee."

"Why would I want to do that, Mr. Cohen?"

"Yet another question I can't possibly answer. I repeat that I will gladly help you eradicate criminals from our cities and towns, but you sound more like a country bumpkin on a fishing trip. Do you have anything specific about any crimes that have been committed that you want to ask me about?"

"Your impertinence is noted, Mr. Cohen, and at this time I will not be presenting any evidence to the committee of particular criminal malfeasance. The purpose of these hearings is to paint a picture of how crimes are taking place across this great nation, which is controlled by a group of key individuals known as the mafia."

"And I have already told you I am not, nor have ever been, a member of the mafia. Senator, if there is nothing else of any substance you will add then the American taxpayer deserves to hear from a different voice because you've finished flogging this dead horse."

Alex stood up and walked out of the room, almost before Mendy grabbed his papers and followed him out. As soon as he exited the courtroom, light bulbs popped around him as the reporters grabbed a photo before hitting him with a barrage of questions he refused to answer.

When he got into the sedan positioned for him out front, Alex waited for Mendy to catch up and then Ezra drove the vehicle away at high speed before any press car followed them back to the Last Frontier.

40

"I SAW YOUR performance on the television, Alex. You did very well. Congratulations."

"Thank you, Meyer. I'm glad to hear you were watching—the last time I was in court, nobody was there to support me, apart from Mendy here."

The three men chuckled and sipped at their drinks; Alex had chosen his usual Scotch on the rocks.

"Did you think I appeared too aggressive? The pinhead rankled me—I didn't want to react, but I couldn't leave it alone either."

"I've spoken with the fellas back east, Alex, and they were mighty impressed with the way you handled yourself. Mendy, I think you need to make a phone call, right?"

"Sure, Meyer."

The lawyer set off to walk around the block as he didn't fancy pretending to speak on a phone while his clients held a private meeting. Meyer waited for Mendy to be out of sight before continuing.

"First, you were not alone in court when Dewey took you down for tax evasion. How do you think your sentence was kept short? I made a payment to your judge's benevolent fund."

"I never knew. Thank you, old friend."

"Second, the syndicate members have been talking about you. I have been pleading your case for years, as you know, and I reached a deal with them last month—depending on how you did today. Alex, I can't tell you how happy I am to invite you into the syndicate again. You will have full voting rights from now on. Welcome back."

Alex squeezed his tumbler until, realizing it might shatter, he released his grip. His words caught in his throat and all he could do was nod in acceptance. Meyer put a hand on his friend's arm as Alex wiped away a solitary tear from his left eye. Five minutes later, Mendy returned and hovered in the periphery of Alex's vision until Meyer beckoned for him to sit down.

"Mendy, we have something to celebrate—Alex just got a promotion. Does the Last Frontier stock any French champagne, Alex?"

A SECOND BOTTLE of bubbly later, Meyer suggested they go out to eat instead of staying at the Frontier all evening.

"I got the concierge to book us a poolside table at El Rancho—I know how much time you spent there before you had this place to run, Alex."

Massimo drove them the few blocks to Benny's first hotel investment in Vegas, and Alex recalled those early days when Meyer dragged him over from LA to work with Benny and build up business in this desert town.

The maître d' took them to the table Alex knew only too well, but there was already somebody sat there. Meyer waved as they approached, and it took Alex a minute to recognize the fourth guest—Sarah. Alex's face formed a query.

"I brought my executive assistant with me as we have business to discuss tomorrow. Do you mind that I invited her for dinner?"

"Not at all."

As they arrived at the table, she stood and beamed, heading straight for Alex to give him a kiss on the lips. Then she shook hands with Mendy—the way they smiled at each other showed they had met before.

"How are you, Sarah?"

"All the better for seeing you, Alex."

AFTER DINNER, MEYER and Mendy made their excuses and left while Alex and Sarah finished a bottle of red.

"Sarah, you know I hadn't turned my back on you and the boys, but the work I was doing was dangerous and I didn't want to repeat past mistakes."

"Meyer's been keeping me up-to-date with your exploits. After Benny died, I thought you might have reached out then."

"At that point, it felt too long and I wasn't sure you'd have wanted me to show up, anyway. How are the boys?"

"The men have all flown the coop—I've missed you, Alex Cohen."

"Straight back at ya. It's been a lonely few years…"

Sarah nodded as Alex's voice trailed off and he thought about Rebecca, recalling the moment when she died.

"I told you I ended it with my lawyer guy, Kameron? Not everyone behaves as well as you."

"If I had known then, you wouldn't have had any trouble from him. You mentioned he was just remote. You should have said."

"Alex, a woman can't run to her ex-husband every time her current boyfriend lays a hand on her."

He ground his molars as he imagined somebody harming his Sarah.

"Did that go on for long?"

"First time I put it down to his drinking. The second, I threw him out. When he tried to return, two of Meyer's colleagues discussed matters with him and I have never seen him again. Actually, that's not true. I saw him in my neighborhood the following week and he turned tail three hundred feet from me and ran away."

"Has there been anybody since?"

"Not even close. These have been lonely times for the pair of us."

"If you ignore the occasions I put you and our children in mortal danger, things weren't that bad when we were together."

"Apart from the near-death experiences, I loved the time I spent with you."

Alex looked deep into Sarah's eyes and held her hand. She smiled and squeezed his fingers.

"Would you be so kind as to accompany me to my hotel? Somehow, I don't want to be in this restaurant any more."

"You know something. We should go on vacation together and see how we get on. Meyer keeps telling me how Havana is a great party town if you have the gelt."

"One step at a time, Alex. Let's find out how we feel by the morning."

Alex grinned because Sarah was right. He might be a syndicate member again, but he was rushing ahead of himself. First, a night in Sarah's bed, then the next day they could plan the rest of their lives together.

BOOK FIVE
CUBAN HEEL

January 1952

1

"WHAT I LOVE about America is that the sidewalks are paved with gold."

"That's what I was told when I first arrived in New York, but the reality is different, Mr. President."

Alex Cohen and Meyer Lansky, members of the organized crime elite, sat with Carlos Socarrás, the Cuban president, as they sipped coffee and compared notes on the differences between their two great nations.

"I have seen the photographs, Alex, the walkways are so hot that the gold melts. I saw the steam, so it must be true."

Alex glanced at Meyer, who maintained his fixed grin and stared at this excuse of a man before him.

"Maybe it's in Harlem. I spent little time up there..."

The conversation continued in its stilted fashion for another five minutes before Meyer allowed it to slide away from the painful small talk and on to more important matters.

"I appreciate you are a very busy man, so I will get straight to it, if I may?"

A presidential nod indicated Socarrás was bored with pretending to care about the lives of the other people in his office.

"Cuba is a fabulous country, but it is on the cusp of becoming a great nation."

"There is no need to flatter me, Meyer. The people of my land have been neglected for far too long. They are impoverished, tired, and hungry. I hope that I may find some ways to ease their lot during my time in office."

"And we think we can help you with that. I will not pretend that we'll wave a magic wand and fix the difficulties you have here, but we offer a route for a sustainable revenue stream in the long term with the opportunity to secure foreign investment now and in the future."

Socarrás leaned back in his velvety chair and mulled this thought around his head as he inhaled deeply on his cigar.

"Fine words, Meyer, but what is it you are proposing?"

"I don't need to remind you that Havana is a quick plane ride away from Florida, which means we have an opportunity to encourage Americans to fly over here and spend their hard-earned wages."

"By any chance, do you have an idea what would attract those flies to travel to this midden?"

"Gambling. Alex and I created modern Las Vegas, which was nothing more than a desert town before we built casino-hotels and watched the money roll in."

Alex was surprised that Meyer had omitted the work by Benny Siegel, the real creator of gaming Vegas, but the fella was in full sales pitch and not concerned with historical accuracy.

"Mr. President, we can make the same thing happen here. Build casinos and other sources of entertainment to attract American tourists to spend US dollars–with your approval, of course."

Meyer sat back on the couch and gave Socarrás time to ponder the proposal. Alex couldn't tell if the guy was counting greenbacks in his mind or was concerned about the impact of American culture on this perfect isle.

"Foreign currency always interests the president."

"Inward capital flows are healthy for a country."

"I was speaking personally, but what is good for the president is good for the people."

"The investors I represent would want to build several casinos. The model would be to replicate what we have already achieved in Nevada, only with less scrutiny of our day-to-day operations from the authorities."

"Meyer, I understand your situation. The American government has tried to shut down or curtail your business activities in Las Vegas several times, and you want to be left in peace. You see Cuba as the place where you can make your money without hindrance."

"More or less, yes."

"But I still represent a government and the Cuban state needs to be compensated for allowing you the freedom you seek."

"Mr. President, we would want to pay our taxes and contribute to the fabric of this nation. All we ask in return is that we are not hampered by excessive regulation or undue scrutiny of what we do within the casinos themselves. We need to be left alone to make our money."

"Exactly, so, I am sure you will have outgoings too and wish to have a level of privacy around the payments you make."

Meyer nodded and leaned forward, elbows resting on his knees.

"There is also the matter of how we show our appreciation to you for facilitating these arrangements."

"Half a million US dollars in small denominations, no consecutive serial numbers delivered to an address of my choosing before I lift a single finger to help you gentlemen destroy the moral fabric of my country."

BACK IN MEYER'S suite at the Hotel Nacional de Cuba, the two men discussed the morning's events. Meyer had been the underworld's financier for decades and funded the operations of organized crime across the United States. He did business with the Italian Mafia, the Irish, the Jews. Meyer didn't care who you were, where you came from, or how you earned your money, provided you paid what you owed when you said you would.

Alex was also a syndicate member, but he earned his money through hard work and a steely resolve. They had worked together since the start of Prohibition and Alex had dispatched Meyer's close friend, Benny Siegel, and a catalog of other known and less well-known figures.

"I like a man who knows his price."

"Meyer, the president had a figure in his head and was keen to ensure we got the message loud and clear. Does that mean we can trust him?"

"Alex, to be honest, I had a better feel for his predecessor, Batista, but the people voted the general out of office."

"That's politics, Meyer."

"That, my friend, is not putting enough money in the hands of the right officials on polling night. I have visited this place regularly since the war and the one thing you can be sure of is that everyone has a price and most will take at least ten percent less than it."

"So it is like doing business in America, only with a Spanish accent."

"Funny, Alex. If the president wants half a mill' then that is what it will cost to get our piece of Vegas in Havana. Only on this occasion, we can make sure our interests are put first and not our Italian friends."

"Not even Charlie Lucky?"

"He won't be leaving Sicily any time soon, which means other members of the mob are vying for the top job. Charlie's influence is waning and we must both accept that."

"Will you wire him the money, then?"

"There are elections in a few months and this president might not be around much longer. I'd prefer to wait and see who sits on the other side of the table once all the votes have been counted."

"A true democrat."

"I just don't wish to waste a bribe on that man."

"Why have the meeting now, Meyer?"

"Because you've only recently arrived in town and I want you to meet all the players. Besides, the promise of that much money in a private bank account might be the motivation our illustrious president needs to make sure he rigs the election his way."

2

ALEX HAD ONLY just arrived in Havana before meeting Socarrás, having used the opportunity since returning to the syndicate to further his interests in Las Vegas and extend the Trans-American racing news wire across the country. In those two years, he felt as though he had not spent any time with Sarah and was looking forward to being with her while they remained in Cuba.

"Have you any idea how long we're going to be on the island?"

"Can't say, hon'. It might be a few weeks or months, maybe longer."

"I asked Meyer the same thing, and he was as noncommittal."

"At least you know that when we tell you we have no clue, we mean it."

The couple sat on a veranda overlooking the city and tried not to guzzle their fruit cocktails. This was a country that enjoyed mixing its drinks, and Alex wondered if this was so they could hide how much they were cutting the alcohol. Then he remembered he was a far cry away from the blind pigs he used to supply during Prohibition.

"Alex, you know we haven't been on vacation since our trip here just after they brought you back into the syndicate?"

"Yes, sorry. Running Vegas took more of my time than when I was strong-arming johns who were chiseling the house."

"It wasn't a complaint, more of an observation."

"Sarah, do you think I'm reverting to my old ways like when we were married?"

"Oh no, Alex. Almost every weekend you've flown over to Jersey to visit me. You would never have done that before. I couldn't face the thought of living in Vegas and you have been very accommodating."

"I want you to be happy and also I understood you needed to be near New York to help run Meyer's office."

"That as well. He expects you to be on call day and night."

"Tell me about it. I've been with him for… thirty years now."

Alex knocked back the rest of his banana daiquiri and waited for the liquid to settle at the base of his stomach.

"Meyer has allowed us the weekend to be tourists before he sets you to work on Monday. Where would you like to go?"

"Show me the entire island, Alex."

"I've been inside a couple of hotels so far and not much else. So, we can discover the sights together."

THE NEXT MORNING, they hired a car and drove the two hours to reach Varadero, Cuba's second-biggest city, east of Havana.

"Remind me why we've come here, Alex?"

"Years ago, my friend Alfonse told me he had an enjoyable vacation here, so I thought we should check it out."

"If it was good enough for Capone, it's good enough for me."

The crowds were quieter in Varadero, which was no surprise, and the couple wandered around a market before settling down in a *taverna* for a bite to eat.

"We never seem to see where people live, do we, Sarah?"

"Well, that's because we spend our time near the visitor areas and hotels. The locals' homes will be somewhere else."

"Do you fancy looking behind the tourist facade?"

"If you like. Why the sudden interest in the ordinary john?"

"Don't worry, I haven't developed a heart overnight. If we are going to run a string of hotels eventually, then we need to understand how we shall ship in our staff."

"Alex, you always have an eye on the prize."

"Keep telling yourself it's one of my better traits you fell in love with."

"I'll bear that in mind, although your kindness was one of the first things that drew me to you."

Alex raised an eyebrow and Sarah squeezed his hand.

"Let's see what kind of world your staff exist in."

AS ALEX DROVE out of Varadero, there was a sudden falloff in the quality of the housing and the surface of the road. He had noticed it on the way into the city, but by heading south and avoiding the main artery to Havana, the effect was accentuated.

Instead of solid brick structures, walls and ceilings were made of corrugated iron and the outskirts of the city appeared more like a shantytown. Sarah placed a hand on Alex's shoulder to give herself comfort because the sights before them were far from pleasant.

"Just drive through, will you?"

"Sure thing. This reminds me of Alabama—the deprivation is immense. Everyone here is living in such squalid conditions. Meanwhile, Socarrás is happy to take a half a million bribe for the sake of us building a casino or two. That man deserves to get a bullet between the eyes."

"Instead of letting your blood boil, let's go back to Havana, Alex."

"There's no justice in this world."

"Since when have you been concerned about justice, Alex?"

He was silent for a spell as he ruminated on Sarah's question.

"If you can then you do, but we got to help those who can't help themselves."

"Is that how you've lived your life?"

"Not at all, but when I needed help after the Great War, who was there to help me?"

Sarah's cheeks reddened in recognition of the time she spent tending to Alex until he could walk again.

"Are you going to overthrow the Cuban government?"

"There's an election soon—the people's will shall prevail."

March 1952

3

ALEX AWOKE TO hear a rumble in the streets, and he wondered what the hell was happening. He got out of bed as Sarah opened her eyes.

"What's going on?"

He stood out on their balcony and saw a mass of soldiers on the sidewalks, on the road. Everywhere.

"The army's arrived."

She whipped on a dressing gown and planted herself next to him. Before she could say anything, the phone rang, and he went inside to answer it.

"Have you seen what's happening?"

"The army is on the march, Meyer. Do you know what they are doing?"

"Stay indoors and you two'll be safe. From what I've heard, Socarrás won't be president by nightfall."

"What do you mean?"

"We are witnessing a military coup. The dust will settle by the morning and then we can deal with the new leader."

"Some trumped-up general with medals and no sense?"

"Let's not be too quick to judge. As soon as it's safe, we'll meet up, but don't go out today. Understood?"

ALEX PACED AROUND the living room of their suite until Sarah couldn't take it anymore.

"Please sit down. It's been thirty minutes since you spoke with Meyer and the day won't happen any faster if you wear a hole in the flooring."

He stopped, shoved his hands in his pants pockets, and shrugged.

"I can't stand being cooped up in here and don't you find the noise from outside deeply unsettling?"

They both craned to listen through the closed balcony doors. The constant stomping of military boots on paving stones was impossible to ignore, and there was a continual drone of voices interspersed with occasional cheers from onlookers.

Alex sighed and slumped into an easy chair hoping somehow this would make the sounds disappear, but he was wrong. A minute later, he stood up and walked onto the balcony. Sarah looked up from her book as she sat on the bed and carried on reading. Then she sauntered over to be with her man.

"Are you worried that this coup will kill off Meyer's plans?"

"For sure, but Meyer sounded remarkably calm for a fella who was about to have his dreams beaten to a pulp."

"What does he know that you don't, Alex?"

"Many things, Sarah. He always uses his noodle and never his hands. How he has survived all these years given the circles he's in is astonishing."

"Not when you consider how much gelt he has made. Meyer throws gelt at any problem he has. If the price is right, you can get anyone to do anything for you."

Alex nodded as he thought about the litany of people he had killed for money in his life. Big names, unknown men, but there was invariably a roll of greenbacks at the end. The only time he hadn't been paid was in the Great War and even then he'd come back with a Purple Heart. His ears pricked up as the crowd on the streets roared once more.

"I've gotta get out of here."

"Don't be a fool, Alex. Just wait it out, like Meyer said."

He shook his head and strode for the door before Sarah could put herself between him and the exit. As he walked into the hotel corridor, she tried to grab his sleeve, but he was too fast and carried on striding to the elevator.

The lobby was packed with concerned guests as Alex wove his way through the crowd and headed to the entrance. The doorman put his palm on the handle but didn't open it and refused to budge.

"Let me out."

"I'm afraid that's not possible, sir. Look outside. You will not be safe there and I cannot allow you to pass."

"That is not your decision to make."

He seized the doorman's hand and yanked it away from the handle. Before the guy knew what happened, Alex stood on the sidewalk and closed the door behind him.

HE MIGHT NOT have known much Spanish, but you didn't need to be a native speaker to understand what the locals thought of him as they went by. The soldiers continued to march in the road, but the men and women waving them past took only a few moments to shout and jeer at Alex.

He stood there for no more than twenty seconds and looked down briefly in disgust to see that his jacket was damp with spit. A globule landed on his cheek and Alex's eyes darted everywhere to find the culprit but no-go. His right hand formed a fist and Alex wanted someone to hit. He gritted his teeth and searched for a likely candidate for a pummeling, but he had no desire to punch a woman in the face, and he did not know who had perpetrated the crime.

He considered his next move and, despite himself, he knew there was only one thing he could do as the sea of people in front of him pinned him to the wall. He sighed again, turned round, and returned to the confines of the hotel.

BY THE TIME the couple woke up the following morning, the streets were quiet and mostly empty. Room service delivered their breakfast, and they sat on the balcony while they ate.

"I think it best if we take you back to the States in case it gets more dangerous here, Sarah."

"Is that your way of telling me you are going to repeat your foolishness from yesterday and don't want me to see you doing it?"

"Not quite. You were right, and I was wrong. I told you that when I got back to the room. Despite Meyer's optimism, the chances of this being a bloodless coup are remote. I know how men think and their propensity for violence. I would rather you were out of harm's way—only for a short time. As soon as I judge it is safe, I want you with me. But if there is trouble and Meyer needs my help, then I can't have a corner of my mind haunted by the possibility of you getting hurt."

Sarah was silent for a spell as she stirred her coffee and ate her cinnamon swirl.

"You must promise me not to do anything stupid. I don't want to go to your funeral."

"That's a solemn vow. We live together, we love together…"

"And we die alone."

With the decision made, Alex went inside to place some calls and make the arrangements. The airport was open, although the army was restricting access to flights.

"Meyer, have you any influence to get Sarah over to Florida until the heat dies down?"

"I've already opened lines of dialog so safe passage shouldn't be too difficult to organize. Will you be going with her?"

"Yes, but only to make sure everything is all right. My plan is to turn tail and get the next flight back in."

"Returning will be easy. Flash some dollars and customs will lie down and beg. Getting out needs a quiet word in the right ear, which is exactly what I can do. I'll let you know when you are safe to leave. In the meantime, pack your things and wait. You'll be out of here before the evening."

Yet again, Alex paced up and down in the living room, waiting for a call from Meyer Lansky.

WHEN ALEX AND Sarah landed in Miami, a fella with a black limousine greeted them and took them straight to a mansion on the edge of the city. Sam Giancana opened the door as they arrived.

"Thank you for helping us at such short notice, Sam."

"I am always happy to help a friend of Meyer's and fellow syndicate member. And this must be Sarah. Good to meet you."

"Meyer has spoken highly of you over the years."

"Pleased to hear it. Do you know him well?"

The confusion on Sam's face reflected his assumption that she was Alex's skirt.

"Sam, I have been his executive assistant for a decade, more or less."

"And to make matters more complicated, Sarah and I were divorced before I first went out to Vegas but reconnected two years ago, around when I got back into the syndicate after the Kefauver hearings."

By the time the story of their lives was complete, the three had sauntered into the house and sat in a living room.

"Would you like to freshen up, Sarah?"

"Thanks, Sam, but there's no need to worry on my account."

He nodded but said nothing, staring at Alex and creating an uncomfortable silence until Sarah tutted, asked for the bathroom, and left the room.

"How are things in Havana, Alex?"

"The military swept into power yesterday, so who knows what is going on. Meyer is optimistic; he probably funded the coup, knowing him."

"I couldn't say. What's important to me is that the potential to entice American tourists over there remains undiminished."

"Too early to determine. I don't know who, if anyone, is in charge, let alone what their response will be to foreign money. In a week or two, we'll see. Meyer is staying put, so I'd guess it'll be all right. He hasn't made a poor investment yet."

"Alex, even the Flamingo turned a profit in the end."

"With and without Benny's help."

Sarah returned and Sam stopped talking.

"Sam, please discuss matters in front of Sarah. She knows Meyer's business inside out and appreciates the importance of omertà."

"Apologies, Sarah. I am not used to conducting business in front of women."

Sam offered Sarah the use of a guest cottage in his grounds, and Alex stayed long enough for a bite to eat before heading back to Havana.

4

THE NEXT DAY, Alex met up with Lansky as the coup had all but fizzled out. The army was in charge, and Cuba's citizenry was being encouraged to remain indoors when they weren't going about their lawful business.

"Great to see you, Meyer. How has the place been in my absence?"

"Calming down. You were right to want to get Sarah away, but the new president has done a good job of protecting American tourists from any angry locals."

"Sounds quite open-minded, not like one of those fascists who were running around Europe."

"Not at all."

There was a glint in Meyer's eye that meant Alex couldn't decide whether he was being serious.

"Do you think we can carry on doing business with these army guys, Meyer?"

"I never deal with soldiers. I'm always more interested in speaking with the organ grinder and not a bunch of monkeys."

"Is there an obvious leader in the armed forces?"

"It's most unlike you not to read the morning papers, Alex. I'm surprised you haven't heard that Batista kicked all this off."

Alex stopped for a second to take stock.

"The same guy who you were schmoozing when Benny was still alive?"

"One and the same. He didn't like losing the popular vote a few years ago and figured the best way to make sure he became top dog again was to seize power before the next election. It saves on all the effort of counting votes and declaring winners."

"How long have you known Batista was behind all this?"

"Alex, where do you think he got the money to afford to take over the country in the first place?"

"Sometimes, I don't know why I am ever surprised about anything you do."

"Too kind. I like to make sure I have all bases covered, that's all."

WHAT LITTLE OPPOSITION there was, Batista crushed within a week, and he consented to an audience with Meyer and Alex almost immediately. The three sat in the same room occupied by his predecessor; the only significant difference was that Batista wore military dress instead of a suit. Alex wondered which of the medals gleaming on his chest he had earned and how many he'd added for effect.

"Thank you for taking the time to see us, Fulgencio."

"Meyer, you are most welcome as you know. I am glad I have been able to return my country to a leadership that will be strong and have the best interests of Cuba in his heart."

"Indeed. Let me introduce my business associate, Alex Cohen. He owns and runs several businesses in Las Vegas and has direct experience of the hotel and casino world. Given what we have already discussed, I thought you would both gain advantage by discussing the future of Havana."

"Very pleased to make your acquaintance, Mr. President."

"Meyer has spoken of you to me before. Your control of Las Vegas and your knowledge of gaming and other matters may prove highly lucrative for us all and beneficial to the humble people of Cuba."

"From what I have seen of your wonderful country so far, I am certain we can find more ways to lure American tourists over here to part with their greenbacks."

Batista laughed at this comment and Alex wondered how a powerful man like the general could have such a small head. A second glance showed him that the man's jacket had puffed up shoulder pads to create the illusion that he was bigger than he was.

"If you gentlemen are prepared to make appropriate investments, then I am sure we shall all prosper from your endeavors."

"Naturally, we will want to help you give the opportunity to enjoy this fabulous country to as many Americans as we can."

Alex listened and eased himself into his seat with every word Meyer spoke. This man before them didn't care about his people otherwise they wouldn't have been able to get to see him so early in his tenure. Lining his pockets was his highest priority no matter what he said.

The meeting continued with Meyer blowing smoke up Batista until there was nothing more to say. Alex recalled his days sat in oak-lined rooms in Tammany Hall when the Bowery was the extent of his world. Politicians were the same wherever they lived—fine words leave their lips, but it is their wallets that shape their thoughts and deeds.

As they walked out of the palace, Meyer turned to Alex.

"You should arrange for Sarah to come back. She'll be as safe here as in Sam's guest cottage, and there's much to accomplish."

"What's there to do? I didn't notice any deals being struck with Batista just now."

"We need to structure an offer to him that means we will take control of the gaming interests in Havana. That is going to require an amount of money and significant planning. With this trumped-up dictator in charge, we have got a green light to do whatever we want to establish a Cuban Las Vegas, but with none of the hassle from any local or federal authority. It's time to make some gelt."

March 1955

5

"IT'S GREAT TO see you, David."

Alex looked at his son with admiration. The young man had made something of himself and could fund a trip to Havana.

"Likewise, Pop."

"How's business?"

"Good, thank you. Lawyers and funeral directors. Somebody always wants one or the other."

"And who wants to hang around dead bodies, right?"

"You should know, Pop."

Alex eyed David as he crossed his arms but let the comment slide even though he took offense at his son's words. Alex figured the kid wouldn't have traveled all this way just to get under his skin. Besides, he called David a kid but as Sarah reminded him, the guy was a man, from the set of his jaw to the clothes on his back. The puppy fat had long since been shed and a lean joe sat in front of him in the Cantina Lima Hastiada, a local bar around the corner from David's hotel.

"If you had called ahead, we would have been happy to let you stay with us."

"That's all right. I didn't know I was coming over until the day before and even then, I don't want to be a bother."

"How could that be? You are our flesh and blood."

"To be honest, Pop, I thought it might be hinky, what with you and Mom back together. It just did not feel right, and I can't live under my parents' roof anymore. At some point, you must let your children stand on their own two feet."

"Wise words. I'm glad your mother brought you up well."

"So am I."

They clinked their drinks—Alex's coffee and David's tequila—and continued to talk the afternoon away.

"Would you compromise your independent spirit by agreeing to eat with us this evening? I know Sarah would rather cook for you than hop to a restaurant. It's a mama's right."

"Of course. Please don't be offended, but I'm not sleeping under your roof."

"I'm teasing. I'd want to go out and party in this town if I was your age too. Shall we say seven, then?"

"Sure thing."

A hug and Alex left the cantina, although he gave instructions to the bar owner that David could continue to order without getting charged a peso.

FROM THE MOMENT Alex arrived back home to the minute David knocked on the door, Sarah filled her day with cooking, laying the table, and preening in the bedroom mirror. Alex couldn't remember the last time she'd seemed so concerned to make everything perfect unless he counted her preparation of Meyer's general ledger.

"It's been so long," she uttered as soon as her tears of joy had subsided enough for her to regain her breath. Alex shook David's hand and offered another hug.

"Can I make you a drink?"

"Only if you are having one."

Alex poured two Scotch on the rocks and a glass of red wine for Sarah, who finally sat down after scurrying in and out of the kitchen for the first five minutes.

"What did you get up to this afternoon, dear?"

"Nothing much. I spent most of the time sipping a coffee and watching the world go by outside the hotel."

"Oh, to have no responsibilities."

"I'm sure you could retire whenever you wanted to, Pop."

"Good to hear you have such faith in my past success, but if I could stop, I surely would."

"Whatever you say, Pop."

David glanced at Sarah whose eyebrows rose up her forehead and he thought he heard her molars grinding. Alex ignored the disbelief on her face.

"I've set a little aside so that your mother and I can look after ourselves when we get old, but don't hold your breath for any inherited fortune from me."

"That's not what I was angling for, Pop. The only money I want to spend is the gelt I have earned myself."

"Pleased to hear it and I may even take you at your word one day."

David inhaled as if to respond, and Alex pointed a finger at him.

"Gotcha."

They laughed, and the conversation continued in a lighter vein until Sarah announced she was ready to serve dinner.

AFTER DAVID HELPED his mother to clear the table, the three sat back down and took simple pleasure in their coffees. Alex stared at his son and his chest puffed up. Most of his memories of the children were from when they were toddlers. After that, he was absent from their lives—prison and living on the other side of the country does that to young minds.

"You never said how long you were going to be on vacation here."

"No, Pop. That's because I don't have a good answer."

"How so?" Sarah intervened almost without thinking, the words squeaked out for both men to hear.

"I am on sabbatical."

"What does that mean, son?"

"My firm has let me take a month or two off and I can return afterward."

"Why do you need such a long rest? Have they been working you into the ground?"

"Nothing like that, Mom. I've left on good terms."

Alex's ears pricked up.

"Are you on sabbatical or are you unemployed? There's a world of difference between the two."

"There sure is, Pop. Let me explain my situation and then you'll both be able to breathe again."

David shot a glance at Sarah, who didn't appear to have exhaled since she uttered her last words.

"I have been very successful at Bernstein and Bernstein. They have treated me well and I have learned a tremendous amount from them."

"And..."

"But the idea that I will spend the rest of my life helping corporations avoid tax fills me with dread."

"Accountants and undertakers, kid."

"Yeah, the thing is I want to give back."

"Work for a charity, you mean?"

"No, Mom, closer to home. You guys are cooking up some fantastic schemes here and I'll bet that the deals that are concocted will require a trained professional eye over them. And those eyes need to be ones you can trust, right?"

"If a deal is good enough for Meyer, it gets my seal of approval."

"I'm sure it does, but do you not think at some point your business partner might prioritize his own concerns over yours and Mom's?"

Alex sat back in his chair and mulled that thought over. He had never considered the possibility that his and Meyer's interests would be anything but aligned. The fella had looked after him since before he went to Sing Sing in '36.

"Suppose you are correct, David—and I'm not sure you are, mind—what are you proposing?"

"Let me come and work for you, Pop. When I look back on my time on this earth, the two people I owe everything to are sat at this table and I have done nothing to repay you."

"Apart from all the joy you and your brothers have brought me and your father over the years."

"Mom, a smile on your face doesn't pay to keep a roof over your head."

"Now you are sounding like Meyer—a true accountant. Besides, we didn't become parents for our children to pay us back. That's not how life works."

"I understand. I wish to work in the family business. I am sick and tired of making money for other people and want my kin to benefit from what I do."

Alex's back stiffened at David's words.

"Have you any idea what I do for a living?"

David laughed and nodded.

"When we were kids, we were regularly strafed with bullets in our bedrooms at night, so we had a pretty good sense before we reached double digits."

A heat in Alex's cheeks made him shuffle in his seat and he looked away from David for a moment.

"It happened once, to be fair to your father."

"True, but let's not forget that Arik was kidnapped, and he talked through every minute of the ordeal for us."

Alex's shoulders sagged, and he stared at his glass as he swilled his Scotch around. Sarah reached over and placed a hand on his arm, and his lips curled upward for a second before slumping on his face.

"Pop, I mention this not because I want to rub your nose in the past, but you need to understand that I know how you make your gelt and it isn't as a sales rep. Also, I am thirty-three and I've been able to read the newspapers for several years now. You forget you get mentioned almost every time some mobster gets killed on the streets of LA, Chicago, Las Vegas, or New York, and in places you've probably never even visited."

Alex exhaled and looked at Sarah before staring at his son. He saw her bite her lip and rock in her chair.

"David, let me think about your proposal for a while. Enjoy the sights and sounds of Havana and we'll talk in a few days. This is a big decision and I do not want to rush to any conclusion."

◆ ◆ ◆

"IF YOU LET him into your affairs, you might as well sign his death warrant."

Sarah had waited until Alex drove David back to his hotel and the words burst out of her before Alex sat down in the living room.

"Sarah, he's a tax lawyer. The worst that might happen is that he is surprised by some of my financial affairs or gets a paper cut from a ledger. I will not ask him to take a bullet for me."

"Don't even joke about such things, Alex, but I am worried about him. We have spent his entire life trying to protect him from what you do and the life I left behind. Now he turns up at our door, demanding to be allowed into our dark world. And it is filled with the bad and the ugly. That's not what I want for our son."

"Nor me, Sarah. But it sounds like it is what David wants. If he were to come on board, then I would only involve him in my legitimate deals. Nothing that could link him to anything criminal."

"Don't you think that if he even touches our world then he will be tainted for the rest of his life?"

"The apple has already fallen from the tree and it hasn't landed very far, it would appear."

6

THE NEXT ORDER of business was to introduce David to Meyer before they met with President Batista. Alex had visited the same office many times over the previous couple of years. His comfort in the room was in marked contrast to David's response to the same furniture, and the general sat on the other side of his large oak-lined desk.

"Fulgencio, always good to see you, my friend."

Batista nodded and his medals jangled on his chest. Sometimes Alex couldn't look past those lumps of cheap metal and notice the guy behind the stern grimace.

"Meyer, there is nothing I enjoy more in this world than catching up with you and your business partners."

The head of state glanced at Alex with a flicker of acknowledgment and ventured a disdainful slit-eye for David. He had been alerted to who would be in attendance, so there was no need for this childish response to the man.

"President Batista, let me introduce my newly-appointed head of legal affairs, David Cohen."

"I see nepotism isn't the sole preserve of Latin American countries, it would appear."

"Yes, he is my son, but I employ him because he is a qualified lawyer with vast experience in international law."

"And so young with it."

Alex let Batista's comment fall to the floor unnoticed because the dictator wanted to score points, and Alex knew there were far more important matters at hand than winning an argument with this *farbissener momzer*.

Before they completed the preliminary pleasantries, another man entered the room and sat on a chair near Batista. "This is the Mayor of Havana, Francisco."

"Do I detect a family resemblance?"

"Yes you do, Alex. Francisco is my brother."

A quip about nepotism flashed through Alex's mind, but he let it go.

"We want to follow up on a conversation you and I have had several times over the years—investment in the entertainment sector in Cuba."

"Meyer, we both know that we just need to find the right way of working, and then we can both have our dream of a Latin Las Vegas become a reality. Last time we spoke, you said you would come back with a proposal."

"And that is why we are all in the room today. As a reminder to you and to ensure your brother is up to speed, the issue I face is that we require a considerable amount of money to build and maintain a casino and hotel complex before we realize any profit. This is millions of US dollars."

"We are aware of the scale of the investment needed."

"Then you understand that people who own those amounts of capital do not want to put it at risk before they can gain a return on their largesse. This means we need to have the right environment in which to place our investments."

"Environment?"

"Somewhere safe where the government will support our efforts and where we can rely on the local police force to protect our building and staff."

"You want us to guard your casinos?"

Batista raised a finger to quieten Francisco who had interrupted Meyer.

"I call for you to prevent any harm befalling my hotel, but this is not a free service. You have personal costs to cover and the local and national agencies must be supported too so that the wheels of commerce may turn."

"How much, Meyer?"

"If I were to make a payment to one of your Swiss bank accounts of, say, half a million, would that help us receive presidential authorization for the first casino?"

"A million."

"And what consideration would you think appropriate for your ongoing support?"

"Thirty percent and we can get licenses made up within a week."

Meyer smiled and sat back in his seat. David looked at Alex, who had let Meyer do all the talking. After all, the man had been schmoozing the *meeskait* since before the Havana conference where Benny Siegel's fate was sealed.

"And what about me?"

All heads turned to stare at Francisco, who had contributed less than David to the meeting; at least the boy had taken copious notes. Meyer cleared his throat.

"Naturally, we will take care of all our partners in the hotel and casino. What do you foresee as your role?"

He was floundering to demand that the brother justify his existence without saying it in so many words. Batista saved them all from the embarrassing situation they'd been drawn into by his craven sibling.

"The mayor is concerned to receive some appreciation for his local efforts here in Havana."

"Fulgencio, I am sure the president will safeguard Francisco's consideration. Besides, as we build more casinos and the number of American tourists increases, I imagine you'll ensure his office is responsible for gathering revenues from parking meters and slot machines."

Alex bit the inside of his cheek to stop himself from laughing, but Meyer seemed deadly serious with his offer. Batista responded by nodding and standing up to shake his hand. The deal was struck and included the pesos from the slots, although Alex knew that Meyer would exclude any machines in his casinos from Francisco's reach.

"HOW DID YOU think the meeting went, David?"

The three men sat in Meyer's suite in the Hotel Nacional to review what had transpired in Batista's office.

"You appear to have got what you wanted as he agreed to your terms, but I'm guessing this isn't over just yet."

"What a very astute son you have there, Alex. I would agree that I got what I asked for, which makes me wonder if I was asking for the right thing."

"To what extent do you trust Batista?"

"Good question, Alex. The man is driven by his ego and his wallet, and not much else that I've noticed over the years I have known him. So any appeal to either of those things usually gets you what you want. He changed the price of his consideration but he had no problem giving up a casino for thirty percent."

"Have you ever paid more for a casino, Meyer?"

"No, if we don't count the Flamingo which had its own set of issues."

Alex's cheeks flushed red as he recalled the night he sent a bullet flying into the head of Benny Siegel, the man who invented modern Las Vegas.

"So why are you bothered? If your plans come good, then you will own a string of hotels and casinos in Havana away from the hold of our Italian friends which will deliver more gelt than any of us can dream of. What difference will a million going into Batista's pocket make in the overall scheme of things?"

"Alex, you may well be right, but so is David. I am concerned he dragged his brother into the discussions. The guy is a cockroach and nothing more, but what was the point of him showing his face?"

Sarah arrived at this moment to catch up on some paperwork, and Meyer invited her to join the discussion.

"Do you think Batista is lining up the brother to take over the casinos once we've built them?"

"You may well be right, Sarah. He wasn't there by accident."

"Is that why you offered him the slots?"

"Nickel and dime stuff, Alex, and he didn't flinch. If anything, his eyes widened as he imagined counting his ill-gotten gains."

"Sounds like nothing is too modest for Francisco Batista to dip his beak into."

"Fashioning him a small bird table might be the best thing to keep him out of our way and it will let the adults get on with their business."

In the distance, the sound of an explosion and the shattering of glass was barely audible, but both Alex and Meyer noticed.

"Students. They are letting off a little steam."

"Meyer, when people throw Molotov cocktails in the street, they are doing more than partying hard. These kids can see what Batista is doing and they are not happy about it."

"Maybe so, Alex. But that doesn't mean we need to be concerned about them. Not everything is certain in life, but anyone who tries to stand between the general and his ability to earn gelt will discover why this general has an army."

7

MEYER SMILED AS he asked for the check in the Lima Hastiada once Alex and Sarah had finished the dregs of the bottle of local red wine. The food was at best average, but they congregated there out of habit rather than love for the place. It sure wasn't Lindy's.

"What are you so happy about, Meyer?"

"Alex, good things come to those who wait."

"Now we're hooked, just tell us your secret. You look like you're fit to bursting and want to share."

"Sarah, as the minister for the entertainment industry in our president's fine government, I have been helping him devise a strategy to encourage American tourists to vacation in Cuba."

"That's why we are all here, Meyer. Have you waited until the end of the meal to tell us what we already know?"

"Patience, Sarah. All in good time."

Meyer glanced around the cantina and leaned into the table, forcing the couple to do likewise.

"He is about to enact hotel law 2074."

"You should have told us earlier, and I would have ordered the finest Californian champagne this place could offer. I mean, if it's the 2074 then we are on the home straight."

"Alex, there is no need for sarcasm to mask your ignorance. If you hadn't interjected, then I could have told you that this gambling rule allows foreigners to have direct holdings in Cuban hotels and casinos."

Alex sat back in his seat, thought for a minute, and let out a slow whistle.

"Finally, he is letting us in to play at the table."

"The investors must have a million to their name otherwise they don't get past the threshold and there is a quarter of a million fee per gaming license."

"So nothing too onerous, Meyer."

"Listen to you, Alex Cohen. You've got to a point in your life where millions of dollars are easy pickings."

Sarah squeezed Alex's arm. She tried not to show physical affection to him in front of Meyer, but she was proud of this moment and her lover's achievements.

"Don't worry. My feet are still planted on the ground. There is always a corner of my heart harboring memories of Broska and another special place for the tenements in the Bowery."

"If you two are finished blowing smoke then, Sarah, please organize a wire transfer in the morning for the government fee. And I'll need a large briefcase for a withdrawal from one of my safety deposit boxes then too."

"By how much will you fill Batista's grift box?"

"Another quarter of a million. The peaked cap might not earn it, but the gelt we'll generate will make it all worthwhile, Alex."

"Politicians are like every one of us—always interested in number one first and the rest of the world second."

"We live together. We love together…"

"But we die alone."

"DID YOU THINK it strange that we walked the money over to Batista?"

Meyer nodded as they sat down at the board table which occupied most of the space in his dining room. Sarah was still wrangling with the bank to organize the gaming fee transfer, and Alex was at a loose end.

"Some matters are best left the old-fashioned way. Cash speaks volumes and is not the least bit traceable."

"With foreign investment possible, how long do you think it will take our friends in Little Italy to pay us a visit?"

"Not long. You know how the syndicate works now that Charlie is no longer in charge. While I might not have fed all the details to the board, close associates understand what's been going on and are ready to make a play."

"Moving large amounts of gelt which Uncle Sam can't see or investigate is an appealing prospect, Meyer."

"We can all see the benefit in that, wouldn't you say, Alex?"

The two men clinked cups and sipped their coffees.

"What are you going to call your first venture?"

"Montmartre, Alex. I've found a prime location with a run-down shack on the current site. It's a hark back to a chi-chi area of Paris."

"No need to tell me, Meyer. I went there while I was fighting the Great War."

"Sometimes I forget, we only met after you came back."

Alex nodded, and a flash of memory of those goddamn trenches ripped across his brain. The bright lights as the shells landed. Deafening tearing metal. Blood pouring out of a solitary hole in the kid's head. They gave him the Purple Heart for shooting a child. Snap and back in Havana.

"I wish I could forget."

"Alex, I meant nothing by it."

"I know that, Meyer. Don't worry, everything is good. The sooner we get the Montmartre up and running, the sooner we can make some real cash in this town."

Meyer nodded and took another swig.

"I am thinking of bringing in David to focus on my interests in this. If he's earning some gelt from me, then he needs a contract to review. Just so's you know, I only want him working on legitimate business. Our syndicate work is out of bounds for him."

"I completely understand, Alex. I won't talk about money laundering in front of him."

"Thank you, Meyer. I just need my boy to stay clean."

"I'VE LOOKED OVER the contracts as you asked, Pop."

"Why are you looking at me so strangely? You can't hold my gaze."

"They need a lot of work before I could recommend you sign them, that's why, and the other party is Meyer, who is no fool."

"What kind of work are we talking about, David?"

"Bolstering your interests almost entirely. Meyer has protected himself well, but at your expense. To deflect liability away from himself but still keep Batista happy, you are the fall guy if anything goes wrong. Mostly, it is your wallet that will hurt, but my professional opinion is that you shouldn't climb into bed with Batista because there may be more than your gelt at stake."

Alex nodded and listened.

"When I read the documents, they seemed reasonable to me."

"Did you see what was typed in front of you or did you rely on your memory of conversations with Meyer where intentions were stated but not papered when they were recorded? I only have what is written and nothing else. And that is what a court would look at too if anything were to go wrong and Batista sued you."

David was right and wrong in equal measure. If matters soured between them, there would be trouble, but the president was unlikely to resort to the law to resolve any difficulties they may have. The man controlled an army and the secret police, he wouldn't wait in line for a date in front of a judge.

Given that the generalissimo would tear up the contract without a second thought, all Alex had was the intentions of both parties as they were written. No more and no less. Meyer was so keen to create his Latin Vegas that he was satisfied to skip any cracks in the sidewalk. David was making sure there was firm ground for him and Sarah to walk along.

"Your advice is well noted, son. We should try to even out some wrinkles but we must be careful not to insist too strongly otherwise Batista might decide to throw his toys out of the playpen."

"I serve at your pleasure."

"No need for that, David. Just see if you can get the more offensive elements watered down. If Batista reneges on the deal, we'll need a plane ticket and not a court date. This contract is only a statement of intent. It's what you do that you are judged by, not your words."

8

ALEX MET SAM Giancana and Santo Trafficante at the airport, one syndicate member to another. Both fellas were based in Florida and the short hop was nothing special, but Alex took care to treat them as honored guests as soon as they arrived on Cuban soil.

"When can we expect to see Meyer?"

"He'll be over as quickly as he can, Santo."

They were ensconced in the Lima Hastiada, Alex's latest favorite lair. Before they reached the cantina, the two Italians had dropped their bags off at their comped rooms at the Hotel Nacional.

"Sam, thanks again for looking after Sarah a couple of years ago."

"Happy to help. Besides, who wants to put their family in danger? Batista's revolution could have turned ugly on the spin of a dime."

"Thank you, anyway. I can't think of the last time the syndicate met in full. It's been a while."

Sam and Santo glanced at each other, and both men smiled.

"Life ain't the same now that Charlie Lucky is back in Sicily. Other fellas are in charge of the Italian outfit nowadays and they have different views about how to conduct business, if you see my meaning."

Alex wasn't sure that he did, but Sam was right. Without Charlie, the Italian mob had become much more insular. Meyer had commented on it just the other week.

"Sometimes, I get the powerful impression that the Italians are holding their own meetings behind our backs. It's as though the syndicate is no longer the place for bosses to come to discuss matters and reach sensible agreements."

"What do you mean, Meyer?"

"I think they might have set up their own commission to settle mafia issues. If you're not Sicilian by birth or by ancestry then you are not welcome."

"Rules me out."

"Tell me about it, Alex."

He had thought little of the comment but if there was a mafia-only commission, then that would explain why the syndicate had almost ground into silence. The other possibility was that he and Meyer had cut themselves off from the day-to-day workings of the syndicate by moving over to Cuba. There may only be a few miles between the island and America, but it is an enormous stretch of water if you let it be.

"You guys over here for a few days? I can show you some sights, if you like."

"I'm here for the week, but Santo is about to move here."

Alex knew better than to ask Santo why he was fleeing the US, as it was unlikely to be because the Florida climate disagreed with him. His mansion was extremely comfortable according to Sarah, and she had spent enough time there to know for sure.

"In that case, the least I can do is to take you fellas out to eat tonight to celebrate."

ALEX NOTICED THE stilted silence between his dinner guests almost before everyone had sat down at the Nacional restaurant table. Neither Sarah nor Meyer appeared to behave any differently and Alex was left to decide for himself whether it was his imagination or if there was an underlying tension between Sam, Santo, and the rest of the group. The slurping sounds of their soup kept him focused at the start of the meal.

"Sam, how is Vegas holding up without me?"

"All good."

"Do you see much of Ezra and Massimo, my lieutenants?"

"Now and again. I don't spend a lot of time in Nevada."

Alex glanced at Sarah, hoping she might weave a conversational line, but she stared at the bowl in front of her. Meyer gave no sign he wanted to help either.

"Well, let them know they are in our thoughts."

"I'll be sure to do that."

Sam's eyes flitted up at Santo's but everybody continued to focus hard on glugging down their minestrone. Alex thought about Sam's intonation—did he detect a note of irritation? These Italians were giving nothing away and one was going to be their neighbor.

Once the dessert had been wolfed down in record time, Alex felt no need to force anyone into being together a moment longer than was necessary and asked for the check before the waiter could offer them a liqueur or cup of coffee.

"Would you gentlemen like to share a brandy up in my suite?"

Meyer's suggestion received nods of agreement, and Sarah sensed this was her opportunity to escape.

"I'm sure you fellas have business to discuss and don't want a woman to get in the way of some of your more robust conversation."

She understood these Sicilians well, and they smiled and shook hands before following Meyer and Alex out of the hotel restaurant, into the elevator and settling into Meyer's living room in his penthouse apartment.

SAM ACCEPTED A Scotch on the rocks, and Santo preferred a twelve-year-old brandy. Meyer poured Alex his usual Scotch and gave himself a vodka tonic; he liked to keep a clear head.

"Alex, thank you for hosting dinner, but next time, your skirt can stay at home."

Alex's cheeks flushed red at the Italian momzer's words—Santo's eyes showed he meant every word he uttered. Meyer opened his mouth and then closed it again, deciding not to engage with the situation and let it pass if Alex didn't take the bait.

"Santo, she is Meyer's executive assistant, but I accept your point and will remember in the future."

"I appreciate your understanding. Now let us get down to business."

Sam pulled out a sheaf of papers he had stuffed in his inside jacket pocket and attempted to flatten them before placing them on the coffee table in front of him.

"There are several matters we'd like to discuss, which should be of mutual benefit."

Alex and Meyer sat forward in their seats, and Giancana outlined how he and Trafficante planned to exploit the Havana entertainment industry for their own ends, and the benefit of other Italian gangs.

"Meyer, we will support your attempts to build casinos, but we do not wish to be direct investors in these properties."

"If we are to make something out of this country…"

"Hear me out, Meyer. We decline to be direct investors because we need to place a series of shell companies between us and the hotels. You might not look over your shoulder at the Feds, but we sure do."

"I know how that feels."

"Alex, I heard how you kept your mouth shut and your conscience clean when you went up the river—respect."

"I did what was right, and Las Vegas was the appreciation I was shown by the syndicate."

"Anyway, our interest in the building reflects our desire to keep a proportion of our assets offshore but still under our watchful eye."

"That's right, Santo. We ain't gonna act like Benny Siegel and use Swiss bank accounts."

The Italians chuckled to themselves and ignored the fact they were joking about Meyer's childhood friend and that Alex had pulled the trigger on the fella. The Jews exchanged glances but gave no other reaction.

"Forgive us, he was one of your men, we understand that, but he was foolish to rely on a woman and a foreign banker when there were places and people closer to home he could have used to hide his stolen money."

"Santo, let's move on to explain our actual reasons for wanting to invest in Meyer's casinos."

"Naturally, no offense intended."

"None taken."

Alex shot another glance at Meyer to judge whether he meant his terse reply. There was a reason he never played poker with his friend.

"The skim from our Vegas casinos alone is sufficiently large for it to have gained the attention of the Internal Revenue Service, as I mentioned earlier. Those vultures are circling overhead, and we are seeking legitimate locations to place our money beyond the reach of the IRS."

Even a mention of those three letters sent a shudder down the spine of every man in the room. They each took a swig from their drinks.

"Meyer, we hope we are your first choice when you look for funding in each of your ventures in this country."

"Sam, the purpose of the syndicate is to ensure we scratch each other's backs."

"It certainly was."

They were silent for a spell as each man reminisced about his time spent in the past twenty years as a member of America's first organized crime board. Alex thought about all the hits he had undertaken for Murder Corporation, the arm of the syndicate created by Charlie Lucky to handle any disagreements between syndicate bosses.

"Is there anything else you want of us, Santo?"

"Once you have got Batista to agree to the creation of the hotels, we can provide the people to build the places. Some of the finest masons in the world have been Italian."

"These accommodations are always possible, we just need to make sure that there is benefit traveling in both directions. So if you want my influence in the allocation of building contracts, please don't be surprised if you are asked to provide the payment for the gaming license and any other financing that is made directly to Batista's personal bank accounts."

A clink of glasses and Meyer agreed to take Giancana and Trafficante's gelt to help build his Vegas in Havana. Where Sam and Santo came, Alex knew the likes of Frank Costello and the other New York bosses would be sure to follow.

9

ALEX SAT AT the bar, while tourists placed bets on the outcome of the spin of a wheel in the Sans Souci gaming room. The Spanish-style restaurant and stage was packed because of the appearance of some local singer he'd never heard of but he wasn't in the outskirts of Havana to take in a show.

He watched and waited to see what would transpire. Meyer had asked him to pay the place a visit because takings were down in the casino room and there was no obvious reason that should be the case. Fifteen minutes with a cocktail in Alex's palm delivered the answer.

When a seat became free, Alex strolled over and perched by the green baize of one of the three poker tables and bought himself some chips. There were four other guys already playing—all Americans. Two hands later and he noticed the remarkable skills of his left-hand neighbor. He wondered if his were the only eyes to see the cards speeding from the bottom of the deck and onto the felt.

Alex wished Massimo and Ezra were with him as he decided whether to focus on the dealer or the player. When the guy folded and cashed in his chips, Alex chose to follow the cardsharp. The dealer would still be standing at the table in an hour's time.

Out of the gaming room and into the main bar, the tourist ordered a mojito and sipped it while perched on a high stool. Alex stood next to him and waited with a beer in his hand.

"Been a good night for you?"

"Can't complain, Mac."

"We were at the poker table together."

"Uh-huh."

"You had some lucky hands."

"No luck about it, Mac."

"Well, we can agree on that. You had more than a little help from the dealer, didn't you?"

For the first time since Alex struck up the conversation, Norman Hawkins turned to face him, menace in his eyes.

"What you talking about?"

"The name's Alex Cohen and I'm saying I saw the dealer pass you cards from the bottom of the deck, so your winnings weren't down to luck at all."

Norman straightened his back and Alex considered whether he was going to take a swing at the one-time leader of Murder Corporation. The spine curved again and Norman relaxed into his drink, with a smirk on his face.

"That's what you reckon, is it?"

"Saw it with my own eyes. I mean, you're not denying it, are you?"

"Talk is cheap, Mac."

"Call me Alex. Tell me I'm wrong about you."

Norman twisted round again to glance at Alex and took another swig from his mojito.

"Say what you like, Alex. I don't have to respond to wild accusations."

"You have two options. Either you admit what you've done or you continue to lie to me. Do the former and I'll let you keep your fingers intact. Carry on pretending that there is nothing to answer for and I'll give you a personal guarantee that you will scream for mercy before I kill you. The choice is yours."

Alex leaned forward and placed a shoe on the footrest of Norman's stool so that the two men were inches apart as he spoke, but it also meant that Norman couldn't make any bid for escape. The man swallowed and sipped his drink, replacing it on the counter.

"Little man, I suggest you take a walk with me into the office so we can continue our conversation in private."

"If I do that, I'll never be seen again."

"We can stay here if you prefer, but that'll only make me more annoyed and you will receive the consequences of my unhappiness. What's your name?"

"Norman Hawkins."

"What have you decided, Norman? You are an American and so am I. We don't go killing our own on foreign soil."

Norman nodded and Alex grabbed his wrist to help him off the stool and pulled him in the direction of the lobby where a door marked *Staff Only* stood straight ahead. Down a corridor and into the manager's office, Alex led Norman to a chair on one side of the desk and he sat in the boss's seat.

"How long have you been coming to this place, Norman?"

"About a week."

"And you've been winning ever since you arrived?"

"Yep."

"How many people are you working with?"

"I don't want to get anyone into trouble."

"Of course not, but please do not lie to me, it offends me and indicates you are not showing me sufficient respect."

Alex let those words hang in the air for Norman to catch and consider. After thirty seconds, Norman opened his mouth and closed it again.

"Well?"

"There's one dealer."

"He approached you or the other way around?"

"First night I came here, we got talking, and I mentioned I was down to my last Jackson. When it was just the two of us at the table, he suggested I help him make some money on the side. So I agreed."

"How much you make?"

"Five hundred. We split my winnings fifty-fifty."

"Very noble. Do you still have the dough?"

"Nope, blew it on the roulette wheel."

Alex snorted. This schnook deserved to be put out of his misery, but he knew that was disproportionate to the offense. Instead, he inhaled deeply.

"Under ordinary circumstances, I'd demand the money back from you, but you do not have it. When are you scheduled to leave Cuba?"

"The day after tomorrow."

"No, you take off in the morning on the first flight out of the country."

Norman looked as though he was about to argue the point, but Alex's steely gaze put paid to that idea.

"Get out of here."

ALEX RETURNED TO the gaming room and stood behind the players facing the dealer, named Joel Sala, judging by the button on his shirt bearing those two words. After ten minutes, Joel was relieved, and he sauntered off for his break. Alex caught up with him after only five paces.

"Come with me, Sala. We need to have a conversation."

"Who the hell are you?"

"I'm with the management, so don't make this any more difficult than it needs to be."

With Sala's elbow cupped in his palm, Alex escorted the croupier into the manager's office and placed him where Norman had sat only a short while before. The dealer swallowed hard and waited for him to begin.

"You know a man called Hawkins?"

"Don't suppose I do."

"Funny, because he knows you as the guy who has been feeding him cards all week. Does that ring a bell?"

"I dunno what you are talking about, mister."

"I'm Alex Cohen and I'll start beating on you if you continue to lie to me. Have you heard of Hawkins?"

"I don't know the name, but there is a tourist I've been helping."

"Is that what you call it? Stealing more like."

"I had some debts of my own and needed to clear them."

"Who else you been pulling the same stunt with before Hawkins breezed into town?"

"Nobody, I swear on the souls of my grandchildren."

"Don't go dragging your family into this. How much you make from this American?"

"Thousand dollars."

"Are you sure?"

"I know how much money I got."

Alex blinked as he realized Hawkins had stiffed him. It didn't change a thing right now, though.

"Listen to me carefully, Joel. You should consider that money the most generous severance pay you will ever receive in your life. Leave the premises and I never want to see you again. Understand?"

"Yessir."

He escorted Sala out of the rear staff entrance. When they were round the corner, Sala turned as if to ask why Alex was still with him. He got his answer when Alex pulled out a shiv from his jacket and plunged it deep in his chest. Two more stabs and the guy slumped to the floor, a red pool gathering around his corpse before Alex cleaned his blade on the man's sleeve and walked back inside.

NORMAN HAWKINS TOOK a taxi straight to the airport as soon as he woke up the following morning, just as he'd promised, but had to wait three hours for the first flight home. He hit the bar to kill some time and was surprised to find Alex waiting for him.

"I wanted to make sure you kept your word, Norman."

"Don't worry, I got your message loud and clear last night. I'm outta here in a short while."

"You certainly are. Let me pay for your drink so you know there are no hard feelings."

Norman shrugged and Alex threw some notes down on the counter which the barman scooped up. The two men sat in silence while they consumed their drinks. Once Hawkins' glass was empty, Alex suggested they go for a walk. Norman looked around as though judging the safety of the idea.

"This is a public airport, Norman. What could happen to you here? I want to give you a proper send-off. Perhaps I was too abrupt with you last night."

"What are you thinking of?"

"A parting gift. You select something and I will pay for it."

Norman sat still for two seconds, then slapped the bar like he'd reached a conclusion and stood up. Alex showed him the way to the souvenir shop and purchased Hawkins a leather wallet. After he led him away from the main concourse to an exit. Norman scrunched his face but followed Alex dutifully, nonetheless.

On the other side of the door was the airstrip with vehicles moving along prescribed routes around the terminal building. Norman turned to go back inside, but Alex leaned on the exit to prevent that happening.

Ten seconds later and a baggage car zoomed past. Alex grabbed Norman's collar and swung him round into the oncoming path of the automobile. His body bounced off the front and landed on the concrete. The driver screeched the vehicle to a halt and leaped out.

"He's fine. There's nothing to see here. Go on about your business."

Alex's instructions were met by an incredulous stare, but the revolver in his hand convinced the guy to keep on driving. He strode over to Norman, who was groaning but had not moved since hitting the ground.

"Hawkins, I told you not to lie to me, and you failed to mention the correct size of your winnings. That was a big mistake."

Two shots rang out, muffled by the general sounds of airport activity. Norman's chest billowed blood and Alex walked into the terminal for a coffee before he drove back home.

10

IF ANYONE HAD told Alex that he was going to get a visit from his eldest son, Moishe, then he would never have believed them. He had been estranged from David for all of his son's adult life, and the same was true of Moishe, only the boy still bore grudges from before his teenage years. His other sons had been so young when he stopped seeing them that he was no more than a distant memory to them.

When David offered to take out Alex and Sarah for a meal, he was surprised but thought no more of the suggestion than to accept it at face value. The venue was their local cantina, Lima Hastiada, and the fourth empty chair was nothing out of the ordinary. Just as their drinks arrived at the table, so did Moishe, who sat down, nodded at his brother, and riffled through a menu.

"I bet you weren't expecting to see me here today."

Alex dragged his eyebrows down from the top of his head, stared at his prodigal son, glanced at Sarah who appeared equally mystified, looked back at the recent arrival at the table.

"You got me there, Moishe."

Moishe reached out to shake his father's hand and then stood up to give his mother a hug. At this, Alex raised himself to his feet and gave Moishe a manly pat on the back, which was reciprocated, for the first time that Alex could ever remember. He wiped the corner of one eye as they all sat down again.

The waiter returned to find out what Moishe wanted to drink, and he said he'd try whatever the old man was having.

"How are you, Pop?"

"Just fine. All the better for seeing you. What brings you into town?"

THE MEAL COMPRISED the usual average food and excellent casual conversation. Moishe allowed the others to talk at him and refrained from expressing any of his typical views about his father and how Alex treated Sarah and the rest of his family.

Alex was thankful for that small mercy but as happy as he was to see the boy again, he was waiting for the punchline. The guy hadn't uttered a word to him since the day Alex visited New Jersey before he moved to Vegas. And that was at least two lifetimes ago.

He and Sarah invited their boys back home after dessert and both accepted, although David was more reticent than he would have expected. Alex served them all drinks in the living room and settled in next to Sarah, one hand on her knee while she draped her arm on his.

"In the cantina, you didn't answer my question."

"Which was that, Pop?"

Alex felt Sarah stiffen beside him and caught her mutter under her breath, "Don't start."

"I can't remember you saying how long you are going to be out here. We'd be honored to have you as our guest instead of you paying tourist rates in a hotel."

"Pop, I was vague because I'm not too sure."

"A day, a week, a lifetime…?"

At the last word, Alex glanced over to David and winked.

"Before I can answer you, I need to ask for your help, Pop."

Alex's cheeks went white, and he swallowed hard.

"Me?"

"I know. It's surprising for me to hear myself say it too."

"Moishe, what has happened?"

"Mom, I'm not sure you should listen to our conversation."

"I am your mother and work at the heart of your father's business operations. Anything you have to say to him, you can say to me. Besides, he'll tell me the minute you walk out of the door anyway whether he has sworn himself to secrecy or not."

Alex nodded to confirm Sarah's analysis and reminded himself that Moishe hadn't seen them since they got back together.

"You haven't asked for David to leave the room though."

"No, Pop. That's because he was the one who suggested I should come here. He already knows the trouble I'm in."

"Moishe: spill."

His eldest son took a deep breath and explained the mystery of his arrival in Cuba.

"I'VE BEEN HAPPY at the accounting firm where I work from the day I started. They have looked after me well and accommodated me when times have been tough, which has been rare. Not all their clients are on the up-and-up, but I figured they pay their bills just like anyone else."

"You mean their ways of doing business weren't always kosher?"

"Yes, you of all people know how I feel about criminal enterprises. I say this out of respect for you and how you've treated my mother. Everyone sat in this room knows what you do, and I have made my peace with that. You took the hand you were dealt and played it for all you were worth. When I was a kid, I did not know about the sacrifices you both made."

"So some of your clients are not just minimizing their tax position?"

Moishe laughed at the memory of seeing his father's face in the newspaper when he was sent up to Sing Sing for tax fraud.

"No, Pop, but who are we to judge?"

Alex felt his cheeks warm but he said nothing more on the subject.

"You are not alone in having unpleasant customers, isn't that right, David?"

Alex aimed a smirk at his lawyer son long enough to be certain that they had all seen his joke.

"Criminal lawyers defend whoever walks through the door, I get that, but I am in a very different situation."

David raised an eyebrow.

"For the last four years, I have been representing a particular client and working hard to help them maximize profit while still operating within the law. I cannot pretend to have asked the details of their operations and they have never told me. Suffice to say it is a family business of Italian descent—I don't judge."

Alex shook his head in dismay.

"There has been no trouble between us all this time, but in the past month, they have raised questions about whether I share information on their business activities. I have assured them that their file remains confidential, my reputation relies on that, but they don't believe me."

"How do you know that, son?"

"Last week they told me that if I mentioned to anyone about their affairs, then I would end up at the bottom of the Hudson wearing a pair of concrete boots."

"Who said this to you?"

"Donnie Cavallo."

"Give me the details of his family members and I will pay this meeskait a visit."

ALEX FLEW OVER to discuss the matter with Cavallo in Little Italy and went straight from LaGuardia to the area just west of the Bowery—the place he grew up in and made a name for himself. Despite the years, Mulberry Street had hardly changed. Sure, there were fresh signs above the restaurants, but the same Mediterranean faces walked the sidewalks and perched at tables watching the rest of the world pass by.

Moishe had furnished Alex with Cavallo's address, which was at the Canal end of the street. Alex sat and ordered a coffee at a cafe opposite Cavallo's home to check the lay of the land. One-and-a-half cups later and Alex knew the fella had arrived. Everything that Moishe had told him showed he was a big fish in a small pond. He was no boss, just a regular mobster running his own crew. His mistake had been to use an accountant but Alex understood the fella's family was worried about having undeclared income that could not be vouched for. Alex had experienced their difficulties himself.

Two gorillas stood outside the front of the building and Cavallo walked inside, so Alex paid for his drinks and hightailed it round the back and up a fire escape. How did he figure out where Cavallo lived? Simple. He listened for the shouting and headed for that story. Sure enough, he spied on the man as he argued with his wife over who knew what. Five minutes of berating the woman and she left the room and ran out of the apartment.

Cavallo remained still for a second and that was when Alex kicked in the windowpane, causing the fella to turn around in response to the shattering noise in his home. Alex pushed his way in and reached out to grab Cavallo's throat.

The guy flailed his arms and fended Alex off, giving him enough time to run to the sideboard, open a drawer and pull out a gun. Alex was too quick and punched him square on the jaw. Cavallo lost his balance and landed on the floor, banging his forehead on the furniture as he collapsed. Alex stood over him, one foot leaning on his wrist until Cavallo released the pistol.

"Listen to me, Cavallo. I have no intention of killing you, otherwise, you'd be dead already. Instead, I wish to give you a simple message: leave Moishe Cohen alone. Change your accountant and never threaten to harm him again in his life."

"And why should I do that, old man?"

"You have threatened someone who you must leave alone. That is enough."

"What are you talking about?"

"Moishe Cohen. He has sought my guidance and I have promised to sort this matter out."

"You go back under whatever kike rock you crawled out from and let me be."

While he leaned on Cavallo's lower arm, he didn't notice the younger man's other fist had formed until the guy punched him between the legs.

Alex crumpled instantly and Cavallo ran out of the apartment and away before Alex could recover to chase after him.

ALTHOUGH HE RANSACKED the place, Alex found nothing he could use as leverage against Cavallo, but a framed photo at the back of a drawer gave him a powerful idea of what to do next.

That afternoon, Alex waited in a different cafe just below Canal until a black-haired girl sashayed into view. He stood up, crossed the street, and tailgated into her apartment block. She turned her head as he followed her in, but Alex smiled and tipped his hat to put her at her ease.

Alivia Bicchieri ignored him as she walked up the two flights of stairs to her apartment and was pleased to have a helping hand to fight her lock open, what with the landlord not being prepared to spring for a new key, the cheapskate. He stepped back to give Alivia the space to walk inside. Alex looked up and down the corridor, saw there were no witnesses, and pushed Alivia square in the back, making her stumble onto the living room floor. Alex slammed the door behind him and grabbed her by the nape of the neck.

"Please no…"

These were the last words Bicchieri uttered before Alex whipped out his gun and blasted three slugs into her body, two in the chest and one between the eyes. He dragged the corpse into the bedroom, careful not to allow any of her blood to land on his clothing.

He pulled open the bathroom cabinet door and removed a couple of items and shoved them in his jacket. Then a quick look through Alivia's handbag and Alex walked out of the building to find himself an anonymous fleapit to spend the night.

After a rough night's sleep, he headed back to Cavallo's, only this time he knocked on the door as politely as he could. When the fella answered, Alex was ready for him.

"I think you left these in Alivia's apartment."

He thrust a whalebone comb and hairbrush into Cavallo's hands, who looked down and blinked. As soon as he recognized what he was holding, his eyes widened and his jaw dropped.

"You'd better come in."

Alex sat down while Cavallo used a nearby dining room chair.

"I believe condolences are in order, Donnie."

The man looked straight through Alex, so much that he wondered if the boy had heard him at all.

"News travels fast, old man."

"Call me Alex. We had some unfinished business from yesterday. First, let me apologize for my abrupt behavior. I misunderstood the caliber of fella I was dealing with. I should have asked for you to sit down with me and discuss Moishe's situation man-to-man."

"Things have got out of hand."

"That they have, Donnie, but I am here now so that we can resolve any outstanding issues."

Cavallo wiped a tear from his eye and went over to the kitchenette to prepare a pot of coffee. "Want some?"

Alex nodded consent and continued. "I would like you to find a different accountant to look after your business interests and those of your family. To ease the transition, I am prepared to make a modest contribution to your costs and I will, of course, pay for your girlfriend's funeral. Such a tragic loss and she was so young."

He glared at Cavallo, who stirred cream into his drink as he listened.

"Did you have to murder her?"

"I never said I did, Donnie. But you must understand that if you threaten my son, you can be damn certain I shall execute some skirt of yours without a moment's hesitation. Imagine what I would do if you attempted any kind of retaliation at this point."

"You don't have to threaten me, Alex. I've asked some fellas about you and I won't cross you again… She was sweet, you know?"

"I'm sure Alivia was the apple of your eye, but you must believe me when I tell you that you'll find somebody else to warm your bed at night. Whatever you do, my children are off limits, especially as they are not even part of my business. Capiche?"

Donnie nodded and Alex finished his coffee before leaving an envelope with cash on the dining room table.

11

ON THE WAY back to his Havana home, Alex took the opportunity of listening to his taxi driver while taking the hop from the airport. Like every cabbie he had ever met, the guy was hacking for a living because there was nothing else for him to do. He spun a story about his choice to work nights to pay for his daughter's upcoming wedding, but Alex wasn't buying it. He listened, anyway.

"Have you heard about the trouble down south?"

"No, I've been out of the country the last few days. What's happened?"

"The news isn't too clear about the details, but there were a couple of attacks in Playa Las Coloradas, one night after the other, that left two soldiers dead and fourteen injured."

"Did they mention who did it?"

"Not on the radio."

"You know anyway?"

"Fidel and Raul Castro are forming a people's army, they say."

"Should I have heard of these guys?"

"You're a tourist, so no."

"I've lived here for a few years."

"No disrespect, but given where I'm driving you to, you ain't gonna have come across the Castro brothers on your travels."

Alex cast his mind back to his arrival in America and the slum tenements his family called home, while they eked a living out of nothing. There wasn't much difference between his background and the Castros. Why would the brothers bear arms against their government whereas Alex had taken a different path and made the streets his own?

"Apart from giving Batista a bloody nose, is there anything to these compadres?"

"They might not be much now, but I heard Fidel speak a month ago, and he knows how to rouse a crowd."

"You think he'll stand in the next elections?"

"You're kidding, right? There won't be any free elections while Batista is in power. That's what Fidel said, at any rate."

"And you believe him?"

"You say you've lived here a while, so you tell me. What has Batista done for the ordinary joe?"

Alex nodded and allowed the conversation to be devoured by silence. His driver was saying what he had thought from the moment he met the generalissimo. Only now it sounded like there might be someone who intended to do something about it.

"WHAT DO YOU make of Fidel and Raul Castro, Meyer?"

"Haven't met them, but, Alex, I'm not that bothered."

"From what I've heard, they've punched Batista in the stomach."

"More a graze of an ankle, according to the man himself."

"You've spoken to him on this?"

"Of course, Alex. I am pumping a lot of money into this country and I need to know my investments are safe. I have faith that Batista knows what to do about the Castros."

"And you believe he'll carry through with his plans?"

"I don't know if you noticed, but he has a ruthless streak."

He paused for thought and realized that Meyer was correct. The guy may not be much more than an ego in a uniform, but he was a predictable jumped-up long streak of lokshen. Meyer stirred his coffee some more, and Alex noticed the corner of Meyer's mouth turn up into a half-smile.

June 1955

12

ALEX COULDN'T REMEMBER seeing Meyer shine up so well. His tux made his pale skin glow in contrast. With Sarah on his arm, he walked into the Montmartre casino on its opening night with a spring in his step. This was the first venue his friend had built from scratch in Cuba and Alex had also put his fair share of blood, sweat, and tears into its creation.

It felt like those early days in Vegas, only without the tension that Benny Siegel created wherever he went. Meyer offered a steady and sure pair of hands while Alex figured that if they could make this joint work, then they would only be limited by their imaginations. Batista might be a schlemiel in a suit, but he was delivering on his end of the bargain.

Alex smiled at the thought that Meyer had been appointed minister for entertainment by the general and was receiving a salary of twenty-five thousand dollars for his troubles; that some of Lansky's bribe money was wending its way back into his own wallet almost made Alex chuckle.

"Share the joke."

"It's best if I don't, Sarah. You probably won't laugh."

She shrugged as they continued to walk the red carpet through the Montmartre entrance. Well-known faces from the big screen crammed the lobby, along with some less recognizable men who had never set foot in California. These were Meyer's business partners and associates—the Italian mob bosses and other senior figures in American organized crime.

The toasts of Hollywood greeted Alex like he was their best friend and he ignored their vacuous pretense while acknowledging to himself that many of them had performed in his Vegas hotels and were showing their appreciation the only way they knew how.

"Darling, so great to see you here. And who is this fabulous woman on your arm?"

Alex introduced Lana Turner to a star-struck and tongue-tied Sarah, then she blinked and the actress carried on down the line and into the casino.

"How many other autographs am I going to miss out on tonight?"

"Beats me, but don't forget that these people with their big grins and coiffed hair are just a bunch of actors who have done me favors over the years."

SARAH CONTINUED TO stick to Alex's arm throughout the night as they bobbed and weaved their way around the guests and their cocktails. Meyer ensured the casino was open all the time his patrons were on the premises and so Alex looked at the Hollywood high rollers throw chips like they were going out of fashion.

As they watched Johnny Stompanato lose his shirt at the roulette wheel, Alex noticed Santo Trafficante on his other side from Sarah. Alex nodded again at the dealer at Johnny's table to allow the guy who used to run with Mickey Cohen more leeway with his losses.

"You're showing much generosity to Stompanato, Alex."

"A friend of Mickey's is a friend of mine and if Johnny doesn't bounce back of his own accord, then I am sure Meyer will be happy to ignore the debt as a favor to Mickey."

"Johnny is no longer one of our friends, Alex. The guy manages actors nowadays, at least the ones he sleeps with."

"Mickey is still a friend of mine and I'll get the money back in other ways. If he sets foot in a Vegas casino, then he'll be standing on my turf. I can afford to wait to recoup my losses—the house always wins, right?"

Santo chuckled briefly, and Sarah sought fresh beverages for the three of them.

"How's business with you, Santo?"

"Can't complain. The move to Cuba has been good. I am making more money than I used to when I was based in Florida, and there is less scrutiny from Uncle Sam. What's not to like?"

"I understand. I'm in the same boat. Ezra and Massimo, my lieutenants, look after my Vegas interests so I see the same revenue stream but this place is all gravy."

"You talking about the Montmartre?"

"It's only just opened."

"That's what I thought, Alex."

"No, I meant Cuba. The potential in this country is immense, you know that for yourself, and Meyer is one smart cookie with the vision to create a Latin American Vegas."

"There's money in those cocktails, for sure."

As Santo spoke, a waitress arrived with a tray for the two men and Sarah returned to sit next to Alex with a pina colada in her hand.

"To success in Havana."

All three clinked their glasses and sipped their chosen beverage. Just before Santo moved off to speak to some fellas on the other side of the room, he leaned into Alex's ear.

"Don't be too generous with Stompanato if you are a friend of Mickey's."

Alex nodded and the next time the dealer looked at him for permission to take the uncovered bet, Alex declined. As Johnny was about to open his mouth to complain, Alex stepped forward and placed a hand on the fella's shoulder.

"I think you need to try a different game. Let's get your glass filled and see if there is something else that interests you."

Stompanato looked up at Alex and recognized him. His eyes shifted left and right until an item caught his eye.

"I want twenty minutes with her."

Alex turned in the general direction of Johnny's line of sight and spotted a waitress.

"No problem. You go to the bar and I'll arrange everything for you, Johnny."

LATER, ALEX NOTICED the throng was thinning out, and he glanced at his watch.

"I thought they'd have stayed a little longer."

"Senators always leave early, Alex."

"Sarah, that's not what I meant—people are leaving."

They stood still as the sea of tuxedos and evening dresses flooded past. Within twenty minutes, half the room had emptied, and the couple walked back to the lobby in case everyone had tired of gaming for a bit. They met Meyer with his hands in his pockets, smiling and wishing his guests well as they departed the Montmartre.

"Do you know why the rats are fleeing the ship?"

"Alex, it's showtime."

He looked at Sarah and back to Meyer, then it clicked. There was other entertainment to enjoy around the corner. Trafficante owned two venues within a block of the Nacional; the Tropicana's outdoor floor show was due to start in thirty minutes. And for those who preferred a more intimate feel, there was the Red Room at the Capri, indoors but air-conditioned. The Montmartre was a fabulous casino, but that was all it was, apart from the odd room for private parties.

"As brilliant as this joint is, we've missed a trick, Meyer."

"What do you mean?"

"Remember Benny's dream of the Flamingo?"

"Thanks for dredging that memory back into my consciousness."

Alex stared Meyer cold. He needed no reminding of the dire end of their mutual friend, the man who created Las Vegas.

"The Flamingo was a hotel, casino, restaurant, and theater. All under one roof."

"You want us to bring Shakespeare to Havana?"

"Don't be ridiculous. Let's bring showgirls, crooners, and some comedians to the city—the sort of entertainers who'll attract American tourists and make them want to bring their wives along to spend money with us too."

ALEX AND SARAH walked away from Meyer in the Montmartre and followed the herd into the Tropicana to see what they would compete against. Alex noticed Santo propping up the bar to the left of the stage in the gardens and spotted several fellas sprinkled around the edge of the auditorium, positioned in case any trouble broke out.

Tonight this was quite unlikely, as the place was packed to the rafters with mob members and Hollywood faces. Alex recognized almost everyone from the Montmartre earlier that night.

The show began with a woman singing her lungs out as the band accompanied her big opening number. She wasn't as great as Rebecca, Alex's girlfriend and childhood sweetheart who had made him so happy during their time in Vegas, cut short by her assassination. Those bullets should have peppered his body.

"You might not like to admit it, but this is a fine performance."

Alex agreed with Sarah because he knew she did not want to hear about Rebecca's singing prowess. Was all that ten years ago? He couldn't remember anymore, and he welled up, just for a minute until he felt Sarah's hand squeeze his fingers.

"She might not be with you, but I am and this man wants to take our order."

Alex regained focus and saw the waiter standing there, wanting them to supply the names of two drinks for him to retrieve from the bar.

"Scotch on the rocks and a pina colada."

"I thought you only had local brews, Alex?"

"Sometimes you need a piece of home."

She smiled and kissed him on the lips.

"Sarah, our shows must be more entertaining than this. Whatever Santo Trafficante can afford, we shall buy better."

13

ALEX WASN'T SURE he recognized the woman sat at the other end of the living room; he could count the time since they'd last seen each other in decades, not years. When he'd received her phone call, he didn't know what to make of the request.

Sarah reminded him that the least he could do was to invite her round to their home as she had traveled a thousand miles to see him. When the doorbell rang, Alex leaped to his feet and scurried to the front door. Esther smiled and Alex responded in kind.

"Are you going to let me in, then?"

"Sure, Esther. Allow me to introduce you to Sarah."

"We've met, but I was still in pigtails."

Alex cast his mind back to his teenage life in the Bowery and recalled how Sarah had been the one to encourage him to visit his family when he returned from the Great War. That was the last time he'd seen or heard from them until yesterday when his sister called to tell him that their father was dead and that she had flown over to Havana to speak with him.

Sarah put out some cakes and offered Esther a coffee or something stronger.

"A java would be lovely, thank you."

"When was the funeral?"

"Two weeks ago, Alex. It took me a while to find you."

"How did you even know where to start, Esther?"

"I saw your face in the papers a few years back when they took you to court. And I knew enough neighborhood people to ask the right questions."

"You're still in the Bowery?"

"None of the rest of the family ever moved away, Alex. You were the only one to escape and look how far you've come."

"Did you leave the family home?"

"I live round the corner in my own place, but somebody had to stick around to care for Mama and Papa."

"And now he's gone, Esther."

"The reason I'm here is that I am worried about Mama and we need your help."

Alex sipped his coffee and stared at his sister, so much older than the person he had framed in his memory, but the little girl had grown over the past thirty years. He just hadn't seen it happen, so there was a massive jolt between what had been and who sat before him. She looked middle-aged and Alex wondered to what extent she might think the same of him.

"How can I help?"

"Mama won't leave the tenement."

"Her husband has just died. She should spend a few weeks wallowing in her grief. The woman's ability to generate histrionics is second to none."

"That's not what I mean, Alex. Of course, she takes a stroll around the block every day. It's a great excuse to gossip with everyone she knows. It is not that, we have a problem with the landlord."

Alex's neck stiffened at hearing those words, and he sat upright in his dining chair.

"What does the *schnorrer* want?"

"Jurek Sokolov wants to sell the property and turf Mama out onto the streets. He's been threatening Mama and Papa for the last two months, and I believe that's what did for Papa's heart in the end. Now he has given Mama four weeks to get out, but she is having none of it. She says she won't budge and I'm afraid of what he will do to her. Everyone else has already fled the building. She's holding out because she thinks her real-estate paperwork gives her the right to stay. But Alex, I know that man'll hurt Mama rather than let a contract stand in the way of a good real-estate deal."

"Leave it to me, Esther. You do not need to worry about our mama."

"HOW DO YOU fancy a brief vacation in New York, Massimo?"

"I haven't been there for a couple of years, so sure, why not?"

"I'd like you to go back to our roots and check out the Bowery while you're there."

"You recommend any place in particular?"

"Visit Jurek Sokolov and make him a reasonable offer for some of his real estate. If he doesn't bite, make it a generous one, and if that fails to work then let's hope he doesn't meet a tragic end crossing the street while you're in town."

"Have no fear, Alex. Everything will be resolved before I return to Vegas."

"Once we get better established here, I'd like you and Ezra to come over and help me run our investments. Right now, I trust you two to oversee Vegas for me."

"Any chance of you popping over here for a vacation yourself?"

"Not for a while, but I'd like to. Sometimes I tire of the sunshine and constant warm temperatures, the incessant rum-based cocktails…"

"Enough already, Alex. Why don't we both visit New York if Vegas is too unpleasant for you?"

Alex pondered the proposal for three seconds and realized it sounded like a great idea.

ALEX MET MASSIMO in their hotel. The smell of New York had hit him before he'd stepped off the train. Massimo suggested meeting him at the airport but Alex knew that these forays into Manhattan were best made as anonymously as possible. The last thing he wanted was to be seen with a kingpin of Vegas just as he got off a plane from Cuba.

They spent the evening in Alex's suite in the Waldorf—chosen for nostalgia's sake, as it was Meyer's home for so many years. Massimo couldn't understand why the airport was a no-go, but one of the most famous hotels in the world was acceptable to Alex.

"Two reasons, my friend. First, I am too old to shack up in the fleapits we used to sleep in, and second, the place is so big that anyone could come and go without being seen. The only person you have to take care of is the concierge and you can buy him off for less than a hundred bucks."

Despite the lavish lifestyle enjoyed by the rest of the guests, Alex insisted he and Massimo grabbed some pizzas and eat in his room.

"I don't wish us to have to worry about prying ears, Massimo."

"Understood. Part of me thought you'd like to go to Lindy's and grab a slice of cheesecake."

Alex smiled as memories of Arnold Rothstein flitted through his mind, until he recalled the afternoon when Thomas Dewey strode in on him and Charlie Lucky, leaving a sour taste to their cheesecake and the threat of federal prosecution. But all that was in the past and Alex did his best to live in the present and enjoy Massimo's tales from Nevada.

Once they finished the pizzas, the two men licked their fingers clean of tomato sauce and Alex suggested they get the concierge to fetch two slices of cheesecake.

"Why not buy an entire round? You won't be back in these parts again for a while."

Alex nodded and issued the instructions to the other end of the phone.

"Now, let's talk about tomorrow, Massimo."

"How do you want to handle this Jurek Sokolov?"

MASSIMO HAD WASTED no time since his original call with Alex and found Sokolov's address before he arrived in town. A taxi to the Bowery took twenty minutes, and they dropped themselves off two blocks away from their destination at Grande and Suffolk, two buildings from Mama Cohen's apartment.

There were still a handful of Yiddish signs above some stores but the sights and sounds were so different since the last time Alex had walked down these streets.

"It's been a long while."

"A *gonif* is still a gonif, as you used to say."

"That would have been Waxey Gordon, not me. I have always believed people can change, only they have to do it in the blink of an eye or I take matters into my own hands."

"Alex, remember we said last night that we'd play this nice and softly."

By the time this advice had been issued, the pair had stopped and were staring at the Suffolk Street residence of Jurek Sokolov. He might have kept the tenements around him, but Sokolov had converted all the rooms in his building into one sizeable home. Rat-a-tat-tat and a housekeeper let them in and invited Alex and Massimo to wait in a front room while she found Mr. Sokolov. Two minutes later, a middle-aged man with a long beard appeared and held out his hand, but neither stood up to shake the proffered limb.

"Thank you for taking the time to see us and for allowing us into your home, even though we have business to discuss."

Massimo nodded and allowed his boss to continue. Sokolov sat in the only armchair left in the room and tilted his head to the right.

"I am listening, Mr. Cohen."

"Two doors away is a piece of real estate that is important to me. Not because of the fabric of the building or its location. Not because of the number on the door or the memories it offers me of my childhood spent in the Bowery. Do you know why I care so much, Jurek?"

"I have done some asking around since your silent friend contacted me and I am told your mother lives there. I assume that is the cause of your interest."

"Exactly right. You are astute and sensible, Jurek. And why do you think I have traveled from out of town to talk to you this day about the building in which my mother eats, sleeps, and spends her life?"

Sokolov swallowed hard and lowered his eyes, scanning the wooden floorboards for an answer.

"I am informed that you have been putting my mother under undue pressure to leave the home she has made since the day my family arrived in America. Is that true, Jurek?"

"I wouldn't describe it as undue, but I would be a liar to say I hadn't encouraged her to go."

"And why would she want to do that? I mean, I understand she has been very clear to you she has no desire to go. Is that your understanding too?"

"She certainly seems set in her ways, Mr. Cohen, but progress waits for no man—or woman."

"This progress you talk of, are you concerned about the state of the Bowery or the profit you hope to make on the sale of your real estate?"

Sokolov thought for a minute, his eyes scanning from Massimo to Alex. He passed his tongue over his lips to moisten them before he responded.

"To be honest, it is the gelt. I have been offered a significant sum and all the other tenants have moved out."

"Apart from my mother."

"Yes. I hoped I might… encourage her to go, but she is a stubborn woman."

"You don't have to tell me that, Jurek."

Both men laughed, but Massimo remained straight faced.

"If I found another buyer who merely wanted to maintain the existing building, would you be prepared to sell to such a person?"

"Mr. Cohen, the offer is high. I doubt if you would find such a purchaser, especially given the overall state of the building."

"I do hope you are not going to tell me you failed to maintain the building in order to drive the tenants out."

Sokolov's eyes returned to staring downward, and Alex ground his molars. Massimo opened his mouth as if to begin speaking, but Alex beat him to the draw.

"The buyer I have in mind will pay you fifty percent above whatever offer you have in writing, and the deal can be struck this week. The condition for sale is that my mother stays where she is, you run the building on behalf of the new owner and you maintain the place to the highest standards and to the best of your ability. Are those terms acceptable to you?"

"Run the building for free?"

"Oh no, Jurek. I will pay you the going rate on top of the cost of any labor and materials necessary for the upkeep of the joint."

"You?"

"Why yes, can you think of anyone better to own my mother's building? Besides, if you know who my mother is, then you appreciate my reputation. I will make you one promise beyond the contract we will sign. If any harm befalls my mother while she lives in that building from now until the day she dies then I shall hold you personally responsible."

"With all the consequences that implies." Massimo's sole contribution contained just the right amount of menace to make Sokolov swallow hard again and agree to anything that Alex wanted.

14

ALEX COULD HAVE insisted Massimo handled the Sokolov situation by himself, but then Alex wouldn't have had an excuse to swing by Miami-Dade and break bread with Vito Genovese. The underboss of one of New York's five families was vacationing in Florida while a small local matter blew over back home; a state cop can't arrest you for homicide if you are a thousand miles away. Sometimes the trick was just to beat a hasty retreat for a few months and run your empire from the county in America with almost as many casinos as Vegas. The two men met at a restaurant in the Italian area of Miami Beach.

"Good to see you, Vito. Thanks for taking the time to visit me."

"Alex, we share too many interests to need an excuse to eat a bowl of pasta."

"How is Albert?"

"Anastasia is doing just fine. He's propping up Frank Costello in New York."

The corner of Alex's mouth curled upwards, but he tried not to let his pleasure show on his face. This was the same Albert who'd stolen Alex's heroin supply back in the day and who would have been happy to see him floating down the Hudson.

"Vito, it sounds as though you'd rather someone else was top dog."

"Don't put words in my mouth, Alex. You're not wrong, but Italian infighting has been a way of life ever since the first Mustache Pete set foot in this marvelous country."

"Anastasia has been a thorn in my side too, and I've been around long enough to know that the Italian families have their own Sicilian rules to play by."

"Just so you understand it is nothing personal, always business."

"I tell myself that, but personalities arrive on the scene that make it hard to believe."

Vito raised an eyebrow and paused as he shoveled another spoonful of tagliatelle into his mouth.

"Albert has been, is, and invariably will be a pain in the butt."

"Vito, he exerts a lot of influence within his territory and is a made man. Some fellas know how to behave and others do not."

Vito nodded agreement and the two men continued their entrees until their bowls were wiped clean with bread.

15

WHEN ALEX RETURNED to Havana the next afternoon, Sarah suggested he should visit the Montmartre Club.

"I'm tired. Why are you hustling me out of my home?"

"Trust me, you will thank me later."

One thing the man had learned over the years with Sarah was that he should always attend to her. They might have had their differences in the past, but nowadays Sarah's voice was filled with reason and excellent sense. They ate dinner together and before Alex could settle on the couch with her and listen to the radio, Alex made his excuses and headed out to Meyer's casino. He collected David on the way as he wanted some company, and Sarah was adamant she was staying at home.

The two men wandered around the poker and roulette tables until Alex spotted someone he recognized on the other side of the room. David nudged him in case the point hadn't become obvious to him.

"There's Aunt Esther."

Alex nodded and meandered over to stand five feet behind her and the roulette wheel, so he couldn't be spotted by her unless she twisted all the way round. Her elbows leaned on the edge of the green baize and she stared straight ahead. She only glanced away from the wheel long enough to take a slurp of her cocktail. Alex ground his molars and watched his sister lose a month's salary in a matter of minutes.

She mumbled something to the dealer who raised his eyes to Alex—she'd asked for credit. He shook his head and took two steps nearer to the situation. Even if he hadn't walked forward, Alex would have heard Esther's response because her voice was heightened with an ugly undertow of anger.

"Gimme some more chips. You know who my brother is?"

"Yes he does, Esther, and this gentleman may not provide lines of credit. It is time for you to step away from the table."

Esther eyed her sibling and nephew, then inhaled as if she was about to start an argument. Instead, she hiccupped and shrugged, almost falling off her stool and into Alex's arms.

"Let's go to the bar and get you a drink."

"Now you're talking, Alex, my boy."

"I meant a java, Esther."

"But I don't want a coffee."

ESTHER, ALEX, AND David sat at a table near the back of the bar with three coffees deposited by the waiter who left them alone as soon as the crockery landed on the tablecloth.

"By your bloodshot eyes, I'd say you've been here since I left the country and have been knocking back the liquor for the duration."

"Do you have a point to make?"

"Esther, you've been in town for barely a week and already you're drowning in the neck of a bottle."

"Alex Cohen, you are the last person on this planet to lecture anyone about the evils of booze. From what I've read, you made your first fortune bootlegging."

"What I did back in the day to provide for my family and how you are behaving now are two different things."

"Keep telling yourself that, bud."

Alex sighed. There was no point arguing with a drunk. Esther's head swayed on her shoulders as she attempted to maintain focus on her brother. David sipped his coffee and kept his eyes trained on his cup or the tablecloth.

"I reckon it's time you were leaving, Esther."

"Let me at least finish my coffee before I go back to my hotel."

"Yes, for sure, but that's not what I meant. You should go back home."

"Nah, I'm having too much fun here. You don't know what it was like being tied to Mama's apron strings. It's one thing to do that when you are a kid, but all my adult life too? She needed me, I understand that, but I put my entire existence on hold for Mama and Papa."

Alex wondered how much Esther's words were the mojitos talking. He'd walked out of his parents' home when he was in his teens—to be in Sarah's arms—and Esther could have left just the same if she had wanted. He had surprised himself at being so happy to see his sister. Thoughts of his family rarely permeated to the top of the pile, and as he considered this, he smiled.

"What's got you tickled pink?"

"How good it is to have you around, Esther. But we can't have you penniless and spending your life in a casino, even if it is one where I exert some influence."

Now it was David's turn to smirk.

"If you are going to stay in Havana, then why don't you work for me—some light admin, nothing more—and then you can enjoy yourself one bit at a time?"

"I want to go to bed."

Esther's head slammed onto the table and the two men grabbed her and dragged her out of the Montmartre Club and into a waiting taxi.

"HOW WAS FLORIDA?"

"Sunny, Meyer.

"I thought that might be the case. The weather's been good here too."

Alex stared at Meyer, unsure whether the fella was being serious as they sat in the Lima Hastiada. His friend behaved strangely once in a while and made Alex wonder if their investments were safe in his hands.

"Did you get matters sorted out about your mother?"

"Yes, thank you, Meyer. There'll be no bother over her accommodation from now until the day she dies."

Meyer nodded, and a smile flashed across his face for the briefest of seconds.

"If only everything could be resolved so easily, Alex."

"What are you talking about?"

"Some of our Italian friends are late with their monthly payments."

"Anyone in particular?"

"I'd rather not say at present as you have dealings with these fellas and I don't want you to change how you treat them, at least for now."

"There might be some trouble ahead, Meyer, judging from the way Vito was talking."

"What do you mean?"

"Friction between Vito and Albert Anastasia to begin with."

"This has been brewing ever since Charlie left for Sicily."

"Meyer, it all started the day Albert stole my heroin route and nobody did anything to stop him."

"Don't dredge up the past. What's done is done."

"I know, but that doesn't make it right. Besides, reading between the lines, Vito sounds as though he has his eye on Frank Costello's job."

"Boss of Luciano's old mob?"

"That's what I'm hearing, Meyer."

"All my life I've worked with those Italian fellas and the relationship has been good for me, Alex. From the days when the Big Bankroll found the gelt to finance our efforts during Prohibition through to our adventure in Cuba. We wouldn't have our casinos in Las Vegas if it wasn't for Sicilian money. Same in Atlantic City. You know what I'm on about."

"Sure thing, Meyer, but why mention it today?"

"Because in Havana I thought I'd be able to carve out a little block of something to call my own without the Italians getting involved. These new boys always have to sour everything they get their grubby hands on."

"And you're still relying on their money now."

"It's not the gelt, it's the way they ask for an inch and take a mile. First, can a nephew visit for a few months until the heat dies down in New York? Then he's shipping in heroin without anyone dipping their beak in the trough. Finally, you're asked to give him a controlling interest in a club or restaurant."

"Whatever they ask, you agree otherwise they'll perceive it as a lack of respect."

"Yep. And I don't need the Italian mob to make money anymore. I have Batista and I am a member of the government. Break the law? I pass the laws so I can do whatever I want and still I'm handcuffed to these meshuggener fellas."

16

BATISTA'S OFFICE HADN'T changed at all since the last time Meyer and Alex were sitting together on the other side of his oak desk. This time, Alex noticed their chairs were lower than his; a pathetic attempt at reinforcing his superiority.

"There's a fly I'd like you to swat."

Alex glanced around for the insect in the room but knew to let Meyer handle the conversation.

"Where and who are we talking about?"

"Castro is still roaming my country, causing havoc and discontent wherever he walks. I need you to snuff him out."

Meyer looked at Alex, who turned his head to one side, unsure of what to make of this request for an assassination.

"With the utmost respect, Mr. President, if it was so easy to remove Castro from the scene then better men than ourselves would have done it for you by now, don't you think?"

The dictator glared at Meyer and Alex wondered what his friend was playing at. He agreed to anything the chest of medals asked.

"His devils are everywhere and I want you to stop them."

"I understand he has taken control of some southeastern parts of this island, but I imagine he has plans in place to protect himself from open assassination."

"You are right, Meyer, which is why I need you to deal with this cockroach. Every day he lives, the people trust me less. This must not be allowed to continue."

"Mr. President, Alex and I do not have a vast army to bring to bear on this matter. We have always been careful to surround ourselves with only our small circle of friends from America, in order to protect you from the eyes of the FBI."

Batista continued to stare but Alex thought his expression had softened as Meyer reminded him of the reality of the situation.

"May I make a suggestion, Mr. President?"

"We are listening, Alex."

"Meyer is perceptive to note that he and I have no army to call on, but your soldiers are already in place. Perhaps we could provide some advice and support to your military leaders in the area on how best to deal with this beetle of yours?"

Both Batista and Lansky sat back in their seats to ponder Alex's proposal. After ten seconds of silence, Batista propped himself forward with his elbows leaning on that desk of his.

"Cohen, your idea is good. You can be my military advisors. I'll send word that you'll start with immediate effect tomorrow. Castro won't know what's hit him."

Before either man could utter another word, Batista dismissed them as he picked up the phone to inform his captain to expect guests in the morning.

"WHY THE HELL did you say that, Alex?"

"Because your president thought we were going to send an army we don't have to the other side of the island and strafe every field, village, and town until the Castro brothers were dead. You and I know that would never happen and then you'd be forced to explain how we failed him. And that would have been a conversation where I stayed home that day."

Meyer opened his mouth and decided not to argue.

"Besides, we can offer the best advice in the world and, hand on heart, report back, that is what we did. Batista needs to treat his soldiers better than he does if he wants to get results like Uncle Sam achieves."

Alex's mind took him back to the foxholes of the Great War.

"Alex, I wouldn't say that Korea was a big win for the US."

"What? No, perhaps not, but would you prefer to be fighting against Castro with a gun in your hand or talking to the schmucks who will have to fight Castro?"

"Put like that, I'll be a military advisor for Batista."

"That's what I thought too, Meyer. Now, I can doubtless convince Ezra and Massimo to take a week's vacation down here and they can talk tactics until the sun goes down."

"Alex, you weren't paying attention to Batista carefully enough. He named us both, but he was looking straight at you. That means he wants you to do it and with no substitutes. Call your lieutenants to join you, it'll look a lot more impressive, but the president issued an instruction that you are taking a trip tomorrow and won't be back until the military feel equipped to deal with the insurrectionists."

ALEX MET EZRA and Massimo on the first flight in from the States the following day and the three men drove to the other side of the island, through the Sierra Maestra mountains, and over to the Moncada Barracks military camp located outside Santiago de Cuba.

They were greeted by the sight of a ramshackle force whose distance from the center of power had increased their disinterest in Batista's proclamations and bluster. Instead, they were introduced to Captain Isidro Leocadio Chávez, who supplied each man with a cigar and poured the first shots of rum before they sat down.

"Izzy, have you received orders from Mr. President informing you of our arrival?"

"Yeah, in this morning's dispatches. Good of you to come all this way, Señor Cohen."

"Call me Alex. When Batista makes a pronouncement, what else are we to do?"

"Havana is far from here and we operate on a different wavelength, Alex."

"So it would appear."

Alex looked around at the makeshift camp that had been in place ever since the Castro brothers had blown into town, causing murder and mayhem to the Batista government.

"Don't be fooled by my casual demeanor. I might think this is a fool's errand but I still value my life and that of my family and ensure we send units out every day into the foothills of the Sierra Maestra to root out the rebel scourge."

"Any luck so far, Izzy?"

"None whatsoever. Every few weeks they attack us with mortar fire or booby trap a road with grenades, but we haven't captured or killed a single one of the twenty-sixth of July Movement."

"How big a force are the rebels?"

"Alex, we believe there are around twenty of them."

Ezra snorted at the number.

"I thought there were hundreds of the guys."

"No, Ezra. You don't need an army when you have right on your side, and that's what Fidel Castro believes. He and his brother say Batista is stealing money from the people of this land and want retribution."

Ezra shuffled in his chair.

"Sure thing, Captain Chávez, but it'll take more than twenty outraged men to control this place. You can't run a country when you're hiding in the hills."

"For now they bite at Batista's heels, but one day…"

Alex raised an eyebrow.

"Izzy, do you think they'll win?"

"I couldn't say, but the people are behind them. There's no food where they are hiding, yet they eat. There's no munitions, but they have guns, grenades, and mortars and bullets. The locals assist them at every turn."

"Have you any idea who in the town is giving them help?"

"Massimo, no we don't."

"Then I suggest you send one of your privates undercover and find out who is in contact with the rebels. Once you identify the individuals, you can take them in and torture them until they tell you what you need to know."

Massimo took another shot of his rum. The simplicity of his idea created a well of silence in the room.

"I don't want to appear rude, but do you have any whisky? Rum really isn't my drink."

Chávez grinned and called for his batman to find some ice and a bottle of Scotch for his newfound friend.

THAT NIGHT, AN unmarried soldier, aged only nineteen, was sent into town to keep his ears to the ground and to seek out any locals who were sympathetic to the rebels' cause. Two days later his body was found on the beach with his throat slashed.

"You were right, Izzy. Castro has mighty big cojones and the townsfolk support him. Perhaps you can exploit their loyalty."

"What do you mean, Alex?"

"Take any man in town, just make sure he has a family. And announce you will execute him unless Castro or one of his men surrenders. Then you kill the guy and repeat the exercise every day if no one appears to save the man or you get yourself a member of the rebel army."

"And if nobody shows, then won't that make me an enemy to the townspeople?"

"I don't think you have to worry about that. If the people supported Batista, then they wouldn't be helping to kill your soldier boys."

"As much as I can see the logic of your thinking, I can't attack my people. If the president ever found out, he'd throw me in jail—or worse."

"Having met Batista, I would say he doesn't care too much about what happens to his countrymen, but I understand why you don't want to follow my suggestion. Do you mind if we stick around for a few more days? I haven't seen my friends in a long while and I'd like to take advantage of the opportunity as we are in the same place together."

August 1955

17

ALEX SAT WITH Meyer in the Lima Hastiada, catching up and enjoying a mug of the local java. Lansky appeared to spend most of his time in government buildings.

"Meyer, it feels like I'm recreating my old gang from Nevada, only in a different country."

"What do you mean?"

"Seeing Ezra and Massimo reminded me of the fun I had looking after Las Vegas for the syndicate."

"Good times."

"And part of the pleasure was having my lieutenants nearby. This may sound soppy, but I miss the fellas."

"Alex, you've worked with those men for how many decades? Of course, you miss them, like I still think about Arnold."

Alex recalled his early days in Lindy's, waiting to have a word with the Big Bankroll. Happy times indeed.

"But, Alex, we live in the here and now. Remember, those times are gone. Our present is in Cuba and Batista is our meal ticket into the future."

"Do you not think that the rebels will come good?"

"Twenty men, you said?"

"Yep. More or less."

"I can't see them bringing an entire country to its knees."

"The people are behind them, Meyer. That counts for a lot."

"They had a revolution in Russia when we were kids and look what happened there. Same in China. Revolutions are for saps. What we are doing is building something that'll last. By the end of the year, we will finish the Riviera. That's not us refurbishing some old Cuban wreck. It's erupting out of the ground and its rooftop bar is so high up, you'll be able to see America."

"Meyer, I admire your optimism."

"This isn't blind faith that you're hearing. I walked into this with my eyes wide open. Batista is a thug, I know that. He rules this country with an iron fist and the citizens get nothing while he and his family line their pockets at every opportunity."

"And this is a sustainable proposition?"

"Alex, the president pays me for my government role. I pick up twenty-five thousand dollars each year to devise ways to generate gaming income for him. If there's a law that gets in our way, he changes it. That is the power we dreamed of having in the States, and here it is in the palm of my hand."

Meyer's eyeballs popped out of their sockets as he spoke. Alex had never heard his friend speak with such passion before.

"You've been warming up Batista for almost twenty years, haven't you?"

"Yes, he vouched for our safety during his first term in office when we held our conference here with Charlie after that scumbag Dewey sent him packing to Sicily."

"Has he ever double-crossed you?"

"No, I trust him as much as I do… Albert Anastasia."

"So not at all, then."

"Not quite. You may be certain that Albert will make money for himself and if your interests are sufficiently aligned, then you can put some gelt in your own wallet at the same time."

"Meyer, do you think Batista'll outlive us?"

"I don't have a crystal ball, Alex, so I have no clue. Besides, I do not plan that far ahead. In three years, we should have set ourselves up in Havana so that we can sit on our haunches and live off the cash flow forever."

"Or until Batista is deposed by the next dictator."

"There's no one waiting in that line, Alex. The closest you could say is his brother, but he doesn't have the brains to remember to wear pants around the house."

They both sniggered at Meyer's insight as David entered the cantina and caught Alex's eye.

"What's so funny? Can I buy you gentlemen a drink?"

"We're good, thanks."

"You still have smiles on your faces. What gives?"

"Nothing much, David. We are planning our future empire in the sun."

"That's nice for you two. Is there a seat for me at the table or am I going back to the US with my tail between my legs?"

"Of course, you'll be by my side."

Alex touched the sleeve of David's linen jacket and squeezed his arm.

"Once we've got the empire running smoothly, there will only be legitimate business enterprises and you are my consigliere in all legal matters."

"Just checking you weren't planning on deporting me."

"All immigrants are welcome at this table, David."

◆ ◆ ◆

ALEX WAS CALLED into a meeting with Meyer and Francisco Batista. As much as he disliked the president, he despised the brother more because the guy was clinging to the shirttails of his more powerful and corrupt sibling. Alex recalled the first occasion he'd met Francisco and the fact he had been put in charge of Havana parking meters—and was happy about it. Penny ante stuff.

The guy maintained a broad grin on his face almost the whole time—Alex imagined what he looked like when he was told his mother died and there would be the same stupid expression glued to the front of his head.

"We anticipate a little local difficulty which we are hoping you will help us with," explained the fixed grin before him.

"It depends what we are talking about. I'm only one man."

"You undersell yourself, Alex."

He gave Meyer a long, hard stare because his friend knew exactly what Alex thought of Batista Junior.

"Next week I will impose a window tax in Havana, and I need someone to oversee its collection. Meyer tells me you were involved in a similar process in the United States."

Alex's mind flashed back to his teenage years collecting protection money from store owners on behalf of Waxey Gordon at first, and then for himself later on.

"I have a passing acquaintance with the task, Francisco. Forgive me, but what is a window tax?"

"If your home has a window, then you must pay tax on it to me."

"Isn't the revenue from parking meters enough?"

Francisco's grin faltered for a second, and then he laughed.

"Let's just say I am a touch cash poor at the minute and have a new girlfriend to wine and dine."

"And you wouldn't want her to know you can't support your lavish lifestyle?"

"Something like that, Alex. Please remember that you might be Meyer's business partner, but don't be impertinent. I do not appreciate that tone."

"Francisco, sorry if I have caused you any offense. My comments were my attempt to find out the background to the rush to tax the citizens of this fine city. Besides, apart from the pleasure of helping the brother of the president, there has been no discussion as to any fee for rendering this service."

"Apology accepted, my friend, and we are not communists. For the time you assist me in this task, you will receive twenty-five percent of the revenue you generate."

Alex nodded consent, they shook hands, and then he left the other two men to their conversation.

◆ ◆ ◆

"MEYER, WHAT THE hell were you thinking of? Why did you put me in that position with Francisco Batista?"

The two friends had resumed their usual perch in the shadows of the Lima Hastiada.

"I didn't know it was going to be such a problem. You've made accommodations for Batista before."

"Meyer, I've helped your business partner, the president. Not that piece of longe lokshen. He's a complete waste of space."

Alex's friend stared at him, stony faced.

"Am I going back to him to say you aren't willing to do the work?"

"Meyer, at this point, I honestly do not know. I feel you railroaded me into agreeing a deal with that man, and I had to count my fingers after we shook hands."

Lansky took a mouthful of his coffee and allowed the liquid to slosh around his mouth before responding.

"I should have spoken to you first, but I didn't realize the extent of your dislike for the man. Had I known…"

"What's done is in the past. We live together, we love together…"

"…but we die alone."

"Exactly, Meyer. You and I are good. Perhaps I could supervise without getting my hands too dirty."

"He does only expect you to oversee, that's what he said."

"I imagine he thinks I have this large mob swanning around Havana waiting for me to snap my fingers and intimidate the local population."

"Alex, back in the States…"

"I'm not saying I didn't used to have that set-up, but I left my best men behind in Vegas."

"Perhaps you should invite some friends over?"

Alex thought for a moment and then smiled.

"It would be a great excuse to drag Ezra over here, Meyer."

"And he could bring some company with him too."

18

VITO GENOVESE VISITED Havana and looked up his old friend Meyer and his more recent pal, Alex. The Montmartre Club was the venue of choice for their first meeting.

"I thought you'd stay in America, Vito."

"We all deserve a vacation, Alex. Besides, Meyer and I have some business to attend to this week."

"Would you rather have a private conversation? I won't take offense, Vito."

"Thank you for your kind consideration, but we can relax this evening and talk business during daylight hours."

Meyer passed over a pile of chips to Vito, who nodded and palmed the lot. "Shall we find a poker table?"

"Why don't we go into the VIP room?"

The three sauntered out of the bar with Meyer leading the way and on to a private door to the side of the main casino space, down a short corridor to a dead end with a reception desk and three rooms, one left, one right, and the other straight ahead.

"Any busy at the moment?"

The receptionist shook her head and Meyer smiled, choosing the middle door, explaining it was the biggest of the three.

He pressed a buzzer when the other two had settled into their chairs, and a minute later a waitress showed up to take their drink orders. After they had been delivered, a valet appeared to remove the extra seating that surrounded the green baize table in the center of the windowless room.

The men sat down and played a few hands with little conversation other than an occasional comment about what was visible on the cards.

"Meyer, you are one smart cookie, the way you spotted the potential in Cuba before anybody else."

"Thank you, Vito. I have my moments."

"It was more than that. This place offers tremendous opportunities that we can't achieve in the US. We are out of sight of the Feds to begin with."

"The lack of American jurisdiction means the FBI can only guess at what we might get up to here. But, Vito, almost everything I am involved with is legitimate. I'm a member of the government, after all."

"You have Batista under your thumb?"

"We have an understanding. He doesn't involve himself in my business enterprises too deeply, and I make sure he keeps getting richer. A simple transaction that works well for both of us."

"Like I said, Meyer, you're smart. My interests in the States generate more than enough income for me, although sometimes it is hard for me to spend my money."

"Vito, when we are unsure of the provenance of our gelt, we need to take great care where we spend it."

The corner of Meyer's mouth rose and Vito snorted consent.

"Which brings us to Cuba with its casinos and hotels under your control, Meyer. You have the perfect vehicles to convert uncertain cash into clean money, right?"

"This is not something I bother myself with at the moment, but you are correct, we could use my Cuban entertainment venues for money laundering."

"If I offered you ten percent of the cash flow, would we be able to come to some arrangement?"

Meyer swallowed a mouthful of his cocktail before placing his cards on the table and stared straight at Vito Genovese.

"A dime on the dollar is low for what you are proposing. For a friend, I'd accept a quarter, but no less."

"Twenty-five percent is acceptable, but I would need your assurance that this would be an exclusive relationship."

"Now you are asking me to leave a lot of money on the table. Let me think about it and come back to you before you end your vacation. Shall we carry on with our card game?"

THE FOLLOWING MORNING, Alex and Sarah had breakfast together on their veranda.

"You were home late, Alex."

"I was schmoozing Vito Genovese with Meyer. We let him win at cards."

"Since when do you trust that weasel?"

"When he's offering Meyer a cool ten million a year to launder. That's worth a few hours' poker."

"Won't that place us squarely in the firing line of the FBI?"

Alex put his silverware down and washed his mouth out with a swill of juice.

"They could trace the gelt to the US border, and then it would be a mystery. When Vito repatriates the cash, it'll come in through a different country, so the Feds will have a hard job proving anything, assuming they could see the connection."

"How certain are you that what you're saying is true?"

"Meyer and I have thought it all through."

"He sure has, but I don't want him to hang you out to dry."

"Don't you trust Meyer, Sarah?"

"Of course, though his interests and yours are aligned but not the same. He won't intentionally put you in harm's way, but you'll be the one left holding the baby."

SANTO TRAFFICANTE, MEYER, and Alex tapped their toes to the show taking place in Santo's Sans Souci Cabaret around the corner from the Montmartre. The man, and his father before him, ran Florida, and he had moved over to Cuba two years earlier.

"We don't sit down with each other as much as I would like, Meyer."

"Santo, you're right. There are times we forget we are neighbors."

"It's a two-way street, Meyer, and I appreciate you coming over to visit me this evening."

Alex was intrigued by what Santo might be up to. He'd stolen Meyer's gaming customers with the lure of a show and the sight of a Hollywood star, yet here he was acting like there was just a piece of tarmac between them.

"There sure is money to be made out of American tourists, and there are so many ways to do it."

"Meyer, the more attractions we can put on in this fine country, the greater the numbers will fly over here for a weekend or even longer."

"A rising tide lifts all boats—that's for certain."

"I agree, and it also offers men like us other opportunities too."

"What are you thinking of, Santo?"

"We both know you have ensured there is no oversight of our gaming activities by Batista's government. Congratulations on engineering that situation. I cannot recall anyone who was in Cuba before you, Meyer…"

Alex's friend raised a limp hand to swat away the compliment.

"…and that means you are in a unique position to help those of us who still have the majority of their assets held in the US."

Meyer smiled and nodded while Alex thought about the deal only recently struck with Santo's enemy, Vito Genovese.

"Money laundering is one of the many services I offer those who I am close enough to call my friends."

"Meyer, would you do me the honor of cleaning our casino skim from Vegas and Florida?"

"My fee is a quarter on the dollar and I would not want us to fall out over something as trifling as gelt, so let's not get involved in any unnecessary negotiation. That is my offer. Take it or leave it."

ALEX STARED AT Sarah over breakfast the next morning.

"Enjoying the view?"

"Of course, Sarah, but I didn't mean to stare, I was just thinking."

"And then you pulled the rug from under my feet. You could have pretended to be in awe of my beauty."

Sarah laughed and Alex continued to look blankly until she couldn't joke his rudeness away any longer.

"What's on your mind, Alex?"

"Meyer has struck a deal with both Vito and Santo for money-laundering services in Havana. The good news is that both are being charged the same rate, so there is no favoritism, but the bad news is that he has promised both men that he will not launder anybody else's cash while they work together."

Sarah stopped eating her toast, putting her current slice back on the plate, and she stared into the middle distance like Alex.

"What are the chances of either side finding out?"

"Right now they are vying for power in the Italian mob, so I doubt if they are spending Sunday afternoons together playing pinochle."

"But, Alex, if you have men working the docks who are your eyes and ears then it is only a matter of time before they notice you shipping out crates of cash."

"There is that point, yes. And if you and I can work that out, why hasn't Meyer?"

"No idea, Alex. But Meyer is not a foolish man. He has the angles covered even if you don't know how."

"Meantime, guess who's caught in the middle as Meyer's placed me as the frontman for this escapade. Yeah, I receive a piece of the action, but when they figure out their exclusive terms ain't so unique, who do you think will get it in the neck first, Sarah?"

"We could go back to the States, Alex."

"And do what? We can make our fortune on this grubby little island, but not if we leave now."

"Better alive and poor than a rich corpse."

"If we hang on for another couple of years, we'll never have to work again. I could become entirely legitimate, shed all my illegal investments, and still live the good life."

"Or wind up dead before we have time to spend one red cent."

Sarah stared back into the distance and Alex followed suit. For a second he thought about how beautiful she looked with the sunlight shining from behind her, but then he remembered the vast amount of money he was hoping to make and gazed into the space just beyond her right shoulder.

19

"THERE IS A new opportunity I want to offer you, Alex."

Like Lindy's before, a booth at the back of the Lima Hastiada was the location for the conversation between Alex and Meyer.

"What have you got cooking now?"

"Nothing yet, which is why I want you to be in on it at the start."

"Hit me, Meyer."

"I thought that as you are about to get an additional revenue stream from laundering mob money from New York and Vegas, you should invest in a new casino and hotel complex I'm going to build."

"The gelt hasn't even landed in my account and you've already spent it."

Alex chuckled, but Meyer's expression remained stony-cold. He never joked about gelt.

"If we knock down a couple of houses two blocks away, we can create a space overlooking the seafront with a casino, restaurant, theater, and one-hundred room hotel."

"Won't the residents mind?"

"We'll pay them off or Batista's thugs will ship them out—that doesn't matter. It's the value of the real estate you should focus on."

"And why me? Surely, Vito or Santo are your obvious first ports of call."

"Alex, I've told you before that there is no need to cut the Italians in on every deal that goes down. I think some ventures should just be with my Yiddishe friends."

"How much are we talking about?"

"First, there's the government license and Batista's payment—that's a couple of million. The construction itself will come in at a little under three million. So call it five million plus the running costs for six months but you'll only need to spring for two million up front."

Alex whistled at the amount of money Meyer was asking of him.

"Meyer, the amount I make out of Vegas is only around a million a year and nowadays, most of that seems to go on maintaining our lifestyle over here. Do you believe I've a hidden stash I can just pull out of a wall and hand over to you?"

"Those days are long gone, Alex. And anyway, I expect you misunderstand. I'm giving you the chance to be a frontrunner for the deal. You are welcome to tap anyone you know to come in on the investment, but it is your name that will be on the deeds."

"And, Meyer, you think I can cash flow this out of the money laundering we are about to embark on?"

"I'm doing the laundering and you are taking a percentage from the proceeds to liaise with Vito and Santo."

"Be a buffer between you and the heads of two mob families, you mean?"

"That's what I said, Alex. Think about it. There's no need to rush. I'm giving you the chance to turn five million into ten within a year if you include the kickbacks that running a casino and hotel offer a man in your position."

"Sounds mighty peachy."

"Just remember that every day you don't decide is one less day to produce money. What would you call the joint?"

"The Panama."

"Why's that?"

"I like the cigars."

"WHAT DO YOU think, David?"

"Pop, you take on all the risk and Meyer makes money off your hard work before you even get a sniff of any profit. What's not to like if you're Lansky?"

"We live together, we love together…"

"And the liability is all yours."

Alex sat back in his dining chair as Sarah entered the room and deposited a pot of coffee on the table before sitting down next to him.

"Are you commenting as my legal advisor or as my son?"

"At the moment, I represent your legal affairs to the world and unless you tell me otherwise, this is a legitimate business, albeit one that you would never get to own in the US because of your checkered past."

"The deal itself is on the up-and-up, David."

"I assume that means the sources of funding are not, and I don't want an answer to that, otherwise you won't let me near any of the paperwork once it is generated."

"David, I will look to you to handle the administration of the real estate purchase and the building project initially."

"If you go ahead."

"There may be ancillary activities to which you should not be party but we can worry about those details later."

"Have you decided to proceed, then?"

"There will be no paperwork from Meyer—that's not how he operates. The man has owned nothing for thirty years to my certain knowledge, yet he swims in cash. He and I will have a handshake and nothing more than that."

"For that reason alone, I must advise against getting involved in this project. If you want to spend five million without having a sheet of paper to back it up if things go sour, then you should know not to do it."

"David, if matters get out of hand and there is a disagreement between Meyer and myself over this, then we will not sue each other and legal advice will not be required."

David swallowed hard at the menace in Alex's voice and he glanced over at Sarah, who ensured she kept her eyes on her coffee cup.

"You can call me risk averse if you like, but any disagreement which ends in violence…"

"This is why you only handle certain aspects of my business dealings, David. Sometimes there are things you do not want to know about."

David's eyes darted left and right, then aimed straight at his father.

"Don't do it. If you don't think the risk of being left holding the baby is too great, then consider what proportion of your current wealth Meyer is asking you to put at risk."

Sarah lifted her head.

"What do you mean, David?"

"Meyer wants Pop to pay government fees upfront to the tune of two million US."

"That'd be all our savings."

"Sarah, let's not get ahead of ourselves. I've asked David for advice—I haven't agreed zip with Meyer."

"And when would I have a say in the matter?"

"If it is something I feel seriously about, then we will have a discussion. We are not at that point yet, not by a long way."

"It sounds like we are."

"No, Sarah. If this had happened six months ago, then I would have paid the gaming license fee to Batista as soon as I walked out of the cantina with Meyer."

"What's changed since then, Alex?"

"As you know, Meyer has got me involved with the Italians and I am not comfortable with the situation which is why I hesitate now."

"Wheels within wheels?"

"Exactly, David. Meyer keeps track of all the various deals and accommodations he has made with every person completely in his head. There is no paperwork for sure, but there is little trace of how interconnected any conversation you have with him is to the rest of his empire. I admire this trait in him but the only way to do business with him is to trust him totally and utterly."

"And do you?"

"Sarah, I don't know. For ordinary situations? Of course, but The Panama will put me in the big league or six feet under and you'll be saying *Kaddish*."

"Would you want to be buried back in America?"

"David!"

"Sorry, Mom, but you know I'll be the one who has to organize it when the day finally comes."

"Stop talking as though your father is dead. I will not have that happening in my house… Alex, look at what this deal of yours is doing to us and we don't even know if it is going to happen."

"We live in unusual times, Sarah."

October 1957

20

ALEX SAT IN a diner just outside Providence, Rhode Island, at Meyer's request: "Charlie Lucky called from Sicily and would like you to do him a favor and meet with a guy."

They reminisced over the good times the two men had spent with Charlie Luciano over the years before Special Prosecutor Dewey tried to tear their Manhattan world into pieces. Alex realized he hadn't seen Charlie since the day the syndicate agreed the hit on Benny Siegel and a weight grew in the pit of his stomach as he recalled his first few months while in Vegas. The best of times and the worst of times.

For a second, Alex thought he smelled Rebecca's perfume in the diner, and then he snapped out of his reverie. Joe Gallo had appeared from nowhere and sat opposite him in the back booth.

"Thanks for visiting me in my hometown, Alex."

"My pleasure. When our mutual friend inquired if I could take a vacation, how could I not want to pop over here?"

They both smiled and Joe ordered a coffee and a cookie while Alex asked for a piece of cheesecake.

"You can drag the man out of New York..."

Gallo nodded.

"How long has it been since you lived in Manhattan?"

"A lifetime, but we didn't come here to talk about the places I've called home."

The waitress returned to their table to fill up Alex's coffee mug and deliver the rest of the order.

"Joe, what am I doing here, apart from the courtesy call?"

"There is a contract we need completing and Charlie thought you'd be the one to execute it."

"Why me?"

"You are incredibly reliable and a safe pair of hands, if even half the stories about you are true."

"Who's the hit?"

"Your old friend from Murder Corp… Albert Anastasia."

Alex dropped his fork on the plate and remembered to close his mouth. Then he sat back and took a sip of coffee.

"Someone finally woke up to the fact that the fella's a *verstinkener momzer*."

"Who?"

"Albert's a no-good snake-in-the-grass who deserves everything that's coming to him."

"So can you stay over for a few days until we get this matter sorted?"

"Happily, but there's been no syndicate meeting to approve this."

Joe laughed.

"You are right, there's been no syndicate meeting, but it has been authorized."

"By whom?"

"The commission has given its approval. The Italian bosses keep in touch and smooth out any problems between themselves."

Alex wondered why the Italians felt the need to create what sounded like their own version of the syndicate, but now was not the time for that discussion.

"I'll kill him."

"You and me both, Alex. It's a two-man job."

"No disrespect, Joe, but I work alone."

"Understood, but on this occasion, we must have an Italian witness to the proceedings. This is no sleight on your abilities, it's just the way of the world nowadays."

"When does it need to be done by?"

"The end of the month, so we have a plenty of time to play with. I suggest you hole up in a motel until tomorrow when my driver will take you to New York and we can meet up again in Manhattan."

WHEN ALEX WAS dropped off in the Five Boroughs, he grabbed a cab to the Waldorf Astoria and took a room rather than a suite; he didn't want to appear too ostentatious. Then he awaited Joe who was scheduled to arrive the next day. For old times' sake, Alex walked across town to Lindy's and waited in line with everybody else to get a table.

He asked for a booth near the back, but the maître d' explained that none were available at present and that one of the side tables was as good. A coffee and a thick slice of cheesecake and Alex got the nostalgia out of his system before he sauntered back to the hotel to remain in his room until Joe called him that evening.

"You could have been hosted with a fella I know in Little Italy."

"I don't get out much and besides, I prefer the anonymity of large buildings over the beady eyes of some fella's wife, who'd pick me out of a line-up if her husband needed a fall guy."

"There'll be no patsy for this trip—you have my word."

"Joe, I believe you, but in three years' time when Anastasia's brother comes looking for revenge, can you protect me then?"

"Alex, you are one cautious man."

"We live together, we love together…"

"And we die alone. I get it."

ALEX WOKE EARLY and enjoyed his room-service breakfast: two cheese blintzes, bagel, fruit salad, juice, and coffee. Then he put on the suit the hotel had cleaned overnight and padded downstairs to the lobby. A guy arrived, wearing a charcoal suit and a black fedora, and Alex somehow knew this was his driver.

Without a word, he was deposited on 55th and Seventh Avenue and strolled to the corner of the building, rested the sole of his shoe against the wall, and lit a cigarette. His wait was short-lived as Joe arrived two minutes later; enough time to finish his smoke and not much else.

The streets were as busy as you'd expect them to be on a Friday morning, and the men hustled up one block to reach 56th. Then Joe guided them over toward the Park Sheraton Hotel and nudged Alex as they walked past an olive-skinned guy, hands in his pockets.

"That's Albert's driver," he whispered.

"Where's he off to?"

"The last three days he's spent with a lady friend who suggested they meet up for a quick *drink* while his boss gets his hair cut."

"On the payroll?"

Joe nodded and winked.

"To the barbers?"

Alex buried both hands in his coat pockets and felt the cold metal of the two pistols as his fingers wrapped around the grips. They stood only twenty feet from the barbershop entrance, and still, the crowd was thick. The main hotel lobby was fifty feet to their left, and you'd have thought more people would have headed there than hang out near the slew of stores that supported the hotel guests and also took custom from passersby.

Joe looked up and down the street and stopped, pretending to tie a shoelace. Alex remained vigil until Joe returned to his full height.

"Let's walk past and decide."

Alex nodded, and they both turned their heads to face the window, but all they saw was a man in the barber's chair, his head wrapped in white towels. He could have been anyone.

"Keep going."

When they reached the corner of the building, they stopped and lit a cigarette each.

"That might not be him."

"Joe, his driver has gone for some fun with a skirt, you know he is having his monthly haircut and that is the joint he goes to. Who else do you think it is?"

"Alex, we can't have him escape. If this is not the time then we should wait until later in the day, but if we shoot and miss then the whole deal will be blown. And that can't happen."

"It's him. Follow my lead."

Alex strode down the sidewalk, back to the barbershop, ten feet away. He thrust a hand in his left pocket and pulled out a scarf which he used to cover his face before he pushed open the door. A quick glance along the street to check that Joe's face was covered too. He walked inside and pulled out his revolvers to take aim, but the barber stood between him and the chair.

Alex yanked the guy to one side, and he lost his balance and fell onto the floor. As soon as the barber was out of the way, Alex kicked the swivel chair to make it spin around and as the fella's torso hove into view, Alex let rip with both guns, causing red pools to appear through the white chair cloth. Before he fired a fourth shot, the chair continued to rotate and Anastasia somehow ripped off the protective sheet, aimed his pistol, and fired twice.

The wall mirror shattered because he was looking at Alex's reflection. Joe hit him once in the back of the head and Alex joined in as they both kept plugging slugs into the body until the only movement was a twitching leg.

All this time, the barber quivered on the tiled floor. Alex noticed he faced the ground—he wasn't stupid enough to make any identification possible. A tap of Joe's shoulder and they stowed their firearms back in their coats as they rejoined the crowd on the sidewalk.

Or rather, with all the gunfire nearby, everybody had scattered, leaving an emptiness for the two men to cross before they ran to a waiting car, parked outside the entrance. As it sped away, they removed their scarves.

"I'd lose the guns if I were you."

"Joe, they'll be in fragments across the city before the day is out."

"I would offer to do it for you, but I respect that you'll want to guarantee that the job is done and the pieces will never come back to haunt."

"You know me so well and we only met a couple of days ago."

ANASTASIA'S FUNERAL SERVICE took place at Green-Wood Cemetery in Brooklyn, and Alex made sure he was one of the few people to attend. Even though the meeskait had lived in New Jersey since '47, his local church wouldn't bury him so his family hunted around until they found a diocese that would take the corpse and shove it in the ground.

Alex expressed his condolences to Elsa, Albert's wife, who thanked him for coming all this way to show his respects.

"I was in the neighborhood and we go a long way back—from before the war."

"Then you know how hard he worked to build his empire and protect his family."

"I know exactly what that man did and will never forget while I have breath in my body—you can be sure of that."

21

FOUR DAYS AFTER Alex's return to Havana, Lansky called him and they met an hour later at the Lima Hastiada.

"Why the rush, Meyer?"

"Haven't you heard?"

Alex's expression remained calm, one eye scrunched up as the question piqued his curiosity.

"There's been an attack on Francisco."

"Who?"

"Alex, the guy's the president's brother. One trip to America and you've come back with mush for brains."

"Don't be like that, Meyer. You spend your life with these people. I see them twice a year and you want me to know what's going on inside your head. Give me a break."

"My apologies. There's been a hit on Francisco Batista."

"Has he survived and do we have who squeezed the trigger?"

"Yes, and no."

Alex saw a sadness overtake Meyer's expression and understood that his friend was hurting even though he himself thought nothing of this nepotistic nobody.

"Will he pull through?"

"He's in a coma right now. It wasn't a bullet, but a bomb."

"For your sake, Meyer, I hope it comes good for him. How can I help?"

"We need to find out who did this—and fast."

"Can't Batista's secret police sort this out?"

"There's not much evidence left, just shards of metal. Besides, both brothers have acquired numerous enemies over the years, so if they rounded up the usual suspects, the jails would be full and they'd be no nearer getting the guys responsible."

"You think I stand a better chance?"

"With Ezra over here permanently, you've got a network built up which is not aligned to Batista. You might have more luck if your fellas make some discreet inquiries."

"I'd have thought everyone knows I dip my beak in the same trough as you and Batista."

"Not the ordinary joe in the street. He knows *gornisht*."

As little as Alex cared whether Francisco Batista was alive or dead, he was very much concerned about the health of his family and the safety of his assets. All his eggs were in one Cuban basket and when he woke up the following morning, Alex understood he needed to find the bomber, not for the sake of either Batista, but for his friends and family.

With that thought ringing in his head, he spoke with Ezra and asked his guys to inquire in the cantinas and brothels around Havana; they could widen their search if they found nothing in the city.

"WHAT YOU SEE and what you hear, Ezra?"

"Alex, men never cease to amaze me. They can get as drunk as they like and remain tightlipped but put them in bed with a stranger and a guy'll sing to a *nafka* until it's time to go home to his wife."

"Weak husbands are never to be trusted. Now I see the trips to the brothels were of value. Do you mind sharing what you know?"

"The twenty-sixth of July Movement was behind it. The night before the bombing, two of the rebels spent gelt in one of your cathouses and spilled their guts to a set of twins."

"You believe the story?"

"The nafkas gave up the two guys before there was even a hint of a reward and described them exactly once there was gelt on the table. Also, they know that if we find out they've lied, I'll slit their throats from ear to ear. They are definitely telling the truth."

"Some retribution is in order. I shall check in with Meyer, but do you fancy popping over to the other side of the island with me?"

"Yeah. I've hardly spent any time outside Havana since I arrived here."

"A road trip it is then."

BACK AT THE Moncada Barracks, Alex introduced Ezra to Captain Izzy, and they sank a few beers to keep everyone happy.

"We still don't get visitors very often, Alex, so it is good to see you and your friend."

Alex smiled and clinked his whiskey glass against Izzy's beer can.

"Always great to meet with old pals, as I think we can help each other."

"I thought there might be something when you rang to warn me of your arrival. What gives?"

"We want to bring back two of the rebels for questioning."

Izzy snorted a mouthful of beer out of his nose.

"Good luck with that. We've been on their trail for years and haven't snared one of them. You come down here and announce you're going to take two home for your supper."

Alex's back straightened and Ezra put his drink down on the rickety table in front of him.

"These are responsible for the attempted assassination of Francisco Bautista."

"I am sure they are—doesn't make them any easier to catch though."

"Let's just say that you follow the army code. You have to, otherwise, every soldier would do whatever they want whenever they want, but we don't have any such restrictions on our behavior."

Izzy's grin left his face, and he took a swig of his beer.

"What do you want of me?"

"All we need is for your soldiers to lead us into the foothills where you last know the rebels were camping and we'll take it from there."

"No disrespect, Alex, but do you really believe that two old men such as you are going to escape detection from those rebels? I have never come across any fighters more terrifying than them."

"And no disrespect to you or your men, but Ezra and I grew up in the Bowery and you don't get a tougher neighborhood than that. Show us the route to the rebel encampment and we'll do the rest."

ALEX AND EZRA borrowed some khakis from the barracks' supplies and followed two boys in similar clothing into the woodland half a mile from the camp.

"Another quarter of a mile up to that ridge—that's where the rebels were seen yesterday. We spotted the smoke from their fire, so either they are getting careless…"

"Or they just don't care."

A smile ripped across the boy's face before he and his companion scurried through the trees and away from the 26th of July Movement. Alex nodded at Ezra and they zigzagged over bushes and under branches until they were three hundred feet away from where the boy had pointed. They hunkered down and waited an hour.

As the stars lit up the sky, Alex saw white wisps above the tree line—the rebels had returned to their previous resting place. A nudge and a finger point to Ezra and he got the joke.

The two men inched their way forward, more concerned with remaining silent and not snapping a twig than making quick footage. After another hour they had halved the distance between themselves and what Alex believed was the edge of the camp. There were a bunch of heads sitting still; it must be mealtime.

Thirty long minutes and they were less than one hundred feet from the nearest head. Then Alex froze as he saw two bodies rise and walk towards them. Ezra crouched under a large bush and buried himself into its center while Alex swiveled his head left and right, desperate to find somewhere to hide—he was a sitting duck where he sat.

Ten feet to the west was another dense man-sized bush, so he tried to get inside it before the men got any nearer. No sooner had he buried himself under the leaves than the two rebels slunk past, talking about nothing much that Alex could decipher.

"Do you think Fidel's plan will come good before the end of winter, Ernesto?"

"Don't talk strategy to me when there's man's work to be done."

And without another word, Alex watched as Ernesto relieved himself over the bush containing Ezra while the other guy stood three feet behind him, both hands on a rifle. As the men faced away from him, Alex slowly rose upright and stepped two paces forward, covering the rebel's mouth with his hand. A slicing motion cut open the guy's throat, and he allowed the body to drop to the ground.

The thud made Ernesto swivel his head to see Alex standing in place of his escort. He tried to find his pistol, but Ezra had removed it from the holster on his hip and covered the guy's mouth, pinching his nose between his thumb and first finger.

Alex strode over until he was inches away from Ernesto's face and raised his knife until the point of the blade was by the guy's eyeball. Then there was a crack, and a bullet whizzed past their heads. Ezra slammed Ernesto onto the ground so that he and Alex could make a break for it. Two more bullets flew by their ears but they could tell that these were random shots in the air. It might have taken them over two hours to get there, but after twenty minutes, Ezra and Alex were back at the Moncada Barracks.

22

VITO GENOVESE POPPED back to Cuba to escape some problems in the States; the Feds were seeking to arrest him on narcotics charges and his lawyers needed time to oil the wheels of justice. Meyer was happy to see his business partner again, but Alex was less enthused. He had nothing against the fella but he knew that Genovese's old rival, Frank Costello, was also in town and that could only spell trouble. Meyer was oblivious, as he had no direct business arrangements in play with Costello.

"Let's take Vito out tonight and give him a good time, Alex. We could have dinner with Sarah, then we men could enjoy a show at a club."

Alex wasn't comfortable with the suggestion as he had already arranged to eat with Costello, but there was no shifting Meyer's opinion, so Alex booked an early meal to give himself a chance to break bread with Costello too. He explained his plan to Sarah, who agreed there was nothing but trouble in store that evening.

THE TABLE FOR four was ready at the Montmartre Club by the time Vito and the gang appeared at the joint. They enjoyed a cocktail at the bar and then settled down to read the menus. Even before their pasta dishes had arrived at the table, Alex was getting restive with half an eye on his watch as he slurped down a bowl of spaghetti hoping everyone else had somehow not noticed him eating at double-speed.

As soon as the crockery had been removed by the busboy, Alex said he needed to make a call and when he returned three minutes later, he apologized and explained he had a matter to sort out and hoped to catch up with everybody later in the evening.

A peck on the lips for Sarah and handshakes for the other two and Alex was out of the club faster than the bullets from the gun barrel that had clipped Albert Anastasia earlier that month.

"THIS IS A swell place, Alex."

Frank Costello looked around the Hotel Nacional and couldn't help but notice its luxury. This was the venue that heads of state and other dignitaries stayed in, as well as any Hollywood stars who were performing in town. If you sat in your chair long enough, you were bound to see someone famous. It saved Alex from having to make too big an effort at keeping the guy entertained too.

This was where the syndicate last met and sealed the fate of Benny Siegel —before Charlie was forced to return to Sicily and Alex had been given Vegas to manage on behalf of all the mob bosses. A nostalgic smile appeared on his face, just for a second, and then his expression flitted back under control.

"I'm glad you like the joint, Frank."

"I'm starved. Is there a dish you can recommend on the menu?"

Alex looked down and could think of nothing less he'd like to do than have another dinner.

"The veal is excellent, but you won't go wrong here with anything you choose."

The conversation flowed well enough throughout the meal and as they were finishing up, Frank opened up the discussion to include his fellow countrymen.

"You see many people from Little Italy round this way, Alex?"

"A few. You know how it is, Frank. Cuba is outside of American jurisdiction and Meyer does business with a lot of different people."

Frank nodded and shuffled his silverware around his plate before returning his knife to its original position.

"You heard about the situation in the commission?"

"Frank, I am not Sicilian or even of Italian descent, how am I going to know anything about what happens in your commission?"

"You have ears and people talk, I thought, you know…"

The man wanted to say something but wasn't prepared to express the idea. Alex felt no desire to help dig him out of the hole of his own making—the second dinner was sitting on top of his spaghetti. He must remember that steak and pasta don't go well together.

"So what's happening in the commission, not that it is any of my business?"

"Alex, have you seen Vito Genovese round here of late?"

A blink and he inhaled before answering.

"Not recently. Any reason I should expect him?"

"Nope, I was just wondering."

How Frank refused to make eye contact showed it was more than a passing fancy, but he wouldn't be drawn any further than that.

"Would you have a problem if Vito turned up in Havana?"

"Let's just say I would not be happy with anyone who was wining and dining him—that mutt ain't no good. If I had my way, he'd have been put down years ago."

Alex raised both eyebrows. He could not remember a time before when one Sicilian badmouthed another outside his family. There must be bad blood between those two and Meyer and Sarah were doing the one thing Frank couldn't abide.

"Alex, the concierge told me that the Kitkatt Club is worth a visit—what do you say?"

Frank's hotel had offered excellent advice. While most of the stage shows in Havana were well known for raunchier dance styles than you might find in Vegas, the Kitkatt was renowned even in Cuba. Its dancers wore nothing that would force your imagination to work overtime, and the waitresses were always happy to take you to a private room on the second floor to entertain you in a more personal fashion.

It was perfect—other than one minor detail: that was where Meyer was taking Vito after they ditched Sarah following a show at Santo's Souci nightclub.

"I've got a better idea, Frank. Why don't I make a phone call and invite some girls back to your room? That way, we can enjoy ourselves until the sun comes up and we won't have to bother about bumping shoulders with any sap tourist who's carrying a roll and wants to show off how he's spending it. What do you say?"

"Alex, I don't know. The Kitkatt sounds cool."

"The girls come from there. You'd be getting a Kitkatt act in your own bed and, believe me, no one else can ever claim that has happened to them before."

A twinkle lit up in the corner of Frank's eyes and he rubbed his hands together.

"Then what are we doing here? Let's go."

NOVEMBER 1957

23

"I SPOKE WITH Massimo yesterday afternoon."

"Oh?"

Alex and Meyer were having a quick lunch at the Lima Hastiada; Meyer perused the paper while Alex sat and watched.

"Guess where he's off to tomorrow."

"No idea, Alex."

"That's my point. There's a meeting of the bosses and you have no clue about it."

Alex's friend dropped his newspaper onto the table and ground his molars.

"What are you talking about?"

"You heard. Their banker has not been invited to a get-together of the bosses of America."

"Did Massimo mention who was on the guest list?"

"He wasn't told who would be there. When he got the call, they gave him the location and said to bring only one fella with him. Although he didn't say this to me, reading between the lines, you have to be Italian to have received the golden ticket."

"Alex, Charlie Lucky understood the Jews and Italians succeed more by working together than apart, but this new breed doesn't get the joke."

"I doubt if the ones in charge are that young. Isn't it more likely to be someone like Vito or Frank calling the shots?"

Meyer thought for a moment and nodded. This wasn't the handiwork of some up-and-coming joe. Then he shared his thoughts.

"It would be Genovese, not Costello. When he was over here, Vito told me he was planning a big push to convince the other members of his gang to proclaim him their new leader. Costello has tried his best, but it isn't working out."

"Says the fella who wants to topple him."

They both laughed.

"Meyer, when I had the pleasure of spending time with Frank, he came across as a lightweight, you see? Stand him next to Charlie and you have a cockroach next to a man."

"Nobody stacks up against that Sicilian."

"You know if Frank received an invitation?"

Alex shook his head—the financier was working out the odds. But of what?

THAT NIGHT, MEYER came over for dinner with Alex, Sarah, and David. He remained incensed.

"I've a good mind to gatecrash their party."

Sarah looked up from her chicken and wondered what was going on.

"Meyer, do you think that's a sensible idea? If they don't want you there, you will not do yourself any favors if you turn up unannounced. That's not good business."

"Alex, I know, but the amount of time I have spent with Vito, and the amount of money we've made together, you would think he'd at least acknowledge my existence."

"We are not Italian and should let the matter rest there."

David nodded while he chewed.

"Meyer, my professional advice to you would be to only attend a meeting if they have invited you. No good comes from upsetting people."

"I placed a call to Sicily this afternoon and spoke with Charlie."

Alex stopped eating and stared at Meyer.

"How is he?"

"The fella is well. From what he said, he still has influence over here. I thought he'd focused all his efforts on the Italian end of things."

"Influence?"

"He is installing Vito as the head of his mob. That's the primary purpose of the convention."

"Massimo mentioned it's taking place in Apalachin."

"Alex, that's upstate New York—they held a meeting there last year."

"Did you go to that one?"

"Yes, I was welcome then, when there was money laundering to organize through Cuban hotels."

"You sound bitter."

"Alex, call it resentment for now."

"You'll lose your appetite at this rate."

"Sarah, this is business. My ego is dented, but this is about how I am treated as a partner by these Italian hoods."

"Are you including Charlie in that?"

"Alex, I honestly don't know."

"MASSIMO, I HEARD there was some trouble. What happened?"

"It was an ambush. The Feds arrested dozens of fellas."

"How did you get away?"

"I ran fast—seriously. We arrived at Joe the Barber's house. He'd set up a boardroom in his summerhouse and his men were at the main gate to check everybody in."

"So far, so good."

"Yeah. When I drove through the town, I felt as though there were more local cops on the street than usual, but I thought I was being paranoid."

"And when you were at the meeting?"

"Alex, we were settling down to discuss business—Genovese announced it was time to start the meeting—when one fella shouted and pointed out of the window. There was a horde of cops running through the wood beyond the summerhouse, heading straight for us."

"How did Vito respond?"

"I've got no idea. We stared through the glass for a second or two, and then everybody ran for the door. I was lucky because I was on the third row of chairs on the outer ring—the made men who are members of the inner circle of the commission couldn't push past us."

"And how did you get out of Joe's grounds?"

"My first thought was to rush at the main gate, but as soon as I got out of the summerhouse, I saw that's what was in everyone else's mind. So I took off in the opposite direction to the house and the woods. Over a wall and kept on running. I ditched my gun in a stream at some point, in case I got picked up later. Then a long walk back to town and a taxi to the nearest station."

"You find out what happened to the rest of the fellas, Massimo?"

"The Feds arrested most, from what I heard when I reached Apalachin Main Street."

"Vito?"

"Wouldn't be surprised. I mean, the chiefs were the last out of the summerhouse and the speed of those Feds meant those fellas must have been caught."

"So that means they've arrested every boss in America?"

"Not by a long way. There was nobody from Chicago or California that I could see. It was a select band of a hundred or so, but not everyone."

"MEYER, I HAVE to ask you something."

"Go ahead, Alex. No secrets between friends. We live together, we love together."

"Did you drop a dime to the Feds over the Apalachin meeting?"

Meyer stirred his coffee as the two men sat in his home that night. Their respective families had long gone to bed, and the men were alone. Meyer smiled at Alex and sipped his drink.

"I'm surprised you need to ask me such a question, Alex."

"And I'm noticing you haven't answered me."

"What benefit would I gain by having Vito's nose bent out of shape when he would have taken over his mob and prevented those Italians from splitting up Anastasia's narcotics business operations?"

"You tell me. Costello was out of the top seat, and Vito needed to consolidate his power base. When you spoke with Charlie, did he explain to you what his plans were regarding Genovese?"

"Alex, Charlie Lucky wanted a smooth handover of power from Frank to his successor."

"I'll ask you one more time. Did Charlie want that person to be Vito?"

Another curled lip and nothing more.

"I was fortunate not to get invited in the end, wasn't I, Alex?"

"Sure, Meyer. The price of it all is that Hoover can't pretend there's no such thing as organized crime—not with his men charging fifty or more with attending a mob meeting."

"Alex, whoever chose the same venue as the previous commission meeting is a marked man—what a *schmendrick*."

"You think the syndicate will ever meet again?"

"Not in our lifetime. All that's left is the Italian commission and we are not welcome at the table. Be grateful we are living the high life in Havana. Times in America are only going to get harder, my friend."

24

"HAVE YOU SEEN Esther?"

"Not in the last couple of weeks, David. Why do you ask?"

Alex's son stared at the floor and the kid had trouble written all over his face, mixed with the embarrassment of telling his father that his sister was in desperate need of help.

"She's almost fallen into a tequila bottle and I'm not sure she will ever swim out, Pop."

"Booze?"

A nod from David.

"Anything more than that?"

A shake of David's head and Alex relaxed. There was so much else Esther could have got involved in.

"Where does she prop up a bar?"

"Montmartre Club. It's one reason there's only alcohol coursing through her veins; nobody would try to do anything to a family member of Alex Cohen in the middle of Meyer Lansky's joint."

"Do you think she'll be there now?"

"The place is open, isn't it? Then you can find her with an elbow on the bar and a cocktail in the other hand."

"How long has she been like this?"

"When did she arrive in Havana? About a week after that."

"This is no joking matter, David."

"You're right, Pop."

Alex discerned the edge of disappointment in David's voice, but neither made of it any more than that.

◆ ◆ ◆

ALEX HIGHTAILED IT over to the Montmartre and discovered Esther just where his son had predicted. As he approached, the barman nodded at him and walked to the other end of his station to allow the two Cohens to talk in private.

"Hey, Esther."

"If it isn't the great Alex Cohen. What a hero of the people you've become."

He couldn't understand all that she said, but she swayed on her stool and Alex knew not to worry too much—the woman was drunk.

"Good to see you too. Can I buy you a coffee?"

"There's no need, Alex, my-dear. Jose has been looking after me all this time."

He looked round to find Esther's benefactor, but there was nobody else there, just the bartender. Alex pointed at him.

"Is that Jose?"

"Sure is." A hiccup erupted from deep within Esther and she seemed quite surprised it had emerged from her body.

"His name's not Jose—he is Hector."

"The barmen here are all Jose to me. Saves me having to focus on what they're called and frees me up to think about what I want to drink next instead."

With that, Esther raised an arm and waved at Hector, who tried to avoid acknowledging her motions, but Alex nodded and he sauntered over.

"Another mojito, if you'd be so kind, Jose."

"Sure thing. For you, sir?"

"Two coffees and no more cocktails for the lady."

Sometimes, being Meyer's business partner had its advantages; Hector needed no other instructions to do Alex's bidding.

"Aw, don't be like that, Alex, my boy."

"I'm not being anything, Esther. I'd like to have a conversation with you, is all."

"Then let's talk and drink."

Alex drew up a stool and sat next to his sister.

"This place isn't any good for you."

"It's a decent bar when you let Jose do his job properly."

"Not the Montmartre, I'm talking about the country."

"If it's good enough for you, then it should be all right for me."

"Esther, I have business interests here and you've been on vacation for longer than either of us can remember."

She swayed some more and sipped the last vestige of liquor out of her cocktail glass, just as Hector arrived with their hot drinks. Esther eyed her mug suspiciously as wisps of steam scurried upward to the ceiling.

"I have nothing to go back for, Alex."

"You have your life to live—the rest of the family to spend time with. Here, the most you can do is tread water."

"Let me work for you then. That'd give me something to do—a reason to live here."

"I have Sarah and David already working for me. Any more household members and we'd have to form a union."

"And the problem with that is…?"

Alex was silent for a spell because he didn't want to be forced to say unkind things to his sister when he knew the truth would hurt.

"There's no room for you, Esther. It's time you went home."

"Then come back with me, Alex."

"No can do. I have investments here to look after. You are the one who must go home."

A drop of liquid departed Esther's eye and meandered around her cheek before dripping onto the knee of her dress. Alex raised a first finger toward her and wiped the moisture off her face.

"Don't worry. I'll take care of you and make sure everything is okay. I owe you that much and it's what I do."

"Not since we were kids, Alex."

"You'd be surprised."

THE FOLLOWING WEEK, David took Esther for a last dinner at Alex and Sarah's before she flew off the next day. The mood was somber, and they served no alcohol with the meal.

"You look well, Esther."

"Ever since the Montmartre stopped giving me credit, it's been impossible to get a drink in this town. Nowhere else would serve me."

"These places all clam up. It's almost as if they are run by the same bunch of fellas."

Alex winked at Sarah, who acknowledged the gesture, and David cleared his throat.

"I'm flying over with Esther to spend some time in New York. Just for a little while until she's settled back in. Isn't that right, Auntie?"

"Don't you call me that. You make me sound too old, but yes, it'll be nice to have the company, if only for a few days."

"Good idea, David."

Alex smiled and basked in the glow of having so many members of his family around him, even if it was only for one evening. He was missing Esther before she'd left the country, and he wanted some way of maintaining the connection they'd formed while she buried her head in the neck of a bottle.

"Esther, how would you like to do some work for me in New York?"

"What do you mean, Alex?"

"Well, I still have investments and ventures that need tending in America. I can't think of anyone I would trust more with those confidential matters than my sister. What do you reckon?"

"I am not convinced. I've spent most of my life looking after the family, not doing paperwork."

"You're a smart woman, Esther. I'm sure you'd be able to get the hang of things pretty quickly," chipped in Sarah.

"While he's in Manhattan, David can find some office space to your liking and we can take it from there. He can show you the ropes and only come back when you're comfortable with what you're doing. Would that be all right with you, son?"

"Sure thing, Pop."

"What do you say, sis'?"

"I don't know…"

"We'll get you set up and you could do a trial month. If the work's not to your liking then—no harm, no foul—you just tell me and I will get someone in to take over for you. If not, then we're all in clover."

"I guess I've nothing to lose."

"And in case it's not obvious, I'll pay you top dollar for your efforts. This isn't charity—it's important work I need doing and I trust you to do it for me."

"Then when you're in town, we'd be guaranteed to meet up and talk business."

"That's the spirit, Esther."

25

ALEX RETURNED FROM dropping Esther and David at the airport, which had given him an excuse to wave Esther off with an enormous hug. Sarah was sat in the living room listening to the radio when he walked in and turned it off because she knew Alex was not a fan of the local beats—he had gained a tense relationship with music since the passing of Rebecca, from what Sarah could make out.

"I hope Esther can get things straight now she's left this place, Alex."

"Yes, me too, it was as though she dived inside a tequila bottle and never got out."

"That might have been what it looked like, but you know that wasn't the reason she tried to drown herself."

"Huh?"

Sarah sighed because Alex was so good at reading people apart from those who were nearest to him; then he was incapable of seeing beyond the nose on his face.

"She came over here because she was desperate to rekindle a relationship with you, Alex. Why else would she search you out after all these years?"

"And I spent most of her stay here without even giving her the time of day."

"We both know how happy you were that she'd made the effort, how glad you were when David and then Moishe returned to your world. But it takes more than hosting a meal to forge a relationship with someone you've studiously ignored for your entire adult life."

"You're talking about Esther, right?"

"Yes. I have never doubted you wanted to be close to your sons—no matter what circumstances conspired to prevent you from being there. But when you walked away from that tenement in the Bowery, it was as if it vanished in your mind as soon as you'd turned the corner at the end of the block."

Alex was silent as he rested next to Sarah, his hand holding hers.

"Did I cause her that much pain, Sarah?"

"What do you think?"

"Is that what I'm like to my family. Am I that toxic?"

"That's not quite what I meant, Alex."

"But I took a quiet, unassuming lonely woman and turned her into a drunk within a week of seeing me again. And what of David and the other boys?"

"He's remained sober all the time he has been with us in Havana."

"That's not what I meant, and you knew that. Am I destroying him too?"

"If you remember, when he first came over, he was a shell of a man. And you've brought the sparkle back into his eyes."

"But now he has been witness to all sorts of conversations about matters which an ordinary lawyer should not hear."

"That's a decision you make every time you talk about money laundering with Meyer in front of him. Have you allowed him to be within earshot of some of your other, less savory, discussions?"

Alex thought for a minute and then shook his head.

"Not that I've noticed, but I had stopped worrying about keeping him away from those aspects of my business life. You are right, I should be more circumspect for his sake."

"If you want him to keep his nose clean, then you shouldn't rub it in the dirt."

"David must only touch legitimate contracts and nothing more. I should be more careful in future with what I expose him to. The boy deserves to be kept away from Genovese and fellas like him."

December 10, 1957

26

THE NEWEST RESORT in Havana was Meyer's Riviera, which boasted more rooms than any hotel outside Vegas with a sea view for every guest. Meyer moved to the top floor and lived in the presidential suite from the moment the place was built and furnished. He had nothing against the house he'd bought when he arrived in Cuba but saw no reason to live in such a small place when he and his family could roam around a penthouse whose footprint matched that of the entire hotel complex.

During the second week of December, Meyer officially launched the hotel with a star-studded show featuring local dancers but with an American headline act: Ginger Rogers. Tourists flew in just to take advantage of the chance to see this Hollywood icon in the flesh. Meyer knew how to put on a good party.

After she stepped off the stage, Lansky went to her dressing room, along with Alex and Sarah who was a huge fan, and made small talk and gave compliments until the hordes of tourists clamoring for her attention got too much to ignore. Only when Meyer had thanked her for the umpteenth time and shut the door on the way out did he express his real opinion: "That woman might wiggle her ass, but she can't sing a goddam note."

"Oh, Meyer, what do you know? She was brilliant."

Meyer threw a glance at Sarah to show he disagreed, but they both left it at that. No one was looking for an argument—the feeling in the building was joyful, and there was no need to burst that bubble.

ALEX AND SARAH left Meyer on the ground floor to continue to schmooze with his guests—mainly mob bosses and other business associates. Instead, the couple headed for the second-story restaurant to break bread with

Moishe, who had traveled over to the island for the occasion. Perhaps he'd gained a love of Ginger from his mother.

"Good to see you, my boy."

"Did you catch the show, Moishe?"

"Of course I did, Mama."

"She sang so beautifully."

"Better not let Meyer hear you talk like that."

Moishe looked askance at his father.

"Not a fan then?"

"Maybe he prefers Fred Astaire," added David and everyone apart from Alex laughed. Alex wasn't sure he could pick the guy out of a line-up. When he went to the movies, he preferred westerns. The amusement died down when he suggested they check their menus before the waiter returned to collect their order.

"Moishe, how long are you in town for?"

"Not sure right now, Pop."

Alex raised an eyebrow but carried on staring at the menu, pretending he was having difficulties deciding what to eat. He and Sarah both knew he would take the steak because that is what he always ate if he had the chance when they were out.

"That's funny because when your aunt visited us, I asked her the same question and got the same evasive answer. Turned out, she wasn't planning on going home."

Moishe put down his menu and a red tinge entered his cheeks.

"You too?"

He nodded slowly. Alex sighed and sipped his Scotch.

"Spill."

"I'm not running away from the States, but I'd like to come to Cuba and work with you."

"Has everyone decided what they want?"

Alex sidestepped responding to Moishe's statement, and he took his cue from being ignored. Sarah glanced at Moishe, who eyed David and his mother before trying to understand what was going on in his father's mind. The conversation twisted and turned, but Alex avoided saying anything to Moishe about his reasons for coming to Havana.

Once they had eaten, Alex handed an envelope to both his boys and wished them well. Each one contained some chips on the house and he led them all to the casino. Once the two men were settled at a roulette wheel, he and Sarah left them to it and headed over to the bar for a nightcap.

"DO YOU WANT Moishe to join the family business?"

"That depends which of the two family businesses you are talking about, doesn't it, Sarah?"

"Would you want him involved on the same basis as David?"

"At most, yes."

"Why the note of caution, Alex? If you are okay with David operating the legitimate side of your affairs, what's wrong with Moishe doing the same?"

Alex thought for a moment. He sounded hypocritical when she said what he believed out loud.

"David came to me because he wanted us to connect again, then we found him work. The only time Moishe has come to me during his adulthood has been to ask for me to save him, and now he wants me to pay him to work. There is the difference, I'd say. Besides, whenever someone says they are not running away, you find that is exactly what they are doing, and lying to me is not the greatest start to a business relationship."

ALEX SAUNTERED BACK to the casino and found that Moishe and David had separated; Moishe had stayed at the wheel of fortune and David had sought the pleasures of a poker table. His father tapped him on the shoulder and indicated he wanted to talk. Moishe looked down at his not inconsiderable winnings, thought for a second, and cashed in his chips, being careful to return Alex's seed capital with ten percent interest.

They walked out of the casino and Alex found a quiet staff room where they could take the coffees Alex had bought along the way and talk in private.

"Pop, I have a wide range of business experience and from what David has told me, it sounds like you could benefit from some sound financial advice."

"Could I?"

"Aw, it's not a criticism. I just mean that he mentioned you were looking to make some significant investments in Cuba, and I thought getting information about tax matters from a trusted source would be useful for you, and I'd love for us to work together. To be honest, I'm resentful of how happy David has been since he moved here. I want some of that."

Alex stirred his coffee. Moishe was right. David and he had got closer since the fella's arrival in town, and the work was the glue that kept them together. After all, Alex was not a natural family man and had spent his life keeping himself to himself and protecting his family from the evils of his work.

"Moishe, to be honest, I am not too sure if that is the best thing for us to do. And before you pull that expression, let me explain my thinking."

His son tried to remove the sulk from his face but looked as though he was having a mild seizure and Alex couldn't help but raise a smile.

"When you last visited me, it was to ask for my help, which you received with a glad heart on my account. We had both been foolish to allow the silence to build between us, and as your father, I allowed that situation to occur. I apologize to you for that. I thought I was doing the right thing by having nothing to do with you boys so that the business I was in would not taint you."

Another sip and Alex wiped his lips on the back of his hand.

"Now, we are both men and you come to me asking to work for me, to be my accountant. And I respect you for doing that. I do not imagine for one moment that it has been easy for you to approach me and ask such a thing when in earlier days, you were so appalled and disgusted by what I do. That takes balls, son."

Moishe allowed a half-smile to flow across his mouth, but he knew he was being prepared for a kiss-off.

"I believe you when you say you are not running away from anything, despite the issues you had with a certain client in the past. But I wonder, why now?"

"There's no particular reason, Pop. I'm in a lull at the moment and having only one client appeals to me. The idea of getting deeply involved in the full details of one business sounds great. Sticking around throughout the year and seeing the complete consequences of everything you do. When you are a jobbing accountant, you mostly prepare end-of-year accounts and tax returns."

"Moishe, I can see how your experience would be useful to me and you are right to play on my old dealings with the internal revenue, but that is not enough. I would be thrilled for us to see more of each other and you are welcome to stay here as long as you want, but I believe you should return to the United States."

"Why do you trust David with your business affairs and not me?"

"That is not the situation. I am happy for you to look after my fiscal affairs… but in America. At the moment, your aunt Esther is settling into our New York offices and I would like you to join her there and manage my US finances."

At the back of his mind, Alex didn't like the idea of all his closest family huddled on this one small island. Despite his faith in Meyer's plans, a part of him wanted to secure a base back home.

27

MOISHE AND ALEX sauntered back to the casino and checked how David was faring. When they'd left, there were only a handful of chips in front of him, but his eggs were sunny-side up on their return. He was smiling as he sat behind a wall of ceramic discs. Despite David's broad grin, his father bent down and whispered in his ear.

"I know you want to stay here but you, me, and Moishe have some business to discuss."

As soon as the words had left Alex's lips, David folded his hand and walked away. The chips could wait until later, and no one was going to steal them from the son of Alex Cohen.

He took the two men to the bar where the maître d' secured a quiet booth at the back, half-lit and away from the other guests—just the way Alex liked it.

"First, David, let me introduce you to our new recruit."

"Mazel tov."

"He will manage my American financial interests from an accounting perspective. Of course, you continue to be my US legal eagle."

David slapped his brother on the back to welcome him to the legitimate Cohen crew. The only other member was Sarah, and she had gone home after the excitement of seeing Ginger Rogers and the concerns about Moishe's safety. Alex reckoned she'd be pleased with the outcome. He'd look after his son without tying him to Cuba like the rest of them.

"Meyer keeps making me an offer he says I shouldn't refuse, but I am not too sure. He thinks I should invest in a new entertainment resort in Havana. It's called The Panama and will be the usual mix of hotel, casino, restaurant, and stage—just like Benny Siegel envisaged for his Las Vegas joints."

David and Moishe glanced at each other as neither wanted to be the first to speak. Alex noticed their reticence and filled in the silence with more details: the upfront size of the investment, the opportunities to achieve profit, and the risks as he saw them.

"As minister for entertainment, Meyer will wave through any paperwork we generate, so that end is fine, but we need to make certain payments to Batista in order to grease the wheels of government."

"Are you saying you have to pay off the president to get a gaming license?"

"I don't call it a bribe because Batista doesn't. He prefers for everyone to think of it as a personal donation paid directly into an overseas bank account. And if you don't make the payment, then you don't get the license, even if you pay the gaming fee in full at the time of the application."

"Well, that is a legitimate business expense as you are making a political contribution, right?"

"You're the accountant, Moishe."

"As your legal counsel, Batista's description doesn't sound like a bribe, especially if at some point we could generate some paperwork to confirm the donation took place."

"David, that won't happen and you know it, but we are missing the bigger picture here. Should I invest in an entertainment complex in Cuba?"

His two sons looked at each other and remained silent until David broke ranks.

"What's the upside, Pop?"

"Casinos make millions a month—that's dollars I'm talking about. Once the place is running at full steam, I'd only need to keep it ticking over for, say, three or four years and I would never have to worry about money again. More to the point, none of us would have to work another day as long as we lived."

Moishe whistled because a new world was opening up to him as the conversation progressed. Alex chose not to mention that most of the profit would be generated by skimming the house take at the casino and earning income from laundering gelt for other business associates.

"If everything is as good as you say and the money will flow like wine out of a bottle, why are you asking our opinion?"

Alex smiled at David's caution.

"I don't know how far I trust Batista."

"With the donation? To keep his part of the bargain?"

"Oh no, all that would be safe. Batista makes money along with the owners of every hotel in Cuba. He would be happy to dip his beak in yet another money-making scheme. You should visit the other side of the island. In Havana, Batista has an iron grip on his people, but that's not the case all around the country. The rebels control entire towns and the outlying regions. If they topple the general, then we'll be left with nothing but the shirts on our backs."

David was the first to respond.

"If you believe the rebels will take over, why are you even contemplating buying into The Panama?"

"That's an excellent question. I guess the reason is that right now the rebels are nowhere near Havana and Batista remains in power. Every day that situation carries on being the case is another one for us to make money. If we build the joint and we hold out for three or five years, then you'll find me in Florida with my feet up by the pool."

"Pop, first, I can't imagine you ever sinking into retirement. Second, from the way you've spoken, the twenty-sixth of July Movement won't take five years to attack this city. My advice would be to stay clear of The Panama."

"I may have only been here a few days, but all the risk you've just described sounds like a thing you should want to avoid. A better plan would be to take your money and build something in Vegas or Atlantic City. They are known quantities without the need to worry about insurrection."

"Moishe, what you are not taking into account is my relationship with Meyer—you too, David. He judges people on how much they are prepared to go into business with him. If you refuse him, then you are diminished in his eyes and I have worked with him since I was a young man—from the days of Prohibition. This is the first time he has ever offered me an investment opportunity of my own. There have been many ways we've made money together, mainly through his seed capital and my hard work. This occasion is different. If I say no to him on this, he might never offer me another similar chance as long as he lives. And the fella knows how to turn gelt into more gelt."

The three men drank their coffees and stared at the center of the table, not making eye contact, to consider all the angles as dispassionately as possible.

"You are my sons and I love you, but you need to say something otherwise you are failing me as advisors."

David chipped in.

"The way I see the situation is that you either keep Meyer happy and risk everything you own or disappoint the man, but remain safe."

"Is losing every cent you possess worth the price of making Lansky feel more positive toward you?"

"Isn't that too simplistic, Moishe?

"Not based on what you've said this evening. If there is more to this, then you should explain it, but I can't see why you'd want to put that much capital at risk. We're talking a seven-figure amount, right?"

"Yes."

"And the money is yours, which you've saved over the years as a financial cushion—what the rest of us would call a pension?"

"That's the sum of it."

"Invest in US blue chips and save yourself the aggravation."

"Spoken like a true accountant, Moishe."

"That is what I am and only a few hours ago, you made me responsible for your American assets. What else did you think I was going to say?"

"David, do you agree with your brother?"

"I see things differently, perhaps because I've seen how you operate in Havana. What Moishe is unaware of is the power you wield and the influence you have with the Italians back home. These men run swathes of America and make up an important source of future revenue for you. The fact the cash might not come from legitimate sources is beside the point in this discussion."

Alex added, "One reason that The Panama is so attractive to me is that the profit it will generate can be entirely legal. We would become like any other wealthy family—like the Rockefellers."

"Only with less foreskin."

They all laughed at Moishe's comment and took a minute to settle down.

"Pop, you asked for our opinions and now you have got them. Moishe advises against The Panama and so do I. There is too much risk and not enough upside for the *tsoris*."

Alex still thought the hassle was worth the effort, but the idea of risking everything—including the lives of Sarah and the boys—was too high for him to commit to the deal just yet.

28

HAVING TOLD HIS kids to go home to bed, Alex walked through the casino one last time in case there was a star to schmooze before hitting the hay. Something about a poker table on the other side of the room made him head over and take a closer look.

As Alex approached the four men holding their cards, one face stood out: Merrick Townsend, who he'd last seen at the launch night of the Flamingo in Vegas. No, that wasn't right—at the Kefauver hearing. A touch of the shoulder made Townsend glance away from his cards, and the frown transformed into a toothy grin as soon as he recognized his assailant.

"I didn't know you were in town, Alex."

"Good to see you, senator. How long are you in Havana?"

"I fly out the day after tomorrow. This was a quick trip to show Meyer some support and then back to the States."

"You still enjoy a game of stud. Do you fancy playing a few hands in more private surroundings?"

"Now?"

"Unless you have something better to do. I reckon we can rustle up three or four other interested parties."

Merrick threw in his hand and walked off with Alex, only to be stopped twenty seconds later by a busboy who had collected his chips from the table.

WITHIN FIFTEEN MINUTES, Alex, Merrick, Sammy Davis Jr., and Peter Lawford sat in a room on the first floor with a pack of cards on a table sporting a green baize surface. Many of the big-name stars had already gone to bed, but Sammy and his friend had been hanging at the bar, keeping the crowd entertained with their impromptu Vegas schtick in Cuba.

The group had only played two hands before Merrick opened up the conversation beyond commenting on which cards were face up for all to see.

"Alex, some of our Italian friends are making a name for themselves back in Newark."

"That so, Merrick? I thought you were responsible for the good people of Massachusetts."

"I was, but I ceded my seat to Jack Kennedy and now I represent New Jersey."

The singers stared at their cards and tried not to show their disinterest in Merrick's chatter.

"Yeah, over the last year, the chief of police has noticed a marked increase in criminal activity in certain parts of the city, shall we say?"

"Any particular names come up?"

"New Yorkers who have never seemed to be interested in my state but who are stretching their wings."

Merrick glanced at Sammy and Peter, and Alex could see he wasn't comfortable being too explicit in front of these men who he counted as strangers. In contrast, Alex had known them both since the Flamingo launched and Benny attracted Californian celebrities to perform on stage for him.

"And are these friends causing you any issues?"

Another glance at the singers by Merrick.

"Let's just say they have a different way of doing business than we are used to, and that caused some feathers to be ruffled which I did not appreciate."

"Would you like me to intercede on your behalf over these difficulties or have they been resolved?"

"Thank you for the kind offer, Alex, but at present everything and everyone has calmed down. Last month was a different story."

Alex raised an eyebrow.

"Some mom-and-pop stores were refusing to recognize the right of our New York friends to provide insurance services direct to the door, and sufficient unpleasantness ensued that the local police asked my office to get involved."

"You called out the state troops over some fellas running a protection racket?"

Now it was Merrick's turn to move his eyebrows upwards.

"To be blunt, Alex, I can live with a few guineas coming into New Jersey and shaking down a general store or two. When that causes blood to run on the streets, that's where I draw the line. There was open gang warfare, and every day there was some mobster or other gunned down on the sidewalk. It got to a point where ordinary folk were too scared to step outside after dark."

"And you can't lose an entire neighborhood of voters, Merrick."

"You understand how American politics works."

"I do my best." A smirk appeared on Alex's face as he recalled his first year in the US when he walked bags of greenbacks over to Tammany Hall for Waxey Gordon.

"Did our Italian friends tread on anybody else's toes when they shipped into Newark?"

"You know they did, Alex. What made matters worse was that the FBI has a watching brief over organized crime—ever since the Apalachin arrests. I couldn't ignore the situation. Not only would I be seen to be soft on crime by my voters, but Hoover might have suspected I had a closer relationship to the gangsters than was real."

"Well, unless they've paid you off in the last week or so, it sounds as if you have no business transacted with these newcomers; pardon the observation."

"For sure, we came to an accommodation, but that's not the point. The last thing I want is for Hoover to figure that out. If he does, I'll be ruined."

"And that would never do, Merrick."

Sammy laid his cards down to reveal a royal flush and everyone else whistled out of respect. Alex had seen it build up for a while, or so he thought, but Merrick had been too engrossed in the conversation to pay sufficient attention to his own hand.

"If you guys are going to carry on talking shop, Peter and I might as well go back to the tables outside."

"No need for that, Sammy. Merrick and I can wait until later before discussing more business—isn't that right?"

"Oh yes. No offense to you, gentlemen, but I had to get that off my chest. The intention wasn't to put a crimp in your evening."

"None taken, Merrick."

AN HOUR LATER and Merrick was up a few hundred and the two singers were doing much better than that. Only Alex was down, but he had decided not to win a penny even before the deck was first shuffled. He had hosted the game to make them happy and not to take the shirts off their backs. Alex glanced at his watch, saw how late it was, and stifled a yawn. Merrick checked the time for himself.

"Well, gentlemen. There comes a point in every evening when a gentleman should stop playing cards and seek other pursuits, wouldn't you say, Alex?"

"I'll see what I can organize, Merrick."

A brief call to the reception and five minutes later, a knock at the door interrupted the men's conversation. Six girls in various states of undress stood before the card sharps and introduced themselves to the group. Then everybody moved over to more comfortable surroundings on the other side of the room, where large armchairs and couches gave each man the opportunity to be joined by more than one woman whose aim was to see to their physical pleasures. Alex made sure he was on the edge. Besides, the girls knew better than to inveigle their way into his arms. He was the host, not a participant.

Once shirt buttons were undone, Alex wished everyone well and went home to lie next to Sarah, who needed no fishnet stockings and corset to warm the depths of his heart, although as he slipped under the sheets, she let out one of the loudest snores Cuba had ever heard.

MARCH 1958

29

ALEX PUT SENATOR Merrick Townsend out of his mind over the following months, and he doubted whether the man gave him a second thought either. Although the fact didn't affect him in the slightest, the first night of the impending Passover was set to take place on Good Friday. A week before, the phone rang with Ezra's voice at the other end.

"Sorry to bother you in the evening, but there's something that needs your attention."

"Where are you and what's the problem?"

"Alex, I'm at the Riviera and you just need to come over so we can discuss the situation in person."

Alex recognized that insistent tone and would have been a fool to ignore it. He apologized to Sarah for running out on her dinner and headed over to the complex, where the hotel dick met him in the lobby and took him up to the seventh floor. Still no sign of Ezra.

In room 705 were two men and a woman. Merrick sat at a dressing table in the master bedroom, and Ezra stood five feet from him. Lying prone on the ground was a nude girl. Dead. From Alex's first glance, she looked as though she might have bled out. Merrick's lap was covered by a corner of the sheet and a pile of clothes on the floor showed that he too was as naked as the day he was born. When Ezra noticed Alex's presence, he stepped away from the senator to have a quiet word with Alex in the living room of the suite.

"Have we worked out what happened, Ezra?"

"Townsend rang reception half an hour ago and asked to speak with you. Instead, they put me on as I was in the building and he told me he needed help of a personal nature. When he let me in, I found Lupita Alfaro as you see her now."

"She is one of the regular nafkas?"

"Yep."

"I assume she didn't bleed to death due to natural causes?"

"No. He says he can't remember what he did."

"Ezra, of course, you were right to call me. I'm going to need you to manage the clean-up and see that everyone leaves the building. Before we get to that, let me speak with Townsend."

They returned to the bedroom and Alex bent down next to Lupita. He eased her long black hair out of the way to see her face and neck better. Her throat was red, turning to purple with recent bruising. You didn't need to be a coroner to spot the holes in her chest and the scissors lying between her and the bed. Alex counted at least three bottles of tequila strewn empty on the floor. He stood back up and turned to the senator.

"How's Sylvia?"

"Huh?"

"Your wife, Merrick. How are Sylvia and the kids? I haven't seen you since the launch night of this place."

He gestured all around him to show that he was talking about the Riviera Hotel.

"Oh, they're fine… What am I going to tell them?"

"Merrick, from what I can see, you aren't going to say a word. This girl will not be missed and her body is unlikely ever to be found. We will make sure of that."

"Can you? I mean, would you do that for me?"

"We are friends, Merrick, and that's what pals do. We look after each other in time of need."

"Alex, we were just horsing around. The next thing I remember I woke up on the bed and there she was on the floor—just as she is now…"

Townsend's eyes stared at the smooth skin of Lupita Alfaro and he cried.

"She was always such a gentle child."

"You'd met her before?"

"Whenever I'd had the good fortune to visit the Riviera, I'd ask for her. To assist me through the loneliness of the nights."

"I understand, Merrick."

"I recall us drinking and joking and getting intimate, and then I must have blacked out. When I woke up, there she was."

"So you said."

"I tried to revive her, but she was already cold to the touch. I didn't know what I was doing."

"Of course not, but we are here to look after you now."

Townsend looked up in between his sobs and mouthed his thanks. Alex indicated to Ezra that they needed to go back to the living room.

"Any idea what that butcher did to the girl?"

"The scissors came from a desk drawer, but why he did it? Your guess is as good as mine. I don't buy that he blacked out though."

"He's very careful to not get too intoxicated. Most of his waking days are spent worrying about what the voters in New Jersey think of him, so he is discreet in his partying. But there sure was a lot of booze drunk next door last night."

"What would you like me to do, Alex?"

"Once we get Merrick out of the way, organize the removal of the body. Bury it somewhere outside of Havana where it will never be found. Is there any evidence connecting Townsend to the girl?"

"The concierge procured her after a call from the good senator and the reception staff know he had an issue that needed your attention. Other than that, we're good."

"Fine. Get a camera from downstairs and take a quick photo of Merrick and the corpse in that room. He needs to see it happen."

"Once I realized the situation, I phoned up for one."

Ezra pointed at a coffee table and Alex smiled.

"Well done. Did he hire this place for the night or was he staying here?"

"He is registered here for another two nights."

"Not anymore. Get him moved to a penthouse suite and change the records accordingly. Get some hush money to anyone who came into contact with this mess. Enough so they won't talk and if you think they can't be trusted to keep their mouths shut, bury them in the same grave as the nafka."

Ezra nodded to show he understood his instructions and without waiting for further conversation, rushed back to take a photo before Townsend moved from his spot. Alex followed him to the bedroom and bent down in front of the senator so their eyes were at the same level.

"Merrick, listen to me. None of this transpired. In a few minutes, we'll bring you to a fresh room, which I will comp. If I had known you were in town, I would have comped your entire stay, but that doesn't matter right now. Once you go to your room, we shall deal with the girl and you will forget this ever happened. At the end of your vacation here, you'll return to your wife and children and nothing will have changed."

"Her name was Lupita, and she was the most gentle person in the world."

"That she was, Merrick. But she is dead and you are alive and we need to think about the living. You, Sylvia, and the kids."

Townsend sobbed again, but Alex's patience was running thin. True, the guy was sitting three feet away from a dead prostitute whom he must have killed in a murderous, drunken frenzy. But Alex wanted to get back home before Sarah threw what remained of his dinner in the trash. Once the man had recovered enough to speak, he asked a simple question.

"Why did you take a photo? There was a flash, and I glanced up to see Ezra with a camera in his hand."

"You are confused. That never happened, and I've been in this room all the time."

Merrick nodded acceptance and looked around for his underwear. When he stood up, the corner of the sheet fell away to reveal he was only wearing his socks.

"Let's find Merrick some fresh things to wear."

Alex rummaged through the chest of drawers in the bedroom and found some shorts for the man to put on, while Ezra fumbled in a wardrobe to fetch some slacks and a shirt. That would be enough to take him to the suite. Once the guy had left the hotel room, Alex asked Ezra to get the film processed by a reliable fella and for the negatives and a print to be sent straight over when they were ready.

"Politicians think they can do anything. One day, that photo of Merrick's schlong and that nafka's body sliced to ribbons will be worth a million dollars. Until then, I'll keep it safe."

By the morning, the room was clean enough to receive its next guest and by the afternoon, Lupita Alfaro was buried in seven feet of soil in some woods fifty miles from Havana.

30

ALEX MET UP with Meyer after Passover; his friend took religious festivals far more seriously than he did and Alex wasn't in the mood for a rabbinical argument about a pile of *matzo* and other unleavened foodstuffs. Although he hadn't seen the fella for almost a month, they picked up their conversation as though they had last spoken the day before.

"Have you given any more thought to The Panama, Alex?"

"Yes, but I remain unsure whether now is the right time for that scale of investment."

"If you are cash poor, I've told you I am happy to advance you the money at more than reasonable terms. This is a great opportunity and I don't want you to miss out."

"Meyer, I know it but I need more time."

"That's the one commodity we have so little of. If I was half my age, then I'd be able to get so much more done with my life."

"It's not over just yet, Meyer." A smile appeared on both their faces.

"If you won't invest in The Panama, then perhaps you'll dip your beak in a less risky venture, although you can bet your shirt on this coming good."

"What's this other deal you're hustling?"

"Don't be like that, Alex. I need to do something about the Nacional."

"But you do not own it, or at least I didn't think you did."

"Yes, Batista's name is on the deeds, ever since his return to the island before he seized power. However, I view it as my hotel and I am tired of watching customers come in to eat at the restaurant and then go off around the corner to gamble or watch a show."

"Is there room to add a stage?"

"If they've handed over their gelt to buy my food, then I'll let them wander off to listen to a song and a joke from the best that Hollywood can provide. It's gaming money that I want."

"You're going to put a casino inside the Nacional?"

"Why ever not, Alex? Just because it is old doesn't mean it can't bend with the times."

Meyer leaned back in their Lima Hastiada booth and surveyed the room. In the middle of the afternoon, there were only two occupied tables, and they were both far enough away for any conversation between Alex and Meyer to fall on deaf ears.

"Imagine a gaming floor overlooking the bright lights of the city at night. Tourists and high rollers will flock to the place to be seen to play in the swankiest gaming joint in town. We are going to turn the most luxurious hotel in Latin America into the greatest casino on God's earth."

"How does Batista feel about your plans?"

"He agreed to give me the gaming license yesterday, and I wired appropriate funds overseas and to the government account today. It's a done deal. As I am the minister for entertainment, how could I refuse my own request to convert some usage of the Nacional over to gambling?"

A grin ripped across Lansky's face—this was why he had spent those years schmoozing with Batista while everybody else focused on Vegas. Meyer's vision was so much broader than Benny's in building an entertainment capital out of nothing.

"Meyer, how can I help?"

TWO WEEKS LATER, Alex met a fella at the airport from times gone by—Gus Greenbaum from Las Vegas. Along with his sidekick Moe Sedway, Gus had taken over the Flamingo Hotel the day after Benny was whacked. That showed how much both Meyer and the Italian members of the syndicate trusted him—the previous owner had not been careful enough with their money.

"Good to see you again, Gus. How's Vegas?"

"All is fine, thank you. Massimo sends his regards."

"Pleased to hear it. We are going to be working together in Havana."

"Really? Meyer led me to believe I'd be on my own, Alex."

"You are running the Nacional project, for sure, but Meyer has asked if I can work alongside you to iron out any local difficulties you may have."

"Are we expecting any?"

"Not yet, but you never know what will happen and if a problem were to appear, then I will make it go away."

"You always were good at solving problems, that's why Benny brought you into Vegas."

"Something like that, Gus."

GUS DIDN'T TAKE long to place a call with Alex and ask for a private conversation, so they met in the Lima Hastiada that afternoon.

"Is the food any good here?"

"Passable, Gus. I've tasted worse."

Greenberg ordered a sandwich and beer, while Alex only took a refill on his coffee and a pile of tortilla chips to nibble.

"How's the Nacional going?"

"Fits and starts, Alex. At the moment, we have some issues with a union."

"I thought we'd driven them all out of town."

"Not so's I've noticed. We are gutting the floor which has gone all right, but now the plasterers, carpenters, and electricians are refusing to work unless we up their pay rate."

"And that's not in the business plan?"

"Nope and Meyer has been very clear to me we cannot go over-budget on this project."

"That's what happens when you work for penny-pinching Jews."

"Tell me about it. I've been employed by them all my life and look where it's got me."

The two men chuckled before Alex focused on the problem at hand.

"Are you sure there's a union involved?"

"No, but their action is orchestrated. I mean, they've all asked for the same amount of gelt and they did it yesterday, every last one of them."

"And there's no wiggle room on their pay?"

"Not a red cent, unless we get the go-ahead from Meyer. If I add to my costs here, then I'll have to cut corners somewhere else, and we both remember what happened at the Flamingo when Benny did that."

"Let me have a word with them and we'll see what happens."

LUCIO RUIZ SAT opposite Alex in the bar at the Nacional. Two beers stood between them. Lucio had downed most of his, and Alex hadn't taken a single mouthful from the glass nearest him.

"How does it feel sitting front of house in this place, Lucio?"

"I could grow used to this life, Mr. Cohen."

"Call me Alex. Yes, physical comfort is worth paying a premium for, wouldn't you say?"

"If you can afford it, Alex, then you are right."

"How did you get the job here to work on the casino project?"

"A friend of a friend, you know how these things operate."

"Lucio, I don't. I am not a builder, but a businessman. When somebody wants me to do a job, he comes up to me, straight up, and asks me to my face."

"Well, that's not how contracts are here, senor."

Alex detected a hint of sarcasm in Ruiz's voice in the last word he uttered. He let it go but didn't forget it either.

"I hear there has been an impasse in the project. An argument over money has stopped the work. You know anything about that?"

"Alex, with all due respect, you know that's the case otherwise I wouldn't be having a drink with you in the bar of the Nacional Hotel. I'd be lucky to be allowed through the front entrance of this joint."

"Lucio, you are right and I apologize. You should be thrown out of this place and I will happily organize that for you, if you want me to. I understand there is a hypocrisy in that you can be here when by my side and not allowed in the building in other circumstances. But you need to think beyond what's left of your beer and consider why we are seated in this booth."

Alex gave Ruiz some time to ponder over what he'd just heard, but the blank expression opposite him showed that those thirty seconds had been a waste of time.

"They have offered you and your friends a very fair wage, and yet you want more. Why is that?"

"Alex, sir, we are not fools. Once the casino is built, then Mr. Greenbaum and his business partners will make a fortune out of our efforts. So we reckon it can't hurt to ask for a few more pesos an hour because we won't see any of the profits that our toil generates."

Alex ground his molars as he had heard this sob story, or one like it, a thousand times before, and on each occasion it annoyed him.

"What you don't seem to understand is that each party takes on different risks and is paid accordingly. The proprietors must pay the staff, heat the building, buy food, and so on hoping guests will stay in the hotel and spend their evenings playing roulette or cards. All those costs have to happen before one customer steps through the threshold. The owners take on that risk."

Alex paused for a second for Ruiz to absorb this information.

"On the other hand, you are being given money to do something short term. You are paid after you have done your work and this is taking place in President Batista's hotel, so you know you will get your money at the end of the week."

Another pause.

"Of course, Lucio, I am not pretending that you have no risks at all. For example, there can be an accident with a hammer or saw. You could fall out of a window and come crashing to the ground. You might find that your family is injured in their home, or worse. Your body could be found in a shallow grave on the beach or thrown overboard a boat in the bay. All these things could happen and some of those risks can be removed."

Ruiz's face was ashen now, and he had stopped pawing his glass with his muscular hands.

"What do I need to do so that my family shall be safe?"

"Go to work at the rate of pay that has been offered to you. If you don't do this, then you can be certain that some harm will befall you. I don't know when or where, but you, your wife, and your children will be in mortal danger."

Ruiz swallowed hard and licked his lips.

"Gus Greenbaum and I worked together in Las Vegas a while back. Ask around about me in case you don't believe my words. I am going to go now. I haven't touched my drink so you are welcome to stay and have the second beer. Then you should leave and come back to work first thing tomorrow morning. If you do, all will be fine and you shall have gained two Nacional beers inside you."

"And if I don't?"

Alex rose and smiled. Then he walked to the bar to settle the check and left Lucio Ruiz to consider whether he should knock back the beer or get out while he still had breath in his body.

May 1958

31

"I'D LIKE YOU to hit someone in Havana."

Alex stirred his coffee while maintaining eye contact with Vito Genovese, who had paid the island yet another of his brief visits. He had flown in that morning on his private plane and was scheduled to depart before sunset.

"Talk me through the situation and I will see what I can do, Vito."

"Sam Giancana and his Chicago friends need their wings clipped and you are the man for the job."

"I appreciate you thinking of me, but I don't want to stand in the middle of any Italian beef. With all due respect, one of the pleasant aspects of living in Cuba is that I do not get embroiled in local disagreements back home. As we both know, the syndicate has faded away and I would have thought the commission was more than capable of handling these sorts of matters without involving outsiders."

"Alex, my friend, you are right that the syndicate has withered on the vine and that we Italians look after our own. But Sam has overstepped the mark and needs to face the consequences of his actions."

"That may well be, Vito, and I am not making any judgment as I am in possession of no facts. This remains an Italian American problem, surely."

"Are you concerned about repercussions?"

"I will not insult your intelligence. Meyer and myself do work with many, and often competing, outfits over here. If I assist you in this matter, then my neutrality may be broken and I'll endure the negative consequences of my decision—either through loss of revenue or someone will take a hit out on me. I do not wish to live in a world where there is a vendetta against me. The safety of my family is too important to allow business to threaten their lives."

Vito's eyes bored into Alex, arms folded and lips pursed. He could see the Italian's muscles twitching in his cheeks. He unfolded his hands and lit a cigarette before responding.

"Alex, we both know you have been instrumental in several high-profile hits over the years. You are too much of a professional to confirm this but Albert Anastasia, Benny Siegel, and Abe Reles are the first three names that come to mind—all dead and buried because of you and I respect you for your work."

"I don't know what you mean."

Vito raised a hand to stop Alex in his tracks.

"And even here in front of me, you continue your denial: bravo. But these men are in their graves and you walk free, so let's not pretend too much, eh?"

Alex shrugged and cast his eyes down at their table in the private meeting room in the Nacional that Meyer had provided for their conversation. The waiters had left a pot of coffee and some food before Alex had dismissed them and Vito had arrived.

"Do you fancy a bite to eat, Vito? I'm going to grab a sandwich even if you are not."

Without waiting for an answer, Alex walked over and piled salt beef on rye onto his plate. Then he refilled his coffee and returned to his seat.

WHILE THEY ATE, Vito refrained from talking business with Alex and the fellas covered topics like the state of gaming in Vegas and prostitution in New York and Chicago.

"Alex, you have avoided answering my question for long enough."

"Earlier you said that Sam's actions needed consequences. While it is none of my business, I would appreciate you telling me what has warranted you wanting him dead."

"I thought the whole point of a Murder Corporation hit was that you asked no questions about the contract."

"Vito, this isn't a Murder Corp deal though, and the fact you have come to me indicates that the contract hasn't been sanctioned by your commission."

He eyed Vito's response to this suggestion because the Italians had kept to their own ever since the syndicate evaporated from view. Suddenly, the fella had flown more than a thousand miles to spend an afternoon with Alex to get him to whack one of their own. There was something queer about this request.

"You understand my role in the commission's hierarchy?"

"Vito, of course I do, and I congratulate you on your coronation, which should have happened at Apalachin but was delayed a few weeks. And I respect you and the position you hold. Like Charlie Lucky before you, I applaud good things happening to great men."

Alex raised his coffee cup as if he were clinking a beer glass.

"But this is not personal. Even if Luciano were to walk into this joint and ask me to do the same thing, I would want to know why I was the lucky one to be chosen for the task. I am a businessman nowadays. I operate and manage several hotel services across Havana. The days of plugging men for cash are behind me."

"Alex, I have come all this way to ask you especially. This should speak volumes about how important I view this situation and the request I am making of you. That should be sufficient answer to any of your questions."

"It is, and it isn't, Vito, and I have listened to what you have said and mean you no disrespect when I press you on this. But the fact you have come here means this is not a commission-sanctioned contract and that can leave me open to reprisals."

"If you are only doing my bidding, then you have nothing to fear from the others."

"Vito, that may well be the case today and tomorrow, but at some point in the future, you may no longer be the boss of bosses and I might still be alive. Then I shall not be under your protection over this murder and bullets will fly aimed straight at my heart."

The Italian opened his mouth but said nothing—as though this was the first time he had considered the assassination of Sam Giancana from anyone's perspective but his own.

"I will pay you handsomely."

"Vito, there is no doubt that the fee would be significant, whoever gets to pull the trigger, but this is not some clever ruse by me to increase my pay. I am not negotiating with you, because were I to do so then you would believe I was prepared to carry out the hit."

"The other thing you should consider, Alex, is whether you wish to turn me into an enemy. After all, this is the first time I have asked you for any sort of accommodation and you intend to refuse my request."

"Please don't put words in my mouth, Vito. And I do not want us to part on poor terms today, no matter what conclusion we reach on your proposal. If you have heard half of what I said, then you will understand the reasons for my desire to pass on it and free you to find somebody else to fulfill the contract. I hope you respect my decision in light of my reasons and that we can still do business together. For example, at present, there are several million dollars a month we launder for you through our hotels and I imagine you would like us to continue to carry on with that, even if Sam continues to breathe well into next year."

Now it was Vito's turn to take the heat out of the conversation and wander off to the side table to refill his coffee and grab another sandwich. He stood and ate while keeping his eyes trained on Alex. After a mouthful of coffee to wash the rye flavor away, Genovese returned to his chair opposite Alex.

"Is there nothing I can do to change your mind?"

"Vito, ten years ago I would have agreed immediately and there would have been no conversation, but I am older now and my family has drawn towards me for all my faults. So this isn't about what I want as much as it is about what is best for them. Agreeing to this hit can only do them harm in the long term, so I must decline with regret and respect."

Vito stared at Alex for five intense seconds, then he blinked, as though he was snapping out of a trance, and lit a cigarette. He inhaled half without uttering a word, flicking ash off the end. Then he stood up.

"Alex, thank you for taking the time to see me today. I must return to New York and make other arrangements. I cannot pretend to be happy with the outcome, but I respect your decision and understand why you are refusing to do this job for me."

"Vito..."

Before Alex could respond, Genovese walked out of the room and into his waiting limousine. Alex called the airport an hour later to confirm that the fella had left the island. If Alex hadn't been concerned with ensuring the safety of Sarah and his boys, then Sam Giancana would have been sleeping with the fishes before the end of the week.

32

ON THE OTHER side of the island, the rebels had been quiet for several months and Alex wondered if they were about to break cover. Batista must have had the same thought because he called in Meyer and Alex to ask them to head over and survey the scene. Like before, this meant Alex and Ezra found themselves sat in a tent opposite Captain Izzy Chávez.

"Have you had much contact with the rebels?"

"Nothing in the last two months. Most weeks, they'll attack a police vehicle or my soldiers on reconnaissance, but there hasn't even been a sound out of them."

"That is peculiar. Any ideas, Ezra?"

"I'm blank. It suggests they are cooking something up though. Izzy, were there any thefts of munitions or arms before they went into radio silence?"

"No major hauls from around here, but that doesn't mean they couldn't ship them in from another part of the island. These barracks are not the only place to get rifles in Cuba."

He was right. Either the rebels had packed and gone home or they were about to descend from the hills and reap merry havoc on the town. The chances were they hadn't given up and returned to their jobs in the fields.

THE ANSWER FROM the rebels came two days later, before Alex and Ezra got back to Havana. They stayed in the Moncada Barracks as Izzy couldn't guarantee their safety if they boarded in town, and regretted that decision shortly before nightfall.

Alex heard a whizz over his head and he recognized the sound from his time in the trenches back in the fields of France. He shouted, "Mortar!" just as the first one landed twenty feet away from his tent. The boom as the missile hit the ground shook through Alex's chest and a plume of soil showered on the canvas. He hit the dirt with his hands covering his skull, like he had received his basic army training only the other day, instead of forty years before.

Screaming and shouting engulfed the air space as the soldiers responded to the attack. Alex popped his head out of the tent and first turned to his left to check on Ezra, but there was no sign of him.

"You in your tent, Ezra?"

"Sure thing, and I ain't coming out until this is over."

Alex took in all that he could see. Men rushed up and down the aisles in between the rows of tents and at the end of the row, a group stood firing indiscriminately into the tree line, but there was nothing to indicate that was where the rebels were situated.

He dashed over to Ezra's entrance and scurried inside.

"It's only mortar. They want us to stay still so we are sitting ducks for them. Trust me and make a break for it. My bet is that they're scaring us but do not want to engage with this army. Izzy is a good enough soldier to have trained these men well."

"Where do you think we should go?"

"To a point of safety. Follow me and stay close."

Out of the tent and away from the trees, Ezra trailed Alex as he wended his way along past the tents to the permanent huts. These barracks were only meant as a temporary measure to keep military control of the southern part of the island when Batista seized power so a few buildings with corrugated iron for walls had been put up and everyone and everything else had to make do with canvas tents. The mess was too important a location and was the first to be erected as a permanent structure—it needed running water to function well too.

They ran past the mess and noticed some troops lying on the floor inside, as though that would stop a mortar from landing on their heads. Then past more tents, enough for a platoon and beyond that… dunes.

The barracks were situated smack on the edge of the island, and Alex figured that heading for the beach would offer them the best protection. Over the ridges and Alex took a quick look at the tide—it was going out so there would be a vast expanse of empty sand if they went far enough and plenty of time to remain there before the sea lapped at their ankles.

Ezra got the idea and pointed at an upturned hunk of wood. When they drew close, Alex saw it was a boat with a massive hole in it. Terrible for sailing but great as cover in case the rebels swarmed the camp and came leaping over the hill.

The mortar fire continued for another twenty minutes, but it was all aimed at the barracks and not at the beach. When everything had quietened down, Alex and Ezra tentatively picked their way back to the camp to see what damage the rebels had inflicted.

"MEYER, THIS WAS not a good sign. The rebels had the entire barracks pinned down by only three or four of their men. We shouldn't underestimate them."

"One well-planned attack doesn't mean that Batista is going to be deposed. I spoke with him yesterday—they call themselves revolutionaries, but they are just a bunch of disgruntled farmers with the Castro brothers leading them around the hills like sheep."

"Those lambs nearly blew my head clean off, Meyer."

Alex's friend looked at him as though he was a foolish little boy.

"I think Batista's iron grip remains on the throat of this land. Those rebels might have made a big noise down south, but the actual onslaught takes place in the city every day of the year. The secret police abduct miscreant citizens at night and they are never seen again. The papers don't report it, and their families are too scared to even talk about it among strangers. That's the real crisis in this country, Alex."

"Meyer, I had no idea you were so concerned about the ordinary joe in the street."

"We live together, we love together, Alex. Everybody must look after their own. Let the saps living here do what they want; all that matters to me is that we can build Las Vegas in the sun."

"Are you more interested in creating something bigger than we dreamed was possible in Nevada or making money?"

"Alex, to do one, you must do the other, as far as I'm concerned. The important thing is that nobody must stand in my way. I don't care who they are or how powerful they might be, Havana is where I shall make my mark."

That night, Alex told Sarah about his conversation and asked her what she thought about Meyer.

"The fella has an amazing vision. A gambling haven in Latin America. If he could pull that off…"

"That's the question, though. Do you think he will?"

"The man is the minister for entertainment, has the ear of the president and you for his muscle. How can he lose?"

"Sarah, I've seen Castro's rebels first hand—those guys mean business. There may not be many of them, but they would give any gang member in Little Italy a run for their money."

"Are you saying we should leave Cuba?"

"No, at least I don't think so. Not right now, I mean. But I believe Meyer underestimates them and that might cost us dearly."

"Alex, is it safe to have David here?"

"Yes, for the moment. If I thought it wasn't all right for David, then you'd need to leave too, Sarah."

"Do you want me to go, Alex?"

"I never want us to be apart, but if this place gets dangerous, for whatever reason, then, of course, I'll need you back in the States."

"Now you're getting me worried."

"Don't be, Sarah. At the first sign of trouble, we'll all be out of here. I've left everything behind me before and I'll do it again, although that's not my plan for Havana."

"You would say, though?"

"Sarah, you have my word."

December 1958

33

MEYER GOT WHAT Meyer demanded and the new wing of the Nacional Hotel was set for its first paying customers before Christmas, or as Lansky preferred to comment, "I knew you guys would get it ready before Hanukkah."

The Casino Nacional was positioned next to the Starlight Terrace Bar and the Casino Parisién night club. They were located so that the clientele would have the shortest distance to travel to flit between gaming, booze, a show, and more gaming. Paradise on earth only a hundred miles from Florida.

Gus had been good to his word and brought the project in on time and under budget, in part thanks to the persuasive skills of Alex, who convinced the workers to take a pay cut in exchange for their families' lives around Halloween when they seemed to be slacking for no good reason that anyone could make out.

Opening night at the Nacional passed without incident. Meyer had made it low key because all he was interested in were the high rollers who would appear as soon as they took the covers off the poker tables. The tourist trade would pick up as quickly as word got out back home that a new venue was open for business and Lansky didn't need to spend any money advertising that fact; the travel agents would do all the work for him.

Although Alex had half-thought he'd bump into Townsend again, he was glad he didn't have to put on a monkey suit for the night. The days of dressing to impress had long since faded in his mind, and he preferred to spend the evening with Sarah and David rather than making small talk with a bunch of strangers. He was getting old.

Instead, Alex remained in the bar and restaurant to save himself from falling foul of the dress code in the casino. The lack of publicity didn't prevent Meyer's friends and partners from coming to town to celebrate the launch, and so it was that Vito Genovese appeared that evening and plonked himself next to Alex, who ordered them both a Scotch.

"So we meet again, Vito. How's business?"

"All good, Alex, thank you for asking."

"Are you over here for the grand launch?"

"I always like to see new places opening up to allow more people to be separated from their hard-earned cash."

"Meyer will do well here, Vito."

"Let's hope so. And how's tricks with you, Alex?"

"Good. There's plenty to keep me busy and, as you said, there's a lot of money to be made in this town."

"From what I've heard, Meyer is the sole owner of this gambling establishment."

"That's what I reckon. The man wants to create Las Vegas in Cuba—one casino at a time."

"A fella with vision. How very old school. The rest of us Mustache Petes just want to make money, launder it and then spend what's left on our mistresses and maybe our wives now and again."

Alex smiled but had no interest in being drawn into a conversation about extramarital affairs. He hadn't strayed from Sarah since they'd got back together after Rebecca's death. He had a flash of Ida's face beneath a pillow as she struggled to breathe before her body slumped still.

"Alex, are you interested in having more money than you currently make?"

"That's a rigged question. Have you ever met anyone who is satisfied with their lot?"

"Not in America."

"So, what proposition do you have for me this time, Vito?"

"All these American tourists you're going to gather at the Nacional, walk in with clean cash and leave poor."

"That's the plan."

"I guess at some point the dollars you accept at the counters get put into bags and deposited in a bank which then wires the money back to the US."

"Vito, you don't have to warm me up. Cut to the chase, please."

"As you know, I have the utmost respect for both you and Meyer and all that you have achieved together over the years, not least what you have done on this island. I would like to launder money from the mainland through the Nacional on an exclusive basis."

"I assume you have a monthly minimum figure in your head."

"We are talking ballpark a million a year."

Alex whistled. That was more than chump change.

"I am glad business is going so well for you."

"Thank you, but what do you say?"

"Vito, this isn't my call. Meyer owns the joint, and he decides who he does business with, not me. You've asked the wrong fella."

"I understand the situation, but you must admit I stand a better chance of getting an exclusive deal with Meyer if you are backing it."

"Sure, but why not just launder the money through here, even if others are doing the same?"

"Meyer Lansky might not be the Big Bankroll, but he is the next best thing. My only criticism is that he acts like a bee, buzzing from one flower to the next. I want him to hover over my plant and give it some special attention."

"Let me think it over. When do you intend to approach Meyer over this?"

"The day after tomorrow. This might be a great place to make money, but there's too much Spanish spoken for my taste and I need to get back home."

"WHY WOULD I want my hands tied behind my back, Alex?"

Lansky and Alex were talking the following afternoon in Meyer's penthouse.

"That's not for me to say, Meyer. The fella came to me with a business proposition, which I am relaying to you. It's your casino and you decide who you deal with, of course."

"Genovese should have come direct to me, then I would have had the chance to tell him what I think of his proposal."

"Meyer, perhaps that's why he swung by me first. But let's be straight. I do not wish to be an intermediary, standing in between you two. If you can't talk directly with each other on this, then I want no piece of it."

Meyer left his armchair and paced up and down in front of Alex, who relaxed into his seat, knowing this was going to be a long ride. After a couple of minutes, Meyer stopped in his tracks and lit a cigarette. Then he returned to his chair.

"Feeling better after your promenade, Meyer?"

"There's no need to be like that. Vito annoyed me with his entire approach. Since when does the fella need an envoy?"

"When he's Italian and doesn't want to lose face if you reject him."

"Alex, that man and I go way back; I funded his first heroin smuggling operation before the war."

"He was a young Turk back then. Roll forward twenty years and Vito has a lot to lose nowadays and is generating over a million a year in cash he has yet to launder. The fella has picked you to do the job, not some Italian from his old neighborhood."

"That's why I don't want him using the Nacional."

"Meyer, I don't get your point."

"All my life I have wanted something to call my own. Since I was a kid, I have been fantastic at lending money to fellas who pay me back—and some. Great, but these joints in Havana are the first opportunity I've had to construct some action for myself from the ground up. This is mine and nobody else's."

"With a little help from the president."

"I told myself when Batista took control that I wanted this to be my *shtetl* —my town, my home—and there shouldn't be Italian money funding it."

Alex thought for a moment, mulling over what he'd heard.

"Hasn't that ship sailed decades ago, Meyer? You've done business with the Italians since the days of Arnold Rothstein and Charlie Lucky. They expect you to maintain that relationship even when you are abroad. You've been swimming with the sharks too long to complain they are in your self-declared inlet."

"Alex, I don't want to use the Nacional Hotel to launder Italian money. This is going to be the basis of all my new ventures, including The Panama. *Yiddishe gelt*."

"I'd be surprised if Vito sees it like that. He will take it as a snub."

"I'll offer him better terms to handle his cash through a different joint."

"Meyer, is it only about the money? Do you think Vito is testing you in some way?"

"Huh?"

"Has he ever asked for an exclusive contract before?"

"Alex, no—not that I recall."

"Then why now? Why you and why here?"

Meyer blinked twice and stared at Alex as he sipped his coffee.

"What do you reckon, Alex?"

"I'm not sure, but the Feds are snapping at the Italian mob's heels and they can now trace the movements of cash like never before. In Cuba, we are beyond the FBI's jurisdiction and Hoover needs some wins to show he can hit the commission hard. If I were Vito, I'd want to ensure I had at least some of my eggs in a different basket. Wouldn't you?"

"Does that mean we can count on him?"

"He is the head of the Italian's commission—the boss of bosses. Of course, you can't trust him. He'd slit your throat as soon as look at you if you stopped being of any use to him. Same as all the Italian bosses—they never invited us to Apalachin, remember?"

34

"I GAVE YOU until the end of the year to sign the Panama contract and here we are in December, Alex. Are you going to piss or get off the pot?"

Lansky might have carried a smile on his face, but his tone was cold—like an impatient teacher talking to a kid who doesn't do as he is told. Alex shifted in the booth at the rear of the Lima Hastiada. Meyer had asked to meet him here rather than in his suite, which sounded off, but Alex paid no attention to it.

"Meyer, David has prepared the paperwork, so this isn't a kiss-off, but I have some reservations about the deal."

"Is that you speaking or your son?"

"David provides me with legal advice and I decide. If you are annoyed with me, please don't drag other people into the conversation."

Meyer sighed.

"What's your concern then, Alex?"

"It is a question of risk and reward. While I have never pretended to you what I think of Batista, I can suck that in if the results are worth it. I am a realist, Meyer, and I know that when you swim in the sea, there are always sharks surrounding you. But I do not want to hand over a million to that man if he will not be running this country."

"Alex, the guy has an iron fist that smashes all opposition."

"Not quite, Meyer. You're forgetting about the rebels. Batista might have total control in Havana, but that's just not true on the other side of the island. You should visit Moncada Barracks and you'd see what I mean."

"I don't need to travel to the other end of Cuba to recognize that the rebels are a small band of nobodies stirring up trouble with no popular support. The Castro brothers are nothing to worry about. Your money will be safe."

"Meyer, it is more than my money that is at stake, it is the future of my family. If I invest in The Panama then the financial security of Sarah and our children rest in the bricks and mortar of one entertainment complex…"

"Which will make more money than you and yours could spend, Alex. There might not be certainties in this world, but you can bet your last cent on The Panama turning a profit within months and generating enough gelt in a year than you have ever had in your life."

"Above what I make out of Vegas?"

"You get ten percent of the skim there and that's nothing to sniff at, but that's chicken feed compared to one hundred percent of a place like The Panama."

"I wish it was that simple, Meyer."

"But it is, Alex. You are overthinking an easy question: do you want to make enough money so that you could retire with Sarah wherever you wanted. No more and no less."

Alex wondered what was really stopping him from signing. Perhaps Meyer was right—wire the money over to Batista today and by the end of the week he'd have a gaming license in the bag and in six months, the hotel would be open and this time next year, he would be in clover. What's not to like?

"David tells me there is too much risk on my side. Batista's name is absent from the agreement and he is the party with the most influence over the outcome of the deal."

"Alex, some things are better done on trust than in any paperwork, and Batista's word is only as good as his deeds. Naming him in a contract would be a futile gesture and would gain you nothing but tsoris. It would annoy him and make him difficult to deal with in the future. Nothing more."

"That makes Batista sound like a cranky child, and that's the guy you want me to do business with?"

Another steely look by Meyer.

"I have been working with that petulant child for years now with no problems. Does he have an over-inflated sense of his own importance? Sure thing. Does that stop me from making money through him? Nope. Nothing is simple when there's gelt involved."

"Meyer, it's not like I think the whole matter is a bad idea. If I did then we wouldn't be having this conversation as I'd have nixed it a long time ago…"

"Great, Alex, so wire the money over and stop grousing."

"But as you so rightly say, nothing is simple when there's hard cash at stake. I want to be clear about the risks involved. For me to fund the venture without having to go cap in hand to the Italians for fundraising, I'm going to have to put everything I own on this horse. If the deal goes south, then I will be left with nothing. *Nothing*."

Alex emphasized the last two syllables to get Meyer to think outside of his admiration for Batista. The slimeball was as keen as Lansky to create Las Vegas in the Caribbean, and their interests had been entwined ever since the Havana conference when Benny's fate was sealed. That was over a decade ago, and Meyer had made significant sums of money out of that generalissimo.

Lansky paused for a second, and Alex wondered if he had got through to his old friend.

"I've told you before, you don't have to go to any outside parties for funding. If you want financing I am happy to offer it to you at more than reasonable rates. I hope that serves as a powerful indicator that I want you on board with The Panama and that I am prepared to back you with my own money in order to secure your involvement. We don't need the Italians because they have made it clear they do not think they need us anymore."

"Charlie has long gone, for sure, Meyer."

"And our future is in this island. Three or four years from now, our legacy will be complete."

"Your legacy, Meyer. I'm only concerned to look after my family."

"In years to come, they'll remember both our names in Havana like the older fellas recall Benny in Vegas, only we won't be skimming the take and getting our girlfriend to fly overseas with the money."

THIRTY MINUTES LATER, Alex thought he had turned the conversation away from The Panama, but Meyer had other plans.

"So is there anything else you need to know from me before you wire the payment to get your gaming license, Alex?"

"How tight are you with Batista?"

"What do you mean, Alex?"

"You're his minister for entertainment and you bought into the Nacional before any of us had even heard of Cuba. Yet there you were going into business with a man who was about to lose an election."

"Alex, I trust Batista enough that he will look after me, but only when our interests are aligned. We both like to make money and while the gelt rolls in, I know I am safe with him and he'll do right by me. But I am not naïve—the day the casinos stop creating wealth is the time I need to leave this island or ask you to fulfill a contract on the guy."

"Meyer, how long do you think you will both board the same gravy train?"

"Business is cyclical. When they banned liquor, we thought bootlegging would last forever, but it didn't. Same here—eventually we will run out of space to build new casinos or there'll be no more tourists to fly over here. At that point, we'll max out and takings will plateau. Sometime around then, I will need to separate my investment interests from Batista. That is many years away though."

Alex pondered Meyer's words. He wanted it all to make sense, but he was aware of a gnawing at the pit of his stomach. If this gamble of his went south, the Cohens wouldn't have a penny to rub together.

"Has David been whispering in your ear, Alex? Is this why you can't commit?"

"We both know my son has had issues with the wording of several of the clauses, and that's all been ironed out between him and you. I don't have a head for paperwork so when he tells me the contract's good enough then I believe him. For me, a handshake is all I ever need. As you've said yourself, a business relationship is all about trust and not much else."

A sip of coffee each and just as Alex opened his mouth to continue, Meyer held up a palm.

"There we have it, Alex. We are all about faith. If you can't trust me enough to invest in The Panama, then I can't trust you to work with me in Cuba and you should go home. Give me your signature on the bottom of the contract by the time the banks open after the holidays or pack your bags and leave."

DECEMBER 31, 1958

35

THE NEW YEAR'S Eve ball at the Nacional de Cuba was the swankiest event in the Havana calendar where Batista hosted a lavish dinner and dance for all his friends, senior government officials, and his extended family. Meyer, Alex, Sarah, and David were honored to be on the top table, albeit ten seats away from the man himself.

Alex surveyed the ballroom and wondered how many people it contained —the sea of bobbing heads seemed to go on forever. For a second, he remembered the times he had spent at Arnold Rothstein's New Year celebrations. Sarah nudged him in the side to push him out of his reverie.

"How many of these people do you know, Alex?"

"Sarah, there's the four of us, the president and his brother. The rest are total strangers or I recognize them and have nodded or smiled at them since we arrived in Havana."

She giggled.

"I'm glad it's not just me then."

"These are Meyer's guys, not mine. I tolerate Batista and his cronies because we can make money here; the man is a disgrace to his uniform."

Sarah's smile evaporated, and she squeezed his hand.

"You do what you have to do. We live together, we love together. Right?"

"And we die alone. Maybe we'll hang on for a couple more years, produce a big pot of gelt, and head home. What do you say?"

"Is that your way of telling me you've signed the papers for The Panama?"

Before Alex could reply, the trumpets from the band screeched into a rumba and all words were lost beneath the cacophony.

"SURE FEELS GOOD, doesn't it, Pop?"

David's face was lit up with enthusiasm for the coming year, buoyed by the copious amounts of champagne poured down his neck by the waiting staff. No expense was being spared, and the lawyer hadn't even got to the end of the soup course.

The rectangular head table ran across the ballroom and all the others spread like tentacles away and down the room. Located near Alex and Meyer were Batista's Italian friends—close enough to lean backward for a short while and exchange pleasantries. Alex and Lansky looked out on the vista while Sarah and David stared at podiums with flowers perched on top of them lined along the back wall.

Alex caught Vito Genovese's eye; the man was at the nearest point on the Italians' table, and he smiled in response. They hadn't spoken since Meyer rebuffed Vito's exclusive money-laundering deal. Alex knew it was nothing personal but aimed at anyone whose family hailed from Sicily, although Genovese didn't share Meyer's perspective. Alex was lucky to get any acknowledgment of his presence at all.

Once the soup bowls were cleared away, Alex excused himself from the table and idled over to Genovese.

"Good to see you, Vito. How's business?"

"All well, thank you, Alex. It would be better if Meyer had seen sense over my proposal, but that's behind us."

"Pleased to hear it, Vito. There's plenty more deals for us to make in the future."

"Thank you for saying so. That might be true for you, but I'm not so certain you speak for Meyer on this."

"Oh, Vito. He likes you and enjoys working with you. From what I know, this is the first time since you fellas began to do business that he has ever refused a favor for you. Even then, it was done with respect and you can be sure that no one received a similar deal. Meyer wants a small piece of Havana to call his own. No more and no less."

"Interesting to hear that, Alex. I thought he snubbed me, but perhaps I shouldn't have taken it so personally. Now that's twice when you guys have refused me."

"They are serving the next course. I'd better return to my seat. Let's talk some more before the end of the night, all right?"

BEFORE HE WALKED back around the head table, Alex put his hand on Sarah's shoulder, interrupting her conversation with David. Alex leaned down and whispered in her ear. "Quite an evening. I love you." She smiled as he kissed her on the cheek, stood up, and returned to his seat opposite her.

"It has been a profitable year, Alex."

"Sure has, Meyer. Even the Nacional is showing healthy numbers and it's only been open a handful of months."

"I'm glad I didn't go into bed with Genovese over the money laundering too. This place is my piece of paradise and I don't want to share it with anyone—present company excepted."

Alex grinned and clinked glasses with his old friend. The fella had been there for him before he went upstate to Sing Sing and had looked after him ever since, one way or another.

"Meyer, what can I say? I'm sat in front of my family—people I might never have seen again if it hadn't been for you—and we are on the brink of greatness. Actually, where's your wife and kids?"

"On vacation in Florida. They'll be back next week."

"That explains why I haven't seen them for a few days... Yeah, what we will do over the next five years will make history."

A sip of champagne each and Alex chuckled.

"What's funny?"

"That we're going to do better than all those Italian gonifs over there, and they don't even know it yet. We'll be retired before they get assassinated; very few bosses survive to old age."

"Don't gloat just yet, Alex. We need the money in the bank first. Talking of which, have you wired the payment to Batista's account for your Panama gaming license?"

Another squealing roar from the trumpet section announced the end of the meal. Alex looked down to see that busboys had cleared the tables, and the guests at all the other tables were ushered away from their chairs so they could convert the space ready for the band to play so the dancing could begin. Naturally, the top table was excluded from these antics and within a handful of minutes, the musicians rose and kicked off with a toe-tapper which drew almost everyone onto the dance floor.

Before Alex could protest, Sarah grabbed him by the hand and dragged him to join her to rumba. He wasn't well-practiced but did his best not to crush her feet. She smiled and wiggled her hips to the beat. But after only one song, Alex was forced to admit defeat. He turned round and caught David's eye, beckoning him over. "Sarah, you deserve someone who knows how to do this." Then he walked off and perched next to Meyer.

Just as he inhaled to start a conversation with his friend, Vito sat down in front of them and lifted his glass. They sipped their champagne, and the Italian leaned forward.

"Another year, another dollar."

Meyer raised a smile.

"Despite our differences, I wish you a long life and every success in the coming year, Vito."

"And to you, Meyer. Although if you disrespect me a second time, I won't take it so quietly."

"I always respect you in all that you do and what you have achieved. Sometimes business partners disagree, and the strength of their partnership keeps them together. That is what you and I have, Vito. It's not just about the money, it is down to character. We are men, not boys."

Meyer glanced at Batista, who remained glued to his seat in the center of the head table. There was no way the most powerful man in Cuba was going to be jiving on the dance floor tonight. Genovese followed Lansky's line of sight and nodded.

"Wearing a uniform doesn't make you a soldier. Isn't that right, Alex?"

"Absolutely, Vito. When you've got your hands dirty with the blood of your compatriots, that's when you are a fighting fellow."

"Gents, let's not darken the mood on this evening of celebration. To our success in the future with General Batista, the greatest man ever to wear that uniform."

With a glint in his eye, Meyer clinked glasses with Alex and Vito as they acknowledged his toast. Alex looked into the sea of couples dancing and saw Sarah and David in the heart of the throng.

As the music wound down, the bandleader took to the mike to remind everyone that it was only a minute before midnight. With that news, Sarah and David headed back to Alex, and Vito made his excuses to return to his fellas.

With ten seconds to go before the new year arrived, everybody in the room counted down… three, two, one. Happy New Year!

JANUARY 1, 1959

36

BALLOONS FELL FROM the ceiling, and everyone howled and whooped for the new year. Alex held Sarah in his arms and they kissed. "Happy New Year, my love." They hugged for an eternity and kissed again until Alex noticed someone hovering near them—David was waiting.

Sarah got to him first and hugged him, so Alex took Meyer by the hand to man-hug him, slapping his upper arm twice. Then Alex reached his hands out to David and wished him well while Sarah gave Meyer a hug and a peck on the cheek.

The band played Auld Lang Syne and everybody crossed arms and sang along until the orchestra stopped and a spotlight aimed at Batista, who had stood up to make his annual speech.

"Another year has gone by and Cuba has got stronger. The economy has grown year-on-year since the people showed their support for me when I took power. Their faith in me has been entirely justified. I stand before you all and I look to the future, filled with optimism and hope. Thanks in part to your investment of time and money in our country, I expect even better things to happen to my state. There will be greater foreign investment in the entertainment industry in Havana, and we shall benefit from the know-how provided by our American friends in the construction sector."

The president inhaled to grab what appeared to be his first breath since he began speaking and, at that moment, a guy who was dressed as a waiter scurried into view and handed Batista a scrap of paper. Then he vanished into the crowd.

The general's expression indicated he was not expecting to be interrupted, let alone by someone so menial, and he paused to read whatever was on the note he'd just received. His eyes widened, and the color left his cheeks.

"Thank you and goodnight. Enjoy the rest of the celebration."

Alex blinked, and the president had gone.

"What's going on?" asked Sarah, but Alex had no better idea than she did.

"Is this some kind of gag, Meyer?"

"Not that I know of."

Alex gazed at the faces staring at where Batista had been standing only a minute before, but he couldn't make out anything that would give a clue to what happened. All he knew was that the president had walked out on his own party.

"WHAT NOW, ALEX?"

"Not sure, Sarah. Stay near me until we figure this out."

His tone had switched to somber instruction. Despite his reassuring words, Alex was not happy. Batista's expression had contained shock and confusion, which he hadn't seen on the face of that trumped-up uniform since he arrived on the island.

Meanwhile, half the band started playing and some guests danced, unconcerned by what had just transpired. After all, it was a New Year's party—the host might have left but there was still celebrating to be done.

"What's Batista up to?"

Vito marched up to Meyer and asked a very reasonable question in an aggressive manner.

"Your guess is as good as mine, Vito."

"I thought you were part of his inner circle."

"We are close, but not so much that he tells me everything he plans on doing. Whatever it is, I'm in the dark like you. All I can advise is that we all stay sharp."

Hearing Meyer say those words, Alex regretted not bringing a revolver out with him. He had allowed himself to get soft in this city.

Although the orchestra continued to play and people danced, a quick glance at the exits showed many guests were leaving. Even members of the band were packing up their instruments and walking away. A waiter hurried past and Alex grabbed his arm for a second.

"Can we order some more drinks?"

"Get them yourself, senor."

The guy wrenched his limb out of Alex's grasp and continued on his journey across the ballroom. He felt Sarah's fingers intertwine with his, and Alex turned to discover that David was only inches away from him.

"Whatever happens, we stick together—just remember that. If you can see me then I can see you. We don't know what's going on, but we must stay near each other."

Then Lansky chimed in.

"Where's Francisco?"

"Who?"

"The brother. And Batista's wife. The entire entourage has left the building."

Alex scanned the room again and found that Meyer was right.

"What was in that note, Meyer?"

The two men hurried over to where Batista had risen during his speech. Alex hunkered down and scoured the floor, and Meyer pulled apart the party debris from the table surface. Among the cigarette ends and spilled booze, Alex's fingers came upon a scrunched-up ball.

He rose and revealed the note: *LEAVE NOW*. Alex showed it to Meyer, who was equally perplexed.

"At least we know he followed the instruction."

Alex stared at Meyer for a second.

"That's not the point. We don't know why he was advised to go and who told him."

The last of the band stopped playing and half the guests who hadn't already left the second-floor ballroom remained on the dance floor, unsure what to do or where to flee.

"Everyone stay here. Do not move. I'm just going to see what is happening outside the ballroom."

"Don't leave us, Alex."

"It'll be fine, Sarah. Trust me."

Before she could respond, Alex let slip her hand and marched toward the exit, matching the slow flow of tuxedos out into the lobby. There was a constant murmur of conversation, but nothing more than that or any sign that anything was happening beyond the confines of the Nacional.

Alex considered venturing down the broad spiral stairs but thought better of it. There was no knowing what might be round the corner, and he needed to make sure his family remained safe. As soon as that thought was planted in his head, the only thing Alex could do was scurry back to be by Sarah's side.

Yet another quick look around and Alex couldn't see Vito or any of the other Italians, which got him wondering if they had been tipped off at the same time as Batista. A squeeze of his elbow and Sarah brought him back to the here and now.

"There didn't appear to be anything happening the other side of that door, but who knows what's going on in the streets."

"Let's find out."

Meyer strode away from the top table and fussed with some red velvet drapes that formed the backdrop to the ballroom wall. He tugged at them with all his might and they opened enough to reveal a set of doors, which led onto a balcony. They followed him out to survey the Havana streets.

A GLANCE AT the world in the early hours of the new year and you'd say there were still hundreds of guys walking along the streets, but as Alex's eyes became accustomed to the darkness and the sparkling light from the stars and lampposts, he realized that most of the ants down below on the sidewalks were stationary. Those people walking along the roads were getting jeered and shouted at. This was not any party spirit Alex had seen since his arrival in Cuba. They stood tens of feet away from the action, but the tone of the voices and the body language of those they could see revealed a menace as far removed from a new year's party atmosphere as you could imagine.

Sarah gripped Alex's fingers tightly, and he felt David edge closer and put a hand on his shoulder. Meyer leaned over the balustrade, keen to hear what was being said, but the voices were too far away.

A crashing sound of splintering glass and a fireball appeared in the middle of the street. People ran in all directions, unsure of the source of the explosion or quite what was going on. Women screamed and a herd of revelers stampeded from the Nacional.

"It's time for us to leave, everybody. No good is going to befall us if we stick around in the hotel. That was a Molotov cocktail, and they rarely come on their own. If those people are as angry as they sound, we need to get as far from this joint as we can."

Sarah and David needed no further explanation, but Meyer was less certain.

"This is my hotel and I can't allow anyone to attack it."

"Meyer, this is Batista's place and the most important thing right now is to make sure we are all safe. Without that, your investment in this building will be worth nothing."

His friend thought for a moment and then nodded consent. Alex led him and his family back into the ballroom, down the stairs, and out through a side entrance marked for staff only.

37

THEY FOUND THEMSELVES in a blind alley to the side of the Nacional with dumpsters, rats, and the stink of sewage within their grasp. Alex led them toward the alleyway entrance where people rushed past. Screams. Elbows jostling. The smell of burned gasoline in the air.

There were two groups in front of them: those wearing evening dress were scurrying away from the hotel and the casino area, fear in their expressions and with good reason. The other group looked like locals and there was hate in their eyes. Some guy who hustled past the alley turned to sneer at Alex and spat in his direction before continuing on his way.

"We've all got to stay real close. There's some ugly goings-on round here and we must all be very careful."

To emphasize his words, Alex pulled off his bow tie and removed his cummerbund to make himself feel less conspicuous while wearing a tux. Meyer and David followed suit while Sarah stood and stared. Alex took her clutch bag and stuffed its contents into his pants pockets and threw the bag on the floor.

"You won't be needing that."

She widened her eyes and then nodded. Her jaw stiffened and the old Sarah returned, the one Alex had met back in the Bowery. They both knew that they would do whatever it took to survive. Sarah seized his hand and Alex led them onto the street.

THEY TRIED TO act as though they were out for a stroll—on the night when the only people on the street were seeking or fleeing mayhem. As Jews, they knew how to be invisible in plain sight and did their best to march along the sidewalk with purpose while not attracting attention.

Throughout this time, Alex and Sarah remained glued to each other's hands as they wended their path down one street and up another. Alex knew exactly where he was going as he had walked the same journey countless times, albeit under calmer circumstances. Whenever they reached a road where there were too many angry locals, he'd switch left or right to keep on going but ensure they kept out of harm's way.

He reckoned they were only three blocks away from their home when he stopped to take stock. They were at a T-junction, and both the left and right streets contained large gatherings. Alex looked around and stood to his full height.

"Where are David and Meyer?"

Sarah turned around to see that the two men were no longer behind them.

"No idea. Should we go to find them?"

"Sarah, let's get you safe before we worry about the other two."

"But, Alex, which way can we go?"

She was right. They were going to have to double back to avoid the two crowds ahead, but there was no guarantee they wouldn't come across the same problem around the next corner. All Alex knew for sure was that staying still was not an option.

They strode back down the street they'd just come from, and Alex spotted a side alley between two houses. He scurried towards the gap and they entered the darkness of the passageway. Although Alex wanted to keep plowing ahead, Sarah slowed him down and he looked at her to figure out why she wasn't running at full pelt. She put a finger to her lips, and he realized she'd noticed a group marching along the sidewalk, past the alleyway entrance and off to the junction they had just been standing at.

Once they were both certain the group would not come by any time soon, Alex and Sarah hightailed it down the alley and out the other side, returning to the glare offered by the street lighting. Alex inhaled and smelled the sea.

"This strip by the coast is filled to the brim with expensive housing and foreigners. We must tread carefully."

Sarah nodded.

"What if they've fire-bombed the house?"

"Let's worry about that later. We've got to get there first."

Although he was right, Sarah didn't appear satisfied with the answer. If they'd burned the place to the ground, then there was no point fighting their way around the crowds to get to it.

"Where to now then, Alex?"

He looked up and down the street—nothing. So they headed back north toward the sea and nearer to their home. Just as they reached the corner to turn left, they stopped in their tracks. Fifty feet in front of them was a gang of thirty or forty men, clubs, bottles, and rifles in hand. The ones nearest them glanced back, saw the couple, and nudged their friends. Even if they bolted for it, they had been seen and there was no way they could outrun thirty guys. They were trapped.

ALEX KNEW BETTER than to reason with a group that large and instead, inched slowly backward and whispered, "Follow my lead, Sarah. No sudden moves to spook those guys and don't make a break for it unless I do it first. If so, do your best to get back to the house, whatever it takes. We'll wait for each other there."

"Got it."

While facing the group, Alex carried on taking a pace or two backward then stopping, all the while ensuring he remained with the front of his torso pointing in the mob's direction. He figured in the darkness, they would find it harder to judge distance and so might not notice the gap between the couple and the group was widening.

They had reversed almost to the corner of the two streets before one of the group nudged his friend and stepped forward.

"What are you doing, senor?"

A machete dangled from one of his hands, practically scraping the floor. Alex stayed silent and moved back one more pace; there were twenty feet between them and the man. The guy took two steps toward them and tilted his head, trying to see who this couple were. Alex noticed there was a streetlight just behind, which meant they appeared as silhouettes to all the people who stood before them.

Alex's Spanish wasn't good enough for him to sound like a local and he didn't want to alert the group that they were within feet of a pair of foreigners, so he ignored the guy's question and took another pace back, along with Sarah.

Loreto Melendez took several steps toward them again and Alex saw his face, the anger in his eyes directed at them, even though they had done nothing to him and his compadres.

"Why don't you answer my question?"

This time the guy spoke in English and there was an edge to his voice. One of his friends stepped forward and shouted out for him to sort out these two strangers. He nodded and jogged forward, blade raised to his shoulder.

When he was ten feet away from Alex, Melendez brandished the machete above head height and Alex let go of Sarah's hand and pushed her away from him to the side. Loreto upped his pace and ran at Alex, swinging the blade straight at his head.

One quick sidestep and the machete swung down and missed Alex by a foot; he grabbed at the guy's downward-plunging wrist with one hand, catching him unawares because of his speed, Alex used his other palm to reach out to Melendez's face or neck. He didn't care what he snatched at as long as it hurt.

Sure enough, Alex's fingers wrapped around Melendez's collar and he squeezed the throat hard. Loreto dropped the enormous blade in response to losing his breath and grabbed at Alex's hand on his windpipe. He kicked at one leg and Melendez overbalanced and fell with a thud onto the concrete road. All the while, Alex held on and landed on top of him, plunging his fingers deeper into Loreto's larynx. With no threat from the machete, Alex put both hands on Melendez's neck and pulled his head up, only to slam it onto the hard surface of the street. Once. Twice. Three times and the body went limp beneath him. Sarah exhaled with a hiss as she recoiled from the murder she'd just witnessed.

Alex looked up and saw her staring at him. Then he shifted his head to check on the rest of the huddle of men. He grabbed for the nearby machete and got to his feet in time for two more guys to step forward. They hung back because the glint of Alex's blade made them extremely aware that he was armed, and he'd already shown them he was dangerous.

"Whatever happens, you must get yourself somewhere safe, Sarah. Do you understand me?"

"Yes, but…"

Alex stood to his full height and waited.

"When I count to three, you are going to run back down the street. I will be right behind you but don't turn around because that'll only slow you down. And be as fast as you can."

He inhaled so he'd know she could hear him under his breath.

"One. Two. Three. Go!"

38

SARAH'S FOOTSTEPS RECEDED into the distance and Alex held his ground, wielding the large blade for all to see. Someone from the crowd lunged forward but Alex clipped his shoulder with the machete. The guy tumbled down, clutching his upper arm, and screaming in pain. The others near the front tried to take a step back—they had not been expecting one of these foreigners to put up much of a fight, but they hadn't encountered Alex before.

"Leave us alone. We've done nothing to you people. Let us pass by in peace and you won't have to suffer the consequences."

He was outnumbered thirty to one, but Alex's chief concern was to buy Sarah enough time to escape from this mob. He waved the machete some more as another guy edged forward from the group, weighing up his chances of getting the better of Alex. He was a little younger than the rest.

"Don't even think of trying it, boy. That is your last warning."

This sufficed to goad the boy into action and Alex knew it. Before the runt got within five feet of him, Alex swiped with the deadly blade and a blood-curdling noise emitted from the kid as he fell to the ground with his hands around his throat but he only had seconds to live as Alex had deftly slashed him from ear to ear. A murmur rose from the gang. They wanted revenge but didn't want to die.

Alex swallowed and focused on taking some deep breaths. He wasn't as young as he used to be, and he recognized the fear in the pit of his stomach. They were hanging back for now, but groups of angry men only wanted blood and he needed to time his next move precisely.

He swung the blade over his head so everyone could see it and as the machete entered the downward phase of its motion, Alex rotated round using the momentum of the knife and hit the sidewalk hard with his right foot. Then he ran as fast as he could away from the mob and down the street. Three seconds later there was a roar of noise as the men chased him, screaming abuse, their boots and shoes thumping on the concrete.

Alex didn't look back because he had the sound of their feet to judge how close they were, and his advice to Sarah was right—it would slow him down. He had one advantage over the mob; he knew where he was going and headed through the alleyway which was narrow enough for him to be sure that it would slow a group that big down a little.

Out the other side and then a choice: left or right. He and Sarah had come from the right and so he went left, hoping that the trouble they'd fled earlier hadn't moved further on. The sound of boots on the ground grew noticeably louder and Alex allowed himself a peek behind. Most of the men had reached the end of the alley but he had gained fifty, maybe one hundred, feet on them.

Alex kept on pelting along the sidewalk, looking for another alleyway or some other way to gain ground on the guys baying for his blood. The answer came in the form of a building in the middle of the street. Just a glance at it and Alex knew nobody was home—the broken glass for windows, the hanging piece of wood for a front door. Its other advantage was that there was no gap on either side. He ran at the entrance, kicked the door off its hinges, and scampered into the house.

WITHOUT HESITATING FOR a second, Alex sprinted through the entrance hall and entered the kitchen, which was strewn with boxes, rats, and who knew what else. In the darkness, Alex bashed into a waist-high cupboard and ricocheted off other unknown furniture until he got to the back door. Then out into the yard and he stopped.

There was fencing all the way round with a gate to the right. Alex pulled the exit open and considered going through it, but halted. By the wall to the left of the kitchen was an outhouse with tall grass and weeds in front.

Alex sprinted over to the outbuilding and took his shoulder to its door, which fell open easily enough, and he closed it behind him. He bent down with one eye peering through the crack in the gnarled wood and waited. Twenty seconds later a horde of men spewed into the yard and the first out of the kitchen staggered and headed through the gate. With the initial three out of the yard, the others followed until there was nobody left of the swarm and their noise subsided.

Alex waited for a count to sixty and then he peeked out: nobody. He skedaddled through the house and out the front, careful not to bump into the mob in case it had doubled back on him. With nobody on the street and nothing to see, he headed back to the alleyway and zigzagged to his home.

There were no lights on inside and he gulped. He opened the door and stepped into the entrance hall. "Sarah!" A body lunged at him, arms engulfed him, and Sarah kissed him hard on the lips. He needed no light to recognize the person hugging him for dear life. She was safe, and Alex allowed a tear of relief to trickle down his cheek.

"WHY NO LIGHTS?"

"There've been hordes running past, and we figured it would be safer if they didn't know we were here."

"We? Are Meyer and David with you?"

"No, Alex. There's only Ezra."

Now that Alex's eyes had got used to the darkness again, he noticed a figure standing in the doorway to the living room. He walked over and shook the man's hand.

"Good to see you are all right, my friend. Where did you get to this evening?"

"After midnight, I tried to make my way to the Nacional, but there were too many people on the street with hate in their hearts. So I figured I'd head straight over here and wait for you to appear; it had to happen at some point."

Alex walked past Ezra and slumped down on a couch, his legs buckling under him, he had been fleeing for so long. Sarah sat next to him and Ezra kept a watchful eye on the scene outside on the street. She brought him a glass of water and Alex relaxed for a minute to regain some much-needed energy.

"No sign of David or Meyer?"

"None."

The sadness in Sarah's voice tugged at his heartstrings, and Alex focused on the problem at hand.

"We can just wait for them to show or go and try to find them. Ezra has done the waiting for us, so I'll grab a gun and go back outside to look for them."

"You can't do that, Alex."

"We have no choice, Sarah. The sooner we get David back in one piece, then the sooner we leave this city."

"Let me go with you."

"No, Ezra, as much as I'd like your help, you have the more important job of staying here and protecting Sarah if any trouble should come calling. Understand?"

Ezra looked unhappy, but Alex knew his lieutenant would follow his instructions until the day he died. Alex knocked back the rest of his water and fumbled around his study until he had a revolver and four boxes of ammo. Then he dashed into the bedroom and changed into ordinary clothes.

He shoved the pistol into his pants pocket and kept the machete at hand. Sarah kissed him and flung her arms around his neck, not wanting to let go.

"Let me leave, Sarah. That way I will be back before you know it."

"Bring him home alive."

He brushed her cheek with the backs of two fingers before picking up the blade and heading out the door.

"If I'm not back in an hour, grab whatever you can and head to the airport. Do whatever you need to do to get off this island."

ALEX'S FIRST MOVE was to return to the Nacional and figure out quite where they'd lost David and Meyer in their rush to leave the area. This proved a short-lived plan as the streets were heaving with people, shouting and smashing any store window selling American goods. After a few minutes' thought, Alex realized he was going about this the wrong way, He was wasting his time attempting to retrace their steps. What he must do was think like Meyer and decide what he'd do if he was separated from the rest and needed to hide out somewhere safe.

Before long, Alex had skirted around the Nacional to the other side of the hotel, away from the coastline, and hopped from sidewalk to sidewalk until he reached the Lima Hastiada. Its frontage was boarded up, almost as though the owner knew there was trouble ahead, so Alex scampered to the rear to see if there was an open window.

All the windows were a no-show, but his luck was in, the back door was ajar instead. He took out his pistol and entered, listening for any sign of life. He edged into a room filled with crates of wine and tequila, as well as cases of beer. There were various kinds of food on a set of tall shelves to his left.

Alex shuffled to the door that led from this glorified store cupboard and into the private meeting area at the rear of the cantina; his usual booth was ten feet away from where he stood. He pressed his ear to the intervening door before slowly turning the handle and allowing it to creak open. He clenched his teeth, inhaled a lungful of air, and pushed the door wide enough to walk into the main bar.

Alex hit the dirt as he heard the click of a hammer being drawn back on a gun. One slug whizzed past his ear in the semi-darkness—the sun was rising outside. As much as Alex wanted to shoot at the person or persons unknown, he hadn't seen from which direction the bullet had come. Four boxes of ammo would soon become none if he sprayed the room indiscriminately.

"We've got the place surrounded," he lied in an authoritative tone. "Cease firing and everyone will get out of here alive."

There was a heartbeat, and then a timid voice broke the eerie silence.

"Pop?"

"Yes. Is Meyer with you?"

"Who else would've taken a shot at you? Not your *fercockte* son, that's for sure."

39

BACK AT ALEX'S home, everybody huddled in the living room in the dawn's half light. They'd closed the shutters on all the front-facing windows. Alex and Sarah sat next to each other, while Meyer and David were in two armchairs. Ezra stood by the door, always with one eye on the main entrance.

"Meyer, I think I understand Batista's note."

"No kidding, Alex."

"Is he still on the island?"

"If I know Batista, he'd have gone straight to the airport and off to the States before we'd inhaled after he exited the ballroom."

"Wouldn't he need to grab his gelt?

"Sarah, he holds almost all his money in private banks in Switzerland and Bermuda. The little he had lying around would've only kept him in chump change for a week."

"Meyer, his spare cash is what most of the men in Cuba call a lifetime's wages."

"That may be so, Alex, but this is no time for a discussion on Cuban politics."

"I wasn't planning on it but you admit that if he'd treated his people better, then maybe they might not have chased him out of the country."

Lansky looked down at the ground, watching his dream of a Vegas in Cuba slip through the floorboards.

"What'll happen if the rebels take over?"

"First thing I'd guess is that Meyer will no longer be minister for entertainment. You've lost that job, my friend."

Meyer continued to stare at the ground and didn't respond.

"Then there'll be a few changes—for the people, by the people. Based on what I saw last night, the guys on the street were destroying American stores. We won't be flavor of the month."

"Alex, what shall we do?"

"Sarah, first we need a better idea of what the hell is going on beyond the confines of this house. Second, we need to get ready to leave. Whatever is happening, I don't think we will be welcome at the minute, at least not until some of the heat dies down. Ezra, I need you to stay here while I go out. Will you need to grab any of your things when I return?"

"I'll live without any clothes I'm not wearing. Looks like I won't be saying goodbye to my girlfriend."

"Write her a letter when we are back in the US. Sarah, pack everything that's important into two suitcases. Anything we can afford to leave behind, then we will. David, do you need to get anything?"

"I have some papers…"

"If they are to do with business dealings in Cuba, forget about it. The regime after Batista can't possibly operate on the same terms as the generalissimo."

Sarah walked upstairs and David went to the kitchen to search for coffee for everybody. Meyer remained where he was, unaware of the bustle surrounding him. Alex sauntered over and squatted in front of him, placing a hand on his knee.

"Meyer, I need you to get it together. With Batista gone, all our leverage has flown out on the same plane. We must be ready to leave. You need to work out if there is anything you have that wasn't on the top floor of the Nacional because there is no way on earth that you'll walk inside that building again."

His friend looked up and stared straight ahead.

"Meyer, I'm going to check out what is happening on the streets and then we shall figure out how to get off this island."

JUST BEFORE HE left the house, Alex tied a handkerchief over his face to shield his less than Hispanic features. The streets in this affluent area were vacant; last night's violence had given way to this morning's calm. He kept to the shadows and did his best to travel behind the houses rather than on the streets to hide from any potential trouble.

Eventually, Alex arrived near the center of Havana, a thousand feet from the casino district, and that is where he found the good people of this fine city. They were marching or listening to men making impromptu speeches about how everything was going to be better now that they had driven the evil Batista out of Cuba.

Alex smiled beneath his mask. Ordinary folk like the ones gathered in front of him never had it any better. People with money make more money and that was how it had always been.

Restaurants and bars had opened up hoping to catch some trade from thirsty and hungry rioters. This contrasted with the broken glass and empty stores where the signage indicated they aimed the contents at American tourists. Alex thought about the Lima Hastiada and decided that it was worth a visit.

Using the same caution as when he'd come into town, Alex sidled his way over to the cantina to see if it was open. Sure enough, there were barflies at the counter and two occupied tables. He headed straight for his back booth and waited. The owner came over and asked him what he wanted.

"Some information and a drink, if you'll serve me."

"You got money? Then I'll bring you a coffee. Anything else and I'm not so sure."

"Just tell me what happened last night. I know Batista fled, but why then?"

"Haven't you listened to the radio, Alex?"

"If I had, would I need to ask you?"

"The rebels took Santa Clara yesterday. Word is that they are now marching on Havana."

"How long do you think it'll take them to get here?"

"Less than a week. The twenty-sixth of July Movement was never a big band, but with victory in the south and Batista out of the way, their numbers will swell."

"So my family and I have time to breathe?"

"Some gasps maybe, but you don't want to be here when Castro arrives in town. The man has spent the last three years making speeches about how all the problems of Cuba are down to Batista and his capitalist cronies. With all due respect, Alex, I think he was talking about you."

THE REBELS MIGHT be a day or two away from Havana, but that didn't make the place any safer for Alex, his family, and friends. The best course of action was to get out that day because who knew what would happen tomorrow.

"We can try to catch a seat on the ferry to Key West or head for the airport."

Alex summarized their options when he got back to the house. Lansky appeared not to have moved the entire time Alex was away, and two cases were stuffed to within an inch of their lives by the door.

"I have a twin-prop."

Meyer broke his silence and dropped a simple piece of information in their laps.

"A private plane at the airport?"

"Yes, of course. When you are in Batista's government, they are one of the perks of the job."

"Is it yours or Batista's?"

"That doesn't matter right now, Alex. We have a means of leaving the island with no customs officer in the States getting his nose put out of joint wherever we land."

"You have nothing with you, Meyer. So why do you care about Uncle Sam?"

"Not now, but I need to empty some safe deposit boxes before I go."

"Meyer, I wasn't planning on taking anything like that. Isn't it more important that we are alive? We can always make more gelt somewhere else."

Meyer sighed.

"To make gelt, you need gelt and, in America, I was always careful not to have any asset in my name—for tax reasons, you understand."

Alex stared at him, not comprehending the implication that Meyer thought so obvious.

"This means that most of my wealth is in gold and cash. I can't get it wired anyway because there are no records that I own it. I am the only one with a key to the deposit boxes. If I don't leave with the money, then I'll have nothing."

"What about your income from your other investments?"

"I put it all into Cuba. This was to be my paradise."

Meyer sank back into silence. Alex's mind raced. They had no idea how long the airport would remain open, assuming flights were still being allowed right now. And the longer they waited to allow Meyer to grab his loot, the more dangerous it could be. The innkeeper believed it would be a few days before the rebels hit town but Alex knew more than him about how armies behaved. He reckoned they'd arrive tomorrow, if not later that day.

Right now there was a vacuum at the center of power in the capital and Castro couldn't afford for anybody like another tinpot army general to seize the moment and take over before the rebels arrived.

40

"THIS IS THE deal, everyone. We'll drive over to the airport or as close as we can get. Then into Meyer's plane and away we go. All of us—not one person will be left behind."

Nods all round and Ezra opened the door and scurried to Alex's car to bring it from where it was parked at the back of the house. With still nothing on the street, they packed the trunk with cases and piled inside, Alex and Ezra at the front and the other three in the rear.

For most of the journey to the airport, there was nobody on the streets and no trouble along the way. The situation altered as they approached the outskirts of the airfield fencing. An armed guard stood at the first entrance and the barrier was down. Alex didn't fancy convincing a bunch of yokels to let him through, so he kept on down the road.

Alex turned right, and the vehicle headed north until they reached another barrier surrounded by a second crew of rebels. He slowed the saloon down and stopped two hundred feet short.

"Keep sharp, Ezra. Let's stay calm but prepare for the worst."

Alex trundled the car forwards and halted in front of the roadblock. One of the group, toting a rifle with the barrel resting on his arm, indicated for him to stop even as he hit the brake. Alex wound down his window.

"Afternoon, what is your business here?"

"We wish to buy tickets to fly out and are hoping we can get away today."

"Where are you intending to travel to?"

"The Bahamas."

"Are you Americans?"

"Yes, we have been working over here and now we want to leave. What's going on in your country means that we won't be able to earn a living until things calm down."

"What do you guys do?"

"We're involved in the entertainment industry."

"I understand why you're wanting to get out of here, but we cannot allow you to do that."

"Can you explain why please?"

"We are restricting the number of flights out of Cuba, and the only individuals allowed into the airport compound already have tickets."

Alex nodded and took another look at the group. There were four, two behind the guy who'd done the talking and one on the other side of the vehicle near to Ezra. Alex tapped on the shift stick to get Ezra's attention and gesticulated his intentions.

"My friend is just going to help me turn the car around, okay?"

"If you don't know how to drive, what's a guy to do. Go ahead but make it quick."

Alex smiled and attempted to imply some humility by not looking straight into the guy's eyes. Ezra hopped out and headed for the barrier while Alex returned the vehicle to the road and then executed a poor reversing maneuver so that Ezra was forced to slam his palm against the back of the car to stop Alex hitting the obstacle. Meanwhile, the crew laughed at Alex's bad driving and chatted to each other, making jokes at his expense. He didn't mind.

The turn signals flipped on and the windshield wipers flashed left and right at high speed before the engine stalled. Alex shook his head and stepped out of the car.

"Sure isn't my day. You got a light?"

Hector Sastre, the chief, laughed at him and fumbled around his pockets until he found a book of matches. Alex took a smoke from his pack and leaned towards him, cupping the end of his cigarette to stop the wind from attacking the fire that appeared in front of him.

As he shifted position to bend down and avail himself of the flickering flame, Alex dropped the cigarette and whipped out his pistol, putting a slug in the center of the leader's stomach. His body recoiled slightly, but Alex grabbed his neck and swung round to face two more of the group. With Hector to shield him, Alex twisted and poked the barrel of his gun under the guy's armpit.

Two clean shots and the men's corpses twitched on the ground. Another shot rang out and Alex looked over. Ezra stood over the last body and kicked it to make sure the guy was dead. They raised the barrier and Alex turned the engine over. Then they thundered inside, following the single-track road until it reached an open space with hangars all around.

"Where's your plane, Meyer?"

"Hangar sixteen."

"And what about the pilot?"

"Good question."

The enormous numbers painted on each hangar let Alex know where to go. Within sixty seconds, they were inside the building and Alex pondered their next move.

"EZRA, DO YOU know how to fly a plane?"

"You're joking, right, Alex?"

"We need someone, don't we?"

Ezra looked around just in case a pilot might appear inside the hangar, but no joy.

"Any suggestions, Meyer?"

"Next door is a rest area away from the customers. We might find one in there."

That was the best idea they had, so Alex stashed his gun and strode through a side entrance that Meyer pointed at. Inside were several tables and chairs, along with some couches and armchairs, the sort of environment a pilot would use to relax in between flights or to catch a nap.

Only trouble was that the place seemed deserted and the sheer number of half-empty cups and glasses showed there had been quite an exodus. Alex walked through an open door on the other side of the space into a room with some beds in it. Sure enough, this was where pilots came to sleep.

Just as Alex was about to leave the suite, an enormous sound erupted from nowhere. On closer inspection, the noise emanated from a man in the far corner whose head was hidden by his sheets. Alex pulled out his gun and aimed it at the guy as he threw off the bedding.

Another snore was the only response, so Alex tapped his chest with the tip of the revolver. An eye opened and then Mike Sniders sat bolt upright.

"Easy, my friend."

Sniders stared at the barrel of the gun and remained still.

"Where is everybody and why didn't you join them?"

"No idea. I've been out cold since the early hours of this morning. I ferried a guy off the island and came back because he said his friends would be over later today."

"Are you from the US?"

"Sure am."

Alex picked up the guy's jacket from the floor and read his identity badge.

"Mike, this country is no place for Americans right now. The rebels are moving in on Havana and when they do, they are going to be more concerned with the lives of the local population than with the likes of you and me."

Sniders stared some more at the gun, and Alex lowered it to help him keep Mike's attention on the matter at hand.

"You prepared to fly a group to the States? We'll pay you a decent rate."

"I said I'd wait for this other bunch."

Alex raised his pistol so Mike could get a good look at it again.

"There's money in it for you and you can still come back and pick up more passengers. We've got a plane for you to use, but we need to leave now. What's your answer?"

"Cash and a plane?"

"Yep. And keep the aircraft once we're done with it. That's got to be worth something to you."

Sniders thought for two seconds and then agreed.

"When are we going?"

"As soon as you're ready for takeoff."

MIKE TOOK A couple of minutes to get himself together and hustled about the kitchenette to make and consume a mug of coffee, all the while watched over by Alex. Then into the hangar where Sarah and David nestled next to each other and Meyer stared blankly into nowhere. Ezra's gun was in his hand; he stood by the entrance permanently on the lookout for trouble.

Sniders entered the ten-seater and Alex followed him just in case he got clever. But the most he did was switch on the engines and check the fuel.

"Someone was here before. You rarely leave a plane lying around with a full tank."

"I'd guess that Batista's planes had different rules."

"Are you telling me we're about to steal an airplane from the government?"

"That's the old management, Mike. The general won't need this jalopy again, he's already fled the country."

"In that case, I'm ready as soon as you guys hop on board."

Alex exited the twin-prop to speak to the others.

"It's time to get on the plane and Mike will take you out of here."

Sarah looked at him quizzically.

"You're coming too, Alex?"

"I'll pay Mike for a return trip and he can bring me tomorrow. If we have any hope of salvaging anything, we must act now but you guys need to be safe on American soil."

"If you stay, then so will I."

"Sarah, this isn't a debate. I need you to get on that plane and make sure David gets back in one piece."

"Alex, gelt is never worth the trouble you take over it."

"I've stashed enough money around this city to keep us in clover if I can get at it all before the rebels arrive."

He hugged her tightly and whispered in her ear. "But I need you to leave now. We'll see each other tomorrow. I promise."

They kissed and Alex led Sarah onto the plane, followed by David and Meyer. Just before Ezra stepped onto the airstairs, Alex caught his arm. "Look after them for me. If Sniders causes you any trouble, kill him when you get on the ground." Ezra nodded and boarded the twin-prop. Alex entered the cockpit and sat down in the copilot's seat.

"Mike, this is the deal. I'll pay you two hundred and fifty dollars to fly my family and friends to the Bahamas. And five thousand in total to come straight back and pick me up here."

Sniders whistled. That was what he'd normally earn in a year, and Alex hoped this would swing the deal.

"You're not coming with?"

"I've got some loose ends to tie up, but I want to leave this hellhole tonight and you're the man to help me."

"How d'you know I won't welch on the deal?"

"You only get paid when I see you again."

Alex beamed at Mike and the guy mulled over the proposition for four seconds until he agreed. They shook hands and Alex hopped off the plane and helped Mike to close the door. Then he stepped back as the aircraft taxied out of the hangar and waited for permission to take off. With no other planes on the wing, Alex watched his family depart Cuba in less than a minute. Now he needed to scoop up as much of his money hidden around Havana as he could before Sniders returned and Castro's men waltzed into town.

41

THE GOOD NEWS was that Alex had access to any tool he might need as the maintenance crews had departed as quickly as anybody else from the airport site. He figured that if the rebels were protecting the boundary fence, then they intended to seize control of the runway as soon as they entered Havana. He used metal cutters to create a hole in the mesh fencing so he could get back in with no permission from anyone at a barrier.

Mike would take a little over an hour to reach the Bahamas, have the inevitable mug of coffee, and return after another hour so Alex needed to ensure he was at hangar sixteen in two hours. This would not be sufficient time to get the job done. A glance at his watch and he made some calculations.

Sniders would need to accept an overnight layover if Alex was to reach all the places he needed to in the city. Until Castro's forces arrived in the vicinity, Mike would not be bothered. No one would be stupid enough to land in Havana today, and the handful of people who could get past the guards at the gates would fly off in their private planes; scheduled flights were off the agenda for the foreseeable future. Revolutions mess with capitalist timetables.

ALEX ONLY HAD about thirty minutes near the city center before having to get back to hangar sixteen to await Sniders' return. Almost three hours after his departure, a plane landed and taxied over. The engines cut and Mike appeared, grinning, along with another man. Alex put a hand on his pistol. This was not part of the agreement, although Mike might not have been as dumb as he looked. If this was a hijacking, then they'd die for their troubles.

"Hi, Alex."

Lansky's voice softened Alex's mood in an instant and he ran over to his old friend.

"What are you doing here, Meyer? Are Sarah and David all right?"

"They are safely holed up in a suite at a hotel. With Mike coming back to collect you, I thought I'd join him and pick up a few things I didn't get a chance to grab earlier today."

There was a light in Meyer's eyes that had been absent from the minute Batista left the Nacional ballroom. Alex smiled, then he turned his attention to Sniders.

"Mike, there's a slight change in the plan. The city is difficult to travel around, which means Meyer and I will need more time to gather our possessions."

"Are you about to tell me we aren't shipping out until tomorrow?"

"You read my mind, Mike."

The pilot looked down and then scanned the far distance of the airport as though he could see Castro's men marching toward them.

"That's not what I signed up to, Alex. And every minute we are here, those rebels are closing in on us."

Alex let him stew for a few seconds.

"I'll double your fee. Ten big ones to go next door to sleep and then fly out tomorrow morning."

Mike held out his hand, and they shook. Alex had known the promise of more cash would help Sniders make the right decision. The only risk was that he and Lansky would need to leave him alone, and anything could happen to him then. Most likely, he'd catch a yellow streak down his back and decide to quit the country without them.

ALEX DROVE MEYER to the outskirts of the city and then hid the car in an alley. There was no point risking the vehicle being found, and they had a wide variety of locations to reach before the morning.

"Meyer, do you have any cash in the banks or is all your money in deposit boxes?"

"Are banks even open today? It's New Year's Day, after all. And yes, there's some hidden around the city."

With all his focus on escape, Alex had forgotten that this was a public holiday and that the banks were closed.

"You're right. We can forget about bank accounts unless you want us to pull a robbery this evening?"

"Alex, I figure that'd be overreaching. I just need to go round a few government buildings and apartments with a jimmy. Then I'll be ready to leave this town."

"I think we should hide out somewhere when night falls. The mood on the street only darkens when the sun goes down."

They used the next half hour to plan a route for the remainder of the day. Alex had an idea where they could rest their heads.

The number of people on the streets increased and when they got near the principal government offices, Alex and Meyer found swathes of men milling around the buildings. This meant at least it was easy to get inside the Ministry of Industry and Commerce, which was where Meyer's office had been located.

The two men walked through the main entrance surrounded by a steady stream of locals. At first glance, you'd be forgiven for thinking this was just another day, but the knives and occasional rifles slung over shoulders belied the fact that the Cuban rebels were beating a march over to the capital.

Meyer led the way up three flights of stairs and right, along a corridor, then left and into an anteroom that Alex recognized. There was nobody in the vicinity, so Alex stood guard while Meyer went inside to rip up floorboards and came out with two cases stuffed with dollar bills. Alex took one look at his friend and slapped his forehead.

"Meyer, we didn't think through the size of our stash. By the time we visit one more place, we'll have our hands full and even a stupid peasant will figure out that something's amiss."

"Let's make our way to the car, perhaps we must risk taking it round the city."

Alex wasn't happy with that suggestion. Keeping it hidden meant they wouldn't need to worry about getting back to the plane. Driving around town with Castro's army on their heels was not a great option, but it was the best they had. By the time they returned to the car, the sun had almost vanished below the horizon.

"Let's hole up for the night."

"Shouldn't we go to check on Mike?"

"Meyer, either he's flown off without us or he is asleep next door to the hangar. We can't do anything about it right now. Tomorrow we must be as quick as we can and sort out our affairs at the earliest possible moment. To do that, we need to be nearby when we wake up and I've got the perfect place where we'll be welcomed with open arms and given a warm bed and hot food too."

ALEX TOOK MEYER to the Plaza del Vapor where even on the day of Cuba's revolution, women stood on street corners seeking men with money to burn. While the fellas had controlled casinos and hotels in the country, prostitution in Havana had remained a local affair with one madam ruling the roost, just round the rear of the Shanghai Theater. Benita Rodríguez greeted Alex and Lansky as they entered her establishment.

"How are you, Alex?"

"Just fine under the circumstances. My friend and I are hoping you might have a room for us for one night."

"Of course you do, and you've come to the right place. These are trying times, but you are welcome here any day of the week, you know that."

Benita supplied girls to all the hotels that Alex looked after and they had made a lot of money together over the years.

"And if you have some bread and coffee, then that'd be wonderful."

"We can do better than that for you, Alex."

She left them in the reception area where at least a dozen women stood, sat, or reclined in various states of undress. Alex chose an armchair and Meyer reclined opposite on a chaise longue. As soon as they eased themselves into their seating, Alex felt a hand rifling through his hair and a girl in a corset and not much else flopped onto his lap.

"Thanks, but we are just browsing."

She shrugged, pecked him on the cheek, and sauntered to the other end of the room to giggle with her girlfriend. Meyer flicked his hand at an arm that had appeared on his chest, which disappeared. They were probably the only men ever to refuse the sexual advances of the nafkas in this boudoir.

Within an hour, they had eaten a fine meal with Benita, away from the working girls, and she had allocated them a room each.

"Would you like some company for the night—on the house?"

"Very kind, but we won't take advantage of your hospitality any more than we need to. All we ask is that you get one of the girls to wake us at five. We've a busy day tomorrow and want to start as early as we can."

"Consider it done."

As soon as Alex's head landed on the lavender-scented pillow, a wave of tiredness hit and he went straight to sleep.

January 2, 1959

42

ALEX AWOKE WHEN he felt someone's fingers inside his pants and he sat bolt upright. A nafka in a negligee squatted on his bed, attempting to get his attention—she'd succeeded.

"Thanks, but you've done your job."

He pulled out a couple of notes, removed her hand from his clothing, and placed the money in her palm. A smile and he pointed at the door. Alex waited in the reception area for Meyer to appear—he needed more time to rouse himself. No sooner had he walked into the room than Alex stood up and they exited the brothel, although he left a cash donation in Benita's hands, despite her protestations.

For the next four hours, they drove around the city while either Alex or Meyer popped into a building or alleyway and grabbed a case hidden under floorboards or in a wall. Although he didn't have time to count, Alex estimated he'd gathered at least two million dollars of his own gelt in the vehicle.

Meyer arrived back from a crash pad he'd kept for his girlfriend and threw a bag into the trunk.

"I have so many happy memories of that place."

Alex held a finger to his lips and Lansky stopped speaking. Something didn't feel right, and Alex couldn't quite say what it was. A low rumble in the distance; he felt it in his chest more than he heard it with his ears.

"It's time to go."

Meyer didn't need to be told twice. Alex gunned the car down the street and around the edge of town. The vehicle screeched to a halt as Alex stared along the straight avenue leading out of the city. All he could see was not much more than a speck of dust on the horizon.

"The rebels are on their way."

For a second, Alex did a calculation based on where they were, the direction of the army, and the location of the plane. Then he gulped.

"They'll get to the airport before we do."

Alex looked at Meyer.

"You'll be proved right if we stay here. What are you waiting for, you meshuggener mensch? Drive!"

Alex's foot slammed on the gas pedal and the vehicle skidded forwards. While he couldn't work out the exact speed of the rebels, the airfield seemed an awfully long way away. He gunned the car along the main avenue which led to the airport. All the while the ball of dust got larger as they headed straight towards it, hoping to reach the plane before the revolutionaries.

Ten minutes of hard driving and the engine screamed as Alex tried to squeeze every drop of speed out of the saloon. They were a quarter of a mile from Alex's hidden entrance, and the army was less than half a mile in front. A solitary vehicle sped ahead of the main group—they'd been spotted.

"Hang on tight."

Fifteen seconds later, Alex slammed his automobile through the wire-mesh fence and carried on hurtling to hangar sixteen. As they reached the entrance, Alex saw a jeep appear from the makeshift entrance and head straight toward them.

Alex hooted three times to warn Mike of their arrival. The car screeched to a halt as close as Alex could take it beside the airplane. Its propellers were already turning and as soon as he got out of the vehicle, Alex felt the airflow caused by the blades. Meyer and Alex grabbed as many cases as they could and chucked them inside the cabin. Then again, and for a third time. A glance showed the jeep five hundred feet away.

"Meyer, get in. There's no more time."

His friend shook his head and went back for a fourth set of bags. Alex grabbed him by the arm and slapped him on the cheek.

"We're dead if we don't leave now."

A bullet flew past their heads as if to emphasize Alex's point. Meyer blinked and ran to the airplane door. Alex took out his gun and fired a meaningless shot in the jeep's direction which was only two hundred feet away. As soon as Alex was inside the plane, Mike taxied forward.

"Get us up, Mike, as quick as you can."

Alex aimed at the jeep's tires but missed due to the abrupt movement of the twin-prop as it trundled onto the runway. A hail of bullets came from the rebel vehicle, but none touched the plane's fuselage. The rear wheels left the ground and Alex held his pistol steady in his hands as he tried to fire off one last round. He hit the windshield, and the jeep swerved to a stop.

Then a change in the sound as the plane wheels stopped making contact with the ground. Meyer helped Alex close the door, and they sat down in the nearest seats and waited for Mike to take them to the safety of the Bahamas.

WHEN THEY LANDED a little under two hours later, the two men offloaded their cases into a waiting car that Meyer had hired for the week. They gave Mike his money and shook him by the hand, then Lansky drove them to Nassau and the Providence Hotel. Up to the top floor and into Sarah's arms. Then a hug for David and Alex flopped onto a couch.

The next thing he knew, he opened his eyes and found himself in bed. A glance at the bedside clock told him it was the middle of the afternoon, but he had no memory of how he'd got there. The bedroom door creaked and Sarah's head appeared. She smiled when she saw he was awake.

"Are you all right, Sarah?"

"For sure, now that I have you back."

"Those few hours were a long hustle."

"So Meyer was saying, especially your overnight stay."

Alex's cheeks felt red hot and Sarah grinned at him.

"What goes on in Cuba stays in Cuba, Alex."

"I can't speak for Meyer, but nothing happened at Benita's apart from a meal and a *shloof*."

Another grin stretched across Sarah's face as she threw her dress onto the floor and wriggled beneath the sheets.

"I believe you, but you'd better work damn hard to convince me you shouldn't sleep in the car tonight."

THE FOLLOWING MORNING everybody met in the Providence restaurant. Alex ordered his usual huge breakfast, and the rest took a selection of bread, cheese, and Danish pastries. A variety of juices and coffee appeared on the table too.

"What are we going to do now?"

"Sarah, I think we should stay here for a few days and have a vacation while we figure out our next steps."

"I can't speak for you guys, but I'm staying in the Bahamas."

"Why, Meyer?"

"Because with the seed capital I rescued from Havana, I'm going to turn this place into the new Las Vegas."

Alex almost spat the coffee out of his mouth.

"Are you serious? After everything we've just been through?"

"This can be paradise on earth for us, Alex."

"Don't involve me, Meyer. I want to get back to American soil. Florida, maybe."

"You think? This is a tremendous opportunity."

Alex turned to David.

"What's your advice?"

"Pop, you didn't listen to me the last time, so why are you going to hear a word I say on this occasion?"

"Who told you that? I never wired the money over to Batista for the Panama Hotel. That's why Meyer wants my gelt now."

Meyer nodded sanguinely.

"It was never a trust issue with me, Meyer. Or rather I'd work with you until the end of my days, but I couldn't trust Batista further than I could spit."

"The offer to invest in the Bahamas is still there if you change your mind, Alex."

"Thank you, Meyer. But right now, I think I'm going to head for Florida and try out retirement. Those collections we made in Havana have to be good for something."

Sarah held Alex's hand.

"I thought you'd work until the day you died?"

"When I said retire, I meant drop a dime to Sam Giancana to see if there's any action I could get involved with."

"Alex, you tread careful with those Italians. You didn't trust Batista, but I feel the same way about Genovese, Giancana, and the rest of them fellas."

"Don't worry, Meyer. With Sarah and David by my side, what could possibly go wrong?"

BOOK SIX HOLLYWOOD BILKER

February 1960

1

"THANKS FOR TAKING the time to see me, Santo."

The Italian boss of Florida nodded his acknowledgment of Alex's words as they sipped their coffees in the back of one of the many casinos owned by the Sicilian in Miami-Dade county.

"Cuba was a terrible business for us all. I am only glad we got out with our lives."

"Santo, I don't think I ever saw Batista travel faster than his last minutes in power. That man knew the right time to flee."

"And he left the rest of us high and dry."

Now Alex nodded as he recalled the final two days in Havana, with his close friend and business associate, Meyer Lansky, as he attempted to salvage the gelt he had secreted around the city; they never trusted the banks.

"That was the past, Santo. Despite all that has happened, I am trying to focus on future opportunities."

"Spoken like a true businessman. How can I help?"

"I am hoping you'll make an introduction for me to Frank DeSimone out in Los Angeles."

"What's wrong with the Eastern Seaboard?"

"Nothing at all, I just want to get as far away from Cuba as possible, at least for a short while. Having spent so many years in the Vegas and Havana hotel complexes, I thought I might check out life in Hollywood. I've mixed with enough of the celebrities to know what they are like and I can see some opportunities for myself, subject to Frank's approval, of course."

"Alex, I will give you the introduction you seek with pleasure. You have proven yourself in the past and I wish you every success in your new enterprise."

The two men shook hands and Alex left the back room, knowing that by the time he contacted DeSimone, Santo would have put in a good word. What Alex failed to realize was that as a former syndicate member and the fella who still ran Las Vegas, his reputation was the only calling card he needed.

Perhaps his seven years spent in Cuba helping Meyer build a casino resort in paradise had left Alex jaded. In the four weeks since his return to the US, he had given no indication that he was a guy sitting on over two million bucks he had brought back to the country.

SARAH AND ALEX arrived at their Boyle Heights home less than a month later. They held hands as they walked up the drive, and Alex felt her fingers squeeze around his palm before he opened the front door.

"How long do you think we'll be here, Alex?"

"Beats the hell out of me, hon'. For now, I am thinking of finding a way to make some gelt and then we retire."

"I thought you'd saved sufficient money from Havana before we flew out?"

"You can never have enough cash. Besides, I'm too young to stop working, don't you think?"

"Without Meyer's accounts to look after, it looks like I will have time on my hands too."

"The first job we've both got to deal with is getting ourselves nested in this place."

They stood in the middle of the emptiness, which was their living room: bare floorboards, and no furniture. Sarah followed Alex as he sauntered to the rear of the house and opened up the doors onto their patio. The swimming pool was boarded over and the summerhouse looked uninviting.

Sarah let go of Alex's hand, dashed into the living room, and appeared on the balcony on the second floor. He waved at her and she laughed. They would do well here, he thought, as he considered what he was going to arrange with DeSimone.

FURNITURE AND SOFT furnishings changed their house into a home. Sarah had not wasted her years with Meyer as she took on the role of project manager for the transformation. She said what she wanted and when it needed to happen, and all the people working for her knew it too. She did not allow a single one to fail her.

Alex spent his time in the summerhouse, hiding from being asked his opinion on the colors of tables and chairs, but also to escape from the chill that hung in the air. They might have been away from Cuba for over a year, but he had still to acclimatize to the less than Caribbean temperatures.

Once Sarah declared the end of her project, Alex spent more time in the main building, although in that short while he had made the summerhouse his office.

"You can move your things into the den. I've decked it out especially for you."

"I like the fact that this has a different path to the entrance, Sarah."

"Is that to have discreet meetings without my seeing?"

"Having a detached place is nice. It means we can separate business from personal. And you are an essential part of the operation. Just because we are back in the US doesn't mean I intend to treat you the same way as when we were first married. My investments are your investments; we sink or swim together."

Sarah's shoulders sagged. "I had plans for the summerhouse: I thought we might turn it into a children's playroom."

"Children?"

"For when the grandkids visit."

Alex nodded, although he couldn't see David or Moishe schlepping over to the West Coast very often. Not that either of them had even met a woman, let alone produced an heir.

"Perhaps we could build a new spot for them."

"Or Alex, you could have an office a little further away from the pool."

He smiled. There was something fabulous about the idea of having a conversation about money laundering and then hopping into the water for a swim. Perhaps he could cope with a twenty-foot walk between the two activities and it would make Sarah happy too.

"Before we settle down too much, do you fancy taking a trip with me to Las Vegas? I have some business I want to sort out with Ezra and Massimo?"

"I'll stay here and leave you to speak to your men by yourself."

"That wasn't what I meant."

"I know, Alex. I'd rather spend some time enjoying the fresh nest I've built before I fly off."

THE NEXT DAY, Alex took one of the new jet planes over to Vegas and one of his lieutenant's drivers met him at the airport. Alex stood at the arrivals gate until a fella in a long black coat and a fedora walked up to him and asked if he had a light.

"Sure, Mac."

Alex proffered a match, and the guy nodded briefly and lit his cigar.

"You need a lift, Mac?"

"I'm waiting for someone, thanks."

"Are they coming from the Sands?"

Alex eyed him up and down and nodded.

"Then you've found your driver, Mr. Cohen."

"How do you know I'm this guy you mention?"

"You look the spit of your photo and you haven't denied being Alex Cohen."

He thought for a moment and decided this fella had made a good point.

"What's your name?"

"Tito Vestri. Follow me."

Tito grabbed Alex's case before he had a chance to protest and pounded out to the sidewalk where his limousine waited by a hydrant. A local cop stood nearby and appeared about to issue a ticket, but he took one look at Vestri and put away his notebook.

"GOOD TO SEE you, fellas, and thank you for making time for me with only a day's notice."

Alex was in his suite with Ezra Kohut and Massimo Sciarra for company. He lounged in an armchair, and the two others sat at either end of a matching leather couch. A bellboy had just left, having delivered coffee and some snacks that Ezra had ordered on his way up to Alex's room.

"We always have time for you, Alex. You should know that by now."

Alex smiled at Massimo for his kind words and his chest puffed out in response.

"How's business with you two?"

"Everything is good, Alex. Are you concerned about your end being short?"

"Not at all, Ezra. Should I be?"

"Oh no, not at all. It's just been a while since you've journeyed to visit us and I thought you might have a problem you wanted to discuss."

Alex's eyebrows took a few seconds to lower from their new high perch, but he relaxed as he took in Ezra's and Massimo's expressions.

"After our troubles in Havana, Sarah and I have spent some time putting ourselves back together. Now we have moved to Los Angeles, I thought the time was right for us to talk about the future. I've had enough of sitting in the Florida sun and want something to do."

Ezra looked at Massimo, who stared back. Neither wanted to say what they were thinking, but Alex knew there was an opinion to be uttered. He allowed silence to descend until one of them expressed their thoughts. Massimo was the first to break ranks.

"Do you want to take Vegas from us?"

Alex laughed.

"Quite the reverse. You have both been kind enough to provide me with my tithe, month in and month out, no matter what has been happening at home or away. While I am looking for my next opportunity, I also am thinking about separating my legitimate businesses from the rest. When I do, I want you two to be assured that I'll do the right thing by you in Vegas."

"You mean…"

"Yes, Ezra. In the near future, I will hand over control of my gaming interests to you and Massimo."

"I never thought I'd hear you talk of retiring, Alex."

"Soon, Massimo, but not just yet."

2

FRANK DESIMONE'S CASUAL dress caught Alex by surprise. He was expecting a suit and tie and was greeted by slacks and a plaid jumper. When he'd last lived on the West Coast, things were different, but that was before his Cuban escapade and America invaded Korea.

"Thank you for taking the time to see me, Frank."

"My pleasure, Alex. Apologies for my attire, but I have just hopped off the golf course as I was running late and did not have a chance to change."

"Not at all. That's a game I've never tried."

"Didn't they have any courses in Havana because they sure as hell do in Miami? Isn't that where you've been holed up this past year?"

"Pretty much, Frank. I guess I've never been bitten by the bug."

"You'll get there, Alex. In the meantime, how are you keeping yourself busy?"

"My interests in Las Vegas are served well by what you would describe as my capos and now I'm looking for a fresh opportunity in California."

"If there is anything specific you want to discuss, then I am all ears, but please don't expect me to throw you some crumbs from my plate."

Alex shuffled in his seat because he'd thought Santo would have primed Frank better. That said, Alex only wanted a little something to keep him afloat until the next big deal came across his lap, if it ever did.

"I was in the Sands Hotel a while back and met up with some old Hollywood friends: Frank Sinatra, Sammy Davis Jr., and Peter Langford. There were doing their schtick on stage when I was shooting through. Do you think you could sanction an import/export business focused on Burbank?"

"What are you looking to move?"

"A small amount of cocaine and marijuana."

"And girls?"

"If I can feed the party set, then it makes sense to fan the flames of entertainment while I am there. Would that be acceptable to you? I don't want to step on anybody's toes and if you've got that action covered, then I'll find something else."

"No disrespect to you, Alex, but it is small fry for us so it's not an area we've focused on. Be my guest, for the usual fee."

"That goes without saying, Frank. Of course, I will show you the appropriate consideration. Despite what McCarthy might have thought, we are not all communists just because we live on the West Coast."

Frank smiled.

"And that is the joke people up in the Hollywood Hills still don't find funny. I wish you well with your new endeavor. Let me know if you need my assistance at any point."

THE PARTY WAS in full swing and Alex found himself standing with a Scotch in his hand talking to Frank Sinatra. The guy had the ear of Sam Giancana, so Alex knew he could be trusted, and he understood why Alex was attending this Hollywood shindig: to catch some customers in his web.

Not that he had a problem with Sinatra. Unbeknownst to the crooner and actor, their paths had first crossed at the Havana conference back in the '40s when the heads of the syndicate had met to decide the fate of Benny Siegel.

The singer had performed on the first night. Then every time Sinatra had performed in one of the Cuban hotels owned by Lansky, Giancana, or Trafficante, Alex had been in the audience or in the group that had gone out for dinner the same evening. Now they were chatting like old friends, while the whole of Hollywood cavorted around them.

"How long are you going to be in town, Alex?"

"I moved into Boyle Heights this month, so you'll be seeing a lot more of me."

"Always a pleasure, never a chore. You know that. Is there anything I can get for you?"

Alex recalled this gathering was in Frank's place. He raised his tumbler and said, "I'm good, thanks."

"That's not what I meant, Alex. Can I get you *anything*?"

Frank's hand swept around the room, palm up, and if Alex didn't mistake the gesture, it appeared as though the fella's fingers lingered only on the women in the room. Alex's cheeks tingled for a moment and he ground his molars.

"Not for me, thanks. Quite the reverse. If you know of anyone who needs a companion for the evening, then let me know in future."

Sinatra returned his hand to his side and stared at Alex for a long second. Then he nodded.

"Sure thing, Alex. I hold a party only once a season, but I will bear that in mind."

"And tell your friends the offer's good for them too."

Another nod.

"Let me introduce you to some of my buddies, Alex. You know the rat pack, but there are plenty more names you can put to faces."

Alex smiled and followed Frank around the room, but he didn't have the heart to tell him he didn't bother with the movies unless it was a good Western.

AN HOUR LATER and Alex had only worked half the party. He recognized most of the names he heard and made a special detour to pass by Ginger Rogers and say hello, but he feigned sufficient concern over the lives of the others to make tens of new friends.

One face that he knew was attached to a curvaceous body and a shock of platinum blond hair. Alex reckoned he had nothing to lose and sauntered over to her and the guy she was with. "Sorry to interrupt, but I just wanted to say how much I love your work." Then he turned to walk elsewhere.

"Hey, bud. Thank you for saying so but there's no need to run away."

Alex stopped, sipped his Scotch, and introduced himself.

"Thanks, Marilyn."

"Tell me, which of my performances did you appreciate the most?"

Alex's mind went blank. Just because he recognized Marilyn Monroe did not mean he'd seen any of her films.

"Some Like It Hot?"

She scowled, and he realized he had said the wrong thing, but he'd heard Sarah talk about it because it was about the St Valentine's Day massacre, and Alex had had a hand in that. That's why it stuck in his head. It was time to deflect the conversation in a different direction.

"And I don't think I've met your friend."

Marilyn's expression relaxed when she turned to the man by her side.

"This is Jack."

"Pleased to meet you, Senator."

The guy had a firm handshake and as soon as he let go, Jack picked the cigarette from Marilyn's hand, exhaled, and took three short tokes. Then he passed it back to Marilyn, who inhaled as deeply herself before offering the roach to Alex, who declined the opportunity to smoke the Mary Jane.

"Call me Jack. No need to be formal when we are among friends."

"I knew your predecessor: Merrick Townsend. He represents New Jersey nowadays."

"Great guy."

With that, Kennedy took Marilyn by the hand and wandered off to the other side of the room to get some more drinks, but Alex saw what had just happened and tried to decide whether the politician had figured out who he was before he blanked him.

A GLANCE AT his tumbler told Alex he needed a refill, so he waited for Jack and Marilyn to move away from the bar then zigzagged over to get a fresh Scotch. As he collected his liquor, a woman sidled up to him and ordered a glass of white wine. He felt her leaning in so their hips touched. Alex turned to face her and clinked glasses.

"Haven't we met somewhere before?"

"If that's your best line, Mac, you're going to have to try much harder."

Alex responded to her comment with a blank expression.

"My name is Alex Cohen, and I meant we met in Havana; at the opening of a casino or hotel. I can't remember which one."

"Sorry, Alex. I misunderstood. Your face is familiar. Call me Lana."

Memories of refusing credit to Turner's then-boyfriend, Johnny Stompanato, flooded into Alex's memory.

"Sorry about all the trouble you've had, Lana."

She stiffened her back and then let her shoulders sag as she exhaled.

"Sometimes you gotta deal with a situation. Do you have anything to smoke?"

Alex fumbled in his pockets until he produced a packet of cigarettes and flicked at the end of the pack to make one pop out of the aperture at the top.

"Not quite what I meant, but thank you, Alex, anyway."

"I don't keep anything stronger on me, but if you tell me what you'd like, then I can always get you a regular supply."

"Whoa, fella. We might have attended the same opening night for Meyer Lansky, but that doesn't make us pals."

"Never said that it did, Lana. It's just that I am new in town and I'm looking to expand my activities in Burbank. Ask Frank about me and maybe we can talk some other time."

"You're a friend of Sinatra?"

Alex nodded and smiled.

"In that case, we can probably do business."

3

ALEX VISITED HIS sons Moishe and David, along with sister Esther, in New York as much to see the family as to talk about his legitimate business interests.

"We haven't seen you since you got back to the US. How was it getting out of Cuba?"

"A few hairy moments, but all was fine, Esther. You're looking good."

"I like the taste of Bowery air in my lungs."

Moishe chortled, and Esther threw him a glance.

"Something amuses you, my boy?"

"No, Pop. How was the journey over?"

"Nothing much to report. The good thing is that it didn't take as long as it used to."

"We live in modern times, Pop."

"Is it too early for me to invite you guys out to lunch?"

Esther had a quick look at the clock on the wall and shook her head.

"If it's somewhere swanky, then we're ready to go now."

"Grab your coats. Let's hop over to the Waldorf-Astoria."

Alex's limo took the group uptown in no time at all, and soon they were ensconced in the five-star luxury to which Alex was very much accustomed. Esther's eyes popped out of their sockets when she looked around the restaurant.

"I don't think I've ever seen so much mink on so many shoulders."

"It makes you wonder how their men got the cash to afford them."

"You are a cynic, David Cohen."

His lawyer son glanced at Alex to show his understanding of how gelt operated in this town. Moishe added his own perspective. "This just goes to show what hard work can achieve."

He looked round at his lunch companions and they all laughed.

"Gelt makes gelt and nothing more," intoned Alex as they settled into their menus.

Once the waiter took their order, Alex turned to what was uppermost on his mind.

"How have you all been?"

"Alex, married life is treating your two sons well and I am much happier since you last saw me."

He smiled at his sister and recalled picking her up with David and dragging her back to her room in Havana. The woman had almost drowned in a bottle of tequila.

"That's good. And Mama?"

"She is slowing down, of course, but she is well, Pop."

Alex wondered what stopped him from visiting her himself. There was time this trip, but he knew he would not do so.

ON HIS WAY over to Hoboken, Alex pondered why it had taken him so long to visit his New York operations. Moishe was right, Havana had been a year ago and all he had achieved since then was to sit on his *tuches* and grow fat. He looked down at his paunch and realized that he might be exaggerating. He wondered to what extent his mind had slowed down in the past twelve months. He was getting old, minute by minute, day by day.

The limo pulled up to a nondescript building in central Hoboken, only six blocks from Alex's former apartment, where the boys would come to stay when they were kids. He got out and entered the lobby to be met by a receptionist, who eyed him up and down for a moment.

"I'm here to speak with Merrick Townsend."

"Is he expecting you, sir?"

"Not at all, but if you let him know I am here, then he will see me."

The pinhead looked at Alex through the bottom of his eyeglasses and pretended to hide his disdain.

"Mr. Townsend does not meet with uninvited guests."

"You should put a call through to his assistant and let her know that Alex Cohen is here to see Merrick."

He held the gaze of the receptionist for a couple of seconds until the guy got uncomfortable. Alex looked around the counter and spotted a name etched into a bronze-colored plate.

"Mr. Garfield. Aiden. I understand many people walk off the street and demand to speak with Merrick. I imagine part of your role is to distinguish these individuals from those who should meet with him. You need to verify that I belong to the second category. You will achieve this by speaking with Merrick's secretary."

Garfield's eyes flitted left then right, and a hand edged toward the phone on the desk.

"Bear with me while I speak with Mr. Townsend's assistant."

Alex smirked and stepped back to allow Garfield to retain what remained of his dignity. Two minutes later, he sat down in Townsend's anteroom with a coffee and an apology from Amy Penn about the wait before Mr. Townsend was ready to see him.

"THANK YOU FOR seeing me, Merrick."

"It is always a pleasure, Alex."

"As I was passing by, I thought I'd drop in. How's tricks?"

"Can't complain. My constituents keep me pretty busy. You know how it is."

"And how are Sylvia and your kids?"

"She is fine, and they have grown up fast."

"Tell me about it, Merrick. My two eldest work for me nowadays."

"You have others?"

"Three, but we haven't spoken for years…"

Merrick allowed Alex to dwell on that thought for a short beat, but that was long enough.

"How long are you planning on being in town? As lovely as it is to see you, I have a schedule, but I can meet up with you for dinner any night this week."

Alex nodded and opened his briefcase, fumbled around inside, and pulled out a dossier. Then he placed it on Townsend's desk, although the senator did nothing with it, apart from giving it a second glance.

"Like I said, Merrick, I'm only passing through, so now is the time when we need to talk."

Townsend leaned back in his swivel chair and lit a cigar after offering Alex one. When he looked at the item in his hand, he noticed they were Cuban and smiled at the irony.

"Let's get this over with then."

"Merrick, I'd like you to do me a favor."

"You know I am always happy to help. What do you need?"

"I want you to introduce me to Jack Kennedy."

Townsend stiffened and attempted to hide his reaction by tapping some ash into the ashtray.

"The guy is trying to become the Democratic nominee for the presidency. With the greatest respect, Alex, I don't think he is going to want to have a conversation with a man of your… pedigree."

"Open the file, Merrick."

Alex waited for Townsend to follow his instructions and then to digest the contents of the Manila envelope.

"May I remind you that the photo was taken on the night when you were in Havana and found Lupita Alfaro sliced to ribbons by the scissors from your hotel room."

Townsend swallowed hard.

"Then you phoned for my help to deal with the murdered prostitute. We resolved all those issues, and I told you that, in the future, I would ask you for a favor. You appear to have forgotten our arrangement, but the picture in your hand has jogged your memory, judging by your expression. You can keep the photo if you like. I have many more copies in case of need."

"She was the sweetest girl I have ever met. There isn't a day that goes by without me thinking about her."

"Touching, but I saw her body that night and there wasn't much care being shown by you with that *nafka*."

Townsend's eyes bore into Alex like he'd just sliced his mother's face open, but the only violence had been perpetrated by Senator Merrick Townsend. And they both knew it.

4

RATHER THAN TRAVEL all the way to the West Coast before heading back to the commonwealth of Massachusetts, Alex took the sensible decision of going straight to Boston to wait a day or so before he could visit Kennedy.

Sure enough, a call from the senator's people relayed the message that the presidential nominee had made time in his schedule for Alex to see him that afternoon for fifteen minutes.

Kennedy's election office was a storefront building nestled among a crowd of mom-and-pop mercantile opportunities for the hapless shopper, near Charles Street and Jefferson. As Alex headed for the entrance, the hustle of campaign workers was all around him.

Out of the corner of his eye, he spotted Marilyn Monroe's boyfriend as he scurried from one side of the building to the other and ducked into an office with a glass wall and blinds for privacy. Alex followed him in.

"Good to see you again, Jack."

Kennedy looked up from the pile of papers he had brought in with him and squinted at Alex.

"We met at Frank Sinatra's party a few weeks back. Don't tell me you've forgotten the thirty-second conversation we had together. It's etched on my memory forever."

Alex proffered his hand and Kennedy shook it like a well-conditioned politician should.

"I'm sorry. You are…?"

"Alex Cohen, Jack. Your people gave me fifteen minutes with you now. You appear confused."

Kennedy stood up, walked out, and shouted for someone to find his schedule. A woman appeared clutching a diary and confirmed the appointment. Kennedy shrugged and returned to sit behind his desk.

"Alex, you have my attention. What can I do for you?"

"First, do you remember Frank's party?"

Kennedy stared into the middle distance and shrugged again.

"I go to a lot of parties. I can't say that any spring to mind right now, but I believe you when you state we met there."

"That's fine, Jack. I only ask because you were sharing a marijuana cigarette with Marilyn Monroe."

Kennedy stiffened, exhaled, and closed the blinds on the glass wall.

"Is this some kind of shakedown or has one of the boys sent you to pull my leg?"

"Neither, Jack. Judging from your reaction though, your memory of the party is improving."

"Don't get fresh with me, Mac."

"The name is Alex and I have a business proposition for you."

"Sounds like extortion to me."

"Such harsh words, Jack, and I have done nothing to you to deserve your mistrust. Far from it. At any point since we met, I could have gone to the papers or the Republicans and inform them of what I saw you do, but I have refrained from such action. Do you know why, Jack?"

"Why, Alex?"

"Because I want to help you win the election. Who knows how far this country will go with you at the helm?"

"You mentioned a business proposition."

"We don't get nothing for nothing in this life, as I am sure you are aware, Jack. I propose boosting your election war chest in exchange for your help with my winning state construction contracts."

Jack Kennedy's glare softened at hearing Alex's offer. Politicians are the same the world over: they want power and aren't that fussy about how they gain it.

"And I suppose the amount of your financial contribution will be less than the value of the building contracts?"

"Let's just say that the more you let me dip my beak in the trough, then the greater my generosity. And, of course, my friends will be eager to support you too."

"Money is always welcome."

"Jack, when I was a kid, my mentor Waxey Gordon had a close relationship with the New York Democratic Party. He didn't put cash in their pockets, but there were other ways he found to help. My business partners will find other forms of support for your campaign efforts."

The senator leaned his elbows on the desk and rested his chin on his palms.

"Are you offering to stuff ballots for me?"

"Jack, I am letting you know that if you help me get state construction contracts, then I will ensure that my friends assist in the election, assuming you get the party nomination."

Kennedy grinned.

"So your money gets me the nomination and your friends deliver me the White House?"

"That's the size of it."

"What makes you think I need that much help?"

"Perhaps you don't. To be honest, I don't follow politics. I have never found the law to be a friend of mine and the people who make laws are of even less concern to me."

Kennedy shuffled in his seat as though the act of being in the room with Alex caused him discomfort.

"But I look across your campaign headquarters and I see a bunch of college kids running around like their asses are on fire. This is not how a winning team behaves, so I would guess that you might welcome my suggestion. Also, the fact you continue with this conversation shows you have some minimal interest in what I have to say."

Kennedy shuffled some more and then stood up and said, "Excuse me one minute," before scurrying out of his office, leaving Alex on his own and unsure what to make of this erratic behavior.

True to his word, Kennedy came back and settled back into his seat.

"Apologies, but I am taking new meds and they are disagreeing with me. You were saying?"

"Let me cut to the chase, Jack. You need me far more than I need you. To make matters clear, I have known many Catholics in my life and, while I am not of that faith myself, I imagine your voters would be unimpressed with a candidate who smoked illegal substances and had an extramarital affair."

Alex lit a cigarette to give Kennedy time to mull over what he'd heard. After three long drags, Alex noticed there was no ashtray. Instead, he leaned forward and grabbed a coffee mug on the desk, peeked inside to find the dregs of Kennedy's last cup, and flicked the ash in it. The man sat opposite him scowled but did nothing to object.

Throughout the time that Alex took to finish his smoke, Jack Kennedy averted his gaze. Alex thought he heard cogs whirring in the man's skull.

"Well?"

"Alex, I have met your kind before and I have never enjoyed the experience."

"I am not asking for us to be friends, but to be business associates."

"Let me finish. Like my father before me, I understand how politics operates; sometimes you have unusual bedfellows. My brother, Robert, sees the world in black and white, whereas I live in the penumbra."

"Gray is my favorite color."

"Alex, if you can deliver what you say, then we have a deal. If you fail me, then you must understand I will call the FBI and they'll cart you to jail."

"Prison isn't that bad, Jack. It's the waiting to get out that'll hang you every time."

"And I suppose you'd know about that, wouldn't you?"

"Jack, don't be so hasty to judge a man. What I do is put bread on my family's table and provide a roof under which they can sleep safe at night. The only difference between you and me is that you care what people think of you. I only care about results."

Kennedy maintained the smile he'd plastered across his face since he returned from the john.

"By the way, Jack. The next time you are visiting Marilyn, let me know and I can supply you with anything to make the party go with a swing, from a discreet venue to grass and coke."

"If I ever pass that way again, I'll bear that offer in mind."

The grin somehow got broader and Jack's chest puffed out.

"And, you never know, I might have a different girl in tow."

"What you do in the privacy of someone else's home is of no concern to me. Like I told you, I don't follow politics and I do not care about the private lives of politicians. It's what you do that matters most to me, Jack. I shall judge you on your actions."

"In that case, we will get along just fine. Give me your contact details and next week you'll receive a call. That'll be for the first contract. If you send a check to my campaign the same day, then we both know the deal is sound. If not, you can kiss my ass."

April 1961

5

SARAH AND ALEX settled into a simple routine. In the mornings, they enjoyed breakfast together, on the patio if the weather was in their favor. Then Alex would hustle into his recently built office and she remained in the main house. Together for lunch and then they'd take Alex's limo over to Burbank to attend to business in the afternoon and evening.

"To what extent do you trust your coke connection, Alex?"

"He appears to have been reliable since DeSimone introduced us last year. Why do you ask?"

"There's a discrepancy in the books between the amount you've paid for and the quantity you have received. It might not be much, but if you look after the pennies…"

Alex tilted his head and smiled.

"I will check that out, hon'."

"There might be nothing to find apart from poor record keeping on our part."

"Sarah, you mean me, don't you?"

"Alex, I'm not accusing anybody yet."

"Only a matter of time, though, right?"

"Listen, mister. I wouldn't put it past you not to note every few bags you receive, but if it becomes a habit, then we'll never see if we make any money at this game."

Now it was Alex's turn to smile.

"And I was running drugs while you were changing diapers."

"That is very true, but you still need to record what you buy and sell if you want me to look after the books."

"Remind me again, why we are keeping such excellent notes of our criminal activities. If the FBI gets hold of this paperwork, then I'm sunk."

"Alex, we must ensure we make money. And there is only one copy of these records. The only way the Feds can get their hands on them will be over my dead body and if that is the case, then you've got more to worry about than a tax fraud investigation."

He drew on his cigarette and nodded, not wanting to think too much about the implication of Sarah's words.

"Let me change the subject as I don't like the way the last one was heading. How are the girls?"

Sarah leaned back in her chair and sighed.

"Everything is going all right. The two cathouses we own are doing solid business. From what I've calculated, every bedroom has a nafka on her back for at least twelve hours a day."

"And how's the Hollywood party scene?"

"Less productive. It's a function of the number of parties and how many hosts we know and deal with. The problem we have is that everybody wants to do a line of white powder but only a small proportion want to have call girls hanging around A-list stars. They think it'll cramp their style."

"It's the lonely headline acts that are grateful for the attention without needing to worry about anybody growing any attachments."

"You don't have to convince me, Alex. It's the likes of Sinatra who needs to hear your sales pitch."

Alex laughed because they both knew that Frank would do anything to keep on the right side of the mob and had been requesting a steady supply of ass every time he held one of his parties. It was the rest of the rat pack that needed to be turned. If they all sourced tail from Alex, then other actors in Hollywood would follow suit.

HOW LUCKY WAS Alex to bump into Peter Langford the next day as he arrived at the movie studio to film some interiors for a new Sinatra picture? He made sure he parked right by Langford so they could walk and talk until they reached the sound stage.

"What brings you round these parts, Alex?"

"Haven't you heard? I'm back on the West Coast. Sarah and I came over more than a year ago. I thought you might have spotted me at the far end of the room at one of Frank's parties."

"I'm afraid not, but you're not the sort I'm sniffing out when there's a party in full swing, if you get my meaning."

"Sure do, and no offense taken. You're looking out for someone younger and prettier all round."

Peter guffawed.

"You know me too well, Alex. Now if you could guarantee you had a juicy skirt with you, then I'd give you the time of day at least."

Both men chortled and Alex stroked his chin.

"Now that you mention it, I might be able to help you in that regard. When're you going to your next party?"

"Saturday, of course. Why?"

"How would you like me to introduce you to a lovely girl you can drape over your arm when you walk in the door?"

"With my reputation, Alex, it's not getting the girl that's a problem. They are like moths at night and have the habit of skipping around, flapping away at every light they see in the room."

"This is where the individual I find for you will be more than perfect. Not only can you be certain that she'll make you salivate when you see her, but you can bet your bottom dollar she'll leave with you too."

Peter stopped in his tracks and tilted his head as he thought through Alex's promise. Then he smiled and slapped Alex on the back.

"If you could do that for me, I will make you a rich man."

"I hope you will. And if you need anything to keep the buzz going, tell me because I can obtain substances you can't get in your local pharmacy."

A wink told Langford all he needed to know, and they shook hands.

"If you have a good time on Saturday, then inform your friends because there's plenty of ass to go round and more coke than you can inhale."

Peter bid Alex farewell and entered the stage to tell the rest of the rat pack what Alex was offering. He popped into the studio canteen for a quick coffee and then drove back to the office to let Sarah know they had a special booking.

DAVID HAD BEEN staying in a guest bedroom for the past three months since he'd arrived from New York.

"Tell me, Pop. You don't appear to have much work for me to do."

David, Alex, and Sarah sat in the living room after dinner, a glass of their favorite liquor in their hand.

"Son, the problem is that I am not investing in anything that you can put your hands on."

"Did you tell me that so I wouldn't ask how the family operation is doing?"

"No, I said it so that you would understand why there isn't much for you right now. The only thing I can think of is the operation that flows through New York."

"When I came here, I thought you were preparing to keep only your legal activities. When we fled Havana, you said you wanted to retire and leave the criminal life behind you."

"Almost, David. I announced I wished to go legit but informed you all that I was going to Florida to seek opportunities with Santo Trafficante, who is a man not untainted by the mob. He represents the mafia in that state."

David swilled the brandy in his glass.

"Are you pushing me out, Pop?"

Alex swallowed hard.

"That is not my intention, but we both know I must protect you from some of my business affairs. You cannot be a party to matters which would get you disbarred."

His son took a swig of his cognac.

"I understand, but I am not the least happy about it."

"Of course you are not, but don't forget the importance I place on having you look after Esther and Moishe. They are both meticulous with detail but too naïve in the dark art of business. You must mentor your brother more and make sure your aunt remains sober."

"She hasn't touched a drop since she left Cuba. Those days are passed."

Alex nodded and glanced at Sarah, who remained silent throughout the entire exchange.

IN BED THAT night, just after he switched the light off, Alex turned to Sarah.

"I'd be much happier if David stayed in California, wouldn't you?"

"Of course. The mother hen in me would love it if all my chicks lived near the nest."

"That's not quite what I meant."

"I know, Alex, but you want to have your cake and eat it. Either involve David in all your dealings or clean up your act."

"I can't do that yet. You know that."

"Alex, that is what you believe, and so that is how you behave. Don't tell me you couldn't get a fair price for your Las Vegas interests and for the import/export from Italy."

"Perhaps..."

"And we only have cathouses and drug supply in Hollywood to give ourselves something to do if we are being honest with ourselves. Right?"

"Maybe..."

"So, the only thing stopping you from keeping David in Los Angeles are the decisions you make."

"For sure, hon'."

"The choice is yours. Send David back to New York or sell your more salacious enterprises."

6

TWO WEEKS AFTER David flew back to LaGuardia, Alex heard Jack was in town, so he paid a visit to Jayne Mansfield.

"Do you have any plans for the weekend, Jayne?"

"There is no need to be coy, Alex. We both know I am spending time with Jack."

"And you know that I'm the go-to guy for anyone planning a party that's going to last the entire weekend."

"Alex, why do you think I took your call?"

"I'm flattered, Jayne. What do you need and when would you like me to deliver it?"

"My usual order will be more than ample."

"That's fine. When shall I come over?"

ALEX ARRIVED AT eight, just as he'd promised Jayne he would. He rang the doorbell and waited for thirty seconds until she answered the door with a smile and swanned back to her living room, leaving Alex to close the door behind himself. He followed her inside and stopped in his tracks when he saw Jack on the couch in the pinkest place he had ever seen.

"Good evening, Mr. President."

"Call me Jack when I'm not representing the office of the presidency."

"Congratulations, by the way. This is the first time we've spoken since you won the White House."

"Thank you, and for all your support."

"We made an agreement and I always keep my word, Jack."

"How's the construction business round here? Still doing well?"

"You know that I was only the front for those contracts. They've been putting up buildings ever since the Romans."

"I thought that was the Greeks, Alex?"

"I don't know any Greeks, only Italians."

They both smiled while Jayne removed the contents of the bag Alex had dropped on a nearby sideboard. She tapped some powder onto a mirror on a coffee table by Jack's perch on the couch. Then she cut it up repeatedly until she had four lines arranged. With an arm resting on Jack's lap, Jayne took a curled-up Jackson and snorted one line. Then she swapped nostrils and inhaled the second.

Mansfield passed the note over to Jack, who pushed her off his leg in order to bend forward and take the two remaining tramlines for himself. He looked up at Alex and shrugged. "Nothing for you, Alex," and sniggered.

"I don't imbibe. Thanks anyway, but I would like a quiet word as we've bumped into each other."

"Now is not the time, Alex. I can't tell you how wide of the mark you are at the minute."

"Shall I come back tomorrow afternoon?"

"Whatever…"

As Alex turned to leave Jayne's house, she hauled herself off the floor and slithered onto Jack's lap. They started making out, and Alex closed the door.

AS PROMISED, HE swung by the Sunset Boulevard mansion Saturday around three to start up the failed conversation from the night before. When he rang the bell, this time Jayne took at least a minute to get to the door. She was wrapped in only a bathrobe, which left very little to the imagination. She beckoned Alex in and he padded upstairs to discover that the living room was not alone in being painted pink. He didn't think there was an inch of wall that had any other color on it.

Jayne vanished into a bedroom and Alex followed her, wary of what state of undress he might find the president of the free world in. A flush of the john and Jack emerged from the en suite wearing a matching bathrobe.

She lit a cigarette and passed it over to him, before sitting on the bed. Jack nestled next to her and rested a hand over her thighs. Alex tried to decide whether the man would have done the same if he hadn't been in the room and realized he didn't care. If Kennedy was playing games to make him feel uncomfortable, then it wouldn't work. Alex had seen much more and far worse over the years.

"Take a seat, Alex, if you are going to stay."

"Last night we agreed we would use this afternoon to talk business."

"That's not what was said, but I'll let it go for now."

"Jayne, do you mind rustling us up some coffee?"

The actress smiled at Alex's suggestion but looked at Jack, who nodded consent to give her permission to leave.

"I understand you want to build on our past business relationship, Alex, but your timing is lousy. I only have a few more hours before I am expected back to my work and no matter how enjoyable a conversation with you might be, it pales into insignificance compared to the pleasure I can derive from the same time spent between Jayne's thighs."

"Does your wife know about Jayne?"

"Don't be impertinent."

"I meant no disrespect, Jack. My only thought was whether you had an open marriage, and nothing more. I don't read the comics, so I do not know what gossip is out there about you. I appreciate what it's like to find out about yourself in the dailies and it is never pleasant."

Kennedy's shoulders sagged, and he inhaled on his cigarette.

"No offense taken. I thought you were trying to do a cheap hustle on me… but, I keep my infidelities private."

"The papers are silent so I figured as much."

"Alex, it's time for you to go. Talk to me on some other occasion, but not when I am only wearing a bathrobe in Jayne Mansfield's bedroom."

SINATRA INVITED ALEX to spend a few days at the Cal Neva Lodge as there was someone Sinatra thought he would like to meet. Although the proposal sounded mysterious, Frank wouldn't have wasted his time, so he kissed Sarah goodbye and headed for the lodge, which was on the border of California and Nevada, as its name implied.

The first night he checked in, Alex hit the restaurant. Frank popped over to welcome him to the establishment and they chatted for a short while before the singer flitted off to another table for more schmoozing.

Alex had spent his entire life sitting at the rear of restaurants, in the shadows, but tonight the maître d' had positioned him in the middle of the place. Alex monitored Sinatra as he worked the room. With whom did he spend the most time? A booth at the back housing a man and a woman. The guy was too far into the darkness for Alex to see and although he had never met the young woman before, she had all the marks of a good-time girl and nothing more.

He might have only given Alex five minutes, but the guy received a half hour's attention. As Frank got up to leave, the man leaned forward and his head emerged from the shadowy darkness. Alex understood why he had got more attention; Jack Kennedy was a far more important person than Alex could ever be.

Once the couple had finished eating and the busboy had cleared their table, Alex watched Jack call for the check. As they walked past Alex, Jack stopped to talk, an arm hanging around the skirt's neck.

"Good to see you, Alex. How's tricks?"

"All fine, thank you for asking, but we never completed our conversation from the last time we met."

Kennedy stared back with not even a flicker of recognition in his expression.

"My friend and I are about to have a nightcap. Care to join us?"

Alex looked down at his plate and calculated how long it would take him to eat a third of a steak.

"I'll be ten minutes. Will you be at the bar on this floor?"

A nod from Jack and he sauntered off. His arm slipped off the girl's shoulder and landed on her butt cheek. When you are president, you don't have to worry too much about what a woman thinks of your clumsy moves.

ALEX CAUGHT UP with the happy couple fifteen minutes later when he aimed for a back booth in the hotel's second-floor bar. The lovebirds were cooing when he arrived and he sat opposite them, facing Kennedy.

"Aren't you going to introduce me to your friend?"

"No, babe. There's no need for that. Why don't you powder your nose?"

The girl smiled and left. All the while, Alex watched Jack stare at her ass as it wiggled away.

"I'm looking forward to finishing this drink, you know what I mean?"

"Sure do, Jack. You are one lucky man."

"Luck has nothing to do with it. I earned that the hard way."

Alex couldn't be bothered to argue with the guy and was more concerned with business.

"Now you've left Massachusetts, new construction contracts have trailed off. So I am hoping you will agree to a more relevant arrangement as you have some sway with federal opportunities."

Jack maintained the grin that had appeared on his face from the moment he'd stared at the disappearing ass.

"Alex, we had an agreement, and we both held up our end of the bargain, but that moment is over and there's nothing more to be said."

It was Alex's turn to smile.

"Jack, I understand why you might think that is the case. However, we have become business partners and that relationship persists until the end of time. So I have a new proposal for you."

"I'm listening."

"You swing some federal contracts my way so that my Italian friends can benefit too, and I will ensure that your liaisons remain private from the general public and from your wife. I've met many politicians in my time, but the devout Catholic ones don't go to hotels and have clandestine meetings with cocktail waitresses."

"She's not a waitress. Cheryl is an actress."

"Jack, what she does for a living is of no concern to me. She could be a whore for all I care. The fact remains that you shouldn't be sleeping with her. Do we have a deal?"

Cheryl waddled back to their table in her red stilettos and matching pencil skirt. Jack's eyes continued to pop outside his head. Then he turned to Alex.

"Yes. Now leave me alone to enjoy the delights of this fabulous woman."

They shook hands and as he stood up, Alex bent to whisper in Jack's ear. "Remember to tip her well. Loose talk costs careers."

7

ALEX HAD ONLY been back home three weeks before Santo Trafficante called him and invited him to come to Florida as his guest. That afternoon, a private plane took him from LA to Fort Lauderdale, where a limo ferried him over to Boca Raton. The sun was setting by the time he arrived at a warehouse on the edge of town.

As he entered the building, the saloon turned round and drove off. Alex swallowed hard and licked his lips. All was quiet within those walls and no lights were on, despite the fading sunlight. He kept the creaking door open to minimize the noisy announcement of his arrival, but Alex knew Santo would hear he was there.

He tiptoed through the reception area and wondered where the welcoming committee had got to. Then Alex halted in his tracks and the thought crossed his mind that Santo had drawn him here for darker reasons. Alex had lost count of the number of times he had brought people into similar warehouses to drag them out in a makeshift body bag. Was he about to meet the same fate?

He pushed at a door in the far wall and walked into a large space with some kind of machinery fifty feet away, but it was too dark to make out any details. To the left and right were row upon row of shelving and in front of him was an empty area, comprising only a table and a few chairs. A man in silhouette sat there with a cigarette in his hands.

"Thank you for agreeing to see me, Alex."

Santo's voice was quiet and almost monotone, and a hand showed for him to step forward and join the old Italian gangster at the table. He walked toward Trafficante, where a pot of coffee and three mugs were waiting for him.

"Are we expecting anyone else?"

"No. Why do you ask?"

Alex pointed at the third mug and Santo explained everything by flicking his ash into the receptacle.

"There's no need to make a mess in your own place, is there, Alex?"

"I don't suppose there is, Santo. Could we not have met somewhere less... stark?"

The fella inhaled his cigarette before dropping it into the trash-mug.

"Until we have had this conversation and I find out if you are interested in my proposal, then this meeting never happened and the fewer people who see you in the state, the better."

"Now you have me intrigued, Santo: spill."

"If you ignore the end, we had fabulous times in Cuba, wouldn't you say?"

"Sure. We were hotel neighbors and did good business together."

"That's what I thought too. You and I have had no beef either have we?"

"No, I can't say that we have, Santo. But why this interest in reliving the past? What's done is done."

"It is, and it isn't. A friend of mine has asked for my assistance and I think you can help me with his request."

Alex exhaled.

"Is there a hit you want me to do? Because if there is, let's talk about it without hiding in a crummy warehouse in the middle of nowhere."

Santo raised a smile and shook his head.

"Close, but no cigar. My acquaintance would like some help in Cuba. Would you be prepared to go back there for a short while? A few days only."

"Thank you for thinking of me, but Santo, I am too old to be gallivanting around that island to rob a bank or whatever you have planned. I prefer easier ways to make my money nowadays."

"Oh no, Alex. We don't want to hit a savings and loan. Nothing as tawdry as that. We wish to take out Castro."

"Whack him?"

"Yep."

"Santo, you and whose army?"

Trafficante lit another cigarette and offered one to Alex.

"We were thinking you would recruit your own army. Well, troop of men anyway."

"And do what? Fly over to Cuba, parachute in, and assassinate Fidel Castro?"

"Plane, boat. How you do it is less important right now than whether you're prepared to try."

Alex smoked his entire cigarette in silence until he inhaled roach and he tossed it into the mug. Santo poured them another cup of dark brown coffee each.

"Who's behind this? What is the name of your friend?"

"If you are in, then I will tell you, but we can't afford for anyone to know if they are not involved. It's for your own good."

"No can do, Santo. With all due respect, if you want me to kill a foreign leader, I must have the name of the person who is paying my wages."

Santo thought for a moment, then nodded.

"It is a mutual friend. A man of power."

Alex stared at the Italian, none the wiser. Santo snorted his disappointment.

"Jack Kennedy, you dolt."

"I thought the CIA did covert operations."

"They do, but Kennedy has asked us to help because we've lived in Cuba and we are renowned for successful hits."

"And you want me to work with the CIA to assassinate Castro?"

"They've recruited an army of exiles in Miami and are training them in Guatemala."

"So what do they need me for?"

"You have military experience and you know the island, the towns, the streets. Besides which, this wouldn't be your first assassination and we need somebody cool in the face of enemy fire when we kill that bastard."

"And why haven't the CIA come to me directly? What skin do you have in this game?"

"Alex, let's just say that Jack and I have reached an understanding, a working relationship you might call it."

"I have a similar set-up with him too."

"We would all like to return to the casino business in Havana. And Kennedy wants a base in the Caribbean that relies on the US for its success. Jack wins, the mob wins, and so do you. What's not to like?"

"How much to kill Castro?"

"Half a million to cover your expenses. And another half on his death."

"What if we fail?"

"Then you don't get the second payment."

"And I'll come home in a body bag."

"If you are lucky, Alex. Yes."

"I hope you don't expect an answer tonight, because I need to think this through before I respond."

"Take all the time you need. I'll get some food and bedding delivered here."

"No, Santo. I need to leave this place. There is no way I can think properly cooped up in this excuse for accommodation. I shall hole up somewhere discreet, but I am not staying here. Trust me on this."

"You have two days. If word gets out about this operation, then I will know it was you who spilled your guts."

"Santo, there's no need for such words. I understand the responsibility of omertà. If I didn't squawk to the cops when I was in Sing Sing, why would I start now?"

"Just remember that Kennedy is a man we can work with. He is pliable and open to sensible business arrangements."

"That I know for myself, Santo."

"And by keeping Jack close, we get him to place brother Bobby on a short leash. That guy wants to take down organized crime."

Santo laughed aloud but before Alex joined in, Trafficante stopped and looked dead-eyed into his Cuban neighbor.

"And we can't let that happen, can we, Alex?"

8

"GOOD TO SEE you, Alex. Come on in."

He smiled at Thelma Lansky and followed her as she took him up to the guest bedroom. When he came downstairs, she showed him to the living room where Meyer was watching the baseball on television.

"The Minnesota Twins are making short change of the Yankees."

Alex nodded and sat in an easy chair while his friend enjoyed the game, although, for a lifelong Yankees fan, the result was about as bad as it could be.

"To think they've only just come up from Washington. You'd imagine the Twins would be tired from the journey."

The problem was that Alex knew little of the rules of baseball and was even less interested in discussing it, given what Santo had asked him to do.

"I need to stay a night or two, Meyer, if that's all right with you and Thelma."

"That woman is a peach."

"Meyer, I have an important decision to make and I came here because I value your opinion. Do you mind if we switch the TV off?"

Meyer suggested they take a walk around the block, but Alex explained he had promised not to be seen on the streets.

"This is sounding dangerous before you've even told me what is going on, Alex."

"Right now, I'm in the clear, but there is a lot riding on this if I agree to Santo's proposal."

"Is he involved? The *meeskait*."

"You and he have done enough business together over the years. Is he such a bad fella to work with?"

"You know my feeling about the Italians so don't get me started."

Meyer led Alex out through the patio doors and to a table and chairs by the pool.

"You swim, Meyer?"

"Of course not. It's for Thelma, and the kids if they ever visit. But you know what it's like—they don't write, they don't phone…"

A nod and Alex allowed the conversation to slide into oblivion so he could keep Meyer onside. They soaked in the warmth of the sun and enjoyed each other's company, talking about nothing as Lansky seemed unable to focus on anything serious.

AFTER DINNER, THELMA left the men alone after she had washed up the dishes and headed into the living room. Meyer and Alex wandered back to the patio.

"I'm visiting you because I am interested in your opinion, and you know all the parties involved."

"Is this the Santo business?"

"Yes, Meyer. He approached me and asked me to help him take Cuba from the revolutionaries."

Meyer almost spat his coffee back into his mug.

"Are you serious? What does that Italian think you're going to do? Fly over, parachute in, and assassinate Castro?"

Alex laughed.

"That is one plan on the table, from what I hear, but the bigger issue is whether I should do it at all."

Despite his promise of complete secrecy, Alex fleshed out what Santo had said to him, from the involvement of the CIA to the Guatemalan training camp. If he was to receive a meaningful judgment from Meyer, his friend needed all the facts at his disposal.

"Alex, I can't pretend that I wouldn't benefit from Cuba opening up to US tourism again, although, with a different leader in charge, we might not operate on quite the same terms."

"That only happens if the plan is successful. Do you think we have a good chance of whacking the old buzzard and should I be the one to do it?"

"Killing Castro shouldn't be that difficult if you spend time on the island and monitor his movements and routines. The chances are that he'll have grown complacent. The bigger issue is whether you'd be able to get away after the deed is done. We both saw first-hand how loyal his people are to him. They are unlikely to let us go to the airport and take the first plane home."

"Meyer, if it was me going through the streets of Havana, I'd believe I had a very good chance of a lucky sniper shot piercing his skull. Santo and the CIA appear to have got themselves a small army. I can lead the men, but Castro's execution will be that much harder with a squad under my command."

"Remind me again why Santo wants the hit?"

"It's come from Kennedy."

"Sure. Right..."

IN THE MORNING, Alex sat with Lansky in the dining room and they consumed yet another pot of coffee.

"All these deals boil down to trust, Alex. You know that, right?"

"Yes, Meyer. My attitude to the Italians differs from yours. Santo and I have got along just fine over the years."

"When you do business with one, you do business with them all. You might think Santo is a good fella, but can you say the same of the rest of the mob bosses, even the ones you haven't met?"

"Of course I can't, but does that mean I shouldn't touch the hit? If you felt this strongly then why did you launder mafia money for so long?"

"Sometimes two people have an alignment of interests. When you walk along the same sidewalk as another fella, then you both have a vested interest in ensuring that the path ahead is smooth because neither of you wants to trip up. After a length of time, interests diverge and then you are walking on your own and no one is looking after your back."

"And, Meyer, I suppose in Cuba you both were on the same path?"

"I wanted cash flow, and he needed clean gelt, but now we are both in Florida and I no longer have a series of casinos to launder his Vegas skim. Do I get a call from Santo? No, I do not. Instead, you hear his voice on the line and he flies you over to hire you to kill Fidel Castro."

Meyer stirred his coffee without purpose, as he had added neither sugar nor cream. Alex pondered for a second.

"By that reasoning, Santo and I should do fine. He wants the guy dead to keep Kennedy happy and to reopen Cuba to US investment. I want the money Santo will pay me."

"You have forgotten to factor in the CIA, Alex."

"When the mob and the CIA work together, the government agents can't do anything about any of our other business enterprises because we'd have no reason to keep our mouths shut. Imagine what the papers would say if they found out a president had hired organized crime bosses to murder Castro."

"Alex, I see the alignment of interest between you, Santo, and the CIA handler keeping the matter silent, but is that enough for you to work together to hit Castro?"

"What else do you think we need, Meyer? We would all be looking for the death of the man who stole our property and chased us out of the country."

"Alex, that is a connection between you and the Italian. My question was whether you trusted the CIA."

Alex thought for a minute.

"They will only do what Kennedy tells them to do. No more and no less."

"Are you implying that you trust Kennedy? I mean, he has been good to Israel, I agree, but I'm not sure that means he'd always have your back, no matter what."

"Meyer, if that was all there was between Jack and me then you'd be right."

"What ace do you hold up your sleeve?"

"I supply narcotics to the president of the free world when he flies into California to see his girlfriends. And a shell company set up by David and Moishe has won state construction contracts. We have an arrangement so that some federal contracts will head my way too."

Now it was Meyer's turn to sink into somber thought.

"What *chutzpah*. You are walking a dangerous tightrope, my friend."

"He has been feeding me contracts since we returned to the US, so I wouldn't say I trust him. He is a politician, but there is an alignment of interest. We walk on the same sidewalk; he wants my silence and I want his contracts."

"Alex, we have waited all our lives for a president in our pocket and you moved to the other side of the country and picked one up along the way."

"You take what you can find."

"That leaves us with the Italians, then."

"I think they are there for the ride because of Santo's history in Cuba. The CIA could rustle up some soldiers, a few Marines, and enough air power to blast the hell out of the island."

"So, Alex, why do you need him at all? Why not make the same deal direct with Kennedy and cut out Santo as the middleman?"

"If I do that, then I will create an enemy out of Santo and there is no need to create unnecessary foes in this life."

"I've told you before, you cannot trust Trafficante. Were you invited to the Appalachian conference?"

"No, Meyer."

"Because they don't want Jews at the top table. If there are any problems, then Santo will turn his back on you at the earliest opportunity."

"The gelt will help me retire and look after my family for the remainder of their lives."

"Look around, Alex. What little money I salvaged from Cuba is in the bricks of this house. Do I have cash coming out of my ears? I do not, but I can still spend the rest of my days in quiet comfort. If you have any sense, then you should do the same as me and save yourself all the *tsoris*."

9

ALEX PLANNED TO spend a week with Sarah as he wasn't sure when he would see her again. Despite Meyer's protestations, the lure of Santo's money was too great.

"Must you put your life on the line just for the sake of a bag of cash, Alex?"

"Tomorrow is always difficult to predict and I need to be certain you will be well provided for, no matter what happens to me."

"Don't talk like that, Alex. You sound as though you have a death wish."

"I have no desire to die, Sarah, but at some point, I shall. Until then, I plan to stay alive as long as I am able and that means I must make provision for you so that when I am gone, you need worry for nothing."

"If this is just another hit, then why won't you tell me what you are going to do? Your reticence makes me feel as though you are involved in something far more dangerous. Tell me I'm wrong."

"Let's enjoy the next few days together, Sarah, and let the future unfold before us at its own pace."

Alex stepped onto the patio carrying a pot of coffee to lure Sarah from the dining room. She shrugged and followed him out, perching herself on the edge of a sunbed. In contrast, he lay down and shut his eyes for a spell. A minute later, she relented and copied him until they both soaked in the warmth of the afternoon sun.

ALEX'S FIRST STOP was to Useppa Island, just west of Lee County in Florida. The place used to be a resort, but the last hotel had closed its doors a year or two back. Manuel Artime, a Cuban national, met him at the pier and showed him around the small-town buildings.

"Manuel, thank you for the tour, but what are you doing here?"

"Alex, I taught at the Havana military academy after the fall of Batista, but soon I realized that the revolution was being thwarted by the leadership."

"Castro, you mean?"

"Let's just say I needed to leave Cuba in a hurry and here I am working with some of our mutual friends to rid my country of the vermin who are turning it into a rotten state."

"Castro has a lot to answer for. I'd be happy to see the back of him and return to Havana."

"What did you do there, Alex?"

"I was involved in the entertainment industry."

"Singer?"

"Not quite, but I knew a few. I helped to run a hotel or two."

Manuel stiffened.

"So, Alex, you'd like the country to return to its capitalist ways?"

"I don't believe in revolution if that is what you are asking, but I want a change of government over there. Our interests are aligned and that should be sufficient. If we are successful, then we can argue about what sort of state Uncle Sam allows later on."

Artime walked Alex over to a ramshackle hotel. There was no one still living who could remember its glory days. The Cuban introduced him to Elías, Paquito, and Juanfran, who had been recruited by a guy called Gerry Drecher.

"Paquito, are you hoping for a new dawn once we remove Castro from his people's throne?"

"For sure. I want to get back to my import/export business."

"How about you, Elías?"

"If I were in charge, then I'd call General Batista to be president again."

"Me too," added Juanfran.

The conversation flowed for another five minutes and then Alex decided he wanted to rest in his room for a while. Manuel showed him his second-floor quarters and Alex invited him inside.

"You appear to be the only revolutionary. Is every other member of the crew seeking to reinstate Batista?"

"Depends who recruits them. I want a new nirvana; Drecher is less choosy."

"When do you expect that I'll meet him?"

"Tomorrow maybe, or the day after. He is due back soon."

"You know much about him?"

"Nothing. He recruited me, sent me to this island, and spends his time on trips to Miami, finding disaffected Cubans to join our group. Then he goes back and repeats the process. Just one thing, what is your role here? Gerry told me you'd be arriving but gave me no idea why you were joining the fight."

"I am here to run the show. You can direct the men as much as you want, but we will all be executing my plan, once I've figured out what it is."

"We had better find you a uniform."

"When I left the army, I was only a private, and that was a long time ago."

"Well, you're a general in Brigade 2506 now. Congratulations on your promotion, sir."

GERRY ARRIVED ON the island two days later and Alex seized the chance to meet him before he scurried back to Miami. He checked into Alex's hotel so they could have lunch together with no effort.

"Good to see you in the flesh. Everyone talks about you in hushed awe. You are the guy from the CIA and that is the only thing people know about you."

"Alex, that is how it will stay. I turn up, I do my job, and then I leave. The rest doesn't matter."

"Gerry, if that's your real name, how well do you know Cuba?"

"I've stared at enough maps to be comfortable with the terrain."

"Ever visited? Even as a tourist?"

"That would be classified, Alex."

"No, it wouldn't. You might believe you aren't authorized to talk about clandestine jobs Uncle Sam has sent you on, but if you went somewhere on vacation, then that is fair game for our conversation. Gerry, have I been recruited just because I have driven on some of the roads?"

"Not entirely, but it sure does help us. Almost all the men are Cuban, so they'll know every nook and cranny of the island. From what I've heard from our mutual friends, you have the experience of fleeing the country while being chased by Castro's forces at the airport."

"Are you talking about Santo or somebody else?"

"Now, that is classified."

A broad grin swept across Gerry Drecher's face and he chuckled.

"I shall need to bring in some of my own people, Gerry."

"Show me a list of names and I will vet them. When I give the go-ahead, then you can contact them."

"That is not the way it is going to be, Gerry. If the two fellas aren't with me, then the deal is off and the brigade can kill Castro without me."

The grin flung itself onto the floor and Drecher stared at Alex, who lit a cigarette to give the man time to reach a decision.

"I must insist, Alex."

"No, you don't. Let's just say that they do not need the level of scrutiny from the US government that your background check will entail."

"What makes you think we didn't do the same with you?"

"Gerry, my invitation to join this party did not come from the CIA or any government agency. In case you are unaware, Santo Trafficante asked me to assassinate Castro, and I agreed as a favor to him and other interested parties far more senior than you can imagine. I want Ezra Kohut and Massimo Sciarra or I'll take the next ferry back to the mainland."

"Alex, can we trust them?"

"I have trusted my life and the lives of my family members to them more times than I can remember. They need no CIA authorization, as I have known them for over forty years. If I couldn't rely on them for anything I may ask, I would have put a bullet in their skulls decades ago."

Gerry considered his response.

"Let me make a call and confirm they can join the brigade without formal vetting by my department."

"That's fine. I understand you have protocols with which you must comply. Only don't mention them by name. I want no record of their involvement in this project, apart from their salaries. Tell your superiors they will receive half the amount I am being paid. Take it or leave it."

"I like you already, Alex. No messing about, a man after my own heart."

With the main order of business out of the way, the two men ate their buffet lunch. As Alex mopped up the pasta sauce from his bowl, he dragged the conversation back to the brigade Gerry was forming.

"I understand why you'd want the likes of Artime in the brigade, but why fill the ranks with Batista supporters? He did nothing for the country except bleed it dry."

"Alex, if the guy is anti-Castro, then that is good enough for me. What happens after we remove Fidel is not my concern. We shall create the power vacuum and somebody else, with way more stripes than I possess, will choose the next Cuban leader."

"And open up the place for American tourists?"

"In an ideal world, why not?"

10

WITHIN TWO DAYS, Ezra and Massimo arrived in Florida, and Alex picked them up from the airport. They were stationed in rooms on either side of his, which meant they could spend time together, away from the other men. All three helped Gerry whip the brigade into shape through a mix of PT and classroom sessions on war strategy.

Most of the guys who had signed up to the show knew a trade, but some were professionals: doctors, lawyers, accountants. They picked up the war games quicker than the rest and were destined to join the officers, but they were klutzes, almost to a man.

"Gerry, we need fighters, and the guys we have who want to see Batista reinstated are not much to work with. They'll get killed before we jump out of the plane."

"Alex, you worry too much. This is only the first stage of their training. By the time my men have worked with them, this raw material will be transformed into something brilliant."

Alex was not convinced and he could tell by Ezra's and Massimo's expressions that they shared his concerns.

"We are leading these guys into slaughter. If you are serious about toppling Castro, we are going to need more than this bunch to achieve it. I remember seeing the hate in the peasants' eyes, and that was before the revolution began."

"Ezra is right. Americans were spat on in the street. Gerry, you underestimate the size of the task at hand."

"Alex, you seem to think we do not already have assets on the ground. The Company has more than one plan underway for Operation Mongoose."

"Are you telling me you have agents on the island and you still need us to swan over and take him out? Why not use those fellas to do the job?"

"An intelligence officer is not the best person to carry out an assassination, Alex."

Massimo cleared his throat. The fella generally let others talk and he listened, but not today. "We are missing the point here. Just because you have found some Cuban exiles who want to see the end of Castro does not mean we can train them well enough to cope with a military attack. Gerry, you need to rethink your plans."

The CIA operative inhaled. "You are not listening to me. We have put in place several initiatives, all of which are geared around killing Castro. By the time we head for Cuba, this ragtag band of brothers will be a well-oiled fighting machine. It is our job to all make certain that is the case. When we move to the second camp, then we shall introduce you to our other assets who will work on these men until they come up to the mark."

Alex finished his coffee and lit a cigarette. These CIA guys were sure of themselves, but Gerry had done nothing to show why he should be so certain of his abilities.

THEIR MILITARY PLANE touched down in Guatemala three days later. It had not been a comfortable journey, especially when compared to the private jet Alex had enjoyed before, but they were safe and installed in their barracks within hours of arriving in the country.

"Do you think the men are prepared enough, Alex?"

"Ezra, they'd be lucky to take over a local bar and get a free drink."

"Gerry stores a lot of faith in the CIA training."

"I overheard him say they had the go-ahead for the invasion, so it can't be long now."

"Massimo, keep your ears close to the ground. It sounds as though Gerry wants to keep us in the dark."

The three men stood watching the brigade as it mustered for morning reveille. There may have been thirty-five men who had come over with them from Florida, but Alex counted almost thirteen hundred in front of him. If he had believed this was going to be a small sortie, with him at the helm sneaking into Castro's quarters, then the sheer scale of the army before him showed he was mistaken.

"Would our mission not be better served if we made a clandestine landing and positioned a sniper in a well-located building, Gerry?"

"We considered that option and decided against it as that puts all our eggs in one basket. With this many men, we have a stronger chance of getting at least one guy into the center of Havana and putting a bullet in Castro's brain."

"You are setting us up for a bloodbath. Even to land all these guys is going to take a miracle."

"Alex, that is the easy bit. We can send them onto the beach under cover of night. As you know, there are many weaknesses in the island defenses and insufficient troops to maintain patrols at every piece of the coastline."

"Gerry, do you have any concrete plans to reach Castro?"

"You will lead the advance party to find the best routes to Havana and feed that back to the brigade. Some of them will spread out across the country to cause as much confusion as possible and to mask who is aiming for the primary target."

"So no actual idea how to kill the guy apart from throwing a thousand men onto the island and hope that someone gets lucky."

"Alex, we are shipping over enough troops so that Castro's forces will have no knowledge that you and your friends are going to assassinate Castro. Everything else is window dressing."

Alex pondered the proposal before him.

"That still sounds mighty thin to me, especially as I am the one who'll be in the thick of it, while you'll relax, smoking a stogie back here or in Florida."

"I'm not a cigar man, Alex, but you do not need to be concerned. I have seen my fair share of action over the years."

"But I am right? You're not joining us for this trip, are you?"

"No, Alex. I will sit this one out."

"Gerry, we need longer. First, I require a much more detailed and well-thought-out plan of attack. Second, we call them men, but they are nothing but a bunch of intellectuals and store owners. These guys are far from being a fighting force we can rely on. We must have a few more weeks to train them into something useful."

"Time is one commodity we have little of. With my current budget, I could buy each of us a top-flight hooker and still have enough money left to arm everyone twice over. But the launch date remains fixed."

"When are we aiming for?"

"Come hell or high water, we sail on April seventeenth."

Alex sighed and let out a long whistle through the gap between his front two upper teeth. Ezra and Massimo shifted in their seats to indicate their disquiet with the situation Gerry was presenting to them.

"What's the rush?"

"We still have a week, Alex, but there are other factors at play, so the date is set and cannot be changed. Besides, there'll be no moon, which should make the first few hours of the assault easier, especially if you are right and these guys are going to end up as cannon fodder."

Gerry indicated the sea of Cuban exiles in front of them, and Alex shuddered. The memory of leaping out of trenches into no man's land amid a hail of shells and shrapnel ripped across his mind. Then he snapped away from France and back to reality.

"We need more time, Gerry."

"Ask for boats, bullets, planes, or guns and I can get them all in less than twenty-four hours with one phone call, but we can't extend the assault by even a day."

"Why?"

"That's above my pay grade, Alex."

"You are sending these men to a certain death, Gerry."

"In which case, it is your duty to save them. The sooner you get to Castro, the quicker this thing ends."

"The only way it'll work is if I am in the reconnaissance party."

"Whatever it takes to get the job done, Alex. Succeed, and the world is your oyster."

11

TWO DAYS BEFORE they were due to attack what they hoped would be the soft underbelly of Cuba, Alex ran through the plan once again with Ezra and Massimo.

"We lead the three flotillas so that they land half a mile apart. Once we hit the beaches, the enemy will be spread thin along the south coast."

"Alex, Massimo, and I think we need to rearrange matters. We are not happy about you being in the firing line. You should be somewhere less... risky."

"Ezra, I can look after myself. You two are not responsible for my safety."

"Alex, we want you to be alive at the end of the operation. You make your own choices, but Gerry doesn't have to drag you home in a body bag."

"Massimo, I'll be fine. Of the three of us, you should remember that I am the only one to have fought in a war."

Both men looked at each other, and Alex knew they didn't believe his bravado. Gerry had promised him he would arrange air cover from the time they landed until he radioed to say they were pushing through into the foothills.

"You fellas worry too much. This isn't some flight of fancy, we have the CIA watching our backs. Can you imagine that? The US government is riding shotgun on this trip."

"Remind me where Gerry is going to be when we land, Alex."

"Ezra, you know he is coordinating all activities from a gunship."

"So, he won't put his ass on the line then?"

Alex sighed. "No, but we are the ones who are getting paid the big bucks, and all he gets is a service pension."

THERE HAD ONLY been two occasions in his past that Alex had sat in a boat as small as the one he found himself in now. The first time was arriving on a French beach during the Great War and the second was at the start of Prohibition when Arnold Rothstein funded trips from Europe to deliver Scotch to the high-end clientele who could afford the luxury of imported liquor. As the waves lapped far too close to his head for comfort, Alex's thoughts were more focused on his old khakis than when he discovered the taste of whisky.

Ten other men clung on for dear life as their small vessel bobbed and weaved its way toward the Cuban shore. Alex squinted into the semidarkness, wondering how much longer they were going to be stuck in this floating coffin. He received his answer within two minutes when a whisper ran across the lips of every person on the craft. "Land."

He braced himself because he knew what would happen next. Everybody lurched forward as the hull hit the sand with a thud and the boat ground to a halt, listing to one side. The men needed no instruction as they leaped out into the water and scurried for dry land. Alex thought he heard gunfire in the distance and wondered if it was his imagination or if Ezra's and Massimo's flotillas had arrived first and were meeting some resistance.

There was no time to ponder because a hail of bullets ripped into the sand on either side of his feet. Everybody zigzagged toward the tree line, rifles in hand, and Alex did his best to look ahead to spot flashes from gun barrels so he could figure out where the enemy was located.

The trees seemed far away with bullets zinging past his ears, but three hundred feet and a lifetime later, Alex reached the foliage and hunkered down. There was still no sign of where Castro's forces were hidden. He popped his eyes above the bush in which he was hiding and counted heads. Three dead in the first five minutes.

Alex's biggest concern was that whoever was trying to pin them down would radio headquarters to tell them what was happening. His advance party would be the sum total of the invasion if that were to happen.

Then a whistle and Cecilio Guadarrama indicated he had something to show. A finger pointed toward a mound one hundred feet from where they were on the edge of the tree line. Alex nodded and gestured for everyone to stay put. He circled around the trees on his hands and knees until he was only fifty feet away and saw the whites of a sixteen-year-old's eyes. A single crack rang out and he thought about how men still sent children into battle.

Silence. Alex waited a minute before doing anything else and when he was certain they were alone on the waterfront, he signaled out to sea to let the ship know it was safe to send the troops and tanks on shore. With a handful of boats and a shallow beach, landing the whole army was going to take hours to complete and Alex's job was to ensure that his seven men stayed alive long enough to deal with any interference the local militia might throw at them.

For now, there was nothing to do but lie and wait, although Cecilio reported that Ezra and Massimo were under fire.

"Where is their air cover? Gerry told us they'd attacked the airfields yesterday and that the Air Force would continue its bombardment throughout today and tomorrow."

"No idea, but it doesn't look like we've any protection from the skies."

"GET ME EZRA on the line, Cecilio."

Alex waited for his radioman to raise his lieutenant.

"How are you doing, Ezra?"

"We are fine, at least for now. We have been under fire from the moment we landed, but we've hunkered down in positions near the tree line. And you?"

"There was not much opposition when we arrived, although it's heated up overnight."

"I thought Gerry promised air cover."

"Words are cheap, Ezra. Since when did we trust G-men?"

"After they asked us to assassinate Fidel Castro, Alex."

They both chuckled.

"Back to the militia, Ezra. You said they met you as you hit the beach?"

"Yeah, it was like they knew we were coming."

"Well, the Air Force hammered the airport and other military outposts the day before, so you don't have to be a tactical genius to realize that something was about to happen."

"Alex, I hadn't thought about it that way. You're correct. Have I mentioned the lack of support?"

"Let it go, Ezra. You are right, but it will not make a difference. For whatever reason, the bombers have flown back home. We won't be seeing them again."

"Do you think we have a chance in hell of getting to Castro, Alex?"

"I don't know, to be honest. Unless Massimo has broken through and is heading for Havana as we speak, I can't see how we are going to overcome all these militias."

"I spoke with him just before we talked. They landed tanks with his men and have made some headway. He plans to hightail it to the airstrip at Giron and use that as a base."

"If you and I make it off the beach, then we should head for the hills. From there we can wage guerrilla warfare on Castro, just like he did to Batista when the roles were reversed."

"I hear you, Alex, but I don't know how successful I'll be at reaching the foothills. Our positions are safe for the moment, but if the locals get any kind of reinforcement..."

Alex's throat felt dry, and he tried to conjure saliva in his mouth.

"Ezra, if you have the choice between encroaching into Castro's territory or living to tell the tale to your grandchildren, make sure you get back home. No matter what. Cuba's freedom isn't worth dying for."

"Straight back at you, Alex."

FOUR HOURS LATER and Alex's men had dug into positions on the far side of the woods to give cover for the main force behind them as it landed and attempted to make some headway inland. The lookout gave a whistle to indicate troops were coming their way. Ten more minutes and bullets flew past his head and peppered the bodies of two more of his special squad.

"Get word to the beach, Cecilio. Either they send men to support us or we'll have to pull back to the shore."

"Our instructions just in are to retreat, Alex."

"Then what are we doing still talking?"

Alex issued the order and the five men withdrew until there was sand under their feet and not soil. Still the bullets zipped past. The Cuban militia was advancing and there was no time to hang around. The brigade opened fire on Castro's militiamen as soon as they appeared through the trees and Alex's crew zigzagged back along the beach and onto one of the small boats which had disgorged men onshore only a minute before.

"Take me the hell off this island."

The instruction tore out of his throat and the boatman blinked and followed his orders to the letter.

12

"I AM SO happy to see you."

Alex's sister, Esther, gave him an enormous bear hug, while two of his sons, Moishe and David, looked on. After a long weekend recuperating with Sarah from his Cuban escapade, Alex felt a powerful urge to see the rest of his family.

He walked into their New York office without announcing his arrival because he just wanted to meet them with no fanfares or anything fancy. A firm handshake for the boys and a pat on the shoulder each was the most Alex offered for physical affection, but the smile on his face spoke volumes.

"Aren't you glad you're no longer living in Cuba what with all that's been happening over there last week?"

Alex nodded at Esther, but David's expression showed the lawyer guessed there was much more to reveal.

"How is Mom? And how are Ezra and Massimo?"

"She is fine and enjoying Californian life… and they got out by the skin of their teeth."

"Huh?" Esther was naïve but Moishe figured his father had been involved.

"It's been a long time since you've been this side of the country, Pop."

"Moishe, I can't tell you how busy I have been, but it is great to be here with you all now."

"Did you try a mojito before you left?"

"Don't get fresh, David. Whatever you may think, I will not comment. Just be pleased that Ezra and Massimo made their way to an airstrip by a whisker and escaped. From what I read in the newspaper, there's a thousand or more captured by Castro's forces."

"Like I said, Alex. I am so glad that your Havana jaunt is behind you," Esther reiterated.

THAT NIGHT, ALEX hosted a meal in a private dining room at the Waldorf-Astoria on the strict understanding that Lindy's cheesecake would be procured for dessert. The dinner went with a swing, and then they hopped over to Broadway to catch a show. Esther was in her element and couldn't stop squeezing Alex's arm to call attention every time there was some item of note that she had spotted.

David and Moishe were more relaxed about the stars they saw on stage, in part because so many American hoofers had visited Cuban hotels during their time in Havana. Once the performance was over, David suggested a nightcap before they headed home.

Alex's eyes shifted from David to Esther and back, but his son nodded with a gentle smile. She might have left Cuba with a liquor problem, but she could enter a drinking establishment without falling apart. In the Waldorf bar, the three men ordered Scotch, and she asked for a soda and lime, much to Alex's relief.

Conversation twisted and turned for an hour as everyone sipped their drinks, not wanting to finish the evening too soon. Chuckles and stories abounded as Alex caught up on everyone's lives. He did his best not to talk about work because he had no desire to open himself up to the old discussion about how much he should let his sons know about the less reputable side of his business empire. David especially had grabbed a glimpse and might have been in awe of the powerful people in Alex's sway, but the boy was not ready to handle himself in the criminal world that Alex called home.

Esther's eyes began to droop, and Alex suggested he call her a cab, which she accepted without question. They walked through the lobby and out to the front of the building to wait for a hotel porter to hail a taxi.

"It's been great to spend time with you today, Alex. You haven't said how long you are in town for."

"That's because I don't know yet, Esther. At least a couple of days, maybe longer. While the focal point of the trip is to see you guys, there are one or two errands I need to take care of."

"There always is with you, Alex."

She winked at him, and then pecked him on the cheek as the porter opened the passenger door of the yellow cab. Alex took care of the guy, and Esther zoomed off into the night.

Hands in pockets, Alex sauntered back to his sons, who had ordered another round of drinks.

"Hope you didn't mind, Pop, but we don't like to let Aunt Esther see us with too much liquor."

"What's to mind?"

They clinked glasses and Alex called for three stogies to be delivered to the table.

◆ ◆ ◆

THE FOLLOWING MORNING, Alex returned to the Cohen office and talked business with all three of his employees. Esther handled the day-to-day smooth running of the company that Alex had set up to keep her busy once she'd wrestled herself out of a tequila bottle after her return from Cuba. Legal advice came from David and as Moishe was a trained accountant, he was the go-to guy where financial matters were concerned.

"How's the Vegas cash flow, Esther?"

"There's been a dip in the last month. When I called Massimo and then Ezra, they were missing. I asked around, but nobody had a clue where they were."

"With me. We were investigating a new investment opportunity."

"Any good?"

"The entire deal fell through, more's the pity."

"So we can expect your eyes and ears in Las Vegas to be on top of things again?"

"Yes. Let me know if a shortfall in May is likely. Tell me by the end of the first full week. Those two should be able to sort everything out by then and, if not, we will need to hatch a plan."

"Understood, Alex."

Then it was Moishe's turn to join Alex in the meeting room. Alex would have been happier conducting these conversations at the back of a nearby deli, but he hadn't been in town long enough to find a suitable location with a disinterested proprietor.

"Pop, I know you sent me away from Cuba, and I understand your reasons. In hindsight, it was an excellent thing for me."

"You're welcome, Moishe."

"But that doesn't mean I don't want more."

"My boy, has there ever been a moment in your life when that has not been the case?"

"Do not tease me, Pop. I am serious. You have kept me out of harm's way and protected me from whatever it is that earns you all your money. But I could do so much more for you if you let me."

"There is a reason I do not want you too involved in some of my affairs. If you have no clue where my gelt comes from, then you have plausible deniability if Uncle Sam were to come sniffing around into my finances again."

"This isn't about plausible deniability but that you exclude me from too many things. Imagine what I could do for you if you let me inside the circle of trust."

Alex raised his eyebrows.

"Moishe, just because I do not offer you full financial disclosure, please don't mistake that for a lack of confidence in you on my part. Quite the reverse. It is because I know you and believe in your strong moral compass that I trust you with my money, and the future of my family which provides me with the peace of mind I need to know that Sarah will never want for anything ever in her life. Knowing what you do, if you weren't in the circle of trust, then you would never have left Havana alive."

His son swallowed hard and remained silent. Alex lit another cigarette and sipped a mug of coffee, poured from the pot which Esther had made the minute he arrived that morning.

"Moishe, when the time is right, then I will rely on you to tend to all my finances, irrespective of their source. I hope to retire someday soon and then all my cash must be clean as your conscience. Until then, find comfort in knowing that you are one of the chosen few."

ONCE MOISHE HAD left the room, Alex placed a few calls and spoke with Sarah.

"How are you doing?"

"Missing you, Alex, but I pretend I am used to your absences."

"Please don't be like that, Sarah. Everyone here is giving me tsoris. Not you as well."

"You were back for such a short time before you went off again."

"Sarah, I needed to check on the family business. Besides, there are some acquaintances I need to meet. While we might not live in the pockets of the Italians, we still must feed and water their concerns."

David was the last to speak with Alex.

"How goes it, Pop?"

"Your mother wants me to come back home."

"Not before we've had a chat, I hope."

"David, that's the second time you've been fresh with me in the same number of days. Have I annoyed you?"

"Ever since we fled Cuba, I feel you've pushed me away."

Alex stared into David's eyes until he made his son uncomfortable.

"I made a mistake with the Cuban businesses and that was to give you too much insight into how I make my money. It put you in jeopardy, especially with our Italian friends, and I do not want to repeat that error now we are back in America."

"We all know how you earn a living, Pop. I've told you before that Moishe and I made our peace with that many years ago."

"Your Aunt Esther is less certain."

"She tells herself that your investments generate cash flow, and she doesn't for a minute wish to think how that gelt gets generated. What little she saw of you in Havana was enough for a lifetime."

"David, there is another reason I don't want you to be too close to my current activities, you need plausible deniability if Uncle Sam were to pay a visit."

13

ALEX SAT IN an anteroom, smoking a cigarette while he waited to be allowed in to discuss business with Joe Bananas. So far, he had been stuck in the chair for around ten minutes, but who was counting? A short while later, a door opened, and a fella in a suit beckoned him inside.

"Alex, I apologize for making you wait so long."

"Don't mention it. I was pleased you could find time in your day to see me."

Joe indicated for Alex to sit on a couch away from the man's desk. His underling supplied coffee and then left them alone. Alex lit yet another cigarette while he waited for the stooge to go.

"How's business, Joe?"

"I can't complain. You know how it is, if it's not one thing, then it is another, but we get by."

Alex cast an eye around Joe's office and noticed the gold leaf corners on the picture frames, the sheer acreage of the room itself, and the feel of the leather upholstery in his seat.

"Life on the commission must be tough. I rescinded my syndicate membership when people stopped coming to the meetings."

Joe curled the corners of his mouth and sipped his coffee.

"Some of my predecessors should have had the decency to tell you that the days of the syndicate were over."

"Kind of you to say so, Joe. I guess the Appalachian meeting was the nail in that particular coffin."

"Sixty of us were arrested that day and Hoover discovered organized crime for the first time in his life."

Alex thought how wrong Joe was. The Italians were grabbed by the Feds as no Jew was invited to the party.

"Water under the bridge, Joe. I try to look at the future. Do you have any interests on the West Coast?"

"Alex, now why do you ask me that?"

"Forgive my abruptness, Joe. I don't mix in the same circles as you do anymore. Let me explain. I have business in California and hope to expand my activities. However, the last thing I want to do is to lock horns with any person of influence as I grow."

"Do not undersell yourself, Alex. You might not sit at the top table with the Italian families, but you are known and respected. After all, if you were just the small-town operator you claim to be, then you would not be sitting here enjoying our conversation."

"Very kind, Joe. And you are right to say that I have worked with the Italian families over the years, here and overseas."

"Cuba was a tremendous opportunity for us all, Alex. How is Meyer these days?"

"Happy in Florida, from what I hear. I don't see him as much as I used to, besides he's retired and I'm still treading the boards."

"Retired, Alex? That's not the Meyer Lansky I know. That man always has some scheme cooking in the background."

"He told me he lost everything when Castro nationalized the casinos."

Joe smirked and shook his head. "Meyer's not down to his last nickel and dime just yet."

Was Joe jerking him around or had Meyer escaped with more than Alex realized? He had no method of figuring it out at the minute.

"Either way, Joe, you didn't answer my question."

"No? My apologies. Tough business in Cuba. Wouldn't you say?"

"It sure was…"

Alex's voice drifted away as he recalled the terror in the pit of his stomach on the Playa Giron, which then hopped his mind over to France fifty years before.

"Thank you for trying, Alex."

"You're welcome."

He responded on autopilot before he registered the implication of Joe Banana's comment.

"I mean, I'm always interested in finding profitable opportunities with exceptional business partners."

"No need to be coy, Alex. We all appreciate your efforts in returning Cuba to a sensible footing. It's just a shame things didn't work out for us."

"Some you win, Joe, some you lose."

"And that one, we sure lost."

Another sip of coffee, and Joe continued his line of thought.

"I find it interesting you inquire about the West Coast for two reasons. First, I assumed your territory for narcotics and prostitution was restricted to the Hollywood Hills and no further. Second, we are keeping a watchful eye on Frank."

"DeSimone?"

"For sure. The guy has run Los Angeles for six years now, but the area has never been secure for our interests since the days of Mickey Cohen and your friend Benny Siegel."

"Jack Dragna ruled with an iron fist."

"True, Alex, but you made inroads back then without too much opposition if I recall."

Alex smiled. Joe was well informed.

"Joe, if I were to expand my business, would that be problematic for you?"

"Not at all. If you can carve away more of Frank's empire, then you will hear no objection from me or any of the other families in New York. What do you have in mind?"

"Nothing in particular, but I wanted to ensure I wouldn't be stepping on your toes or conflicting with your interests when I make a move."

"Very considerate, Alex."

"We live together, we love together, but we die alone."

"Well said. Is there anything else you wanted to discuss?"

"Just one thing, Joe."

The man raised an eyebrow.

"My lieutenants have returned to Vegas, and I wondered if they should watch out for any issues you are aware of."

Joe stared at Alex without uttering a word.

"Are you on a fishing expedition, Alex? Because that sounded like the vaguest question I think I have ever heard. No disrespect."

"No sleight perceived, Joe. To be honest, I'm asking because it has been so long since I've been involved in the day-to-day Vegas casino operations. I thought I'd check that it remains an open city."

"Sure thing, Alex. Although everyone would like to have their own piece of Nevada, we allow it to remain neutral. Even nowadays."

"So the money should keep on rolling in?"

"If you carry on as you have been. I know I can speak for all five families when I say we continue to be happy with the way you help run the city. The casinos under your control continue to deliver their numbers and you have always been amenable to working with us over the years."

"Thank you, Joe. Ever since the Flamingo, I have done my best to generate money for all my partners in the casino business. Sometimes it hasn't been easy…"

"We all have our differences of opinion sometimes…"

"But I make as many accommodations as I am able. Vegas is an enormous pot of honey and if no one loses their head, then we can all enjoy its sweetness."

"Alex, you sound as though you are taking stock of your business empire."

"It's not quite an empire, not anymore at least. I have a few well-placed interests around the country and at some point, I want to retire."

"The racing wire, an iron grip on Vegas, access to the rich and famous, the ear of the president. These are no mere trifles, Alex. You are right that the days when you ran Manhattan have long since faded, but your influence in America is significant."

Alex felt the warmth in his cheeks.

"Thank you. I do my best. And I wouldn't say I have Jack's ear. We have a business relationship where I act as an agent between federal departments and some of our construction friends."

"Well put, Alex. I will not press you because I respect your privacy, but we both know that you have Kennedy's private line."

Alex did not respond and lit a cigarette instead.

"And on a separate note, Alex, I wonder if you'd be kind enough to get in touch with Sam Giancana over the next few days."

"Any particular reason beyond reminiscing about our time in Havana?"

"Alex, I'll leave Sam to run through the details, but I would see it as a personal favor if you were to do so. My understanding is that he'd like to talk to you about a mutual friend."

"We have picked up many of those over the years. Anyone, in particular, he has in mind?"

Joe Bananas sighed and sipped his coffee for the millionth time since they'd sat down.

"If you talk to Sam, then you'll find out. You don't need me to act as a broker. I'm just asking you for a favor."

"There's nobody else in the room. This is as far from a case of entrapment as you'll get. I'll just find it easier if I know who I'm going to be having a conversation about. Nothing more than that, Joe."

Another breath and a slug of coffee hit the back of Joe's throat.

"Frank Sinatra."

"A great singer, by all accounts. And can act too."

"He's brought plenty of customers to our casinos as well."

"Yeah, you could say that."

The two men smiled at each other and finished their coffees.

14

"HOW ARE YOU doing, Sam?"

"All the better for seeing you, Alex."

The two men shook hands and sat down in the back of a Chicago restaurant owned by Giancana.

"Fancy something to eat?"

"I'm good for now, but coffee would be wonderful. Joe sends his regards."

"It is kind of you to take time from your schedule to see me, Alex."

"Joe Bananas recommended we talk and here I am. He mentioned we had a mutual friend."

The waiter arrived with their drinks and they paused for the guy to be out of earshot before they continued.

"Frank has been very useful to us over the years. His turns in Vegas and Havana helped to encourage tourists into our hotels and casinos."

"We have both benefited from his performances, that's for sure."

"Alex, the thing is that he is hosting a weekend away for Kennedy and I'd like someone to be my eyes and ears when the two of them are together."

"Are you expecting any trouble?"

"Quite the reverse, Alex. My informants tell me that Jack Kennedy is tight with Frank, but Bobby Kennedy continues to obsess over mob involvement in American politics and industry. He's like a dog with a bone who refuses to spit it out. You'd be there to gauge the extent to which Bobby is influencing Jack. No more and no less."

"No disrespect, but why don't you visit instead of me?"

"Because I haven't met Kennedy and you have."

Alex thought for a minute and understood how he was better placed to assess the situation.

"Sam, how can I get an invitation?"

"I'll call Frank tomorrow and tell him he has an extra houseguest."

THE PALM SPRINGS home of Frank Sinatra was lavish even by that town's standards. Far from the city center, Frank's residence stood on two acres of grounds west of South Palm Canyon Drive. Sam had arranged a driver to collect Alex from the airport and fifteen minutes later they arrived at the main gates, where a guy in a peaked cap greeted Alex, then they drove on to the front of the house, away from any prying eyes from the street.

"Good to see you, Alex."

Frank welcomed him as soon as he stepped out of his limo.

"Straight back at you, Frank."

"Have you brought anything to help the house party go with a swing?"

"Don't you worry about a thing, Frank. I'll look after anyone who needs a little kicker."

Frank smiled and slapped Alex on the back then showed him around the enormous mansion he had built brick by brick to his own design. It was palatial, for sure, and there appeared to be sufficient staff to guarantee that every need would be met within seconds of it being thought. After Alex unpacked and came downstairs, Frank introduced him to his guests.

He recognized Peter Langford and Sammy Davis Jr. and met Dean Martin and Jerry Lewis for the first time. Everyone had brought a girlfriend along, and Alex wondered whether he should have got an invitation for Sarah. Then he checked himself because, unlike the others, he was here on business.

Jayne Mansfield swept into the living room and planted a kiss on Frank's lips, so Alex figured out who was his skirt for the weekend. Then two other men entered in quick succession: a young singer, Buddy Greco, and a comedian, Don Rickles. Everybody appeared to know each other and he wondered how well he would fit in and, therefore, how relaxed everyone would behave when Jack blew into town.

"Let me show you the helipad I had built for the presidential helicopter."

Frank took the group out of the back of the house, past the swimming pool, and then beyond the tennis courts, where a circular piece of tarmac had been plopped on top of a raised mound.

"We had to get foundations dug before the surface was laid. Those whirlybirds weigh a ton."

They all nodded and smiled. The men talked about construction for a short while and then their glasses needed to be refilled, so everyone sauntered to the booze at the rear of the house. Alex hung back to allow himself a few minutes' conversation away from the group.

"Thanks for letting me intrude on your weekend, Frank."

"All's good. Besides, when am I going to refuse Sam an accommodation? He wants you here, and why should I ask for any justification beyond that? Of course, that Peter's brother-in-law is due to land here in an hour might have something to do with it."

Sinatra winked at Alex but expected no response and none was forthcoming.

TWO HOURS LATER and no helicopter had landed. A further sixty minutes and still no bird had flown in from the sky. Frank's blue funk settled on him like a shroud, and even the close attention afforded by Jayne couldn't lift his mood. By this point, everyone had moved inside and Alex overheard a valet tell Sinatra that the dinner was well and truly burned. Nobody had wanted to eat before the president of the free world had arrived, which meant that at this rate, no one would eat at all.

Then a housekeeper popped her head around the door of the dining room and informed Frank that he had a telephone call. He stormed out and Alex followed him because the day was not going well and he wanted to keep a handle on the situation.

"Let me get this straight. Jack is staying with Bing Crosby tonight?"

The faint voice at the other end of the line responded, but Alex couldn't hear what was said.

"And when did you say he decided this?"

Muffled noise again and then Frank slammed the phone down, swearing in Italian for several seconds. Alex hung back, leaning against a door jamb. Sinatra stormed up and down his office until he had calmed down enough to be near his houseguests again.

"Jack will not be with us then, Frank?"

"No, Alex. He's staying with that Republican Crosby."

"Any idea why he changed his mind?"

"That rat-fink brother of his. Bobby told Jack he shouldn't be seen to mix with my sort anymore. That it's not acceptable for his image."

"Doesn't the attorney general like singers?"

Frank stared at Alex with an unimpressed expression.

"Let's just say the guy does not appreciate the entrepreneurial spirit, Alex."

"Do you think he understands how politics works?"

"Good question. From the moment the man uttered his first baby scream, he has lived inside the most political family in America. So you would expect he'd get the joke by now."

"Frank, I shall leave before breakfast tomorrow morning, but I might be back before the end of the weekend. Nothing personal, but without Jack here, I am going to be like some spare change and there is no need for me to make your guests feel uncomfortable."

"Alex, I appreciate your concern. Of course, you are always welcome in my home."

"JACK DIDN'T SHOW and stayed elsewhere that weekend."

Sam shook his head.

"The world we live in is very complicated. The Kennedys need to remember how they got into the White House."

Alex remained silent as Giancana continued.

"Let me guess. It was Bobby's decision and not Jack's? The president has always enjoyed hanging out with cool fellas like Frank. Bobby has a broom stuck up his ass, and he has a hard-on for organized crime."

Alex winced but did not respond until Sam had calmed himself down.

"Someone needs to do something about Bobby Kennedy."

Italian eyes pierced into Alex.

"Is that an instruction, Sam?"

"No, but thank you for the offer. I appreciate it."

"If you ever change your mind…"

Now it was Sam's turn to smile.

ALEX HOPPED OVER to Frank's Palm Springs mansion again the following week.

"What are you going to do about Bobby Kennedy?"

"Frank, as much as you want me to take action, I have not been authorized to do anything. And you must respect that decision."

Sinatra glared at Alex but chose not to follow up and changed the conversation to something more fun.

"Been to any parties the last few weeks?"

"Frank, you know Hollywood far better than me. Blink and there's another party to go to. Besides, you film stars like to have an entourage with pretty girls and plenty of narcotics."

"You've always been there for me and my gatherings."

"It's nice to help nice people."

They clinked glasses and settled in for a night of jokes and conversation.

"How does Jack get away with it, Frank?"

"What do you mean?"

"Well, the guy has at least two of Hollywood's biggest stars for girlfriends and somehow keeps both of them dangling on the line."

"Alex, everyone lives in denial. Marilyn and Jayne know about each other, but they tell themselves that the other is one of Jack's friends and nothing more. That way, they convince themselves they are his exclusive lover."

15

ALEX SETTLED BACK into his Hollywood routine with Sarah, supplying girls and drugs to any actor who had a credit on any movie that was on general release. Cannabis was the narcotic of choice although Alex noticed there had been an increasing call for coke over the past few months.

Sarah couldn't say there were any changes in the sexual tastes of their clients: teenage girls. It didn't matter the color of their skin or the shape of their hairstyle. If the skirt was short enough and the flesh willing, then they would do just fine. Alex never judged what any of his customers did with their money; that was their decision and their right. Sarah had a different perspective.

"Alex, do you ever imagine what would have happened to me if we hadn't got married?"

"What do you mean?"

"I'd still be in the old life."

"Sarah, after all these years? Do you think you'd have remained living the nafka life?"

"What are you trying to say?"

Alex was silent for half a second, and then he raised his eyebrows.

"That's not what I meant. You are still an amazingly attractive woman."

"Too little, too late, young man."

"I was attempting to tell you that you were too smart to work for Waxey Gordon for the rest of your life."

Sarah looked at him to consider his words, but her expression gave nothing away.

"Kind of you to say so, but Waxey Gordon only set me free after you paid him off. Without your gelt…"

Alex placed a hand on Sarah's arm and squeezed it.

"What's got you wondering about the maybes of our past?"

"Not much. With you back home, I was remembering how I felt when we first lived together when you returned to the Bowery after the war."

◆ ◆ ◆

TWO DAYS LATER and Alex sat in an armchair in Marilyn Monroe's living room. A housekeeper had let him in and instructed he wait for her there. Ten minutes staring into space and Marilyn appeared in a figure-hugging powder blue dress. He smiled as she walked toward him.

"Sorry for making you wait, Alex."

"Don't mention it. I know how busy you actors are."

"No need for that tone, Alex."

"Only kidding."

She punched him on the arm but didn't even make a dent in his jacket.

"I've got a visitor arriving in a short while. Do you have what I asked for?"

Alex nodded, removed some folded brown paper from his coat pocket, and flicked it with his fingers.

"I think this is what you requested."

Now it was Marilyn's turn to smile, and she shimmied over to a sideboard. She opened a drawer and pulled out a small roll of notes, which she deposited in Alex's hand, with a kiss on the cheek as a bonus.

"Marilyn, is there anything else I can get you for your party tonight?"

"I said I'm expecting one visitor, not a gaggle of friends. Jack wouldn't appreciate coming all this way to share me with others."

That Kennedy sure knew how to keep his ladies happy, despite being president of the United States and having the first lady so much in the public eye.

"Marilyn, will I have time to go before Jack turns up?"

Before she could inhale to answer, the doorbell rang and thirty seconds later, Jack appeared in the living room, followed by the hapless housekeeper. The couple embraced, which gave Alex the excuse to leave the building. The only acknowledgment he received from Kennedy was a small nod before the president fondled Marilyn's ass.

JACK MUST HAVE been busy, because less than twenty-four hours later, Alex bumped into him again, only in Jayne Mansfield's home. His head popped round the doorway of her bedroom and Alex wondered if the two of them ever spent any time in the other rooms of her expansive house. Perhaps the decor was not as offensive as elsewhere, in which case Alex understood Jack's desire to be in Jayne Mansfield's boudoir; apart from the obvious reason, of course.

"Hi, Jack. How's it going?"

"Just fine, Alex."

Jayne pulled on the strings of her nightgown to tighten the front, but the sheer material left little to Alex's imagination and he clenched his teeth until the pressure on his molars became too intense. There was no need for her to behave that way. It felt as though she was playing games with Jack and was trying to place Alex in the middle. Jack's head disappeared from view and Alex was forced to talk business with Jayne.

"Is there anything else you require for your house party?"

"No, it looks like you've brought everything a girl could want for her man."

A wink and a coquettish smile. She padded over to a chest and opened the top drawer. Then she returned and placed both hands on either side of his and stared him square in the eyes.

"That's all for you."

For reasons beyond Alex's understanding, she planted a kiss on his cheek and he looked down to see the green Jayne'd pushed into his hand.

"Time for you to go back to Jack. Enjoy your night of passion. Call me any time if you need anything else."

Another smile and Jayne undid her nightgown to get it to slip on the floor as she turned around to walk into the bedroom.

"Come here, baby," were the only words Jack spoke before Alex trotted down the stairs and let himself out. Had Jayne left the door open for his benefit or because that's the way Jack liked it?

16

FOLLOWING A PHONE call from Jack a couple of weeks later, Alex drove down from Hollywood to Malibu and entered a swanky house on the beach itself. A butler greeted him on his arrival and led him through the building and out onto a patio.

Two men in black suits stood on the other side of a swimming pool with their backs to a summerhouse. Alex noted a pair of figures inside through the windows. A maid offered him a drink, and he accepted a coffee and waited.

Only when she returned and inquired if he wanted a refill, did the door to the summerhouse open and Jack appear. He waved at Alex and beckoned for him to come over.

"Good to see you, Alex. Have you met Bobby?"

The two men walked inside as Jack spoke and before Alex could answer, he was shaking hands with the attorney general. All three sat down in armchairs that surrounded a low table. Alex poured himself a cup from the coffeepot and settled into his seat.

"How's business, Mr. Kennedy?"

"Call me Bobby. The Department of Justice is doing just fine, thank you."

"Pleased to hear that federal law enforcement is protecting the citizenry from the evils of criminal enterprise."

"We do our best to remove all the vermin from our land, Alex."

He couldn't tell if Bobby had a way about him or whether those beady blue eyes were piercing into him especially, as though the brother knew about all of Alex's illegal business. He wondered how honest Jack had been about their relationship.

"Pest control is a wonderful thing, Bobby, and I am glad we have you on our side."

Now it was Bobby's turn to be silent for a moment as he judged Alex's comment.

"I saw that you have had your own trouble with the federal authorities."

Before Alex inhaled to reply, Jack stepped in. "That was long ago. He was a young man and served his time with dignity. We have all had youthful indiscretions."

Bobby scowled at his brother but chose not to continue the conversation. Alex took a sip of his coffee and waited to find out why he had been summoned here on such short notice. Just as Jack opened his mouth as if he was going to start a fresh discussion, he excused himself and left the summerhouse, and padded back to the main building. Alex looked at Bobby and smiled for half a second, but his expression was met with a scowl and a grimace.

"My brother is very forgiving, Alex."

"What do you mean by that, Bobby?"

"You are on record as a felon, like so many of your kind. Jack tolerates you but I do not."

Alex ground his molars. Whenever a *goy* talked of his kind, you could never tell if they meant other Jews or other criminals. Neither was good, but the former was far worse.

"I've paid for my past mistakes and my record has been clean ever since."

"That the authorities haven't indicted you for any crime in the last twenty years is not the same as saying that you have committed no felonies, Cohen. We both know that."

"Bobby, you should be careful about throwing casual accusations into a conversation. I am here because of my business relations with Jack. To cast aspersions on my activities is to do the same to your brother."

"The president is above reproach. You are not. Just remember that I am the attorney general and it is my job to root out all criminal activity in this country, organized or otherwise."

As Alex was about to respond, Jack returned and settled back in his armchair.

"What have you guys been talking about in my absence?"

"Bobby has been telling me of his plans to rid the country of organized crime."

"I'm going to exorcise all criminals from this fair land, Alex."

"A worthy aim, Bobby, and I applaud you but remember that not all business relationships are black and white. Most people operate in the fuzzy gray in the middle."

"You might, Alex. But the majority of hard-working Americans pay their taxes and follow the rules."

Alex allowed that comment to fall to the floor.

"So, Jack, why did you ask me to visit Malibu?"

"WHAT'S GOING ON, Alex?"

A blank expression met Sam Giancana's question.

"That Kennedy will be the death of me."

"Which one do you mean, Sam?"

"Bobby, of course."

Alex leaned back in his seat at the rear of the Miami restaurant where he and the mob boss were sharing coffee and cake.

"He is gunning for us, Sam. That's the simple truth and Jack doesn't appear to want to stop him."

"You just can't trust these people."

"Politicians are scum, have been since the glory days of Tammany Hall."

"And still are today, Alex."

"You said it, Sam."

"Is there anything specific we should be concerned about?"

"Not that I am aware of at present, Sam. Bobby talks the talk but he has done little in his fight against the high levels of the mob. So I think it is more about politics than actual plans. He wants to be seen to be doing the right thing, but he knows he'll end up implicating his brother if he digs too deep."

"We are going to need to do something about this family."

"Sam, what do you mean?"

The Italian sighed and took a swig of his coffee before guzzling half his tiramisu.

"Kennedy would never have moved into the White House if we had not offered our support. Our control of the unions and the influence we have over the Italian American community put him where he is today. And that man knows it."

"I wouldn't say Bobby acknowledged that with his behavior to me earlier this week."

"Alex, he agreed to turn a blind eye to some of our activities for the support we offered. He promised me that Bobby would do nothing to rock the apple cart."

"Then he was appointed attorney general."

"Yes. He got a taste for publicity when he was on a senate committee, but Hoover kept him in check. Now he is acting like he's ignoring what Jack has committed to."

"You know what we'd have done in the old days, Sam?"

A laugh.

"Yeah, but we live in a different age nowadays. I appreciate your offer, Alex. We shall let things slide for the moment. Unless Bobby uncovers any big deals, we can afford to allow a few opportunities to get exposed."

"There's also the minor fact that we are doing business with Jack, and Bobby will not want to besmirch the family name if it were to be revealed to the general public."

"They are both desperate for Joe Kennedy's attention. Their father keeps them under the thumb, and he and I worked together a long time ago."

"Sam, will that be enough to keep his boys in check?"

The mob boss weighed the question as he consumed the rest of his tiramisu.

"Let's just say that I am not impressed with Robert's ongoing actions and his implied threat when you met him. But I will watch and wait—for now at least."

ALEX STAYED IN town the next day so he could visit Meyer Lansky. Apart from an occasional phone call every month, the two men had little contact with each other. Alex told himself this was because of Meyer's retirement, but he was never sure that his old friend had stopped financing the mob's ventures.

"How are you doing?"

"All the better for seeing you, Alex."

Once they settled down in the living room and Thelma had left them alone, he cranked up the volume on the baseball match on the television.

"Meyer, I want your advice about Sam Giancana."

"What is that *schmendrick* up to now?"

"Let's just say we are having some issues with the Feds."

"Alex, you don't have to be circumspect with me. Whatever you say will go no further. No one calls, nobody visits."

"Sam has concerns about how far Bobby Kennedy will go in his desire to rid the country of organized crime."

Meyer smiled at the news.

"That family never ceases to amaze me."

"Meyer, are you going to suggest that Joe made his money out of bootlegging? That's what Sam implied to me."

"Don't be ridiculous. Joe's first fortune was generated by preparing well for the end of Prohibition. He sold legally imported booze as soon as the law changed."

"So why does Sam think he did business with Joe back then?"

"Maybe he did, but it had nothing to do with liquor, Alex."

"Meyer, how might I stop Sam from making a poor decision over Bobby?"

"I'm not sure you can, but I don't expect Sam will make any move on his own. The commission would need to authorize any significant action and I can't see that happening."

May 1962

17

ALEX SAT ON the far-left side of the auditorium at Madison Square Garden at a table containing a mix of Democrat faithful and interested businessmen. Sarah was next to him because they'd used the excuse of the fundraiser to hop over to New York to shop and relax with the family.

A single spotlight hovered in the middle of the stage as Peter Lawford introduced Marilyn Monroe for the umpteenth time that night. He'd set up a running gag that she was behind schedule.

"I introduce to you the late Marilyn Monroe."

The crowd laughed and Marilyn appeared in an ermine coat. The instant she removed it to reveal her skintight sequined dress, the audience clapped and cheered.

"Is she wearing anything underneath that thing?" Sarah whispered in Alex's ear and he shrugged in response. Then Monroe sang *Happy Birthday, Mr. President* to Jack, who was sat nearest the front.

As soon as the applause from the crowd had died down, a gigantic birthday cake was wheeled onto the stage and Jack joined her. Alex thought they made a strange couple and looked at Kennedy's table to see that his wife, Jackie, was nowhere to be found.

Once the show was over and every dime had been squeezed out of the assembled donors, Alex turned to Sarah.

"Now it's time for me to go to work at the after-party. I'll see you back at the hotel, but don't wait up. This could be a long night."

THE KENNEDYS AND senior Democrats were gathered in a library away from the main auditorium. A wall was lined with shelves stuffed to bursting with books. Alex took a drink offered by a waiter on his arrival and sauntered around the room to get his bearings.

One circuit later and Alex had spotted Jack and Bobby, along with Peter Lawford and Monroe. Bobby schmoozed some high rollers in one corner and Lawford chatted with Marilyn. A gaggle of senators and governors circled Jack, and everybody appeared to be laughing. Alex headed toward Marilyn with two glasses of champagne.

"Hello, Peter. Marilyn, what a performance tonight. Here's to you."

He passed her the fresh bubbly, and they clinked glasses, leaving Peter to wave his whiskey sour in the air.

"Thank you, Alex. Very kind of you to say so. I wasn't sure that I would hit the right tone, you know?"

"Sure do. I doubt if there was a single person in that audience who was not captivated by your singing."

Marilyn's cheeks reddened slightly, and she took a second sip of her drink. Peter smiled at his companion, and Alex looked around the room.

"Peter, do you mind if I take Marilyn away from you?"

He shrugged and kissed her on the cheek before making his way over to a bar.

"And how do you think I feel about it, Alex?"

"Marilyn, sometimes you just have to trust me and this is one of those occasions."

She smiled back at him and he took her by the hand and led her across to the other side of the room by the incredible book collection. Having reached the edge, they worked their way into the far corner where Bobby was holding sway. As soon as they arrived in the circle of conversation, it fell silent and Alex knew it wasn't because he'd appeared.

Marilyn accepted their congratulations and kisses and ignored the inappropriate fumbling of her ass along the way. Once the wave of admiration abated, Alex took Bobby to one side.

"Marilyn, let me introduce you to Jack's brother, Bobby."

"Very pleased to meet you, Miss Monroe."

"Call me Marilyn. All my friends do."

"Marilyn, you sang like an angel, my dear."

"Thank you. I thought I'd do my best for Jack."

Bobby's eyebrows rose and a crude smile ripped across his face.

"I'm sure you are a constant source of pleasure for my brother."

"We have our moments, Bobby."

Alex detected a hesitation in her speech as if she hadn't quite understood what the attorney general had said, although the lascivious grin was clear to Alex.

"Your singing voice is remarkable. Perhaps later on you might like to give me some lessons?"

"I didn't realize you sang, Bobby?"

"Back in the day, I was a leading light in my fraternity choir, Alex."

"Is that what you called it?"

A glint in Marilyn's eye showed she was getting the joke from earlier and had delivered her own punchline now.

ALEX AND SARAH stayed in town to continue their shopping trip. The following morning, they bumped into Marilyn as she left the Carlyle Hotel via a side entrance and got ready to step into a yellow cab hailed by a bellboy.

"How are you doing?"

"Huh? Oh, good to see you again, Alex."

Marilyn looked askance at Sarah until Alex introduced them. Polite conversation ensued for half a minute, and then Marilyn's eyes darted twice at the open taxi door. Once the vehicle sped away, Sarah commented: "This is an unusual entrance for Monroe to use."

"One of the apartments is owned by Jack, so I'm not surprised Marilyn is departing out of a side door."

Sarah nodded.

"I don't know how Jackie puts up with him."

"Sarah, you assume that she knows what Jack is up to."

She was silent for a spell.

"The wife realizes, Alex. The question is whether she does anything about it."

Now it was Alex's turn to not speak as he mulled over Sarah's comment.

"Was that true for you too, back in the day?"

"I surprised myself when I didn't confront you more, but I believed I would push you further away if I accused you of sleeping with that actress."

"Sarah, I ripped our family apart, not you. And for that, I am forever sorry."

"I forgave you a long time ago, otherwise we wouldn't be here now. We live together, we love together, but we die alone."

BACK HOME, THE reels of Alex's tape recorder rotated while he listened, not moving, not smoking, just caught in the private moments between two people. Most of the session consisted of general noises, but every so often, he heard snatches of conversation as the man and woman spoke between more intimate acts.

"You are so much more of a man than your brother."

"Don't compare him to me. I just want to enjoy our time together."

Muffled sounds followed for ten minutes, but after a while, they stopped fooling around long enough to talk to each other.

"I never want us to be apart. Would you ever be prepared to leave your wife?"

The man laughed, and Alex imagined the look on the woman's face.

"Not while I am in office. The party would never forgive me."

"But later? Then would you?"

Another chortle. "Perhaps, yes. But that will not happen any time soon. I want you to I understand that, right?"

"I guess."

Then she giggled and his breathing increased in intensity, so Alex zoned out and waited for their carnal pursuits to cease.

"I don't know what I'd do if you ever left me."

Marilyn's hushed tone revealed her insecurity as Bobby reassured her that everything would work out just fine.

"Come over here and grab that champagne on your way over."

August 1962

18

"BOBBY DODGED A bullet, wouldn't you say?"

"How d'you make that out, Sam?"

Alex had paid a visit to Giancana in Miami and they sat at the back of yet another Italian restaurant; never the same place twice.

"With Monroe's overdose, there can be no scandal for the attorney general at any point thanks to his roving dick."

"There is that. She was a beautiful girl."

"I never met her, Alex."

"Marilyn could be really funny if she chose to be, but was sad inside. From what I saw of her, she spent her time fighting with Jayne Mansfield over the affections of our president."

"I thought she kept Bobby's bed warm just before the end."

"That's right, Sam. I reckon she only jumped ship because of the way Jack treated her though. She was loyal."

"Like I said, I only saw her in the movies. Besides, an overdose is not a pretty way to leave this world."

"Marilyn was careful with her meds and her narcotics, and I should know because I supplied her."

"What are you saying, Alex?"

"Nothing at the minute. I'm pointing out that I'd be surprised if Marilyn overdosed by accident. And she didn't come across as a suicidal type."

Sam nodded and continued eating his spaghetti with clams.

ALEX RETURNED HOME to Boyle Heights and amassed all the recordings that had been made in Marilyn's haunts. He listened as her relationship with Bobby deepened. At least from her viewpoint.

"I sure love the time we spend with each other, Bobby."

"Me too, babe."

"Do you ever think we could be together? I mean, for always."

"Not right now, but you never know what might happen in the future."

"You're thinking about your political career, aren't you?"

"And my wife and kids."

"I'd love to have children someday, Bobby."

He instigated none of those conversations, not once in all the hours of talking and banging. Then in July, every tape was filled with the phone ringing and Bobby never picked up. There were times when Marilyn spoke to the emptiness at the other end of the line and that made Alex choke up.

"MASSIMO, I HAVE a discreet job for you, if you're free."

"I am always available to you, Alex."

"The attorney general and Monroe. I'd like you to see what you can find out about their last times together. I'm not interested in what they did between the sheets. I need to learn what they got up to apart from that."

"Do you think that anyone will have seen them? Would they not have been careful about being spotted in public?"

"Massimo, that's for you to find out for me. You are probably right, but I want to know what you can discover."

A couple of weeks later, Massimo visited Alex at home in what he still called the new office. Sarah welcomed him inside and left the two men to their conversation. She knew when Alex wanted to separate her from some of his less savory business activities.

"What have you found out, Massimo?"

"Less than you might hope, Alex."

"Spill."

"Either they were hiding in plain sight or Kennedy and Monroe didn't spend a single moment together in the last three weeks of her life."

"Were they ever in the same city?"

"Yes. Kennedy visited LA at least twice and from all my digging, he might have spent time in a dame's bed, but it sure as hell wasn't with Marilyn Monroe."

Alex ground his molars. He did not know why Bobby's infidelity to Marilyn annoyed him so much, but it did. All he was left with was the recording of her final night when she called Bobby on the phone, but he never picked up. A quick check of hotel records showed he had been in, but the man would not take her call. Only tears, a muffled cry, and then Marilyn was dead.

"I can keep searching if you want me to, Alex, but I've got to tell you I don't think there's anything to find."

"You have done your best, and I thank you. One more thing, you've been looking at this for a while now. Do you believe Bobby had Marilyn killed or was it a suicide?"

Massimo exhaled until there was no air left in his lungs. Then he grabbed a cigarette before replying.

"I've turned up nothing to link him to anywhere she was on the day of her death. If he hired someone to take care of her, then that is something else."

"Massimo, the meds they found by her bed weren't her usual prescription and I'd have known if she had acquired anything else because she'd have bought it from me."

"Blame Kennedy then, but there's nothing we can stick on that man."

NOVEMBER 1963

19

"IT'S BEEN A long time since I have seen you in these parts, Alex."

"I've stayed at home over the last year, Sam, but it sure is good to see you again."

Alex and Giancana sipped cocktails before their pasta arrived. The private dining room at the rear of Sam's restaurant enabled them to speak without any concern over stray ears listening in to their conversation.

"I find it hard to believe you've just sat on your haunches and achieved nothing."

"Sam, at my time of life, I am content to let the money flow in and enjoy the days I spend with my wife. Now and again, we fly over to New York and visit family. But this is the most I've done. Of course, Las Vegas has held my attention."

Sam smiled and waited for the waiter to leave the room, having delivered their plates of spaghetti; clams for him, and salmon for Alex.

"You are too modest, my friend. The gaming capital of the world does not run itself."

"Very kind, Sam. Let's just say I've worked hard to keep a low profile."

"And you have been very successful. I thought the way you handled yourself with the Kennedys was exceptional, Alex."

"No need to blow smoke, Sam. It has been so long since we've broken bread, I guess this isn't just a social call you've asked me to make."

The corners of the Italian's mouth curled upward.

"Let us enjoy our conversation and not worry about any business, for now at least."

A WAITER APPEARED to clear the table of debris and the two fellas placed an order for some coffee. Alex thanked Sam for the offer of a Scotch but declined as he still didn't believe he was in the back of the restaurant just to talk over old times. The drinks were delivered, and the men sat there alone. Alex stirred his coffee to kill time.

"Alex, some of my friends regret what happened in Cuba, but we appreciate your effort despite what transpired in the Bay of Pigs."

"We all lament the outcome with Castro. Some of us had plenty more to lose than others, Sam."

"True, but my younger associates don't have a sense of history. They see what is in front of their noses and remember nothing more than the last smell they inhaled."

"Sam, young men have a lot to learn and I am just glad that I won't have to go back to that country ever again."

Eyes downcast, Sam spoke in a hushed tone.

"There is still much for us to do together, Alex."

"Sam, whatever your next plan to free Havana from the communist hordes, I must count myself out. That is no longer my fight. I got what money I could out of the place and now it is in my past."

"Some of my colleagues fail to recognize the tremendous contribution you continue to deliver to our organization. But I don't make that mistake. Our Vegas interests would be diminished if there wasn't the oversight that you offer us in that open city."

Alex nodded, but Sam still did not meet his gaze.

"Sam, I am sure you remind your less experienced compadres of the value an old Jew can deliver to their wallets."

"You do yourself a disservice, Alex. My father is old, but not you."

"Either way, it won't be too long before I set my affairs in order and retire from this business."

"I am surprised to hear you say that. I thought you'd carry on for years to come."

"Cuba beat Meyer Lansky and I am not that far behind him."

"In that case Alex, I have a proposal for you which should help you feather your nest and hasten your retirement day."

Sam raised his eyes and looked straight at Alex.

"I'd like you to take a trip for me. There may be nothing for you to do when you get there, but I need somebody I trust who knows how to handle himself under any circumstances in case there is trouble."

"Where do you want me to go?"

"Dallas."

"Texas?"

"That's right."

"There's no business there that I can help with, Sam."

"You'd be amazed at what goes on down south. Besides, I'll pay you one hundred thousand if nothing happens and much more depending what else I ask of you while you are in town."

"The last time I did you a favor, I was lucky to get out alive, as were my men. The fact you started this conversation by pointing out that some of your business partners preferred you didn't talk to me makes me want to say no to your request. And I say that with all due respect, Sam."

"You refused a favor from me once before, Alex. Do you remember? And I warned you not to do it again."

"Sam, I was sat between a rock and a hard place in Havana with too many competing interests to keep placated."

"I understand, but it was still a refusal. If I return to my associates and tell them that this Jew shall not help an Italian, how do you think they will respond? These youngsters who can't see further than their noses."

Alex shifted in his seat and took a sip of coffee to moisten the back of his throat.

"Is that how you view me, Sam? As a Jew to do your bidding?"

"Not at all, Alex. But neither of us is so naïve as to believe that other bosses don't hold that view. We have spent too many years fighting common enemies for me to think of you that way."

Sam lit a cigar while Alex pondered.

"I won't be so foolish as to ask you about your business, Sam. But the fact you are asking someone outside your direct sphere of influence within the commission shows it is mighty serious and has a significant amount of danger."

"Life is a risk, Alex."

"What are the chances that Sarah will end up a widow?"

"None that I can see, Alex."

Alex laughed.

"I am sure that's what you told me before I sailed off to the Bay of Pigs."

Sam smiled in return.

"Perhaps, but this time we are not relying on the US Air Force for your safety."

"Should I bring a sniper rifle, Sam?"

"Why no, I am not asking you to shoot anyone, Alex. I want you in the city so that there is a safe distance between any action that needs to be taken and the commission members. You'd be mopping up any potential spilled beer and nothing more."

"More expensive liquor than that we sold during Prohibition if the starting price is one hundred grand."

"Alex, I wish to ensure you are more than taken care of. If I need you, then you must wade in at a moment's notice and if you are not, then the money buys your silence for the rest of your life."

"So, I am a safe pair of hands who isn't tied to the Italian mob?"

"That's the situation in a nutshell."

"Let me sleep on it and tell you tomorrow. Is there somewhere discreet I can stay overnight?"

◆ ◆ ◆

"WHAT WOULD YOU say if I spent a couple more days where I am and then flew off for a business trip?"

Alex was ensconced in his motel room on the edge of Miami, far from prying eyes. Even so, he chose circumspect language while he spoke with Sarah.

"Did you enjoy your dinner, Alex?"

"The food was good, and the conversation was interesting."

"Why don't you visit Meyer while you are away?"

"I might well do that, but you haven't answered my question."

"Do you think I'm going to? You are your own man, Alex, and you do not need my permission to go on a business trip."

"I'll miss you, Sarah."

"Why are you so sentimental all of a sudden? Is there more to this journey than meets the eye?"

"Indeed. I am not sure what is expected of me and when you consider who invited me over to Miami, you can understand my concerns."

Sarah was silent on the line for a handful of seconds.

"Now you've got me all nervous, Alex."

"That was not the purpose of my call, but I need to think things through with somebody I trust, who is looking after my interests."

"Well, you sure have my attention, Alex."

"Sorry. The other issue is that despite how I feel about this jaunt, I am not sure I can refuse the request anyway."

"If you have no choice, Alex, then you must do what you need to do and there is nothing to debate. Call me when you know you are safe again."

"I'll ring when I arrive back at Boyle Heights."

"At least tell me when you're in California. I love you."

Alex put the phone down and lay on his bed. He took a whiskey from the minibar to help him get to sleep. The next day, he informed Sam he would take the flight to Dallas that night.

"An associate will drive you to the airport at six. Make sure you are ready by then."

20

"GOOD TO SEE you, Meyer."

His old friend nodded but carried on staring at the baseball on the television. One leg hung over the armrest. Lansky remained silent and tutted when a player was out. Alex had never followed the sport and didn't see any reason why he should start now.

"If you're not careful, then I'll have to go before you've said a word to me."

Meyer smiled and pressed a button on the remote control. A single white dot lingered in the middle of the black screen until it vanished.

"My apologies, Alex. The older I get, the more interested I am in watching grown men hit a ball with a stick."

Alex grinned because they both knew that Lansky would have placed several bets on the afternoon's play around the country. He wasn't as retired as he liked everyone to believe.

"Meyer, it's healthy for a fella to enjoy sports, especially if he has some skin in the game."

"I'm not the Big Bankroll fixing the World Series, Alex."

"No you are not, but then Arnold Rothstein didn't put the fix on that result either, as we both know."

They chuckled to themselves and withdrew into their memories of the man who created the five New York families and, along with Charlie Lucky, formed the syndicate to keep the peace between organized crime factions across the country. The mob's commission was an Italian-only version of Rothstein's vision.

"We live in the shadow of greatness, Alex."

"That we do, my friend."

"And I suppose you were just passing and thought you'd drop by for some conversation and cheesecake?"

"If you've got a slice, then I wouldn't say no, Meyer."

Lansky smiled and shuffled out of the room, only to return a moment later with nothing. Then, after five minutes, Thelma appeared holding a tray with a pot of coffee and two pieces of cake.

"Thank you. Are they from a local bakery?"

"Oh no, I import them from New York."

"You can take the fella out of the Five Boroughs…"

Thelma grinned. "It pays to have a few connections from the glory days."

"And I thought you lost everything in Havana, Meyer."

"That was a tragedy, for sure, Alex. But I always maintained several business interests. I never trusted President Batista."

"You behaved like you did, Meyer."

"Only enough to keep him onside, and to ensure that the wheels kept turning on the bus."

"Well, that's all behind us now."

"Alex, we live together, we love together, but we die alone. How can I help?"

Alex waited until Thelma was out of earshot.

"Sam has asked me to do him a favor."

"Giancana?"

"Yes. And I wanted to know your thoughts on the matter."

"Alex, what is it he wants you to do?"

"He hasn't been too up front with the details. I'm to go to Dallas this evening and await further instructions."

"Then why are you asking me? No disrespect, but you've carried out enough contracts not to be concerned about another notch on your rifle?"

"Meyer, that is the strange thing. Sam assures me it's not a hit. I'll be there in case someone else needs assistance."

Lansky cut into his slice and swallowed his first mouthful. Alex did the same and reminded himself how much he enjoyed Lindy's cheesecake.

"So, Alex, either you are a wingman or the fall guy. Which do you think fits the bill?"

"Meyer, if I knew that, we wouldn't be having this conversation."

"You sure are in a pickle."

Alex stared at Lansky and tried to decide if his friend was roasting him or was not engaged with the problem at hand. He must remember to ask Thelma how Meyer was getting on.

"What do you suggest I do? Should I go to Dallas?"

"Is Sam going to pay your expenses?"

"Yes, Meyer."

"Then you have nothing to lose apart from the time you spend there."

"Meyer, this isn't a high school picnic that Sam is organizing."

"Of course not, but whatever it is, he isn't placing you at the center of the action, so you know you will be safe."

"Is it that simple, Meyer?"

"I have no clue at all. I'm bored with this room. Shall we go for a walk?"

ALEX FOLLOWED MEYER out to the patio and his friend sat down again.

"I thought you meant we'd hike around the block, Meyer."

"Now why would I want to wear out a sidewalk when there's this view to admire?"

Alex cast an eye over the deck and pool and the walls surrounding Meyer's property. It was something to look at, but not what you'd call a panorama. Meyer swept his hands under the poolside table.

"No bugs, we can talk here knowing that the Feds won't hear a word we utter."

"Are they monitoring you, Meyer? What for?"

"I have no idea, but it is better to be safe than sorry."

Meyer had never been the paranoid type, but he was making up for it now. So much so that Alex started checking over his shoulder and felt beneath his seat in case the FBI had planted something under his chair. Nothing.

"Meyer, what do you think then?"

"You know how I feel about the Italians, and my position hasn't changed in the last few years."

"Sam has been straight up with me."

"Alex, have you forgotten what happened in the Bay of Pigs?"

"Sam put me in that situation, but it was the US army that failed to keep its word. We were supposed to get air cover for the whole of the first night of the invasion and they delivered bupkis."

"Alex, you are naïve to let the government take the blame. It was Giancana's plan and his failure."

"Meyer, I think the issue is that you've never forgiven Sam for the position he put you in when you were playing both sides in Havana."

"Those Italians have never liked us Jews, and you have always known that. They broke away from the syndicate as soon as they could and formed their own commission."

"Are you going to bring up the Appalachian meeting again? Because that ship set sail five long years ago."

"That was the end, not the beginning. Those Italians thought they were better than us then and they still do now."

Alex didn't respond and counted to five instead.

"You know the irony, Alex?"

"What's that?"

"Sam and his kind propped up Kennedy and brought him into office, and that man has a real soft spot for Jews."

"I've met him, Meyer, and I wouldn't say he has a natural love of the chosen people."

"I've not had the pleasure, but his approach to Israel has been nothing but good. He supports our Jewish homeland and I can't remember a president who's felt that way before."

"Meyer, do you think Jack is pro-Israel because of his liking for Jews, or is it that that lump of desert is just another card for him to play against the Soviets?"

"Alex, you read too many newspapers for your own good. Jack's fighting the communists on all fronts, but he still has time for the Jews. Make no mistake, that is no accident."

"The Kennedys look wonderful on camera but when you see them in the flesh, they are all too human."

"What do I know, Alex, right? All I'm saying is that you shouldn't trust Sam Giancana, but I can't see what can go wrong for you with the Dallas trip if you aren't the trigger man."

21

A MAN ARRIVED at Alex's hotel soon after six and drove him to a private airfield. There was a solitary plane on the runway and the limo stopped one hundred feet from the airstairs. The fella scooted round to Alex's side of the vehicle, opened the door, and escorted him onto the airplane. Not a single word left his mouth for the entire journey.

Inside the jet, a hostess greeted Alex, invited him to sit down, and offered him a drink, which he gladly accepted: Scotch on the rocks. There were five other seats on the plane with a large table positioned next to pairs of seating. Once Alex's glass was resting on his table, the stewardess closed the door and vanished into the cockpit. Alex spotted two men in there, but could only see the backs of their heads.

When they were in the air, the woman returned to give Alex a sealed envelope.

"Have you looked inside this?"

"No, sir. Our instructions were explicit on that matter."

He waited for the woman to sashay to her seat near the cockpit, and then he tore open the envelope to see what Sam had to say for himself. He had the name of a guy he was to mind and the address of an apartment. All he had to do was to reach out and keep in touch with the fella. If there was anything more to the job, then a message would be left at the apartment.

He ripped a hole in the note and placed the piece with the residential address in his pocket. Then he asked for an ashtray. Alex lit a cigarette and then ignited the paper using his lighter until it was nothing more than ash.

A little under three hours later and the jet touched down on a runway in a private airfield.

"Are we in Dallas?"

"On the outskirts, yes, sir. You have a car waiting by the hangar with keys in the ignition. Is there anything else I can get for you?"

ALEX SAT IN his saloon and turned the engine over. On the passenger seat was a map of the city, and he took a few minutes to plan a route to his hideaway. Then he hit the gas, raced out of the airfield, and aimed for downtown Dallas.

He parked on Elm and walked five hundred feet toward North Griffin before finding the apartment block. Deadbeats filled the sidewalks, which reminded Alex of the Bowery before the war.

Inside, he was glad the front door was locked so that he didn't have to climb through more of the winos and punks who littered the frontage. Up to the third floor and the key unlocked the apartment on the first time of asking. It wasn't much to see, but the bedroom appeared clean and the kitchen was well-stocked. If he was only going to be in town for a day or two, then he wouldn't need to show his face in the local store to buy provisions.

Alex put on a pot of coffee and hung his few clothes in the wardrobe by his bed. A shower to wash the cobwebs out of his mind, and he was ready for whatever was to happen next.

BY ELEVEN AT night, Alex didn't think he could bear staring at the blank walls of the living room anymore. Although he knew Sam would not want him to be seen around town, he took his chances and hit the street. With his coat collar turned up to hide his face, Alex strode along the sidewalk. The drunks congregated four doors down from his apartment block in front of a general store, panhandling for enough money to buy some booze, but Alex was in no mood to deal with them.

Around the corner, the block emptied, and he felt as though this was a different city. Outside each of the buildings stood a concierge waiting for the residents to return and at the far end of the street, Alex noticed a cop walking the beat.

There was no need to head straight into potential danger, so he sauntered along the sidewalk about half a block until he reached Fred's Bar. He entered and aimed for his usual preference, a booth at the back of a drinking establishment, a location often reserved for doting couples and therefore not well lit.

A waitress delivered a Scotch within a minute of Alex placing his order. Efficient service, he thought. Five minutes later and Alex saw the cop meander past the front of the bar.

The place was only half full, the majority couples, but there was one table of four young men who were already rowdy enough to earn annoyed expressions from some of the nearby patrons. Alex took measured sips of his drink and let the world flow by.

Two jugs of ale later and their waitress had had enough. One guy slapped her on the ass as she walked away from the table. She turned back and poured a glass of beer over the offender's head. The guy leaped to his feet, and the bartender ran out from behind the bar. If there had been a piano, then the player would have stopped by now. Alex stayed where he was.

The boy formed a fist and pulled his arm back as if to take a swipe at the barman, who remained still. Meanwhile, the waitress edged out of harm's way and stood next to the bar. They all hovered in this Mexican stand-off for two, maybe three, seconds, and then one of the boy's friends placed a hand on his shoulder and whispered something in his ear. The guy lowered his fist, and the four left without another word or a punch thrown.

Alex finished his drink as slowly as his first few sips. Just as he'd allowed the last drop to flow down the back of his throat, the waitress appeared to ask if he wanted another.

"Don't mind if I do. You handled yourself well earlier on, by the way."

"Thanks. They're good kids most of the time but can get fresh once they've had too many beers inside them."

"So they are regulars, then? Fred knew how to handle himself."

"Who? Fred?" She laughed. "Hank sorted those boys out. Fred's just a name on the sign outside."

"My mistake. No offense to Hank."

"None taken, Mac."

A moment later and Alex's Scotch arrived.

"You're not from around here, are you, Mac?"

"Just passing through."

"Well, I hope you have time to see a few tourist attractions before you leave. There's a parade tomorrow..."

"I'm in town on business, so there won't be much of an opportunity for sightseeing. Thank you, anyway."

The waitress shrugged and walked away, leaving Alex to drink his Scotch in peace.

22

AN HOUR AFTER speaking to Sarah on a payphone the following morning, and Alex had had enough of aimless walking and returned to his apartment. He sat down for two minutes but knew that he needed to walk again. With no other place to go, he headed to Fred's and occupied the same booth as he'd been in the previous night.

Within thirty seconds of sitting down, Amy appeared.

"Hi, I'll start with a coffee. Do you have any cake I could try?"

"Good to see you back. We have a vanilla cheesecake or…"

"That sounds perfect."

She smiled and sashayed away to fulfill his order. The coffee and cake arrived less than a minute later. Alex drew a sip of the brew and almost immediately regretted it: the pot had been on the burner for too long. Fred's didn't have sufficient morning customers to get the filter jug refreshed often enough.

He then took a bite out of the cheesecake and dropped his fork on the plate. This wasn't baked cheesecake. Alex washed away the taste of the cake with the acrid flavor of the burned coffee. This was not turning out to be a good day.

At this point, Hank switched on the television and changed channel to the local news. Somewhere in the city, people were lining the sidewalks. The angle of the screen from Alex's viewpoint was too narrow for him to make out any image that well, but he had a general idea about what was going on. Amy returned.

"How's the cake, dear?"

"Can I be honest with you?"

"For sure."

"It doesn't taste like baked cheesecake and the coffee is burned."

Amy's smile fell from her face. She blinked once.

"I'm so very sorry. Let me get you a fresh brew right away and let me offer you a slice of coffee cake instead?"

"Thank you. A new mug would be great. I didn't ask you what kind of cheesecake you had, so that's not your fault."

"I told you last night, you weren't from round here. That is the only cheesecake Texans know."

"It's not a big deal, but yes, I'll try the coffee cake, but you must charge me for both portions, understand?"

Amy removed everything she'd placed on his table and flew off to the kitchen. Alex heard raised voices over the volume of the television broadcast and she appeared with a large slice of cake.

"This is on the house and I'll have no more talk on the matter."

Then she scurried away and Alex waited five minutes for a fresh pot of coffee to brew and a piping hot mug to be delivered to his table.

"I hope this is better for you."

"I'm sure it is, Amy."

She looked down at her name badge, pinned over her heart, and smiled again.

"You're welcome…"

"Call me David."

Alex beamed back at Amy.

"Let me know if you need anything else."

Alex nodded, and she walked away to the bar, and to monitor the java more closely than she had before.

The cake was a little dry but edible, and the coffee was adequate. This was a local bar: Alex expected nothing more from it.

The barman cranked up the volume of the television and Alex heard a commentator talking about the parade Amy had mentioned the night before. Sounded like it wasn't that far from where he was sitting. He watched as a steady stream of people hastened from right to left, many holding miniature Stars and Stripes on little sticks.

Alex concentrated on his food and drink and tried his best to ignore the rest of the world. His sole purpose in being in this city was a man about whom he had yet to receive any instructions to go anywhere near. He just needed to sit the day out and wait in case something happened.

The commentator on the television let out a piercing scream and everyone else in Fred's stood up. Women shrieked, and the barman put the volume on maximum, but Alex had no idea what was going on. He looked around for Amy, but she was nowhere to be seen.

A man took his wife in his arms as she blubbed away and others slammed their fists on their tables. The ones nearest the front ran outside and headed left—in the direction of the parade. Not wanting to appear different from the rest, Alex stood and leaned forward as his waitress hustled past, a tear in her eye.

"What's happened, Amy?"

"Couldn't you see? The president's been shot."

Alex felt a dull ache in the pit of his stomach and he knew he had to get the hell out of the joint.

ALEX CHUCKED SOME greenbacks on the table and ran out of the bar. He too turned left, but he was not planning on going anywhere near the scene of the hit. Instead, he hightailed it to his apartment and slammed the door shut behind him. He threw himself into an armchair and tried to get his bearings. Sam had taken a contract out on Jack. Alex swallowed hard to find some saliva at the back of his throat and coughed instead.

He switched on the radio to see if he could find out more about what had happened to Jack. The commentator spoke of several shots fired, and that Kennedy had been hit and was on his way to Parkland Memorial Hospital. There was no word on whether anybody else had been injured. Alex rocked in his armchair. Sam had taken out a contract on the president!

Another guy in the car, Governor Connally, had been shot too but was alive. Jackie had survived without a mark on her. Just as the voice from the radio confirmed that Kennedy had been pronounced dead, the phone rang.

"Don't do anything. You might still be needed. Stay where you are for the next twenty-four hours."

"Understood." Then a click, and the phone went dead.

Alex popped his head out of the living room window and saw that all the cars had stopped in their tracks. Drivers stood with their doors open and radios on. A silence had descended on the city as people soaked in the implications of the Dealey Plaza assassination. Soon after, Lyndon Johnson was sworn in as the new president.

As he listened some more, Alex heard birds chirping outside, and he closed the sash window tight shut. Entering the bedroom for no good reason, something made him lift the mattress, always a convenient hiding place back in the day when he ran Murder Corporation and needed a safe location to stash items.

Sure enough, there was a pistol and two boxes of slugs. The butt had tape wrapped around it the same as the trigger. This was to be used for a job where the owner did not want their fingerprints to turn up. Was this gun for him or had it been hidden by some unknown assailant on a previous hit? Alex left it where he'd found it for now, and made the bed again.

He tried sitting in the living room, but within a minute, he was pacing up and down. This was no good, not at all. Alex had lost count of how many men he had killed. Yes, he had attempted to hit Castro and had even whacked his friend Benny Siegel, but an American president? There was no way he wanted to be caught up with anything like that. Sam should have told him, explained the situation, allowed him to make his own choices. Meyer was right, you can't trust the Italians.

Alex grabbed his keys and left the apartment, ignoring what the disembodied voice at the end of the phone had instructed. He couldn't be cooped up in that place a second longer. As he bundled along the sidewalk, Alex failed to notice how empty the neighborhood was. Even the drunks were showing their respect for the fallen Kennedy. He turned the corner and strode toward Fred's Bar.

Inside, Amy was sweeping the floor, and the joint seemed deserted. He pushed the door, but it was locked shut. She looked up from her work and held one finger up, indicating for Alex to wait. She put her mop in its bucket and opened up.

"Are you still serving? I've nowhere else to go."

"Hank doesn't want us to draw a crowd, but as you were in earlier on, I don't see why not."

She twisted her head to look at Hank, who nodded his consent. Alex went back to his booth and ordered a Scotch.

"To Jack," he muttered under his breath and knocked the drink down in one. He sipped his second glass and, having calmed down, he slunk out of the bar and returned to the apartment to await further instructions.

23

THE PHONE RANG soon after Alex finished in the shower the next morning.

"Contact our mutual friend. Monitor him and nothing more, for now."

Before he could ask anything, his instructor had ended the call. The mark owed Sam big time, the result of gambling debts that had mounted up over a matter of months. Small amounts that got out of hand on account of the fella doubling up once too often and the size of the vig Sam's associates charged.

The first port of call was to the Carousel Club, three blocks east and one south of Fred's, which was a simple walk from the apartment. There were a few people on the streets, but it was still quite early. On the same block, there were other clubs and bars and a general store interspersed between the residences.

It might have been eight in the morning, but the place was shut tight. A piece of paper was pinned to the door, announcing that the joint would remain closed for the next few days out of respect for Kennedy's death. Alex tried to peer through the windows, but there was nothing to see. The darkened glass prevented anybody from getting a free view of the interior. If his mark was inside, he wasn't making any noise.

Rather than wait around hoping to find someone entering a closed joint, he hopped a cab over to Oak Lawn and wandered the streets until he reached the Vegas Club.

It was in as salubrious an area as the Carousel; the trendy in Dallas were not Ruby's target market. Judging by their surroundings, Alex guessed the joints would take money from anyone who wanted a drink. They were far removed from Alex's blind pigs when he'd sold liquor during Prohibition. Back then, he'd boasted the rich and the famous as his patrons. Looking at the exterior of the Vegas, Alex wondered what kind of fella he was going to tangle with.

This club was closed too and a similar note was placed on its entrance. He was standing there trying to figure out his next move when a woman appeared and headed for the door. She looked up and stopped in her tracks.

"Were you expecting the club to be open too?" he asked.

"Yes, bud. And you are…?"

"A friend. I owe Ruby money and wanted to pay him back."

A smile. "You owe him green? I don't think I've ever heard that happen since I started working here."

"It's only a hundred bucks, but I sure would like to give it to him. I wouldn't want to get into any trouble."

"He can wig out at a moment's notice."

"Do you reckon he'll open up later on?"

"You can read, bud?" She flicked a finger at the announcement pinned to the door.

"But you thought the club would be open today, otherwise what are you doing here?"

"True. We closed around two this morning and Jack said he wanted us back, but he must have changed his mind."

"At a moment's notice?"

She laughed and nodded.

"Patty Ingham, by the way."

"Call me David."

"Ruby owes me back pay. So if you give him his cash, then I might see some money myself."

Patty gave Alex the same address that was in Sam's note, wished him well, and strolled off down the street. After she vanished around the corner, he went in the opposite direction for a couple of blocks and waited a lifetime to hail a cab.

WHEN ALEX GOT out of the taxi, he recognized where he had been dropped, a short hop from Fred's and one block from the Carousel. He had already strode down this sidewalk earlier in the day. Alex glanced up and down the street until he was certain he wasn't about to bump into his mark. Then he checked again to see if he saw anyone he knew. The last thing he needed was for a local like Amy to spot him and place him in the vicinity.

Still only a handful of people were on the streets and most folk were at home with their televisions on, watching to find out about Lee Harvey Oswald, who had been arrested the same day as Jack was killed and remained in police custody. Alex was not as concerned about Oswald's fate as he was to discover what he would do with Ruby once he caught up with him. Across the street, two doors down, was an alleyway. Alex would have preferred to watch from a cafe so he could at least have a coffee and a bite to eat, but everywhere was shut. The president had been dead less than twenty-four hours and the country had descended into a state of mourning.

He leaned on a wall in the shadows of the alleyway entrance and hoped Ruby would arrive sooner rather than later. One hour on, and Alex's hopes had faded as he finished the last cigarette in his pack. He rotated his lighter in his pocket just for something to do. His patience was wearing thin, in part in reflection of him not knowing what Sam had in store for Ruby at Alex's hands.

Alex told himself to give Ruby another thirty minutes because there was no guarantee the fella would even show. He might be holed up with a skirt somewhere and as much as Alex wanted to earn his fee, there was no way in hell he was going to stand in this alleyway for an entire day and night.

When the designated amount of time had elapsed, Alex stood straight and peered up and down the road. There was only a couple in the distance, sauntering away from him. No sign of Ruby or anybody else in his vicinity. With a heavy sigh, Alex took two steps forward and onto the sidewalk. A glance left and right, and still no one showed. He turned left, strolled to the end of the block, stopped, then looked behind. A man turned up the opposite side of the street, heading toward Ruby's building or the alleyway. Alex fumbled with a loose shoelace so that he could steal a few seconds to figure out if this guy was a person of interest.

As Alex had hoped, the fella stopped in front of Ruby's apartment block, took out a key, and let himself in. Alex sighed again as he realized he would need to resume his position in the alleyway. Of course, the fact the guy lived in the same building did not make him Ruby and he had been too far away for Alex to see his features. Not that he had a photo to work off, but Sam's instructions had been careful to let Alex know that the mystery mark was Jewish. And the guy on the other side of the road had a big enough nose to fit the description.

He skirted around the back of the apartment block and saw motion on the third floor. At the front, Alex scanned the names on the mailboxes and, based on their formation, he reckoned Ruby was a third-floor occupant. The odds were stacking up in his favor, but there was only one way to be certain.

Alex rang the bell of apartment 3D and a gruff voice responded through the intercom.

"Yes?"

"Package for Mr. Jack Ruby."

"I'm not expecting anything… Hello? Hello?"

That was all Alex needed to know, so he left the fella hanging and scurried down the street three hundred feet before crossing the road to get a better view of the entrance.

24

AN HOUR LATER, Ruby appeared at the front entrance and hustled down the street, with Alex tailing him half a block behind. He would have got closer, but the streets were too empty and he didn't want to be spotted. Around the corner and into a liquor store.

Alex held back a few seconds and then used the opportunity to get much tighter to the fella. He picked up his pace, walked into the outlet, and headed straight for the counter.

"Bottle of Scotch, please."

Ruby arrived behind him to wait in line. The store owner shook his head.

"I got Irish but not Scotch."

Alex turned round to face Ruby. "What kind of town is this?"

Ruby shrugged. "The city has been good to me."

Alex shot back and accepted the whiskey. Then he paid and pretended to sort out his pockets while Ruby handed over some green to cover the cost of his milk and pack of cigarettes.

"I'm sorry about before. This whole business with Oswald has got me all shaken up."

"Don't give it a moment's thought. It's bad enough that it happened without the damn thing occurring by your back door."

Alex looked puzzled for a minute, then raised his eyebrows.

"Of course, Dealey Plaza isn't that far from here."

Ruby nodded and eyed him up and down.

"Are you visiting these parts?"

"Yes, I'm here on business for a week."

"With anyone?"

"Nope."

"Nobody should be on their own on days like these. Want to share some of that bottle back at mine?"

Alex waited a few seconds, as though he was pondering the situation.

"Sounds as though we've got ourselves a plan. Call me David."

◆ ◆ ◆

INSTEAD OF TAKING him to his apartment, Ruby led Alex over to the Carousel Club. Once inside, Ruby cleared the bar and arranged a couple of stools.

"This can't be where you live?"

"No, but it is mine."

Alex whistled with approval and appreciation.

"Mighty fine. You've done well for yourself."

"I get by, David. You wanted a Scotch, right?"

A nod and Ruby fixed Alex a shot.

"Ice?"

Alex shook his head and his host placed the glass on the counter and poured himself a vodka tonic.

"Kennedy was a great man, David."

They raised their glasses and Alex knocked back his whisky. Ruby poured him another.

"So, how long have you run this joint?"

"A few years, I guess. Let me show you around."

The main bar stood in front of a dance floor and there was space for a band in the far corner. Through a doorway was a gaming room with two roulette wheels and several card stations. Another impressed whistle from Alex. Then Ruby took him to a third area behind a locked door.

"This is for my VIPs."

Alex surveyed the reception desk and Ruby showed him into each of the private rooms. Most had a massage table and a couch, but there was one with a heart-shaped bed and silk sheets reserved for Ruby's high rollers—men who were prepared to spend more than a Jackson on a girl.

"You sure are doing well for yourself."

Alex offered the lie so Ruby would feel better about himself, but even with this joint, Alex knew he could make it profitable without too much effort. Ruby must be a complete schlemiel in business to be up to his neck in debt to Sam and own at least two bars like this.

"Is this your only place?"

"No, I have another bar and a few other interests."

"I'm surprised you have time to sleep."

"David, there's no need to blow smoke up my ass. You said you're in business too. How do you make your money?"

"I am a troubleshooter, you might say. I help my clients with any problems they may have. And, like you, I have a few interests on the side."

"That sure sounds like an interesting time. Hopping from one place to another. Don't you ever want to settle down and stay in one town to grow roots?"

"I've got that too. I'm based in California and visit my kids on the East Coast several times a year."

"The traveling would destroy me. After the war, I moved here from San Francisco and vowed that was the last time I'd pull up stakes and relocate."

"You get used to the planes and trains. It gives me a chance to relax and take stock."

They wandered back to the bar and Ruby filled their glasses.

"David, I'm keeping my bars closed for another day or two, so there's going to be no action here tonight. Do you fancy sharing a meal at mine? My sister's cooking is to die for and we've always got a spare seat for a stranger in town. Nobody should be alone so soon after Kennedy passed."

EVA GRANT WELCOMED the two men into Ruby's apartment and Alex wondered why she cooked for her brother and whether her husband was still in the picture. Either way, Ruby was right, the food she was cooking smelled great.

"This is David. He's a stranger in town and I've asked him over for dinner."

"Pleased to meet you."

"Charmed, I'm sure. What's in the oven? It smells good enough to eat."

She smiled and mentioned chicken schnitzel.

"Just like my mama used to make, Eva."

Ruby raised an eyebrow.

"Are you a member of the brotherhood?"

"Yes, but not practicing. I hope that doesn't cause you any offense."

"Not at all. My sister and I haven't been to *shul* since we were kids."

"I can't say I've seen the inside of a synagogue any more recently myself."

They all chuckled and Eva announced that their food was ready.

Ruby's apartment wasn't large enough to have a separate dining room, and they ate at the kitchen table. A small yappy mutt sought attention from Ruby from the moment they sat down. After way too much barking for Alex's liking, Ruby relented and threw Sheba a piece of the schnitzel. Eva tutted.

"What was that for? Are you judging how I feed my dog?"

Eva remained silent as Ruby's cheeks reddened.

"I'll do whatever I want with that dachshund."

Ruby cut off another chunk and fed Sheba from his hand.

"Jacko, don't start on me. Not when we have a guest with us."

Ruby looked over at Alex as if for the first time. Alex did his best to placate him with a neutral expression and carried on eating; the schnitzel was a little tough, but he wasn't intending on raising a complaint. The rosemary potatoes were cooked to perfection.

"Do not tut me, Eva. You know I don't like that."

"I'm sorry, Jacko. I didn't mean nothing by it."

There was silence for ten seconds, and then Alex lightened the mood.

"You mentioned you came from San Francisco. Is that where you were born?"

"Chicago."

"Small world. I knew some fellas from there. Between the wars."

Ruby's expression relaxed.

"That so? I had business dealings with some connected fellas too, back in the day."

"Like who?"

"David, have you heard of Al Capone?"

"You're kidding me. You met Alfonse?"

"Once or twice. He was a great guy."

"Sure was."

Alex thought back to the time he'd visited the gangster before his death. A shell of the man who once ruled the Windy City and worked with Alex during the Prohibition years.

"Who else did you know back then, David?"

He had said too much already.

"The usual crew. I'm sure you've got some tales to tell."

"While Capone was sitting in his silk drawers raking in the cash, I was on the street, hustling the great people of Chicago with my racing tips."

"Jacko, don't undersell yourself." His sister nudged Ruby in the arm.

"You'll make me blush, Eva. I'd help the neighborhood bagman to carry out his collections."

"Those must have been exciting times."

"They were, but you'd have had your fair share of excitement if you knew Al?"

"That was a long time ago. I paid the price for my youthful choices."

"Amen to that, David. And there's nothing to worry about with us. Eva and I don't hold a fella's past against him. I've been in the same situation."

"To youthful indiscretions!"

They raised their wine glasses to Alex's toast and resumed the meal with no further outbursts from Ruby.

"David, the funny thing is that nowadays, half the Dallas police force are members of one of my clubs. If they only knew what I was like back in the day."

Ruby chuckled, and Alex smiled in return.

"It must be a good feeling to know that your clubs are protected without needing to rely on other insurance options."

"We pay our dues, same as everybody else, David."

"This is a mighty fine schnitzel, Eva. Thank you for tonight's meal. I do appreciate it."

"You are very kind, David. I always cook more than we need, so it was my pleasure. Besides, Sheba doesn't have to eat a human's portion of chicken, does she, Jacko?"

"Don't get me started again."

They all laughed this time, as there was no edge to Ruby's voice.

25

ALEX OFFERED TO help clear the dishes, but Ruby wouldn't let him; that was what his sister was for. Instead, the men walked out to the living room and settled in with a bottle of Scotch for Alex and Ruby's vodka nearby. Once the splashing noises of Eva's washing up had abated, she sat down to join them, but Ruby's expression showed she was not welcome so she made her excuses and went to her bedroom.

"How long have you and Eva been sharing an apartment?"

"Ever since that meeskait of a husband died on her."

"And you've never married?"

"I have Sheba for company and Eva for meals and laundry. What would I do with a wife?"

Alex opened his mouth to answer and then closed it again. Ruby's eyes sparkled.

"So you meet girls in your bars then?"

"A club is like a babe magnet and if I hit a dry patch, then I just advertise for another waitress."

"You sure have all the angles covered."

They drank a toast to Ruby's success and shot the breeze for longer than Alex could believe. That man could not stop talking: about himself and how brilliant he was in the sack, in business, with his family. If half of what he claimed was true, then Ruby should have been a millionaire and not an indebted bum, which is what he was.

"And another thing… I can't believe how good Kennedy has been for Israel, David."

"How so?"

"I reckon he is the first president to support the country against the Arabs surrounding that beautiful place."

"Have you ever been?"

"Not yet, but I hope to someday. The country is steeped in milk and honey."

"That's what the Bible says."

"I might not be a regular in a synagogue, but I still believe in the *Torah*. Don't you, David?"

"The truth is, I'm not sure what I think anymore. When I was a kid, I think I believed in God, but now? What I saw on the fields of France left me doubting."

"I was in this man's army in the Second World War."

"Did you see any action?"

"No, I was a mechanic in a US base."

"Well, at least you did your bit against the Japanese and the Nazis."

"That's what I'm talking about, David. Kennedy was helping us Jews stand up against today's threat from the Arabs."

"Kennedy will have had his reasons for sure. Do you feel threatened by Arabs in Dallas?"

"No, David, but there's anti-Semitism at home too. I was in the local newspaper office yesterday when Oswald did for Kennedy and I saw some evil adverts the paper was accepting. It made my blood boil."

"What were you doing there?"

"I advertise the clubs to increase footfall."

"People have hated the Jews ever since Moses walked the earth."

"But now, David, we've lost a protector in the form of Kennedy. Lee Harvey Oswald is an anti-Semite."

"You don't know that. If he wanted to attack Jews, then there are many more direct ways of going about it than killing Kennedy."

"The consequence of his actions means the Jews will have a harder time, David."

"You may be correct."

"Listen, David. I told you I knew most of the Dallas police force, right?"

"Sure."

"Well, they let me come and go in their buildings, so I thought I'd head to the press conference they held yesterday after the shooting. If you had heard with your own ears what some of those cops told me who were close to the case, then you'd be convinced that Oswald was an anti-Semite."

"Him and the rest of the goyishe world."

"David, I don't know why you are defending this vermin."

"I am not. I have many reasons for wanting Jack Kennedy to be alive, but that does not mean that Oswald killed him because he supported Israel. That's my point, and nothing more."

Ruby glared at him and Alex took a sip from his Scotch to defuse the situation. After a silent spell, Ruby's cheeks seemed less red.

"I apologize if I caused you any offense."

"That's all right, David. You are a guest in my home and I showed you disrespect by raising my voice. I am the one who should say sorry."

"Then let us both accept that there is more that binds us than can split us apart and not allow a minor disagreement to change that. I think I speak for both of us when I say that Lee Harvey Oswald deserves to die."

EVA POPPED HER head around the door.

"Is Jacko causing trouble, David?"

"No, everything is fine, thanks."

"I heard a ruckus and wondered if you boys were behaving yourselves."

"No, dear, we were just talking politics."

"And with a guest in our home. You should know better."

She shook her head and walked out, leaving Ruby to gaze downward as his cheeks reddened.

"Sometimes, she acts more like my mother than a sister."

"Both are precious to us."

"I'll drink to that, David."

After a sip of his Scotch, Alex decided that now was as good as any other time to cut to the chase.

"You might not know this, but we have a mutual acquaintance."

"Who's that, David?"

"The fella who holds your IOUs."

Ruby's arm lowered just as he was about to take a swig of his vodka tonic, suspicion oozing out of every pore.

"What do you mean, David?"

"Let's not pretend. You owe our mutual friend a five-figure sum."

"Who are you talking about?"

"Are you going to force me to mention his name? I thought we were all gentlemen here."

"How do I know you aren't some sort of shakedown artist?"

Alex sighed.

"Because you are still alive. If I wished you any kind of harm, then I would have done something before now. Either when we were alone in the Carousel Club or when you first brought me home to meet your sister. I intend neither of you any ill will, but you and I have some business to conduct."

Alex allowed his remarks to sink in with Ruby, who was confused and unsure what to say next. His jaw opened and closed twice with no words leaving his lips. After half a minute, a thought departed his mouth.

"Giancana sent you."

Alex nodded and lit a cigarette. He flicked some tobacco off his knee.

"That wasn't an accidental meeting in the liquor store."

A second nod and Ruby knocked back the rest of his drink. Then he sat forward and poured himself another shot of vodka. Alex popped into the kitchen to find some tonic water. When he returned, Ruby stood facing the living room door with a pistol in his hand, aimed at Alex's chest.

"Put that away before you hurt somebody."

"I know how to use this thing and don't tell me otherwise."

"Ruby, if you fire that gun at me, you'd better make certain you kill me straight off because if you do not, then I guarantee you won't be alive in the morning. Second, with whatever breath I have left, Eva will get hers. And if those aren't good enough reasons, Sam will send someone else to visit you and he'll torture you before he kills you, slower than you can ever imagine."

Alex stayed still to let Ruby think through his actions.

"Like I said, put the gun down so we may talk business."

Ruby's arm relaxed, and he slumped in his chair. He allowed the pistol to drop to the floor, and Alex grabbed it to examine the firearm.

"Putz, there are no slugs in the chamber. Next time you try to shoot a fella, make sure you know what you are doing."

Alex placed the gun on the table adjacent to his Scotch and lit another cigarette. Under any other circumstances, this guy would have been dead by now, but Alex used all his inner reserves to control his temper. Meyer was right, every time he did Sam a favor, he ended up risking his life. What if Ruby had fired as soon as he got back to the room? Life was way too short for *gonifs* to pull this kind of crap.

"Have you calmed down, Ruby?"

"Yes, but—"

"If you are going to get fresh with me, then you are not ready to discuss business. And I need to know that I have your full attention before we talk."

"It's just—"

"There will be no questions from you. I have a simple proposition that you must hear and agree to. Assuming that you find it acceptable then we can figure out all the details once you have the offer."

"Let me apologize for my actions, David. I got scared and didn't think through what I was doing."

"Are you ready to listen now?"

"Sure thing, David."

"By tomorrow night, you'll have the debt that you owe Sam wiped clean."

"What do I have to do?"

26

IN THE MORNING, Alex walked over to Ruby's apartment and the local drove them both to Main Street and the location of a money transfer service.

"Put the car in the lot over there."

"But it'll cost gelt, David."

"Ruby, now is not the time to count pennies. Let's get this vehicle off the road."

Jacko nodded acceptance and hauled into the parking lot half a block further on. Alex instructed him to go to the far end of the space so that the eyes of the attendant were not on them. Once Ruby had pulled on the handbrake, he whipped out his revolver.

"Take it easy and put that thing below the dashboard. We can't have you being seen brandishing a firearm."

"Sorry, David. I wasn't thinking."

Alex cleared his throat. "You need to get your head in the game, man."

Ruby continued to point the barrel of the gun in Alex's general direction.

"Anyone would think you're planning on shooting me."

A nervous laugh emanated from the owner of the Carousel Club.

"Remember what I said to you last night, Ruby. You can get out from under a pile of debt and your sister will be looked after for the rest of her life. Killing me will bring down a world of pain and agony for you and her. So check your weapon and put it away."

Ruby lowered the revolver and popped it in his pocket.

"Sorry, but I'm nervous."

"That's as may be but we need you to stay focused. It's going to be a long day and we want you to be in one piece by the end, right?"

Ruby nodded, and Alex lit him a cigarette. They hopped out of the car and the club owner handed over his keys to the attendant. Alex made sure he had already hustled past before the guy had left his kiosk. Then they walked onto the road and headed left.

Half a block down and Alex got Ruby to pop into a general store and buy a pack of cigarettes and a newspaper. Then two blocks on and Ruby went into a bank to take out some green. Again, Alex ensured he stayed on the street. The aim was for as many people as possible to see Ruby, to remember his face and the fact that he was alone.

With the cash in his wallet, Ruby returned to Alex's side, and they carried on sauntering along Main Street.

"Is David your real name?"

"What do you think?"

"I doubt if it is, but it is a strong Biblical name."

"Thank you."

"How did you know I was getting cold feet?"

"What do you mean, Ruby?"

"That I was thinking of welshing on my deal with Sam."

"I had no idea. You seem to think I am something more than a go-between."

"David, from what you've said, you come across as well-connected and sound pretty tight with Giancana, so I just assumed."

"For this job, I'm only a hired hand, but it is no accident that we are together right now. If our mutual friend felt you might not go through with the plan, then I was a natural person to turn to."

"Sam and I have had this agreement in place for weeks, if not months."

"So, Ruby, why did you allow me to think I needed to convince you to get involved in this?"

"David, it amused me. You were coming on so thick and strong, I figured I'd let you play out your hand. Besides, what you said reminded me of why I agreed to do this in the first place."

"I'm glad I have been so entertaining for you."

"David, what I maintained about Kennedy and Israel was all true. I believe his death needs to be avenged. We mustn't let the anti-Semites win."

RUBY BOUGHT A slice of pizza and a coffee from a concession and Alex did the same a minute later and caught up with him around the corner.

"Don't you think it's a bit early for lunch?"

Alex looked at his watch and saw that it was just after eleven.

"Maybe, but we've been up for hours and it is always sensible to operate on a full stomach, wouldn't you say?"

Ruby smiled and nodded.

"It sure tastes great, huh, David?"

"There is nothing like the flavors of street food to keep fellas like us on our toes."

They polished off their pizza, and Ruby slugged his coffee down in almost one gulp. Alex preferred frequent sips to avoid burning the roof of his mouth. Brunch over, the men walked from their South Saint Paul rest stop one block east to North Harwood where there was a fund transfer store.

"I'll stay here while you hand that money over."

Ruby nodded. The least the fella could do was to send Patty's back pay over to her. On the other side of the street, from the corner of South Harwood and Main down to Commercial Street, stood the headquarters of the Dallas Police Department. Alex scuttled over the road while avoiding the front entrance.

Fifty feet toward Commercial, Alex found a ramp leading down to the basement. He scampered down the slope to discover a locked glass door. Alex whipped out a small piece of wire from his jacket pocket and positioned it in the crack between the lock and the jamb. A few seconds later, it was unlocked, and Alex fixed the latch to remain open.

Heading back to the other side of the street he found Ruby waiting, smoking a cigarette. Even from this distance, the two men saw a large huddle in front of the main entrance.

"They must have been damn busy since Dealey Plaza, David."

"And some. Are you ready?"

"Now?"

"They'll be moving Oswald from his cell soon to take him to a holding facility."

"A jail?"

"Yes, until he stands trial. The police headquarters isn't a hotel."

"I suppose not."

Ruby flicked the remnants of his cigarette onto the ground and stepped on its smoldering remains. He put a hand inside his jacket and transferred the gun into his pants pocket. A quick nod and Ruby paced himself as he crossed the street. Alex remained where he was until Ruby vanished down the ramp. Then he wandered over to the main entrance of the police building along South Harwood and joined the crowd.

MOST OF THE people outside police headquarters were doing nothing much at all. They stood and stared at the main entrance, hoping to catch sight of Oswald. On the other side of the crowd, a young man held a radio next to his ear, but he was too far away for Alex to hear anything from it.

A car backfired some way off and the throng surged forward. The kid with the radio ran down the street, followed by at least twenty others. Two cops stormed out of the entrance, brandishing their weapons. The men and women, who had been so eager to enter the building a few seconds before, stopped in their tracks.

"You know what's happening, bud?"

Alex shook his head and noticed that he was in the middle of the crowd. He let others push in front to hear what the cops were saying, and he continued moving away until he was at the back of the huddled mass.

He glanced up and down the street, but the kid and his followers had not returned and were nowhere to be seen. A ripple of applause spread across the group, and Alex was careful to join in, although there was no reason for the appreciation.

A man standing in front of Alex turned to his pal. "They've killed Oswald. That sonofabitch got his."

Alex leaned forward. "You heard who did it?"

"Nope. It happened just a minute ago."

"How d'you know?"

"I was at the front and listened to one of the cops talking."

That was good enough for Alex. Ruby had done what was asked of him, and now it was time to leave. He waited for a count of thirty, put his hands in his pants pockets, and walked up to Main Street. On his way, he passed the ramp, which was now filled with cops and bystanders. Without missing a beat, Alex kept to his plan, turning west, then north until he reached Elm Street.

He ensured he maintained a casual pace to avoid garnering any attention and made one last sweep of the apartment in case he had missed anything in his packing. Baggage in hand, he scurried down the stairs and into his car, then headed north and west until he connected with North Houston and punched the gas to take him away from the center of the city.

Five minutes later, he pulled the vehicle over and lit a cigarette. Then he turned the vehicle around and headed back south—there was unfinished business to take care of.

27

ALEX HAD GOT Patty's home address from Ruby when he was looking up her records to get the wire transfer details. She had seen Alex when he asked about Ruby and that was too close a connection to be left dangling.

He parked three blocks from her apartment and walked from there. To his regret, she lived on the fifth floor. Alex went round the back of the building and started the journey up the fire stairs until he reached her window. Then he stopped to catch his breath; he wasn't getting any younger.

He peered into a kitchen/diner and saw Patty sitting at a table with a mug of coffee. Alex checked out the window frame and pulled a tool from his inside jacket pocket to jimmy the sash open as quietly as possible. Perhaps because she had her back to him, he'd raised the window and swung a foot onto the floor before she turned around and gasped.

"You?"

Her memory for faces vindicated Alex's decision to resolve the matter, and he scrambled in and took one step forward. Patty inhaled to scream, but the rear of Alex's hand slapped her sideways and she bumped her head on the corner of the table as she went down.

He checked her pulse: alive. He raised her shoulders, and she slumped back down. So Alex had some time to think. Ruby had told him she lived alone, so there was no danger of him being surprised by a housemate or a boyfriend.

Alex moved into the bathroom and filled the bath half full with warm water. He dragged Patty's body in and removed her clothes. Then he picked her up and lowered her into the bath, face down. Within ten seconds, she woke up and attempted to remove her head so she could breathe again, but he held the back of her skull with both hands to force her nose and mouth to remain below the waterline.

Patty flailed away for more than a minute before she gave up the fight, but there wasn't a moment when Alex relaxed his grip. He remained in position for another thirty seconds in case there was still some life left inside her, but there was only the quiet of her death to keep him company.

He twisted her body, so she was face up and manipulated her limbs to arrange them the way someone sitting in a tub might lie. Then he went to the kitchen and found two bottles of wine. He opened both and emptied one, throwing it straight into the trash. He only half-emptied the second and poured the red liquid into a glass. Alex placed the bottle and the glass on a ledge by the bath next to the tiled wall.

He collected Patty's clothes and took them into her bedroom. He hung up her blouse and skirt in the wardrobe and stuffed her underwear back in a set of drawers. Then Alex returned to the windowsill and examined the frame to see if he had made any scratches on the outside: nothing.

The stage was almost ready, she drowned in her bath after drinking too much. All Alex needed to do was to walk through each room and rearrange anything which looked like he might have touched it or that somehow indicated Patty had not been alone at the time of her death. He closed the kitchen/diner window from the inside and pulled the bathroom door ajar.

With a bit of luck, she wouldn't be missed until someone opened up the club after Kennedy's funeral. Even if a girlfriend were to come visiting, they'd have no reason to believe anything other than Patty was out when they popped over.

Alex listened at the front door: nothing. He poked his head out into the corridor and strained to hear any sounds from Patty's neighbors. Still silent. So he scurried down the stairs, out of the building, and off down the street to his car.

ANOTHER CIGARETTE AND Alex was ready to drive off, although his cuffs were still damp. He should have rolled his sleeves up a little more. Ten minutes of light traffic and Alex stopped around the corner from Fred's Bar on Elm.

He wasn't too concerned about Hank, but Amy had had plenty of time to see his face and remember it. She already knew he was a visitor to the area, and that was a little too much information for her to stay alive.

Alex entered the bar and took his seat at the back booth. Sure enough, within thirty seconds, Amy appeared to give him a menu and take a drink order.

"Just a coffee, thank you."

"Coming right up."

Most of the tables were occupied as though the death of Oswald had lifted a veil over the city. People were getting on with their lives and Fred's was a place worth frequenting.

Amy reappeared with a steaming mug of coffee.

"Cream?"
"No thanks."
"What can I get for you?"
"Steak and fries."
"How d'you want that cooked?"
"Medium-well."
"It'll be with you as soon as possible."
"No need to rush, Amy."
She smiled and switched off her waitress' expression.

"Hi, David. It's been so busy since they announced Oswald was shot on the television."

"That's fine. I'm glad that business is good for you."

"Are you going to be in the city for long? You said you were only here for a few days."

"I'll be in meetings until the weekend."

Amy smiled again as her eyes glanced over to an adjacent booth where a couple had just sat down.

"Go and work, Amy. You don't have to make small talk with me all afternoon."

She nodded and hopped over so that the man could ask for a pitcher of beer for the table. Fifteen minutes later, Alex's steak arrived. It was a bit too chewy, and the fries needed less salt, but overall he had eaten far worse in his time.

When Amy came to take his dessert order, Alex seized the opportunity.
"Any recommendations today?"
"The tiramisu is good if you have a sweet tooth."
"Then that's what I shall I have, Amy."
"Is there anything else I can get you, David?"
"There is one more thing, more a favor."
"Oh?"

"Would you mind if we had a… private conversation out back? There's something I'd like to ask you, but not here in the middle of the bar. Do you mind?"

She eyed him up and down and thought for a moment.

"I take a break in twenty minutes. I always have a smoke around then. If you are there when I am, then we'll talk and you can ask your favor."

ALEX TOOK HIS cue when Amy sashayed past him, down a corridor, and continued out the back of the building. Before the door had swung closed, he saw she had already lit her cigarette.

The rear entrance led out to two dumpsters, and some trucks parked fifty feet away. Amy sauntered toward them to escape the smell of the trash.

"Hey, you."

She leaned against the wall, one foot resting flat on the bricks.

"Hi, David."

Without her apron, Amy proved to have rather a slender figure beneath her white blouse and black pencil skirt. The blouse had Fred's logo on the chest. Alex lit a cigarette, shuffled uneasily, and smiled. He looked up at the sky.

"It's turned out to be quite nice, if you can forget the tragic events that have unfolded in the last couple of days."

Amy laughed.

"Yeah, the sun's out, David."

"Listen, Amy. I realize this is awkward, but you know that I'm only in town a short while and I was looking for some company this evening."

"Uh-huh."

"And I was wondering if you were free some point after your shift ends."

"Tell me, David. What do you have in mind for us?"

Alex worked hard to make his cheeks redden.

"Oh. I was thinking of a drink, or even a meal if you were up for it. Depends what time you get off, I suppose."

"You're a sweet guy, David, but I'm not too sure."

Alex stared at the ground as though embarrassed and disappointed.

"I understand. Why don't we both pretend that I am just not your type or too old and then my ego won't have to be any more bruised than it already is."

"Aw, shucks. Now you're going to make me feel bad."

"That was never my intention."

"A drink you say?"

"To get to know each other better. If we have fun, then that's a win. And if not, then we've had a pleasant drink and we go home… alone."

"What a gentleman."

"You know I tip well, Amy."

She laughed and finished her smoke.

"Tell you what, David. My shift ends at ten. If you are outside waiting for me, then we can try for that drink. If not, then all bets are off."

"You've got yourself a deal."

Alex leaned forward and pecked Amy on the cheek. She mumbled something about needing to get back and scurried into the building.

AT TEN ON the nail, Amy appeared from the front of Fred's and shouted goodnight to Hank. Alex stood outside and doffed his fedora at her.

"I'm glad you're here, David. I could do with letting my hair down and having some fun tonight."

She had changed out of her waitress uniform and wore an orange shirt and jeans, with a suede jacket on top, with lines of tassels running down the seams.

"Amy, are you into country and western, by any chance?"

"How d'you know?"

He flicked a tassel.

"Just call it a lucky guess. Where are we going?"

"There's a bar around the corner which serves a mean martini."

They walked east along the sidewalk and Alex worried Amy was taking them to the Carousel Club. One block down and they crossed the street to head north, so he relaxed. Up ahead was an alleyway, and Alex halted at its entrance.

"Amy, I know this is forward of me and we haven't even had a drink yet, but…"

He took her by the hand and walked them into the shadows of the alley, maintaining a gentle hold on Amy so that when he stopped, they stood next to each other. She inhaled as if to ask what he was doing and Alex put his first finger on his lips and then transferred it over to hers.

Amy placed an arm over his shoulder and leaned in toward him. She puckered up and closed her eyes. Alex grabbed her head and twisted it with all his force until he heard her neck crack. She fell to the floor and he dragged her corpse into the back reaches of the alley and hid the body under some boxes.

Then he hightailed it to his car and off to the airstrip. He only stopped to drop a dime at a phone kiosk.

"It's done."

"We figured as much."

"And I've made sure there are no loose ends."

Click. Whirr.

28

ESTHER COHEN CALLED her brother on the last day of the month. They spoke often as she and her nephews looked after Alex's interests on the East Coast. However, with his trip to Dallas making him impossible to contact, they had missed their November conversation.

"Alex, I've got bad news: we need you in New York tomorrow."

"What's happened?"

There was something about her tone to indicate this was not a business call.

"Mama fell yesterday trying to reach a top shelf of her kitchen cupboard. I don't know why she couldn't wait for one of us to pop over, but that's what she did. The doctor said she had broken her hip and left wrist, so we took her straight to hospital."

"Go on." His throat was dry, and a dull ache was emanating from the pit of his stomach.

"She rested overnight; that'd be last night. And David, Moishe, and I went over this morning to check on her. We were there for about an hour and she..."

The receiver was filled with Esther's sobbing, and Alex knew the rest. He inhaled and sighed.

"I'll get the first flight out today."

ALTHOUGH SARAH JOINED Alex for the funeral, she could not be next to him, as this was an Orthodox Jewish affair and the men and women stood in separate parts of the room. And as one of the official mourners, along with his siblings, Alex was positioned near the rabbi and close to the plain wooden coffin.

Even though they had arranged the funeral for the day after Ruth's death, the hall was packed with well-wishers. By the end of her life, Alex's mother had only a few friends who had survived the years, but word got out that respect needed to be shown to Alex's family member. If he had bothered to turn around, Alex would have seen some of the old Italian commission members, shuffling with ill-fitting skullcaps on their heads.

After the rabbi had muttered in Hebrew for far too long, the attendants followed the coffin to the graveside. Alex stood next to Esther and Aaron and Reuben, his estranged brothers, and in front of Moishe and David, and his three other sons: Asher, Elijah, and Arik. Again, Sarah was left to fend for herself in the main rabble. Alex clutched Esther's hand but wished Sarah was with him.

He had lived with death all his life, but at this moment Alex was crushed by the loss of his mama. He sniffed twice and cleared his throat. More Hebrew and as the oldest child, the rabbi pointed at a spade standing upright in the mound of earth which had been removed for the burial.

Alex plunged the blade deep into the soil and threw the contents on top of the coffin. As the dirt landed, there was a hollow thud as it hit the wood of the casket. He swallowed hard.

The rabbi leaned into him. "Not so much earth. You don't want to do yourself a mischief, and besides, there are plenty of people after you who must also take a turn."

Alex ensured the second pile still had some of the blade visible to lessen the load. The thud was just as hollow because this time the soil landed on a different part of the coffin. The noise pierced his heart again. For his third scoop, Alex did his best to aim the earth onto one of the two existing sprinkles of mud to reduce the agony of hearing it land, forcing the air to echo around his mother's body.

Then he planted the spade in the mound and moved a few steps away with Esther. His brothers were next, followed by the grandchildren. The rest shuffled back to the hall, but Alex remained by the grave, watching everyone who filed past and contributed to the burial of Ruth Cohen. By the time they reached the end of the line, he acknowledged Ezra and Massimo with a nod each. Then Joe Bananas, the boss of Manhattan, and Frank DeSimone from Los Angeles sidled by.

Alex was surprised to see Sam Giancana at the end of the line, the last member of the funeral party to contribute to the burial of the coffin. Before Alex walked away, from the corner of his eye, he noticed the cemetery workers finish the job off. As he reached the hall entrance, the rabbi stopped him for a second.

"We have had little opportunity to talk and there is one thing I need to know for the next part of the service: will you say Kaddish?"

Alex halted. The mourners' prayer?

"Can I read it please?"

The rabbi proffered him a prayer book, but it was all in Hebrew.

"I meant in English."

Rabbi Gould shook his head.

"It is only spoken in Hebrew."

"Then I decline. I only say things in a language I understand."

"If you think it's best."

Alex stared at Gould for a second and decided not to respond, grinding his molars instead.

ONCE THE SERVICE was over, the congregation formed a line after Alex and the other official mourners sat down in a row. One by one, people shook hands and wished them long life. Under Alex's instructions, Sarah didn't say a word and hugged him instead.

The Italian bosses made certain they were the last, so they could talk with Alex without halting the entire proceedings. Sam Giancana was the first to break the awkward silence.

"Alex, I speak for us all when I say I am so sorry for your loss. Nobody wants to reach the day when they must wish their parents a last goodbye."

"Thank you, Sam. She was a noble woman in her own way. She kept the family together when times were tough and was a rock onto which we all clung throughout our lives."

The men nodded and attempted to make small talk.

"I appreciate you taking the time out of your schedules to see me on this day."

"Alex, it is the very least we can do. But we do not want to intrude on your family's grief any more than we have to and shall take our leave of you now."

They shook hands and, for the first moment in all their dealings, each man gave Alex a firm hug and a pat on the back. Alex wiped a tear from his right eye and the bosses vanished from sight to be replaced by Sarah.

"Alex, we need to leave this place."

He looked past the woman with whom he had spent most of his adult life and realized they were alone.

"Hold me."

As Sarah took him in her arms, Alex cried. His shoulders shook up and down, and he could barely breathe. Once the wave of sadness had abated, Alex sat back down on one of the mourners' chairs and cried some more. Then he coughed and blew his nose.

"Let's get the hell out of here."

ESTHER HAD DONE a good job of preparing Mama's apartment for the funeral party. There were stacks of bridge rolls with a variety of toppings like chopped liver and smoked salmon. While her mother was not a big drinker, Esther had ensured she stocked the drinks cabinet well, with a large quantity of whiskey and vodka.

By the time Alex and Sarah arrived in their stretch limo, hired for each of the official mourners, the place was full of people. He hadn't been in the building since he walked out to join the army as a teenager. He shuddered as he entered the living room and those nearest turned round to check out the latest arrival.

Esther spotted them and dragged Alex over to Aaron and Reuben.

"A terrible reason, but this must be the first time in decades that all my brothers have gathered under the same roof with me."

His two brothers shuffled and mumbled something in such an incoherent way that Alex felt the need to be more forthright.

"Esther, it is a tragedy, but we are together again, right boys?"

"I never knew you had other siblings, Alex." He glared at Sarah for making the comment, but she was correct, he'd never mentioned them and, truth be told, it was a rare moment when he even thought about them. When he'd returned from France, they were still tied to their mother's apron strings and he was determined to make his way in the heady world of the Bowery. He didn't look back.

"My apologies, gentlemen. Let me introduce Sarah…"

"We heard all about her from Mama when you first walked out on us all." Reuben's eyes remained locked on the floor.

"Then when you moved away, she kept a scrapbook of your court appearances." That was Aaron's contribution to the conversation.

"It must have many empty pages. I haven't seen the inside of a courthouse since my federal tax problems."

"Alex, both Aaron and I stopped looking at that scrapbook after we left home. Mama still loved you even though you ignored both her and Pop."

"Given the circles I moved in, I thought it best if I didn't come round. Besides, I moved to the other side of the country."

"Whatever…"

The two brothers walked away, leaving Esther with Alex and Sarah, who squeezed his hand and pecked him on the cheek.

"They bear grudges, Alex, and Mama's death won't bring them near you soon."

"I know, Esther. Our paths diverged many years ago and we've led separate lives since. I don't blame them either. My life has not followed the straight and narrow."

At that point, Asher, Elijah, and Arik came up to their mother along with their spouses. They shook hands with Alex and engaged in polite chit-chat. It felt so strange to see his other boys. David and Moishe were part of his present and he'd lost contact with his other children before he moved to Vegas.

Later in the early evening, Alex and Sarah found themselves alone in a corner, the crowd having thinned out.

"Do you think I am still a member of this family, Sarah?"

"In a way, Alex. But the decisions you made all those years ago had consequences. By turning your back on these people to protect them from your business, you became disconnected from their lives."

"Does that make me an evil man?"

Before Sarah could respond, Rabbi Gould appeared, and Esther hurried to meet him and help him prepare for the evening prayers. She dragged Alex and the rest of her boys onto their rickety mourners' chairs and the service began as soon as they sat down. The rabbi didn't want to hang about.

While his siblings were going to sit the usual seven nights of shiva, Alex informed Esther that one night of praying was more than sufficient for him. So he and Sarah flew out to Las Vegas the following day to get away from everything.

29

AS EVER, TITO Vestri's limo collected them from the airport and deposited them outside the Emblem casino, owned by Ezra, Massimo, and Alex. Located just off the strip, tourists tended not to visit, but high rollers knew about it well enough to keep the roulette wheels spinning. Besides, the penthouse was fit for a president and several had been comped there over the years, including Jack.

Sarah insisted Alex stayed in their top-floor accommodation when they arrived.

"Let's at least take the rest of today to gather ourselves together. As soon as you leave this room, you'll throw yourself back into business, won't you?"

A shrug in response because she was right. Truth was that he had been expecting the call about his mother, maybe now, perhaps next year, but sooner rather than later. What he hadn't expected was the way his estranged brothers and children had treated him. Of course, they had no reason to behave in any other manner, but Alex hurt, nonetheless.

The following day, they ventured down to the restaurant for breakfast, where Ezra and Massimo were already sat at a table. They beckoned them over, and Alex and Sarah joined the lieutenants.

"We thought you would never leave your room."

"Ezra, sometimes even an old couple like us want to spend time together."

The corner of Massimo's mouth curled up and Alex scowled at him.

"I hope you appreciate the presidential suite."

"Massimo, of course."

Alex thought both men were behaving in an unusual way, but he couldn't tell if it was just the grief inside warping his perception. They settled down to breakfast and Alex ordered his usual feast, while Sarah took pancakes with maple syrup and a coffee.

"Careful you don't cut into our profits." Another jibe, this time from Ezra. What was their problem?

"If you are that concerned, then I'll just have coffee and toast."

"A mild roasting and nothing more, Alex. Go ahead. Enjoy. Massimo and I have business to look after, but we'll see you later."

After the men walked away, he leaned forward in his chair.

"Do you know what's got into those two, Sarah?"

"What do you mean?"

"I thought they were being snide."

"Alex, your mother died only a few days ago and you are not thinking at your best."

"I guess you're right... Do you see me as too old, Sarah?"

"What are you talking about, Alex? None of us are getting any younger."

"I know that. But sometimes I get so scared."

"This is the grief talking, Alex. Why don't you play some poker to pull your head back in the game? Meanwhile, I'll have a spa treatment."

THE ADVANTAGE OF staying in a casino you own is that there are chips to play with and a guaranteed seat at a table. Morning is always a quiet time with only nickel-and-dime tourists popping in after breakfast. As soon as Alex entered the room, the floor man pointed out a solitary table away from the entrance where a proper game was underway with three men and an empty chair.

"Do you mind if I join you guys?"

"It's a ten grand ante." The dealer's eyes remained fastened on the cards in his hand and on the green baize, so he failed to notice the owner of the joint stood in front of him.

"That's fine by me."

An hour later and Alex had acquired a pile more chips than when he'd arrived. He was about to cash out when the floor man tapped him on the shoulder and told him that Ezra wanted a private word.

"Alex, we thought we'd discover you in the gaming room. Remember that the house keeps ten percent."

"Ezra, if that is all we make, then you'd better find out who is skimming the take."

Laughs all round but Alex had a point.

"Anyway, what was so important that you needed to drag me away from my poker?"

Massimo eyed Ezra before answering. "We have a local difficulty, which we have tried to contain. We were hoping you could tear yourself from your game long enough to help us."

Alex smiled. Their attitude wasn't in his imagination.

"What's the problem?"

"Orazio Ferraro."

"That sounds like who. I asked what."

"He is a regular guest from Chicago; in here five or six times a year?"

Ezra nodded approval.

"He always pays his way and is a good tipper. Of course, his room and board are comped as the fella spends enough in the casino."

"Fabulous, Massimo. I'll be on my way."

"Alex, not so fast. When he came into town yesterday to play craps, we comped him ten thousand as usual, just as a token. He was on a losing streak and burned through the chips in a matter of minutes, so he demanded more on the house."

Alex blinked, knowing what was coming next.

"We declined but Ferraro insisted and we relented. He carried on that way all night. Then he left first thing this morning."

"And you allowed him to?"

"Alex, we couldn't think how to refuse the accommodation. He is the son of Frank Ferraro."

"Massimo, you would not have wanted to disrespect that fella in public. How much are we in for?"

"Half a million."

"Let me see what I can do."

ALEX KISSED SARAH goodbye for his overnight trip and grabbed a flight to Chicago that lunchtime. By the time he arrived at his hotel, it was five, so he ate a light dinner and headed straight to bed.

The next morning, he went to the South Side and found the area which Italians called home. All he needed to do was to go to a cafe and ask for Orazio, and everything else would follow. No sooner had he uttered the Ferraro name than the waiter fell silent, and the color left his cheeks.

"I don't know who you are talking about. I'll get your check."

The steward scampered back to the till and whispered something to the proprietor, who also immediately looked like he'd seen a ghost. Alex remained where he was, knowing that if he stirred his coffee for long enough then somebody would appear. And so it was. After the owner placed a phone call, a fella in a dark suit entered the establishment. A glance by the guy in Alex's direction and the man headed toward him.

"May I sit down?"

"Be my guest, if you tell me your name."

"Orazio Ferraro. I believe you were asking for me."

Alex beckoned Orazio to be seated with an open palm, indicating the chair next to his.

"Good morning, Orazio. Did you have an enjoyable time in Vegas?"

"Why, yes. How do you know that's where I've come from?"

"Orazio, I have business interests in the Emblem casino where you played."

"Great joint. My congratulations to you."

"The work is done by my partners, who inform me you have an outstanding bill to pay."

Orazio squinted as if trying to recall the name of a long-lost girlfriend.

"I don't think so. We are all square."

"Now this is when matters can get embarrassing for you, Orazio. While we comped your room, food, and drink, we are not in the habit of offering you more than ten large in complimentary chips."

"Do you know who I am?"

"Orazio, it is because I do that I am showing you the respect of coming direct to ask you for the half a million you owe."

"Go to hell. You walk into my restaurant and demand money from me? Get out now before we take you to the back and give your old hide the beating it deserves."

ALEX LEFT AFTER throwing a couple of bucks on the table to cover the cost of his coffee plus tip. Then he dropped a dime at a nearby phone kiosk and strolled around the corner and west two blocks.

The building was nothing to look at from the outside, and the signage indicated it was a private club for men of Italian descent. Alex was at the right place.

Frank Ferraro sat behind a large oak desk but walked around to shake Alex's hand. They sat down on armchairs at the other end of his office.

"Coffee, Alex?"

"Thank you, Frank. Sorry to bother you on such short notice."

"Not to worry, Alex. When you called a few minutes ago, I reckoned you would only do so if there was something important to discuss."

"That there is, Frank. And before we start, I want you to know that I come here offering you the utmost respect. Sam Giancana has only had exemplary things to report about you over the years, while you've been his underboss."

"Kind of you to say, Alex, but there's no need to blow smoke up my ass. How can I help?"

Alex sighed and lit a cigarette.

"A case of theft has come to my attention and I am seeking your assistance in resolving the matter."

"How much are we talking?"

"Half a million. Not a vast amount for men like ourselves, but neither is it chump change."

"Indeed. Who is the thief?"

Alex stared at Frank.

"Orazio, your son."

It was Frank's turn to sigh as he asked Alex to explain what his boy had done now.

"Alex, I apologize to you for my boy's foolishness and arrogance."

"No matter how hard we try, we cannot be responsible for our children's indiscretions."

"Tell me you have business in town other than this issue."

Alex shrugged.

"My mother died a few days ago, and I was taking some rest in Vegas when this situation arose."

Frank's cheeks flushed red and he gritted his teeth as he stormed out of his office. Much shouting ensued with the fellas in the anteroom, and Frank returned some five minutes later.

"Would you like another coffee or something to eat while we wait for my men to find Orazio?"

"He was in his cafe a short while ago."

"Alex, you have already seen him today, and he has refused to make restitution?"

"Yes, Frank. I respect you too much to have bothered you over Orazio's debt if I had not approached him first."

Frank nodded, and the two men waited, talking about old times, and sharing stories about Sam Giancana. The man might have significant interests in Florida, but he ruled Chicago nowadays. There was a buzz of muffled voices outside and Orazio entered the office.

The moment he did, both men stopped laughing and stared at him. Orazio's eyes widened as he recognized Alex from their earlier encounter.

"Boy, you have some explaining to do."

"What is he doing here?"

Orazio pointed a thumb at Alex, who returned the gesture with a smile.

"Alex has come to collect his debt and you are going to pay him."

"Why should I do that?"

"Because I am telling you to do so. Besides, this is Alex Cohen, a good fella who has worked with Sam Giancana more years than you have been on this earth."

Alex maintained his smile. This was just like the old days, and it felt wonderful.

January 1968

30

SARAH AND ALEX settled back into their comfortable life in Boyle Heights. He oversaw a sideline in narcotics, which remained focused on Hollywood, and Sarah ran the nafkas Alex procured for the stars and would-be celebrities. There were still his investments around the country and Alex had never given up his interests in Vegas and beyond. Each day began much the same as the last: with breakfast.

"Sarah, do you think we should retire?"

She laughed.

"Where did that thought come from?"

"I don't know. I'm wondering what's the purpose of dishing out pills and plants to the rich and famous in California."

"It keeps us in clover, doesn't it?"

"Sure, babe."

"Well then. Why change?"

Alex contemplated the question because Sarah had a point.

"I'm bored and want something else to do."

Another chuckle.

"Alex, if you are bored now, how do you think you'll feel after you stop working altogether?"

"I suppose..."

"You used to be involved in politics. Why don't you do some more of that?"

"Sarah, after the federal contracts from Jack Kennedy went away, I didn't have any leverage."

"Try state government instead then. We must have a senator or a governor you can bribe somewhere in this great state."

"Darling, I reach accommodations with people. I do not engage in mere bribery."

"Keep telling yourself that, Alex."

THE ECONOMIC BOOM had generated more construction work than anyone could have imagined. The trouble was that the Italians had got there years before. While he might have been late to the game, Alex had one card up his sleeve—his Hollywood connections.

"Thank you for seeing me, Carl."

"No worries. I am always happy to break bread with you. How's tricks?"

Alex and Carl Newman, head of United Studios, were enjoying lunch in Pietro's, an Italian restaurant on Sunset Boulevard.

"Carl, everything is just fine, thanks. How is the movie business?"

"You don't want to ask. The last couple of years have been very good to us, but right now we are stuck."

"What's the problem, Carl?"

"In a word, Alex, the Transport and Master Vehicular Workers. Nobody has got in or out of the studio in the past three days."

"What does the TMVW want?"

"Money, of course. What else does a union demand?"

"Better working conditions?"

"Funny, Alex. But this is serious. It's costing me tens of thousands every day the cameras aren't rolling."

"Perhaps I might intervene for you?"

"Is this your line of work?"

Alex chuckled.

"Like you have no idea, Carl."

"I'm sorry, Alex. Forgive me, but I've only known you as someone involved in… the party scene, shall we say?"

"One way or another, I have been a friend of the working man all my life."

"Alex, I don't give a damn about the working stiff. I care about my studio."

"Let me have a day to assess the situation. If I can assist, then I will be glad to do so."

"Alex, if you are able to sort this out, I'll pay your weight in gold."

"Be careful what you agree, Carl."

THE OFFICES OF the TMVW were like any other union place Alex had seen since his days in the Bowery. The first floor was filled with desperate men pleading with the receptionist for her to solve their problems. Meanwhile, the guys whose wages came from their dues sat upstairs with their feet on a desk doing nothing. So it had been, and so it was.

"Where do I go to speak to someone about the United Studios strike?"

"Listen, Mac. If you want to join the picket, just turn up and they will put you to good use."

"Miss, that's not what I meant. Who is responsible here for the action?"

"That'll be Emory Bourne."

"Where will I find him?"

"Third floor and follow your nose."

Alex tipped his fedora, wandered to the staircase, and heaved himself up the two flights. When he arrived at the landing, he took a breath and stared at the sign which listed office numbers and their occupants, but not in name order because that would have been too helpful. Instead, he stood and scanned the rooms to find Bourne's suite. No luck. A man hustled past in an open-neck shirt with hands in his pants pockets.

"Is Emory on this floor, bud?"

"Three eleven down this corridor, fifth on the right."

"Much obliged."

Before the passage took a left turn, room 311 was where the guy had predicted. Alex gave a quick rap and entered.

"Listen, bud, if you are here to support the strike, that's great but you've come to the wrong place."

Alex smiled and continued toward Emory's desk. Then he sat down in the only other chair in the office.

"Quite the contrary, Emory. I'm here to talk about ending the strike."

"Have I met you before? I know every studio hack Newman's employed and I've never seen you in my life."

"I am Alex Cohen and you are Emory Bourne. Now we both know each other's names, perhaps we could start talking business?"

"Get out of here. Who do you think I am?"

"Emory Bourne, I just told you."

Alex looked at this poor excuse of a man and waited for him to calm down and think straight.

"Are you from out of town and Newman has sent you over to strong-arm me and my boys into capitulating?"

"I live in Los Angeles and the only thing I wish to force on you is a conversation. Nothing more, nothing less. I am here to talk."

Emory leaned back in his leather seat, then sat forward to light a cigarette and inhaled his first drag.

"We have a list of demands. If Newman meets them, then we go back to work. And not a second earlier."

"Mr. Newman informed me the principal item of contention was money. I assume your brothers want more than the studio can afford."

"More than it is *prepared* to pay, Cohen."

"Call me Alex."

"Whatever. My men get up before dawn to pick up the stars from their mansions and wait around until they deign to leave late in the evening. Others spend their lives hauling equipment across country with impossible deadlines to meet. This is a strike about pay and conditions."

Alex smiled. "I told Carl this would be about more than just gelt."

Emory shifted in his chair.

"You said that to him?"

"Of course, Emory. This is not the first dispute I have worked to resolve and often both sides benefit because that way, everyone gains in the long term."

"You don't talk like a boss's lackey."

"I care about the working man. If he's not happy, then I'm not happy."

Emory nodded his consent at that thought, although Alex wasn't sure he knew what it meant.

"So, Emory, let's cut to the chase. We could spend hours in each other's company chewing the fat, but neither of us needs to do that. I expect what you want is to get a better deal signed and sealed before the end of the day. And I can deliver that to you, if you tell me what it will take to bring your men back to work."

"Improved pay and conditions. I've already told you."

"I am authorized to offer you a nickel on the dollar more in wages and one extra stop for drivers traveling over four hours."

"Not good enough, Alex."

"Emory, that is on the table. Five percent is generous and is more than Mr. Newman has offered until now. Let's face it, the two sides haven't even managed to be in the same room together. This is the first negotiation you've engaged in."

"We had months of discussions, Alex, but the studio would not budge an inch."

"That was when they thought they ruled the roost and that you wouldn't bite the hand that fed you. The TMVW has proved them wrong, but you and I need to work out a way to bring everybody together again. For the sake of your men and the rest of the hard-working crew who rely on the movies to put bread on their families' tables."

"Spare me the sob story. I know how important it is to have greenbacks."

"Emory, I do not doubt it. The funny thing is that when I first worked on union problems, I was young and naïve. I'd enter a man's office and offer some deal and if he refused, I would go to his home and threaten to kill his wife."

Emory leaned forward and the supercilious smirk left his face.

"But I am older and more worldly-wise than I was then. We both know that threatening a man with watching his wife's throat being slashed open by a stranger is an unnecessary experience. Are you married, Emory?"

A nod.

"Kids?"

"Two."

"Then you do not need to worry yourself. I will not go to where you live and terrorize your family. That is contemptible behavior."

Bourne leaned back in his chair. Alex leaped out of his seat and whipped around the desk so fast that the poor sap did not know what was happening. One hand grasped Bourne's throat and dragged him toward the window, Alex's other hand opened it up and he pushed Bourne out into the afternoon's air. A flash of memory of the night Alex killed Abe Reles, then snap, back into room 311.

"I've offered you five percent and an extra stopover. Accept that compromise or your kids won't have a dad."

"Don't..."

"Ketchup on the ground or a deal in your pocket. Decide now."

"HOW DID YOU get the job done so fast, Alex?"

"You were using the wrong kind of reason, Carl. Besides, I figured a small raise was nothing compared to the amount you've been losing every day."

"Let me show you some appreciation. Send me a bill for consulting services, let's call it one hundred thousand."

"Very kind, Carl. And thank you. To be honest, the original reason I wanted to talk to you was to find out if you had a private phone number for the governor. I know you two are close. You need to be, given how important Hollywood is to the state's economy."

"Sure thing, Alex. But I doubt if Reagan is going to be a politician you'll be able to do business with."

Carl wrote a different name and number on a scrap of paper from his pocket and passed it over to Alex.

"Much appreciated. And as you've offered me gelt, I'd be a fool to refuse the friendly gesture."

May 1968

31

THE NEXT DAY, Alex dialed the number Carl had given him and arranged a breakfast meeting with Driscoll Hart. As he drove into the Malibu Golf and Country Club, Alex wondered why Hart had picked this location. At the reception, a boy was sent to take him around to the clubhouse, where another man met Alex and walked him along oak-lined corridors, through the restaurant, and onto a patio area overlooking the golf course.

Hart sat nearest the golfing action, at a table with an enormous umbrella, so that Alex could only determine who it was when he was seated. To his surprise, Hart already had a guest who appeared to have almost finished her meal. Alex glanced at his watch and saw that it was only eight.

"Thank you for taking the time to see me, Mr. Hart."

"Call me Driscoll. There is no need for formalities, especially as you are a friend of Carl."

Alex eyed Driscoll's breakfast companion. She was only half his age.

"We haven't met, miss."

"Elizabeth was just leaving, weren't you, dear?"

She nodded, flicked her long blond hair behind her shoulders, and stood up. A kiss on the lips showed Driscoll and Elizabeth had not been engaged in a business encounter. And with a swish of her tail, she was gone. Driscoll's eyes lingered on her ass as she sashayed away.

"You must enjoy meeting your constituents. Or was that your wife?"

"My wife is at home and still asleep, but you didn't want to speak to me about my domestic arrangements."

A waiter arrived and took Alex's order.

"Over the years, I have built up a name in California."

"Mr. Cohen, you don't have to tell me about your reputation. It precedes you."

"Call me Alex. In that case, you are no doubt aware that I have been able to secure a variety of state contracts to the benefit of all those involved."

Driscoll took a slurp of coffee and swirled it around his mouth before swallowing.

"Alex, from what I've heard, you had some juice with Jack Kennedy and did business with Merrick Townsend. Jack is dead and Merrick has long since retired from politics."

"They are from the past, but I am interested in future opportunities, Driscoll. There is much we can do in this state to improve everybody's lives."

"Let me stop you there, Alex. The people of California elected me to do a job and I am here to serve them. I do not need you to come here and tell me how to work in the best interests of this great state."

"Driscoll, that was not what I was trying to say. My apologies if I have caused you any offense."

Alex's breakfast arrived, and the conversation paused while all the plates were delivered.

"Perhaps I was too circumspect. Are there any contracts I could bid for coming in the next few months, where we both could benefit?"

Driscoll smiled, revealing his perfect white teeth.

"I like a straight talker, Alex. There is always something we can work on together. The trick will be for us to find where our common interests lie."

THEIR NEXT MEETING took place in the same Malibu golf club, although this time there was no sign of Elizabeth. Alex was hustled into a private dining room in which Driscoll sat alone. As a busboy cleared the table, it was obvious that the senator had eaten with two guests. And the fact they were no longer here indicated the politician was careful not to mix his associates.

"Would you like a drink, Alex?"

A Scotch on the rocks was ordered, along with a martini, straight up with a slice.

"I have been thinking about what you said, Alex, and there is a project coming up where we might work together."

"I'm all ears, Driscoll."

"The latest phase of the state water project has delivered vital water supplies to the San Joaquin Valley."

"I read about it in the newspaper."

"Right. So this means that the time is right for us to plan the next stage, which will go under the Tehachapi Mountains and send water to Southern California."

"You are talking about quite some tunnel, Driscoll."

"Tell me about it. There are a number of problems we face to push this through. First, the investment will be tremendous and we'll seek private funding. Second, the complexity of the engineering technology required to ensure that the water flows at a sufficient rate. Third, there is an environmental lobby concerned about the local wildlife."

"If you are thinking about asking me to bid for the construction job, then I can put a consortium together of like-minded entrepreneurs."

"Alex, no disrespect but if I am going to get into bed with the mob, the least I want is to sit in the same room as them when we iron out a deal."

"Do you think of me as a friend of the environment?"

Driscoll laughed.

"That's not quite where I have pigeonholed you, Alex. The way I see it is that I've heard you have a persuasive voice, shall we say, that might be useful to me when dealing with the lobbyists. To be honest, I thought you would be more interested in funding the project. If only half of what I've heard about you is accurate, I reckon you could rustle up a billion or two without too much trouble."

"I know a couple of people. It is true."

"Alex, do not undersell yourself. You are a man of means in your own right, even before we consider how well connected you are with the wealthier element in our society."

Now it was Alex's turn to smile.

"And I assume you want to be seen to be out in front of this Tehachapi Mountains project before the Republicans jump up and down ahead of November's election. You're seeking a second term, I imagine."

"I serve at the pleasure of the people of California."

"Do you anticipate the vote will be tight? You won by only five thousand votes last time."

"Alex, if you'd encourage the unions to back me, then I would appreciate it. After all, the more secure my position, the easier we can get the Tehachapi Mountains project off the ground. Besides, it's good to work with friends."

They finished the last of their drinks, talking about nothing.

"Alex, as much as I'd like to spend the rest of the evening with you, I am expecting Elizabeth to arrive soon."

"Do you have rooms here?"

"There is a hotel as part of the complex."

"Does your wife know?"

"Yes, and she has accepted the situation. I look after all Mrs. Hart's financial, emotional, and physical needs. In return, she understands I will stay with her until the day I die only if I allow myself to spend time with women like Elizabeth."

"Been seeing her long?"

"Alex, your curiosity is getting the better of you. Let me answer the one question you are not prepared to ask. No, there is no opportunity for you to blackmail me over Elizabeth. If you attempted such a maneuver, then there are ways to silence you which would not involve a payoff."

He ignored Driscoll's attempt to threaten him.

"Driscoll, you misunderstood my motive for the inquiry. I supply many things in Hollywood and wondered if you needed anything for your recreational time with the young lady."

"HOW DO YOU feel getting into bed with Driscoll Hart?"

"Sarah, he lives under the same rock as any other politician I've met. He thinks he is different and implied he had some clout with the Italians, but deep down he is as self-serving as any other of those pond scum."

"Alex, remind me again what he wants you to do?

"Ballot stuffing for the November election and then fund a state water project worth a cool two billion."

"But rig the vote first?"

Alex grinned.

"You always have to do something for the cockroaches before they'll do anything in return, Sarah. And he'd like some coke for his girlfriend in the meantime."

"Some things never change."

"She's pretty, I'll give him that."

"Alex Cohen, are you getting ideas?"

"Don't get ahead of yourself, Sarah. I said she's cute, not that I'd want to do anything more than that. From the brief time I spent with her, I'm guessing that Hart isn't with her for the conversation. Besides, my days of two-timing you are long gone."

"Just you remember that. So are you going to put more effort into politics than the Hollywood party crowd?"

"I would like to, Sarah. At least it would be a great opportunity to move away from some of my illegitimate business interests."

"You raise one invoice as a consultant and you're going straight all of a sudden."

"Funny. But disentangling myself from the web I've created might not be such a bad idea. If I am heading to retirement, then taking income from a Californian water project is a better pension than siphoning gelt from the Emblem casino."

32

HART WAS ONLY one piece of the puzzle. For any of Alex's investments to obtain regulatory approval meant that his paperwork had to be in order, and that there would be no attempt to air his dirty laundry in public. He relied on David and Moishe to organize his documentation—they spent so much of their lives telling him to keep accurate records of legitimate business deals. Moishe almost fell off his chair when his father handed over his consulting invoice to Carl. "That's the first time you've ever bothered doing that. Congratulations, Pop."

To ensure his public house remained in good order required a fresh approach. Alex hadn't seen Bobby Kennedy since the night he'd introduced him to Marilyn Monroe. Those were far happier times for the country. Two assassinations later and the promise of the so-called swinging sixties had already been stolen away.

"Thank you for taking the time to see me, Bobby. It's been quite a while since we talked."

"Indeed."

Kennedy's campaign offices in New York showed the presidential candidate was not wanting for money. Alex wondered how much support came from the Italian American community.

"Congratulations on your win in Nebraska the other day."

"Thank you. My team worked hard and my message of peace and hope for the future resonated well with the voters."

"Your family has been successful at the ballot box."

"Alex, there is no need for you to drag my brother's memory into this conversation."

"He was a great man, Bobby."

"Jack lived among the greats and died as the greatest. But he is gone and I refuse to live under his shadow. I am my own man and create my own success."

"Sure, Bobby. I only meant that you were in good company. Nothing more than that."

Bobby glared at Alex as though he had slashed the face of Kennedy's mom.

"My mind is on Oregon now. That is one hard state to crack."

"If I can help in any way..."

"Alex, yours is not the support that my campaign needs or is seeking."

Those eyes bored through him. For someone who planned on becoming president, this Kennedy wasn't trying to win over every single voter.

"Bobby, I am surprised that you turn away help when it is offered to you. Your campaign funds must be fit to burst if you are prepared to refuse my money or more direct assistance."

"We might sit in New York but the days of Tammany Hall are long since over and you would do well to remember that before you offer me any inducements."

"You must think poorly of me, Bobby. You are accusing me of bribing you before I've made you an offer." Alex smiled. "Besides, those thoughts could not be further from my mind."

"I'm pleased to hear it."

"The actual reason I wanted to speak with you today was to talk about the California State Water Project. If Senator Hart is reelected, then he hopes to instigate a new phase of development. This would create blue-collar jobs in the state, especially outside Los Angeles."

"Increasing employment is something we can get behind. Rural areas need our support."

"I thought that was your position, Bobby. And how you would feel if I became the lead investor to the project?"

"Alex, I agreed to this meeting out of respect for my brother's memory. I understood you and he had a business relationship. Although I never inquired about that, I have assumed that it was not on the legitimate side of life."

Alex looked at the senator with a blank expression. There was nothing he wanted to say in response to the accusation.

"Bobby, whether or not you become president, I would still like your blessing on the state water project and my involvement. Are you able to give me it?"

"I could save you a lot of energy, Alex. Senator Hart is a good man overall, but he is a poor judge of character if he thinks he can rely on you as an investor in a major piece of state infrastructure."

"Bobby, I appreciate your honest and direct manner. While you may not believe me, I wish you well in your attempts to become president. My family tells me you have served as an effective senator for New York, especially in impoverished Brooklyn."

"Despite your sympathetic words, Alex, we both know that you and your kind are the enemy within."

"WHAT DID HE mean when he said that he thought my kind was the enemy, Sarah?"

"You were in the room. What did you think?"

"Jews."

Alex ground his back teeth and fumed for a moment. Of all the Kennedys, Bobby presented himself as the most liberal. As attorney general, he had put through several bills to give rights to minorities and the disadvantaged, and instigated projects to help the working man.

"Could he have been talking about the mob?"

"The Italians? They aren't my kind?"

"I didn't say the mafia, Alex. Organized crime, not just the commission."

Sarah asked a good question, and Alex had no viable answer. When Bobby had uttered the words, Alex found himself too shocked to respond and strode out of the office. Then he ruminated on the conversation for the entire flight back to LA and still wasn't satisfied by the time his plane landed.

Jack had been easy to read and easier to do business with. He enjoyed sleeping with sexy actresses and taking drugs while he partied. Whatever Alex may have thought about the guy, Jack never behaved like he was better than you. At least not morally.

He possessed what Alex now saw as a Kennedy superiority to the rest of the world, but when he talked to you, it was with respect. Bobby had none of that. He made a good political speech, but his disapproval spoke volumes when you were in the same room together.

Joe Kennedy, father of the clan, was a renowned anti-Semite, and the apple doesn't fall far from the tree— not this one, at any rate. But Bobby had worked hard to forge closer ties with Israel. Was that just because we needed influence somewhere in the Middle East?

The trouble with taking the high moral ground is that there is only one way to go, and that is down.

"If only I had something on him."

"You have the Monroe tapes, Alex."

"I do, but they don't prove he did anything, not even close. The most important tape comprises Marilyn calling him and Bobby not picking up. That is insufficient evidence to show he did for her that night."

"The senator is cleverer than Jack."

33

"I'M GLAD YOU are back in the land of the living, Alex. We haven't seen you since your poor mother passed away."

Sam Giancana sat opposite Alex in a small bodega in Cuernavaca, smack in the middle of Mexico. Two glasses of red wine stood in front of them.

"A lot has changed since we last saw each other, Sam." Alex gestured around the store, indicating how little the joint looked like Florida, where they had been meeting for at least the past decade.

"Alex, the cops wanted me to squeal, and that was not on the cards. To save myself the aggravation, I moved to this nonentity of a place."

"You think you'll get back to the US at some point?"

"Alex, Charlie Lucky always told me he was working on something, but that fella died in Italy, the land of his fathers. Who am I to make myself sound smarter than that great man?"

"But there's always hope and a talented lawyer, Sam."

"I'll drink to that."

They clinked glasses and continued to talk about the past; the days of Arnold Rothstein and Alfonse Capone.

"Thomas Dewey was a kitten compared to Bobby Kennedy, wouldn't you say, Alex?"

"Now that depends whether you were on the receiving end of his lawsuits."

"Alex, my apologies. I forgot he was the one who snared you for your taxes."

"Me and Alfonse both." Alex smiled and took a sip of his wine. Although he preferred Scotch, this tasted quite fruity and was more than pleasant, even if it hadn't come from a Californian vineyard.

"Why mention a Kennedy?"

"Alex, Bobby Kennedy will do whatever he can to prevent me from getting back to the States. That man might not be Sicilian but he knows the meaning of a vendetta."

"He swore me off a billion-dollar investment only a week ago. It was my opportunity to straighten my affairs so that my family would have a legitimate legacy and not be dragged into our world just to make a living for themselves."

"Bobby Kennedy is a cockroach. Do you have anything on him?"

"Only old recordings of him with Monroe. It's not enough to do him irrevocable harm, but it might help you if he tries to prevent your return to the US."

"I will bear them in mind. Right now, the Feds aren't out for me. I'm here in case they call another grand jury and try to drag me back to testify again. Mexico is a better option than jail. We both know that ratting out your friends is not what fellas do."

Alex nodded. His time in Sing Sing would have been cut short if he had sung like a canary, but he was no Abe Reles. Sam offered him a cigar, and he lit it.

"This is a mighty fine smoke. Local?"

"Cuban. I hope that doesn't leave a foul taste in your mouth."

"I got out with most of my money. Unlike Meyer."

"Alex, do you still believe that story he's been spinning since he landed back in Florida?"

"Sam, every time I've visited Meyer, he has been in this ordinary house and his fancy suits have long since vanished."

"That may be, but have you ever asked him how much the Lansky family is worth? I accept the man himself only has two cents to rub together, but that's because he put everything in his wife's and kids' names. The fella is a shrewd player."

Alex laughed.

"One of you is messing with my head and I can't decide which one it is."

"Alex, surely you don't believe Meyer has no income streams. You know how Vegas operates. Are you saying Meyer doesn't own a piece of at least one casino?" Sam chuckled and shook his head.

"But back to the matter at hand: Bobby Kennedy. What I wouldn't give to be rid of that guy."

ALEX MADE IT his mission to find Bobby on the campaign trail. He chased the man around Oregon until he landed the fish after a meet-and-greet in a diner in Klamath Falls.

"How's the presidential hopeful?"

"I'm surprised to see you again, Alex. I thought you'd turned tail and run away. Like a rat leaving a ship."

"Bobby, I've never been a rat. I honor my friends and am true to my word."

"Keep telling yourself that… I assume our meeting isn't a coincidence?"

"I was just passing through this nothing state and thought I'd drop by to see how you are getting on. I saw that McCarthy's claiming you made illegal recordings of Martin Luther King. Shame on you, Bobby."

Alex smiled at the same moment as Bobby scowled.

"Don't believe everything you read in the newspapers. When I was attorney general, I did whatever was within my powers to keep America safe from harm."

"Bugging King? Was he such a threat to the United States?"

"Alex, you are attempting to goad me and I will not fall for your ridiculous game. Now be off with you."

"Bobby, do you think I came all this way just to roast you? I need to ask you a serious political question."

"Spit it out."

"What is your position on crime going to be if you become president?"

"Alex, that is a stupid thing to ask. I will want to reduce it. There hasn't been a president in history who wanted to do otherwise."

"Bobby, perhaps I didn't make myself clear. When you were attorney general, you had a hard-on for organized crime. Won't you have more important matters to attend to if you move into the White House? I mean, we've got boys in Vietnam."

"A peace settlement will sort that out. And yes, I'd love to put an end to the pernicious effect the mafia has on our country."

34

ALEX MET SARAH in New York so they could spend a few days with their East Coast kin: Esther, David, and Moishe. The night they arrived, David held a large gathering of the extended family, including his wife and children. Moishe brought his girlfriend, having got divorced two years earlier, with nothing more to show for it than an alimony bill.

"Thank you for throwing this party, David."

"My pleasure, Pop. You remember Dorit, don't you?"

"Of course, although on this occasion we are experiencing happier times."

At that moment, Nathan and Jojo ran between the adults, almost knocking Alex over.

"Be careful with grandpa."

"Don't worry about me, Dorit. I used to have children of my own. Now they are all grown up, but they ran around at some point in the past."

Alex winked at David, who responded in kind.

"Sometimes I wonder if they'll ever calm down."

"Dorit, Jojo wants to be like her older brother, so when Nathan slows down, then so will she."

"That's going to be quite a few years into the future, Pop."

"I never said it would be easy, only that it will happen."

David nodded and Dorit scurried away to check on her darlings. She didn't have to search for long as both kids had zoomed straight for their Grandma Sarah. Alex surveyed the vista before him. The people he cared for all under one roof were a sight to behold and he smiled.

Sarah looked up at him from under a lapful of children and her eyes sparkled.

"It's a shame you don't visit them more often."

"You are right, Dorit. My work has taken me away from my family all my life."

"That's a good excuse, but some men would change their business if it meant they were closer to their families. They grow up so fast and there's only a short amount of time to enjoy their youth."

His daughter-in-law walked into the kitchen to prepare the next meal, leaving Alex to soak up the joy in the living room and to mull over what she had said. Soon, another son wandered over.

"How are you, Moishe?"

"Just fine, Pop. You and mom look well."

"We have no complaints. So tell me, who's that girl you're with?"

"Alecia Hefferman. From the neighborhood."

"And which area is that then?"

"She lives in Queens, but I met her in Soho."

"That's where you live, right?"

"Yes, Pop. We've been seeing each other for…" Moishe counted on his fingers. "…four months now."

"I'm glad you're keeping a tally."

"Your son is an accountant. What else am I going to do?"

"Does she make you happy?"

"Yeah, Pop."

"And can you imagine settling down with her?"

"Let's not get ahead of ourselves. We've only just started dating and neither of us knows how long it may last. To me, she's clever, funny, and makes me feel great about myself. What's not to like? But I'm a dull man and she is an attractive woman, and I understand how these things play out."

"Don't undersell yourself, my boy. You are an excellent catch."

"Now you're sounding like somebody from the old country, Pop."

"You know something, Moishe? Sometimes I feel I never left Broska."

"Is this my cue to maintain a fixed smile and nod when you tell me how tough it was growing up surrounded by Cossacks?"

"Not my plan, but I am happy to deliver if you want me to."

Moishe shook his head and moved back to Alecia, but Alex followed.

"Pleased to meet you, young lady. You must be Alecia. Moishe has told me all about you."

"Charmed, I'm sure."

She held out her hand and Alex shook the limp fish.

"It must be strange for you to be surrounded by someone else's family."

"I'm fine, thank you, Mr. Cohen."

"Call me Alex. There's no need to be formal around me. I am only his father."

Alex elbowed Moishe in the side, which made his son giggle for a few seconds. Alecia smiled.

"Sometimes they don't grow up much at all, Alecia."

She smiled again.

"When you don't tickle him, he behaves like a man most of the time."

"Will you two stop? I am standing right here in case you'd forgotten?"

"Son, we both see where you are. Now, do not be rude and interrupt the adults while they are talking." A wink in Alecia's direction.

"And are you working?"

"I'm in advertising."

"Sounds fascinating, but I must admit I have no clue what that means."

"Well, you watch television?"

"As little as possible, but I listen to the radio and read the newspaper every day."

"There you go. The adverts you hear and see don't just appear for no reason. The company I work for devises and makes the promo, then we place it in locations for the potential audience to receive it."

"Like on a billboard?"

"That's the idea."

Dorit came out of the kitchen and announced that dinner was served.

AFTER DORIT AND Alecia cleared the remnants off the table, they returned to the living room with Sarah and left the men to smoke cigars in the dining room. The two kids had long since gone to bed.

"I had an interesting conversation with your wife before we ate."

"How so, Pop?"

"She told me that a grandfather whose work prevented him from seeing his family would change his job to spend more time with them."

"I'm sorry."

"Don't be, David. There was no malice in her words, but her response made me wonder how much she knows of our business."

"That is simple. *Gornisht*. Nothing. I am a lawyer and I don't talk about confidential matters at home. She knows that I do some work for you, but she has no idea that you are my sole client or what that entails."

Alex took a sip of the Scotch that David had bought that week for his father to consume.

"And what about you, Moishe? Have you spun a story to Alecia about your work?"

"Not at all, Pop. I've told her the absolute truth."

Both Alex and David stared at him with jaws hitting the floor.

"I am an accountant and I look after your books. She asks no follow-up questions because in her mind the job is so dull in the first place that anything else she knows will make her fall asleep."

Big laughs all round.

"Are you concerned about a leak, Pop?"

"Not at all, David. I trust the pair of you and your judgment without any doubt. I got to pondering how well you have insulated ourselves from prying eyes."

"Moishe and I have learned from the best, Pop."

"Kind of you to say so, but you fellas must continue to be careful. I'm thinking of retiring soon and we don't want to slip up so close to the finishing line."

"You know that you've been threatening to stop work ever since I was old enough to walk?"

"This time I mean it, Moishe."

"No disrespect, Pop, but I'll believe it when I see it."

"MOISHE LAUGHED AT me tonight."

"Why would he do that, Alex?"

Sarah and Alex were in bed back at their hotel.

"I told him I was considering retiring."

Sarah giggled.

"I am not surprised you got that reaction. This isn't the first occasion you've made such an announcement."

"I'm serious this time, hon'."

"What makes this night different from all other nights?"

"Watching the family together this afternoon. How happy everybody appeared and the knowledge that I am missing out on seeing the grandkids grow up. Just like I did for my own boys."

"Alex, they only have their happiness because of the effort you put in to create the safety which they inhabit. David and Moishe earn a fantastic living because of your business interests. Don't sell yourself short. But the life you have chosen has consequences and there's no denying it."

Alex fell silent for a minute.

"How would you feel if we moved here, Sarah?"

"I prefer the Californian climate, but we might winter there and spend spring and summer here. Is this about coming back to your roots or to see Nathan and Jojo?"

"More the latter. When we left the Bowery, I turned my back on the place. If you recall, I only returned to resolve that unpleasantness with my mama's landlord."

"If we bought a house in the city, then you would need to stop working too. Not being in New York is just as absent from those kids as being on business, away in California."

"It's not where we live, is it?"

"No, Alex. You must face up to the consequences of the life you chose."

"Sarah, it's not only about what I want. You have a say in where we live and what we do."

"Is that true, Alex?"

"I believe so."

"Then when are you going to make an honest woman of me again?"

"You wish to get married to me? When last we spoke about this, you told me you never wanted that to happen as long as you lived."

"Alex, that was twenty or thirty years ago. You can't hold me to something I said when I was half my age."

35

AFTER TWO DAYS, Alex informed Sarah that he was going to have to leave.

"There's something I must do. And then I'll be back by your side and we need never work from that point on."

"How long will you be gone, Alex?"

"That's hard for me to say. A few weeks rather than days."

"You're not going to invade Cuba again?"

"Not this time. There are some matters I must straighten out and then we can live in peace."

"I know not to ask questions, but assure me that this is necessary. Whenever you are away, I worry whether you're coming back in a body bag."

"You and me both, Sarah."

"Don't joke. I would rather you carried on controlling Vegas and running nafkas and narcotics in Hollywood than be dead. There's no need to be a hero for the sake of your grandchildren."

"If we are to enjoy our retirement without interference from the Feds, or any other cops, then I must take care of one loose end."

ALEX FLEW OUT that night and landed in LA before taking a rental over to Berkeley. He might have looked more like a professor than a student, but he knew that if he waited long enough in that hotbed of political unrest, then he would catch the fish he wanted.

Each evening, he checked out society meetings and sauntered around the campus, searching for his quarry. Three fruitless days later and Alex found what he was looking for: a group of young Palestinians gathered by a monument facing Telegraph Avenue. It was only a couple of weeks before the anniversary of the start of the Six-Day War and emotions were running high.

"Zionist America needs to be stopped in its tracks."

"We can never be free in this, our adopted country until our brothers and sisters are free in Palestine."

"Israel must cease its oppression of the Palestinian people."

Alex held back that first time, observing and doing his best to melt into the background. From what members of the group were saying, it met every night at this monument and intended to carry on until their voices were heard.

The following day, he joined at the back again and one girl asked him what he was doing.

"I'm a visiting professor from NYU and would like to understand student grievances. My primary research interest is the mechanisms of political protest."

Rawda Qadir accepted Alex at face value and invited him to speak.

"As a mere onlooker, I do not think it appropriate for me to impose my thoughts on the group. All I ask is that you allow me to listen. Perhaps in the future, you will let me engage you in political discourse."

She nodded and huddled with some of her companions, speaking in a murmur, so Alex could not hear what was said. Every so often, one of them would look in his direction and then their head would bob down again and they resumed their private conversation.

By Friday, Rawda and her friends had accepted Alex and were comfortable talking in front of him about anything that popped into their minds. Most of the time, that was the state of the Palestinians in the Middle East.

"The last thing we need is for the US to prop up Israel with any more military support."

"Nothing is going to happen until January when the next president is sworn in. Do you think Lyndon Johnson will take any action before the election?"

Alex couldn't help himself. "And which candidate would you most like to win for the Palestinian cause?"

"Hubert Humphrey?"

"Why do you say that?"

"Well, no Republican is going to worry about the plight of a bunch of Arabs. And Kennedy is a Jew lover. That makes Humphrey the best of a bad bunch."

Alex nodded and pretended to write something down in a notebook he'd brought for that purpose.

"Anyone but Kennedy."

"Because?"

"If by any remote chance he gets elected, he has promised to send fifty jets over to Israel. None of the bombs on any of those flights will land on Jewish heads."

More fake note taking. The man who expressed this view differed from the others; he was the only one who was not a Berkeley student. The rest of them accepted him because of their commitment to equality and fraternity. Although nobody had mentioned his situation, Alex knew the guy was hopping from one short-term busboy job to the next, because Alex had already staked out his apartment and followed him over to that night's session.

"I WAS THINKING about what you said last night, Sirhan."

Alex pretended to bump into the boy an hour before the next meeting was due to start and offered to buy him a coffee in one of the many cheap cafes on Telegraph Avenue.

"What was that?"

"Of how you saw Kennedy as the worst option of all the presidential candidates. Do you think it'll make any difference to the Palestinians who is elected? Will US foreign policy shift that much if any of the mainstream candidates win?"

Sirhan Sirhan stirred his espresso for a minute.

"Perhaps you are right, George. The Americans will continue to support Israel, come what may, but that doesn't mean that some presidents won't be better than others. Those who are committed to the Jews will put more effort into propping up that regime and shall be less inclined to step in to protect my Palestinian brothers."

Alex nodded. "So what are the chances of Kennedy winning, of your fear becoming a reality?"

"George, if I knew, then I would also tell you everything else that is going to happen in the future."

They laughed, but the question had not gone away.

"Whatever else, that man is a Kennedy, so the mass media will follow him around like baying dogs. And the more he is seen and spouts his Jew-loving agenda, then he will sound strong and people shall be more inclined to vote for him."

Sirhan sipped his coffee and leaned back, satisfied with his response. If he skipped over the anti-Semitic details, Alex agreed. The more publicity the guy received, the more voters would be reminded that Jack's brother was on the ticket. And that was a mighty fine reason to put a cross in the box next to his name.

"Sirhan, what are you prepared to do to prevent Kennedy from becoming president?"

"That's an unusual question, George. You do not sound like a dispassionate academic observer."

"I am here for my university research, but that doesn't mean it is the only reason I came to Berkeley."

"No?"

"Do you believe it is an accident that I spend so much time with your group? There are so many activists at this school. What attracts me to yours?"

"I've not given it any thought, George."

"Well, have a think now."

Alex waited for Sirhan to consider the problem before him. Judging by his expression, there was much staring into the middle distance and few thoughts rattling around his head. After several minutes, he reached a conclusion. "You must care about the Palestinian cause."

"That's correct, Sirhan. And I would say I'm prepared to do more than talk about change. Around the world, students are getting off their asses and doing something for the values they hold dear."

"Like France, you mean?"

"Right. Are you willing to take direct action to protect your homeland?"

"What do you have in mind?"

"First, why don't you speak to the group and see if you can start leafleting the area. Not just students but reach out to residents."

"George, you think we should engage with the population?"

"There's nothing wrong with talk, but it won't save any lives. If there's anything I've learned in my studies, it's that change doesn't just happen. You have to forge it with your own two hands."

ONE WEEK LATER, Alex and Sirhan sat in the same cafe to review how their revolution was shaping up.

"It feels great to speak directly to people and let them know what is going on in the Middle East."

"Is that as much as you are prepared to do?"

"George, what are you asking?"

"How far are you prepared to go to stop Kennedy?"

"The group?"

"For what I have in mind, there isn't any need for everybody else to get involved."

"You're singling me out?"

"Let's just say that I have been watching you and believe you would be perfect for a special project. The question I have is whether you are ready to do more than hand out leaflets?"

"George, I am prepared to do whatever it takes to prevent that man from killing my people."

June 1968

36

THE AMBASSADOR HOTEL in Los Angeles was buzzing and had been all day. Alex and Sirhan were not surprised, as this was the makeshift Kennedy home, at least for a couple of days. The senator had toured South Dakota and California in the run-up to their two primaries and now that voting was nearing the end, the campaign settled into the Ambassador to wait for the results.

On the opposite side of the street to the hotel stood Protean Mansions, a residential block on Alexandria and Wilshire Boulevard. The hotel was set several hundred feet away from its main gates and offered some level of privacy to those who attended the various events that day.

Alex and Sirhan entered Protean with no difficulties. A quick trip around the rear of the building and Alex discovered a door to the backyard with an easy lock to pick. As soon as they were inside, they scurried up the stairs to the tenth floor and onto the roof.

"What next, George?"

Alex provided the answer without words. Instead, he unzipped one of his backpacks, which contained two smaller cases. He flipped open the first of them to reveal a firearm separated into several pieces, which he rebuilt as a rifle. Then he added the scope. He repeated the task with the second case and handed one of the firearms over to Sirhan.

"Now it's time for us to get used to the feel of our weapons."

The boy nodded and held the rifle like he knew what he was doing.

"Bullets, George?"

"Before we pour out the ammo, let's get into position and make sure we have a good enough view of the hotel. There's no point having slugs in the weapon and no way to hit our intended target."

Sirhan nodded again, and Alex walked him over to the right-hand corner of the building, facing the Ambassador. Once Sirhan had kneeled and looked through his scope to confirm he had sight of the Ambassador front, Alex jogged over to the left-hand side and hunkered down too.

Through his scope, he imagined moving from the gates, along the driveway, and a car halting outside the circular frontage. A sign announcing the hotel's name was set on the side of a dome, which pushed out from the main reception.

All of this was familiar because Alex had visited the Cocoanut Grove club on the hotel grounds many times before, often to see Frank Sinatra, Sammy Davis Jr., and the rest of their crew perform. The most important thing was that Alex would have a clear shot at anyone who was disgorged from their vehicle at the main entrance.

He checked his watch and saw they had ages before Kennedy was likely to show. He and his entourage wouldn't arrive until after the polls were closed. Even on election day, there was glad-handing to do. One thing he had learned over the years was that a sniper was never fresh if they'd been lying in wait for hours. He sauntered over to Sirhan and advised his mark to stand down.

"But I'm ready, George. Now is the time for action."

"We'll fight for Palestinian freedom when the sun sinks; that is when Kennedy will show and not before. You are going to get cramps if you sit there all afternoon."

"Should we go and come back?"

"No, Sirhan, let's stay where we are. The more time we spend away from this rooftop the more likely some concerned citizen may make us."

"I don't mind. If anyone sees me, I'll kill them."

"Now listen, Sirhan. We are here for a specific purpose and nothing should deviate us from that plan."

Sirhan looked down.

"And another thing is that not only do we want to get this job done, but we must perform it cleanly. There is no need to leave a trail for the cops to find us."

"There's nothing wrong with being a martyr, George."

"That might be part of your life plan, but it sure as hell isn't mine. I intend to execute the task at hand and walk away. You should aim to do the same. If you wish to carry on the good fight, then that is your decision, but don't jeopardize my ability to assassinate Kennedy and vanish into the shadows."

"George, if that is how you feel, then why do you want him dead? You've talked about the plight of the Palestinians, but your heart never puts fire into your words."

"Sirhan, I have my reasons and now is not the time for us to discuss them."

AN HOUR LATER, Alex passed a bottle of cola over to Sirhan, as well as something to eat. This was becoming a long afternoon and Alex wished he was alone. This felt nothing like any of his previous hits. No one was paying him for a start, but Sirhan was impatient and arrogant in equal measure.

"George, who do you think'll get the kill shot?"

"Does it matter? More important to remember is that we will be lucky to fire off a second bullet, so aim for the heart and not the head, unless he's walking away."

"We need him dead and not maimed, right?"

"If he survives the attack, then we'll have gifted him the election. Who wouldn't vote for an assassination survivor? Sirhan, make your shot count."

"George, he mustn't send those fighter planes over to Israel."

"That is what we are here to prevent. Now listen to me. Soon there'll be a slew of limos disgorging politicos, celebrities, and hotel guests out into the evening. The chances are that many of the men will wear a tux like Kennedy, so don't fire at the first person you see in a monkey suit. Make sure he is the right guy before plugging him."

"Have you done this sort of thing before?"

"That is irrelevant, Sirhan."

"You act as though you have."

"You believe what you want. I'm not answering foolish questions like that when we have business to take care of. The other factor that you must keep in the back of your mind is no matter what happens, if either of us is stopped or can't escape, then there was only one person on this roof. There is no need to kick off a manhunt if you are captured. Agreed?"

The boy nodded with eyes wide open.

"Speak to me, Sirhan."

"I agree, George. At least one of us must get away today so that others may know of the deeds we have performed."

"Don't go bragging. That's all I meant. And don't rat the other fella out. Nobody should conduct themselves like that. Now get ready."

Alex picked his path over the roof and back to his corner. Before getting into firing position, he looked over at Sirhan. The young man was poised, kneeling on the concrete with his rifle clasped in his hand. He might not be a Berkeley student, but he seemed to know his way around a firearm.

A quick look through his scope showed Alex that his prediction of a steady stream of vehicles was proved correct. Car after car disgorged men and women who waited a few seconds for everyone to leave the limos and then walked inside in groups, some in a hurry, others sauntering without an apparent care in the world. There wouldn't be much time between seeing Bobby and squeezing the trigger.

Another five minutes and the caravan of limos seemed to stretch forever. It had backed up onto Wilshire itself, despite the length of the driveway. This gave Alex a chance to survey the waiting vehicles before they vanished behind the hotel boundary walls.

The fourth limo from the gates. Alex was pretty sure he spotted Bobby's head in the back seat, along with a woman and two other men who he didn't recognize. A deep inhalation and he stared hard at that skull. It was still. Now was the time. As he exhaled, Alex's finger moved so that he felt how much pressure he needed to pull the trigger. Just as he was about to engage his muscle, there was a blur in the viewfinder, and the Kennedy vehicle lurched forward.

A deep breath and Alex tried again. This time there wasn't as good an angle, and he knew he'd blown his chance. Shooting at the man's nose would not kill him. Alex gave two short whistles and Sirhan repeated the noise in response, just as they had planned. Not long now and the limo would be at the front of the hotel.

One minute later, Alex had resumed his aim a little below the main signage. By now, the whole thing was illuminated and glowing off-white in the early evening breeze. Through the scope, he saw the woman from before exit the black limo and then two other men. This was it.

A lifetime later, Kennedy appeared and Alex placed the crosshairs in the center of the guy's head; the others who were milling around hid his torso, and he waited for Bobby to exit the vehicle. Inhalation and squeeze.

His bullet flew out of the rifle barrel and zoomed past Kennedy's ear. He must have felt the movement of the air because Alex thought he noticed the senator turn his head for a half-second before the slug buried itself in the soil of a nearby rockery. By the time Alex had steadied the firearm to take a second shot, Kennedy was nowhere to be seen. Alex stood up and hustled over to Sirhan.

"Any luck?"

"No, it all happened too fast, George."

"I got one shot off but was an inch too far to the right."

"What now?"

"We pack up our things and get closer to the man. This fight isn't over yet."

37

ALEX AND SIRHAN walked at a pace along the backstreets to Alex's car, which was parked in a lot some six blocks north. With the backpacks in the trunk, Alex pulled out a couple of revolvers from a sack wrapped inside the spare tire. He passed the first piece to Sirhan, who refused it.

"I already have one. I don't need another."

"Fine, but hide it in a pocket until we are ready. We must not get stopped by any cop for carrying a weapon, got it?"

They headed back toward the Ambassador to figure out what to do next. Alex used the time it took them to make this journey to figure out what they needed to do.

"Sirhan, we are going to walk straight in through the main entrance and join the crowd inside."

"What then, George?"

"We'll seize the moment. At some point, Kennedy will open himself up to our attack and then we shall pounce. You follow my lead and take my instruction."

They walked through the central gates, which created a gap in the boundary wall. Although he had arrived by car in the past, Alex knew his way along every twist and turn of the driveway. As they reached the entrance, the number of people surrounding them increased. Men and women spent most of their time talking about what they'd heard about how the vote was going. Alex stopped in the lobby and took stock.

The general flow was heading toward the main ballroom, and Alex was tempted to follow the majority into the rally. Then he remembered there was a bar on the first floor and took Sirhan there instead.

"Why are we here, George?"

"Because Kennedy won't show up on stage until he knows the results of today's vote, so we'll achieve nothing by standing around with the Democrat faithful."

They sat at a table near the back of the room and Alex asked for coffees for them both and a jug of water. The two men remained silent for a spell, even after the waitress had delivered their order.

"And now we wait, but at least this time we are seated in comfort and have a better sense of where the action is."

Alex nodded at one of the many televisions in the bar, positioned so that every customer could see a screen. Live coverage of the Democrat rally, along the corridor and off to the right, was beamed direct to their table.

"Do you have any idea what we are going to do, George?"

"Be patient. In every evening, there are highs and lows. It doesn't matter if Kennedy wins or loses tonight's races. At some point, he'll need to catch his breath and we will be standing by."

"I'd be much happier if we were doing something."

"We are. It's called waiting."

"You know what I mean."

"Have a sip of your coffee and if it makes you feel any better, have a stroll around the ballroom or see what is going on upstairs. Somewhere in this building are the key players in the Kennedy campaign. Just don't take any chances and try not to talk to anyone. When we walk out of here, nobody must be able to spot our faces in a line-up."

Sirhan smiled for the first time that day and took his leave of Alex. He came back thirty minutes later with a spring in his step.

"I think I might have an idea, George. The third floor is filled with campaign staff: if we wear a Democrat pin, then no one will give us a second look."

"And have you worked out in which room Kennedy is staying?"

"Not yet, but it seems like everybody is walking from one room to another. It is mayhem up there. Each time a statistic is announced on the television, everyone erupts in chatter and people scurry over to a different place to discuss tactics or something. I don't know what, but I covered most of the corridors and rooms without anyone stopping me and asking what I was up to."

"What are we waiting for?"

Alex threw some dollar bills on the table and followed Sirhan out of the bar and up a set of side stairs until they reached the third floor. Sirhan was right. Men and women ran down the corridors, popping heads into one area then another, many of them carrying clipboards and clinging to their pens like they would die without them.

They entered the second room on the left and Alex grabbed two clipboards, passing one of the treasured items over to Sirhan, then they headed into the next room along, where there was a flip chart but no television. The Democrats must have been using it as a store cupboard because there was every conceivable piece of stationery imaginable, including a cup of pens with a campaign slogan on the side.

"Take me to parts of the floor you weren't able to check out earlier."

Sirhan led Alex down the passageway, through a set of double doors, and into the continuation of the same corridor. Only it was much quieter here. The workrooms were near the lifts and stairs and none of the mayhem progressed beyond the doors they'd walked past.

Sirhan tapped Alex's arm and pointed to the far end then he leaned in and whispered, "Kennedy is here."

"How d'you know?"

"When I was up here earlier, I saw him vanish into one of these private rooms."

Alex chose not to ask why Sirhan hadn't bothered to follow the guy more closely. Instead, he focused on thinking about the next steps. The decision was taken out of his hands when a blond woman appeared from a room three along on the right. She held the door ajar. "I'll get those numbers for you, Mr. Kennedy."

Then she closed it behind her and walked toward the two men, who pretended to talk to each other and stare at their clipboards. They carried on with this charade until they heard the doors swing shut.

Alex padded down the corridor and stood with his back to the wall with Kennedy's door only three feet to his right. Sirhan was by his side, mimicking his stance. The thumping in his chest did not help Alex's concentration.

He had no notion how many were inside or if there were any cops in there with Bobby. So the idea of taking his chances and bursting in faded from his mind almost as soon as the notion had formed. No doubt, Sirhan would have considered that the best plan of the day.

At that moment, Ethel Kennedy appeared and Alex sauntered past the door to shoot a glance inside before continuing along the passageway to the end where he disappeared around the corner. Sirhan caught up with him and they waited until they heard Ethel walk down the corridor. Alex popped his head round to check on what was happening; she was gone but might be back any minute.

"I saw one Fed stood in the corner facing the door and picked out two voices other than Bobby's."

Sirhan nodded. Then his eyes widened. "You know Kennedy?"

"This is not the time for questions, my friend. If we kick down the door and go in shooting, the Fed will kill us before we've got into the room and fired a shot."

"Isn't it worth trying, anyway?"

An icy stare and a shake of the head.

"No, Sirhan, not now. This is not a genuine opportunity for us, even though it seemed it at first. If Kennedy was alone with his wife, then maybe I'd chance it. But I am not going face-to-face with a federal cop whose job it is to protect Kennedy from people like you and me."

As soon as those words had left Alex's lips, a roar and a cheer ripped along the corridor. Kennedy's door slammed open and Bobby scurried back toward the mayhem beyond the double doors.

"What was that, George?"

"I reckon Kennedy's just won a primary."

38

ALEX AND SIRHAN kept going, away from Kennedy's room, until they arrived at a stairwell. Back on the first floor, they vanished in the seething mass of people who were surging to the ballroom. Modern politics meant that Bobby Kennedy needed to be on television to celebrate his success and be seen to thank supporters for their effort over all these months. The speech wrote itself.

The two men went with the flow and joined Kennedy's acolytes to listen to the great man. Sure enough, he appeared on stage within ten minutes and droned on to the party faithful about their values and how this and that would be different. And he listened to the voice of the people. Yada yada.

While Sirhan's eyes were drawn to Kennedy, Alex focused on the different options for the senator to exit the stage. Bobby portrayed himself as one of the guys so much that he might try to walk through the crowd—there were enough eager hands to shake if he did.

But the place was packed to the rafters and it might take him a lifetime to get out. If Alex was in charge of Bobby's route, then he would take one of the side entrances and use service corridors. Everyone was so buoyant that Alex wouldn't have been surprised if they lifted the guy on their shoulders and carried him round the city like a king. A side entrance then, but left or right?

Alex's eyes switched from one side of the stage to the other, trying to guess which was more likely to be chosen. The patience he had warned Sirhan about earlier in the day bore fruit now. A busboy appeared on the right-hand side of the stage, which meant the kitchens were there, a perfect route for the senator to take after he stopped blowing smoke up his ass to please the crowd.

"Sirhan, pay attention to me. Work your way around the edge of the ballroom and aim for that service door." Alex pointed for a second and lowered his hand.

"On the other side will be the hotel kitchens. I want you to position yourself at a discreet distance and wait. If I'm right, then Kennedy will leave through that door and you'll be ready for him. Remember, aim for the heart and the head."

"Where will you be?"

"I'll follow behind him and be your wingman. Don't worry, I won't be far away."

Sirhan nodded and started inching his way through the mass of men and women gawping at Kennedy as he droned on. Alex counted to twenty and fought through the same crowd, but he took a different route, meandering through the people, but with the same service entrance as his goal.

All the while, he kept one eye on Sirhan, because he needed the boy to get there first. The last thing he wanted was for Kennedy to walk through those doors and see Alex standing there with a gun in his hand. A knife in the back was a different option, and there was a blade strapped to his ankle in case of need.

Fifteen long minutes later and Sirhan popped behind the door. Alex was ten feet away from the entrance himself and picked up speed to position himself against the wall, eight feet from the door.

"My thanks to all of you. Now it's on to Chicago, and let's win there."

A tumultuous thunder of applause and cheers erupted in the Ambassador ballroom as Kennedy waved to all parts of the auditorium and headed to the left. Alex ground his molars and considered taking a potshot at the guy there and then. That was the wrong direction. One of the entourage rushed out from the back of the stage and spoke with Kennedy, who nodded and turned round to go in the direction that Alex had predicted. He exhaled.

There were twenty feet between the bottom of the stage steps and the service door. The sheer number of people who wanted to congratulate the senator slowed him to a shuffle and Alex waited a full five minutes for one of Kennedy's handlers to open the door and let the man through.

Alex seized the opportunity and elbowed past everyone between him and that entrance so he could join Kennedy in the corridor before a security guard prevented the masses from following their leader into the kitchen.

KENNEDY AND TWO other men walked through an open kitchen area filled with stainless steel shelving stacked with canned goods. Bobby could only manage three paces before someone else stopped to shake his hand. Progress was slow and steady, but there was no sign of Sirhan. Perhaps he'd got scared and run away out the back or he'd chosen a hiding place so far from here that there was no guarantee of Kennedy reaching him at all.

The passageway narrowed and Alex sniffed an opportunity, so he increased speed to be only about an arm's length away from his target. He placed his hand on his gun, which was in his pants pocket. There was an industrial scale ice machine to the left and a steam table to the right. Bobby stopped for the umpteenth time to shake hands with a busboy.

A tray-stacker was positioned next to the ice machine. With no trays stowed, it looked like an empty metal carcass. Sirhan leaped out from its center and lunged toward Kennedy. One of the entourage was ahead of Bobby, clearing a path, and Sirhan brushed past him in his rush to get to the senator.

Sirhan raised his revolver and fired eight shots. As Sirhan began shooting, Alex dropped on his left knee and sent off five slugs toward Bobby. At least three went through the back of Kennedy's jacket, but Alex couldn't see if any had reached their target, despite being close enough to touch his ear. The candidate had taken a step or two back when Sirhan rushed at him.

In an instant, Kennedy dropped to the floor like a rock and Alex let others scoot past him. Under the cover of the fresh sea of bodies, Alex raised himself back on his feet to see a guy punch Sirhan in the face. He teetered but kept his balance in time for two guys to slam him against the steam table. Sirhan faced Alex's direction. His eyes were wide and wild.

He screamed and the two men let go for a second, giving Sirhan the chance to fire more shots, but he wasn't aiming at Kennedy, who was bleeding on the floor. Five people spurted red in front of Alex and Kennedy's guys grabbed at Sirhan and subdued him. This time, they had the smarts to take the gun off him and place it on the steam table, a big mistake, as Alex's accomplice was down but not out. Sirhan wrestled free once more, picked up the piece, and squeezed the trigger over and over, but there were no slugs left. This time Sirhan had no escape and Alex joined two other guys who pushed him onto the floor, face down, while what must have been hotel security cuffed him.

Alex had no chance to say even a word to Sirhan, but the fella blinked in such a way that he knew the guy wouldn't rat him out.

Then the flash of camera bulbs caused Alex to shut his eyes for a second. When he opened them again, the press hounds, who had been on the other side of the service door, had burst through and taken over the narrow aisle.

Alex knew there was nothing he could do for Sirhan and although he wasn't certain how many slugs had hit the senator, now was not the time to stop and ask questions of the witnesses.

He thought of pushing his way back to the service door but realized that would be swimming against the tide, so Alex moved forward along with the reporters, only he carried on past the subdued Sirhan and walked toward the kitchens.

People were rushing toward the senator from all directions, but most of the hotel staff had their work to do, so, within five minutes, Alex was in the back lot with a cigarette in his mouth.

Before the local police could swoop in and ask any unnecessary questions, Alex dashed south four blocks and then slowed down to a casual pace to take the three-smoke journey back to his car.

39

ALEX ARRIVED BACK home by three in the morning and woke up Sarah with a kiss on her forehead.

"Everyone is safe, but we need to pack a couple of bags and leave after breakfast."

They took turns behind the wheel for the drive to Florida. The plan was to aim for twelve hours traveling a day. As they pulled into the first of many motels on their route, the radio announced the death of Bobby Kennedy.

"Alex, how long do you think we will be away?"

"A week or two, Sarah. No longer than that. It's not like we're on the lam. I just would rather we weren't in Boyle Heights right now."

"Do you expect any uninvited visitors?"

"No, but that doesn't mean we shouldn't be cautious."

"Alex, you appear back home without me hearing a peep from you for three weeks and tell me to pack our bags as we're going on a trip. All that on the same day that Bobby Kennedy was shot. Now I love you and this is not the moment for me to ask you about your business, but I am not dumb either."

"Sarah, this is a precaution on my part and nothing more. There is nothing to connect me to Kennedy's death that I am aware of."

"And it is the things you don't know that make you want to leave town."

"We live together, we love together, but we die alone."

Sarah nodded and got out of the vehicle to pay for a night's accommodation. Alex hustled straight from the car and into their room once Sarah had the key.

"Are we going to be stuck in motel rooms from here to Miami?"

"Sarah, tonight is special, because I want to lie low. We've been driving all day and we are both tired. We'll only feel worse over the week. So let's crash out here where nobody will see us or care if we are passing through. Later, we can stay in some decent hotels. But not tonight."

She smiled and placed a hand on his arm.

"I'm glad you've tied up all the loose ends. That's what your absence was about, right?"

"Yes, Sarah. If we can ride the current storm, then everything should be peachy from now on. We must stomach some discomfort on this drive for the sake of our future."

THE REST OF the journey passed without incident and four days later, Mr. and Mrs. Bass checked into the Miami Colonnade Hotel, which overlooked the sea. The city had changed so much since their last trip, which had been several years before.

The same outré individuals still walked their poodles on the promenade that ran along the length of Collins Avenue by the Atlantic shore but with a difference. Martin Luther King and two Kennedys were dead. There was a sadness in the air, at least around any table where Alex and Sarah sat to watch the world pass by.

During the day, the couple stayed by the hotel pool rather than lie on the sandy beach as there were fewer people to recognize Alex within the confines of the Colonnade.

At night, they'd hit a local restaurant, but neither had the energy nor the inclination to visit a jazz club. So they would return to the hotel bar for a nightcap or two and retire to bed early. On the fourth day, Alex suggested they eat in the hotel and Sarah had no objection. The food was better than mediocre and the wine was decent.

"Sarah, have you enjoyed the last few days?"

"Miami has been fun but I could have done without the car journey. Next time, why not take a bus?"

Alex smiled while Sarah laughed. They both understood that they needed to leave the most obscure trail in their wake.

"Sarah, if we come back to Miami, I'll fly you by private jet."

"There is no point in showing off in front of me, Alex. Those days in the Bowery are long gone. You knew your tips meant I wouldn't need any other clients for the rest of the day. Back then, you were a mensch."

"And am I not one now?" Alex winked at her. Whatever moral ground he had stood on when he was a teenager, that mound had shifted, and he was down in the dirt with everybody else.

"Tell me, Sarah. What would you like more than anything in this world?"

"Apart from happiness, my children's success and untold wealth?"

"Put that to one side. Is there something you don't have that you wish you did?"

"Alex, why ask me what you already know?"

He reached out across the table and held her hand.

"Sarah, we have been together for a long time, decades, in fact. When we were young and wed, I caused you sadness and you have been kind enough to say that you forgive me for that. I am not sure I can ever forgive myself though."

She squeezed his hand.

"And when we were older and not married, we have told each other that we have found happiness in each other's arms. I know that is true for me. And you?"

She nodded and smiled.

"Sarah Fleischman, will you do me the honor of marrying me again?"

SARAH WANTED TO wait to tell the family in person, but Alex was desperate to share the good news with somebody. And Meyer was down the road.

"Hello, my friend. How are you?"

Meyer showed no emotion as he greeted Alex and invited him into his home. They hustled through and out onto the patio. Kids were playing in the pool.

"Meyer, have I called at a bad moment? There's no need for me to interrupt your family time."

Alex looked around to see Thelma and three middle-aged women, who he assumed were two daughters-in-law and Sandra, Meyer's only daughter. Their men must have been at work.

"Don't give it a moment's thought, Alex. They are here for the summer, so a few hours on one afternoon will not shake their world apart."

Alex smiled. Meyer had two marriages in the bag and three kids, and he took all of them for granted. To him, family was something that stayed at home while he went out and earned the gelt.

Thelma came over and offered the men an iced tea, which Alex declined and received his preferred Scotch instead.

"Alex, these are unusual times in which we live, wouldn't you say?"

"How so, Meyer?"

"Do me a favor. Don't act like you haven't read the papers. I'm talking about Kennedy, of course."

"Terrible business, Meyer."

"Depends whose business you own. On the television, they said the Arab killed him because of his attitude to Israel."

"Uh-huh."

"But you knew the Kennedys, both Jack and Bobby. What did you make of that?"

"The two men recognized the US needs a foothold in the Middle East. The Soviets have aligned themselves with the Arabs throughout the region."

"I met Joe Kennedy back in the day. I don't think I've met a bigger *verstinkener momzer* in my life."

"Meyer, I suppose you believe that the apple doesn't fall far from the tree?"

"Did it?"

"Jack was respectful of everybody. He was arrogant with everyone who he deemed inferior, but that was based on your station and not your religion."

"And Bobby?"

"Meyer, let's just say that Bobby and Jack were different people."

"That's what I heard. In that case, I'm glad he got his. Congratulations."

"What do you mean?"

"Alex, Bobby Kennedy gets assassinated and you turn up on my doorstep a few days later. Coincidence?"

"Meyer, I do not know what you are implying."

"I respect that you keep to the script, even with me."

They clinked glasses and Alex wondered how much Meyer knew and what was supposition.

"I thought you were retired, Meyer?"

"What are you talking about?"

"You said you heard talk about Bobby Kennedy. If you are no longer working, how come you are having conversations with men who are connected to the Kennedy clan?"

Meyer winked.

"There is not working and then there's retirement. I still maintain interests across this fine land and people are kind enough to visit me, like yourself."

"You've remained in Florida for a long time, Meyer."

"It's a safe state and there's a level of protection I receive in Miami-Dade that is not available elsewhere in the country."

"You remain with the Italians, Meyer?"

"Don't be ridiculous. I trust them about as far as I can spit, but there is an alignment of interests and as you know, that has always been good enough for me."

They sipped their drinks and watched the kids frolicking in the pool, enjoying their young lives without a care in the world.

"Is there any chance that you might make a trip to New York later in the year?"

"Now why would I want to do a foolish thing like that, Alex?"

"Because Sarah and I are inviting you to our wedding."

July 1968

40

ALEX SUGGESTED TO Sarah that he go alone to see Sam Giancana, but she didn't want to be away from him for that length of time. Not while he was concerned enough to hide out in Florida or beyond.

So he bought two bus tickets to Mexico City and from there, he paid near top dollar for a used car that took them further south to Cuernavaca. With Sarah secure in their hotel, Alex drove over to the cantina where he had arranged to meet Sam.

"I am pleased to see you safe and well, Alex."

"And this southern climate is treating you fine, Sam."

"It is still too hot and they do not know how to cook a decent bowl of pasta."

"This isn't Little Italy, but what is, right? I miss Lindy's cheesecake and no matter where I go, I can find no replacement."

"Alex, the world continues to spin on its axis and we must ensure we keep up. Times change, people change."

"The last time I went to Lindy's, they made me wait in line and wouldn't give me a booth at the back when it was my turn to be seated."

Sam grinned.

"If there's one thing I've learned, Alex, it's that you should never dwell in the past. The future is ours to shape."

"Wise words, Sam. With that in mind, I'm going to get married to Sarah."

"Congratulations, although I thought you were already hitched."

"We were, then we weren't. And now we'll jump the broom again."

"I wish you every happiness, Alex, but forgive me if I don't come in person, assuming you are planning on sending me an invitation."

"Of course, Sam. Given your circumstances, a telegram would be more than I'd expect that you do."

They sipped their drinks and spoke about nothing.

"It was a sorry business, Alex."

"What was that, Sam?"

"Do you not remember our conversation during your last visit?"

"We talked about many things."

"There is no need to play dumb with me, Alex. If Bobby Kennedy had won the Democratic nomination, we both know he would have gunned for organized crime. I would have been in his sights. So I thank you."

"Sam, there is no need to thank me, as I have done nothing. The senator is dead, and that is all."

"You are right to distance yourself from this sorry deed because as much as it gives me personal pleasure in seeing that mook buried in the ground, other members of the commission were unimpressed with your actions."

"I did nothing, Sam."

Giancana raised a finger to hush Alex's refutations.

"I will not insult you by pretending that you didn't pull off an amazing job. Respect to you and those who helped you. But you did not seek permission."

"From the commission?"

"That's right, Alex. This was not an approved hit and although the outcome benefits us all, you have angered some commission members."

"Let me get this straight, Sam. The biggest threat to the mob has been removed, but I didn't complete the paperwork right, and some bosses aren't happy because of this."

"Correct. So you and I must never meet again. The only reason you are not dead already is that I interceded on your behalf."

"What about my interests in Vegas and Atlantic City?"

"Make sure there is an intermediary between you and any fellas that you do business with. I am sure that is something you have had in place for many years anyway, but now is not the time to become careless."

Alex's stomach burned, and he grabbed his glass to get some moisture to the back of his throat.

"Then I must thank you, Sam."

"There is no need. You have improved my chances of being able to return to America without any grand jury demanding I rat out my friends."

Now it was Sam's turn to sip his drink.

"But as much as I like you, Alex, and the work we have done together over the years, I spoke for you out of respect for our mutual friend and business partner, Charlie Lucky. If it wasn't for him, then you would be dead. You should have asked permission first, Alex. They would have agreed to the hit on the turn of a dime. But you didn't ask, and that is not forgivable."

41

ALEX DUMPED THEIR jalopy as soon as they arrived back in Mexico City and Mr. and Mrs. Bass paid cash for their flights to the US. First, they went home and then they prepared themselves for a longer stay in New York.

David hosted the gathering again, with Esther, Moishe, and the wider members of the Cohen family. To save Dorit any effort, Alex hired caterers at short notice to supply food and drink, and he ensured his favorite cheesecake was on the menu.

They ate, they talked, they ate some more and then their waiters cleared the desserts from the table and Alex clinked his glass of Scotch with the back of a spoon.

"Thank you, everyone, for popping over today. Sarah and I know you had little time to get ready, but we wanted to share some news with you and sometimes these things are best done in person."

His sons nodded, as though they knew what he was about to reveal, and Esther stared agog at her brother.

"When we were here last, Dorit said something to me that put a fire in my belly. I couldn't shake it off."

David scowled at his wife, and she shrugged back at him.

"What did she say, Pop?"

"Moishe, I'm glad you ask and so I will tell you. Dorit challenged me about why I allowed my business activities to prevent me from spending more time with my grandchildren. It took a barrel of chutzpah to pose that question to me, but we all know her heart is in the right place and she is, above all, a *shayner maidel*."

Dorit's cheeks went bright red, and she pretended to blow her nose to hide her face from the world.

"So the first thing I have to tell you all is that we will leave Hollywood because three thousand miles is a very long way to schlep to see your family."

"Mazel tov."

There was a general murmur in the room, and then their sons came over and hugged both parents. When they had returned to their seats, Alex clinked his glass again to get silence.

"Of course, we all know that living on the other side of the country is just an excuse for not visiting; the plane journey takes no time at all. So there is a second thing I wish to tell you. I am going to make preparations so Sarah and I can retire. Living close and having the time will allow us to be with you. Like I should have been before now."

Alex took a sip of Scotch and watched all eyes stare at him until he placed the glass down again and carried on talking.

"And there's a third piece of news too that is as important to me as all that I've said so far."

With that, he sat down and nudged Sarah. She refused to stand but explained everything in a simple sentence. "We're getting married."

The room erupted with congratulations, hugs, and kisses as the extended family showed its approval. Moishe smiled. "I'm glad she's making an honest man of you after all this time."

AFTER A GOOD night's sleep Alex and Sarah sat in the Cohen offices, still in the Bowery. Everyone remained in high spirits and even Esther had broken out into a smile. Alex called them all to order for their shareholders' meeting.

"We need to plan how we are going to wind down my business affairs, especially those which have fallen outside of the federal tax regime."

"Well put, Pop." Moishe grinned.

"I have held conversations with certain people and while Sarah and I will quit our Hollywood activities, we cannot move to New York."

"Why, Pop?"

"David, you saw my business partners when we were in Havana. Let's just say that some of them have indicated that they not only expect me to wind down my operations but that I won't poke my nose anywhere near their businesses at any point in the future."

"So New York is no longer safe for you?"

"Correct, Moishe. I have worked hard to protect you from the details of my activities and that remains best for you all. If you become aware of what I do, and what I have done, then you and your loved ones will be under constant threat from now until the day they put a hit on you."

Alex stopped and allowed his words to sink in. As ever, David took everything his father said in his stride; he knew how to show a brave face to any situation. Moishe was more headstrong than his brother and prone to let his emotions shine through. He spoke first.

"So your retirement is our death sentence?"

"Not at all. Quite the reverse, in fact. You are all safe providing I retire. But Sarah and I cannot make a home in this state."

Esther chimed in: "Are you thinking of New Jersey?"

"No, and not Atlantic City before you suggest there."

Sarah laughed. "Chicago is out of the question too."

They all chuckled because they might not know the details of Alex's business life, but they read the newspapers and understood he was a gangster. Alex waited for everyone to settle down before continuing.

"Sarah and I had Florida in mind. The weather is good, there are beaches and the Italians might control Miami-Dade, but we would be under the protection of a reluctant patron."

"Is this just an elaborate ruse for you to live near your friend, Lansky?"

"Not quite, but he is about the only person left I know and trust outside of my family, Ezra and Massimo. Everyone else has either died a natural death or, more likely, been killed."

David had remained silent for a while, the finger of his right hand circling his chin and eyes half shut.

"You want us to move to Florida. This office, and our families as well?"

"Yes. There will be a lot less to do because we are only seeking to draw an income from our investments. Provided that money is safe, you fellas have my blessing to expand the legitimate empire as much as you see fit."

"How can I sell this to Dorit and the kids?"

"David, like I said yesterday, if they stay in New York, then I cannot guarantee their safety. If they are with you in Florida, they won't have a care in the world for the rest of their days."

"What about Alecia?"

"Moishe, if your relationship is firm enough, then she will come with you, and if not…" Sarah's words trailed away because she didn't want to disappoint her single son. This was the first woman he had connected with in years.

"And what about me?"

The timid voice of Alex's sister broke into the air. Alex smiled at Esther with a glint in his eye.

"We will always need you near us, sis'."

Sarah interjected. "If you like, we could buy a place with a guest cottage in the grounds so that you can have as much company as you want with us, but still get privacy when you need it."

"For real?"

Alex and Sarah nodded. They had discussed what to do with Esther early in their conversations about moving the family offices out of Manhattan.

"Unless there's any other business, I suggest we call this meeting to a halt and head out for a bite to eat. Anyone fancy a trip up to Lindy's?"

"One thing, Pop. What's going to happen to Massimo and Ezra?"

42

ALEX SAT IN Pietro's, the same Sunset Boulevard restaurant where he had met Carl. The food had been good and even though he wasn't a huge movie fan, he had to admit to himself that he got a buzz being near so many stars. The place was packed with people being seen to be there. Where else but in Hollywood?

He had placed his order for steak and fries two minutes before. When he looked up, he expected to see his waitress returning with his Scotch, but Frank Sinatra loomed above him instead.

"Good to see you, Alex."

"It's been a lifetime, Frank. How are you?"

"Not too bad. The great thing about singing and acting is that I have two careers. So if one is quiet then I've got something else to fall back on."

"If you have the time, join me, Frank."

Sinatra eyeballed the room and sat down.

"Concerned about being seen with me?"

A nervous smile rippled across Sinatra's face.

"Don't worry, I won't talk business to you."

"It's not that, Alex, but you know how this town operates."

"I do, which is why I'm going to be leaving it soon. I've been on the West Coast too long."

"Alex, you had a sideline in Hollywood parties. How will you run that if you aren't in the neighborhood?"

"My associates will take over from me. If any of your friends want to get high with a hooker, then they can still count on me."

They laughed and Alex's Scotch arrived.

"I should be going."

"Order something if you'd like, Frank."

Sinatra shrugged and perused a menu, settling on a steak too.

"Are you in touch with many of our Italian friends, Frank?"

"You know how it is. They never go away, and given the support they've shown me over the years, I am happy to do a few turns in Vegas to show my appreciation."

"We all grease the wheels to keep them running along the tracks."

"Right. For instance, I'm about to cut a deal to enable the sale of the Warner Brothers film studio, in return for relinquishing certain other assets."

"It is always the way, Frank."

"Here's a proposition for you. If you're not running whores anymore, why not take a job as a producer for me."

"Make films? You must be joking."

"Alex, if you can work for the mob, then you can assemble a film project. Think about it. You don't have to decide now."

"THANK YOU BOTH for flying over to meet with me here and not in Vegas."

Alex, Ezra, and Massimo sat in the Boyle Heights office with a mug each, poured from a large coffee pot the housekeeper had brought in from the other side of the pool. Alex thanked her and smiled to himself at the sight of the plate of cookies. "She bakes them herself."

"Maybe later, Alex. We are intrigued to find out what was so urgent."

"Ezra, even though it isn't anyone's birthday, I have a gift for each of you."

They looked around for a box covered in wrapping paper, but there was nothing to see.

"Ezra, I am giving you the narcotics distribution operation I have built up in Beverly Hills and Massimo, you shall have the Hollywood nafka network."

The two lieutenants glanced at each other before Massimo said what they were both thinking.

"Why, Alex?"

"I am exiting those businesses and as soon as I have extricated myself from all my illegal activities, Sarah and I will retire."

"You're kidding?"

"I have never been more serious in my life. Sam Giancana has made my position with the commission very clear to me. From this point on, I shall have no direct dealings with the Italians. No disrespect, Massimo. I mean, I can no longer do business with the mob."

Ezra whistled as he thought through the implication of Alex's words.

"Are you staying in Hollywood?"

"No, the plan is to relocate to Florida and take my family there too. This'll take time, but I intend to pass on or sell my assets as quickly as possible without creating a fire sale. The other issue is that we must manage this process as discreetly as we can, otherwise, some bosses will try to take advantage of the situation and move into our turf and take over our rackets."

Massimo cleared his throat.

"You said you will sell your assets?"

"Some of them, others not. I intend to gift you two most of my affairs, but there may be some elements that aren't worth hanging on to and I shall liquidate my holdings. After all, when I have to live on a fixed income, I want the cushion to be plumped up well."

"If you pass on any operations to us, then we will reach an accommodation with you."

"Ezra, you are kind to offer me restitution for my assets, but if I give them to you, then you must accept them with humility. Of course, I won't refuse any parting emolument, but to be clear, I am not demanding one. You fellas have built up these businesses ever since I visited Sing Sing and you deserve to reap what you have sown."

With their questions dried up, Alex led the men to the living room in the main house, where he poured three measures of Scotch.

"And by the way, Sarah and I are getting married again."

"It's been a long time coming. Congratulations."

"This calls for a toast."

"Quite right, Massimo. And I know what it should be."

"Go ahead, Ezra."

"To life. *Lechayim*."

THANK YOU FOR READING!

Get a free novella

Building a relationship with my readers is the very best thing about writing. I send weekly newsletters with details of new releases, special offers and other bits of news relating to the Lagotti Family and Alex Cohen series, as well as information about my stand-alone novels.

And if you sign up to the mailing list I'll send you a copy of the Alex Cohen prequel, The Broska Bruiser. Just go to www.leob.ws/signup and we'll take it from there.

Of course, if you prefer to jump right into the next book in the series then go to www.leob.ws/mensch to grab your copy of The Mensch now.

Enjoy this book? You can make a difference

Reviews are the most powerful tools in my arsenal when it comes to getting attention for my books. Much as I'd like to, I don't have the financial muscle of a New York publisher. I can't take out full page ads or put posters on the subway.

(Not yet, anyway).

But I do have something much more powerful and effective than that, and it's something that those publishers would kill to get their hands on.

A committed and loyal bunch of readers.

Honest reviews of my books help bring them to the attention of other readers.

If you've enjoyed this book I shall be very grateful if you would spend just five minutes leaving a review (it can be as short as you like) on the book's page. You can jump right to the page by clicking www.books2read.com/alex4-6.

Thank you very much.

Leo

SNEAK PREVIEW

In Book 7, The Mensch…

Alex Cohen stepped out of the shower and stared out of the bedroom window. All was quiet. The only discernible sounds were of his wife, Sarah rattling in the kitchen preparing breakfast. It had been a long few weeks and he was glad to be back home, safe in the knowledge that she was there for him, after all these years.

When he looked back on his life, he thought about the friends he had lost like Arnold Rothstein, Charlie Lucky and Alfonse Capone. The fellas from the days of Prohibition and the opportunities that sprang up around the country after the government bent to the people's will and allowed liquor back in the country. His mind rarely contemplated the hundreds he had killed: Abe Reles the Murder Corporation rat or Benny Siegel who had saved him when he'd left Sing Sing but had stolen money from the Italian mob. In fact, the only person whose death still haunted him was the sixteen-year-old who got a bullet between the eyes in the trenches of France during the Great War. And the army had given him a Purple Heart for that.

Alex got dressed and slipped downstairs into the kitchen. Sarah smiled at him and poured a mug of coffee and passed it to him.

"I thought it would be nice for us to eat on the patio this morning."

"Just like old times, Sarah."

He smiled and gave her a peck on the cheek, while making sure not to spill his coffee.

Alex looked up from his paper and pointed at the picture on the front page. "Have you seen this?"

The photo showed a stream of Vietnamese clambering up a ladder in the hope of escaping from Saigon in a US military helicopter.

Sarah's eyes glanced at the image, but she couldn't bring herself to look for too long.

"I can't imagine what it must have been like fighting in the jungles of Vietnam, Sarah."

"Does this bring it all back?"

Alex nodded and reached out to hold her hand. The Great War was civilized compared to what he had seen on the television the last few years. Everything had gone downhill since Kennedy was assassinated.

"Let's not dwell in the past, Alex. Just remember that we live together, we love together, but we die alone."

"I know. I guess I am sad that it has come to this." He flicked the newspaper. "America was supposed to be the land of milk and honey when we arrived at Ellis Island. Instead it has sent tens of thousands of boys off to be slaughtered and sent pictures home every night to show us what is being done in our name."

"Alex, you are almost sounding patriotic. I thought the perimeter of your concern was your family and your business interests."

"Most of the time, but now and again…"

Sarah allowed her husband to wallow in his thoughts for a few minutes and then she poured him another mugful. Then she lit a cigarette and passed it to him. Alex took three long drags and returned to the present. When he finished the smoke, he smiled and tucked into his breakfast: cereal, a bagel with smoked salmon, two cheese blintzes washed down with a large glass of orange juice, and coffee.

"Where's Veronica?"

Sarah laughed.

"We gave the housekeeper the day off, don't you remember?" Alex shook his head. "That way we could spend some time alone together."

A nod and Alex looked down into his lap.

"I have been a disappointment to you for so long, Sarah."

"Don't talk like that, Alex Cohen. Yes, you have made some mistakes along the way, but you have also done your best to be a good father to our children and be a provider to this family."

"Will you ever forgive me, Sarah?"

"I told you that I have done so already. If I had not, then you wouldn't be sat at this table. You'd still be back in Palm Springs. Let's not rehash old arguments. What's done is done and we have the rest of our lives to look forward to. Together."

"Thank you, Sarah."

"Just remember, Alex, that if you can't move past this then we will never be happy again. You must acknowledge what you have done to yourself and then accept the past for what it is. I know I am doing my best to, and you must do so too."

He nodded and stood up, gave her a kiss on the lips and mumbled about getting more of his affairs in order. Sarah remained on the patio and smoked a cigarette before taking the breakfast things into the kitchen and washing them up. Alex appeared from his office on the far side of the summerhouse, which was opposite the pool.

"I don't know what time I'll be home."

"That's fine. You'll be back as soon as you can."

"Do you have any plans, Sarah?"

"I might have a swim this morning and then visit the boys this afternoon."

"Twenty years ago, you told me off for still thinking of them as boys."

"That's right, but it is a mother's right to always think of her children as her babies."

Alex smiled, kissed her goodbye and walked out the front door. Sarah shuffled back onto the patio and slumped into one of the sunbeds. She shut her eyes for a second.

As soon as her eyelids were closed, the walls of the house shook and the windows rattled. A bang and the smell of burning metal and rubber. She ran to the front of the house: Alex's car was a fireball. Sarah slumped onto the grass and screamed.

OTHER BOOKS BY THE AUTHOR

Alex Cohen

The Bowery Slugger (Book 1)
East Side Hustler (Book 2)
Midtown Huckster (Book 3)
Alex Cohen Books 1-3
Casino Chiseler (Book 4)
Cuban Heel (Book 5)
Hollywood Bilker (Book 6)
Alex Cohen Books 4-6
The Mensch (Book 7–Due Early 2022)

Jake Adkins PI

The Case
I Confess (Book 1–Due 2022)
Habeas Corpus (Book 2–Due 2022)
Luther's Diamond (Book 3–Due 2022)

The Lagotti Family

The Heist (Book 1)
The Getaway (Book 2)
Powder (Book 3)
Mama's Gone (Book 4)
The Lagotti Family Complete Collection (Books 1-4)

All books are available from www.leob.ws and major eBook and paperback sales platforms.

ABOUT THE AUTHOR

Leopold Borstinski is an independent author whose past careers have included financial journalism, business management of financial software companies, consulting and product sales and marketing, as well as teaching.

There is nothing he likes better so he does as much nothing as he possibly can. He has travelled extensively in Europe and the US and has visited Asia on several occasions. Leopold holds a Philosophy degree and tries not to drop it too often.

He lives near London and is married with one wife, one child and no pets.

Find out more at LeopoldBorstinski.com.

Made in United States
Orlando, FL
29 January 2022

14181541R00369